STOLEN LAUGHTER

A GRIPPING PSYCHOLOGICAL SUSPENSE NOVEL

CHARLENE TESS

& JUDI THOMPSON

Books By
TESS THOMPSON

ACKNOWLEDGMENTS

Our heartfelt thanks to our first readers including Roger Thompson, Jerry Tess, Nancy Johnson, Chaz Bourland, Carolyn Wilhelm, and Alice Shepherd. We really appreciate the comments and the suggestions.

PROLOGUE

"Patty Jean! You get your butt down here right now," Ed Campbell said. His tone sounded more agitated than angry. He was standing at the bottom of the stairs, looking up toward the closed door to his daughter's room. Dressed in his only Sunday suit, he had been waiting for at least fifteen minutes Je os and kept fingering his hat and looking at his pocket watch.

Sometimes he got teased about carrying an old-fashioned timepiece, but his job as the foreman on a construction crew made wearing a watch dangerous. He had once rushed a co-worker to the hospital because the other man's wrist had been caught on a sharp, protruding, twisted shaft of steel. The man had been lucky not to lose a hand in the freak accident. Ed threw his watch away that very day and bought a pocket watch and chain.

Touching it often calmed him down, but that was not the

case today. Sometimes his only daughter could make him want to chew nails. She was blonde, beautiful, and bossy. He had tried to do his best with her, but raising a spirited girl wasn't easy for the big guy.

After his wife Mavis died when Patty Jean was ten, he had managed to care for her with the help of kind neighbors and a church after-school daycare located a few blocks from their house. For a year or two, she had been a sweet, obedient, young child. But that was then.

Now, at sixteen, she had suddenly become a different person. One he did not know how to handle or control. He was accustomed to giving orders, not taking them from the likes of her. Even though he stood tall at six-foot-two and weighed well over two-hundred and fifty pounds, this teenage girl had him whipped, and he knew it.

Patty Jean opened the door a crack and then disappeared back inside for a moment as if she had forgotten something. Then she flounced down the stairs two steps at a time. He could smell her perfume before he saw her. It was cheap and cloying.

"What's the big hurry, Daddy? It's not like the preacher is going to say anything we haven't heard a hundred times before. After all, how many times can a person say, *Amen*?"

Ed could feel his blood pressure rising. He took a deep breath and when he spoke, his voice was deep and booming. "If you think you are going to church looking like that, you've got another think coming."

"Like what?" she sputtered, bristling with indignation as she brushed past him and opened the front door. She was halfway down the porch steps when he reached out and grabbed her arm.

"I said, you are not going out looking like that. I mean it, Patty Jean. Don't cross me now, or you'll spend the rest of the day in your room."

She shot him a cold look. "Fine with me. I didn't want to go anyway." She shrugged out of his grasp and turned to go back into the house. A few moments later, he heard the door slam shut.

Knowing he had lost the battle, he got into the car and turned on the ignition. This war was making an old man out of him. As much as he loved that girl, he sometimes wished somebody else would raise her. But there was nobody else. Well, shit, he thought. Tag. You're it.

———

Patty Jean stood in front of the full-length mirror and examined her image. Her pale lavender dress nipped in to accentuate her tiny waist, and the scooped neckline showed off her full breasts. Her long blonde hair looked too good for her to sit here and rot all day, she thought. She decided to go out even though she wasn't supposed to. She wasn't worried about her father finding out. After church, he would usually come home and take a nap. He wouldn't come into her room. She knew that for sure. The last time he had been inside her room, he had seen underwear and bras strewn around and a box of tampons on her dresser. He took one look, turned beet red, coughed, and left in a hurry.

She made her way to the mall and walked around looking in shop windows, hoping to find some of her friends. Today wasn't her lucky day. No one she knew was anywhere around. She was all dressed up with nowhere to go and feeling more depressed by the moment when she heard laughter.

A group of girls from school sat in the food court drinking Cokes. They waved her over. "Well, look at you," a short, dark-haired girl said. She was wearing cutoff jeans and a tank top. "What fashion magazine did you fall out of?"

"Daddy wanted me to go to church, but I was disrespectful, so I'm being punished."

They laughed in unison. "You call going shopping punishment?" one of them said.

She sat down in one of the plastic chairs and put her elbows on the table. "I'm window shopping," she said. "It's not like I ever have any money to spend." Then, knowing how whiny she sounded, she turned to the girls and smiled. "Daddy thinks I'm in my room. He has no idea I'm at the mall."

"You take a lot of chances, Patty. You're lucky your dad is a nice man."

"Is that so? Then you go live with him if you think he's so great."

A few minutes later, the whole group of teens at the table drifted away, and she was left sitting there all alone. As usual, she had quickly worn out her welcome with the other girls. She knew she was in a bad mood, but so what? They were all boring anyway.

She had almost decided to walk home when a tall boy with the bluest eyes she had ever seen took a seat across the table from her in one of the plastic chairs. He had a brown crew cut waxed into a fan over his eyes and an ordinary face – until he smiled.

When his Elvis lips curved upward, and she saw his straight white teeth, she had to stop herself from making a strange swooning noise.

"Hi, beautiful," he said. "Whatca' doin' here all by yourself on a Sunday morning?"

"I could ask you the same thing, but it's none of my business." She was annoyed by the question but basked in the glow of his compliment.

"Well, I'm looking for someone to go to the movies with me and share some popcorn. Know anybody like that?"

"I might," she said and turned on her full flirtatious charm. "I'd like to know your name first."

He grinned again. "It's Danny. Danny Ford."

She reached her arm across the table and held out her hand. Her pink fingernails glistened in the fluorescent lights of the food court. "Nice to meet you, Danny Ford."

———

Danny put his arm across the back of her seat as soon as they sat down in the theater. As he reached across to sample the popcorn she held on her lap, his arm brushed the side of her breast. And then, he gently turned her face toward his and kissed her. The scent of Polo cologne and the salty taste of popcorn on his tongue left her breathless.

From that moment on, they were inseparable. Danny was eighteen and a senior in high school. He worked unloading boxes at an after-school job in a local warehouse and headed straight to Patty Jean's house at five o'clock. He got to second base within a week and was rounding for a home run before Patty's father had a clue what was going on. Patty Jean's virginity was gone, and her libido was awake and hungry.

On weekends, they spent hours alone in Patty Jean's room while Ed was at church, or even when he was at home taking a nap. At night, they often had sex in the backseat of Danny's old car, and if they saw the lights of an approaching vehicle, the whole event had to happen quickly. They could not keep their hands off one another, and using protection was a haphazard occurrence depending on how much of a hurry they were in.

Patty Jean was Danny's date to the Senior Prom and was the envy of every other girl in her sophomore class. Danny was the perfect combination of danger and desire. He held her close and kissed her as they danced while taking sips of vodka he had hidden in a flask inside his jacket.

Patty was looking forward to spending the summer with Danny. They could go swimming in the lake, take long rides at night, get greasy hamburgers and fries at Dairy Queen, and not have to worry about finding time to be alone. Her father would be gone all day, and the house would be empty.

The morning she woke up sick was the last day her world was a happy place. She barely made it to the bathroom before she threw up what little she had in her stomach and ended up with dry heaves.

She told her father she had eaten something that didn't agree with her, and she told Danny she had the flu. She looked in the top drawer of her dresser and stared at the full box of Tampax sitting there. All the white cylinders were lined up in perfect rows. She remembered buying that box at Walgreens. It only took her about three minutes to count backward and figure out that she had not had her period in over two months.

She buried her face in her pillow and let the sobs rack her body. How had this happened? It couldn't be true. Could it?

But it was. She waited a full week to tell Danny. He was so happy about being out of high school, and so excited about their summer ahead, she didn't have the heart to tell him that by the end of summer she would be five months pregnant and showing.

———

Danny put the car in park and turned in his seat to face her. "Okay, Patty Jean, what's so urgent? I've been trying to see you for days and you keep putting me off." He reached over to grope her breast, and she pushed him away. "What's going on?"

She put her hand on her stomach and looked into his bright blue eyes. "I ... I'm ... pregnant."

He said nothing for the longest time and silence filled

every inch of space in the car. He opened his mouth and then closed it again. The second time, his voice sounded more like a croak. "Are you sure? Have you seen a doctor?"

"No. How could I without telling my dad?" She frowned. "I've been sick as a dog, my breasts are sore, and I haven't had my monthly for two months going on three."

"Three months? No way. You waited this long to tell me? Now what the hell are we going to do? I'm sure it's too late for an abortion."

Patty Jean's eyes spilled over with tears. "That's it? That's your solution?" Her voice was shrill. "To kill the baby?" She reached for the door handle on the car and pulled it up.

She had never been more hurt in her life except when she had stood by her mother's grave on a rainy morning and watched them lower the casket into the ground. Did she mean that little to him? Would he not even consider making her his wife and helping her raise the child they had created?

"Patty Jean, wait!" he said. "Let's talk about this."

She took one more look at him and got out of the car and made her way into the house where she would ruin her father's day and break his heart.

Ed's eyes filled with tears, but he sniffed and blew his nose on his handkerchief. He pulled his daughter into an awkward hug. "Oh, honey, I'm sorry. I wish I knew what to say. I sure as hell don't know what to do. I need to ponder it a while, but don't you worry, we'll figure this one out."

He wasn't sure about Danny Ford. Did that young man have the strength of character to stand by his daughter? He didn't think so, but he intended to have a heart-to-heart with the young man and see what his intentions were. In the meantime, he needed to talk to the preacher. Surely this kind of thing was not new. It was just new to Ed. Raising a child was hard. Raising a daughter was impossible without a woman's touch. He missed Mavis more and more every day.

The preacher told him about a home for unwed mothers in

Charleston that provided prenatal care to young, unwed girls and found good adoptive parents for their babies. All the facility expected was a onetime donation and a signature that severed all parental rights after the child was born.

Ed hoped that Patty Jean and Danny would figure it out for themselves, but that didn't happen. Two weeks after he found out he was going to be a father, Danny Ford drove out of town without a word of goodbye.

Patty Jean cried so hard Ed was sure she was going to miscarry, but she didn't, and after she accepted the fact that she was going to be a mother at sixteen and completely lose her chance of having a carefree, teenage high school experience, she agreed to go to Charleston and give the baby up for adoption.

———

Now, nearly seven months later, Ed Campbell downed another cold mug of Budweiser, belched, and tapped on the bar for another round. The surly bartender set another glass of light-gold liquid on the sticky surface. Ed could smell the droplets of old, stale beer that had sloshed down the sides of the pints that were served by the dozen. The light in the room was dim, but he could make out a line of people seated on the high stools and hunched over their glasses.

He wasn't ordinarily a drinking man, but you would never know it tonight. He had been sitting here at the Handle Bar for over two hours, and every time he tried to stand up, his legs buckled, so he decided to stay there on the stool until he could figure out what to do.

What he couldn't understand was how he got himself into this fix. Here he was all alone in this world with a pregnant daughter who was about to pop. He knew there was no way she could care for a baby, and he sure as hell knew he couldn't do it again. Look how his first try at parenting had turned out.

He knew he had made the right decision, but he missed his daughter, and he hated the idea of missing out on his first grandchild's birth.

He tried to pinpoint the moment when he had lost control of his little girl, and the day she started running him in circles. He sat there with his chin cupped in his hand and fought back tears.

Then, after way too many beers, Ed had the bartender at the Handle Bar call him a cab. The night was still except for the sharp bark of his neighbor's dog. He staggered up the driveway and let himself in the back door.

He walked into the dark, empty kitchen filled with the smell of old, half-eaten pizza and saw the red light flashing on the answering machine. Hoping it was Patty Jean, he took off his jacket and made his way across the room. He felt guilty for missing her call while he had been tossing back drinks at the bar. The telephone was his only contact with his daughter after she went to Charleston.

He pushed the play button and listened to the message twice. "Mr. Campbell, this is Doctor Hightower. Please return my call as soon as possible, no matter what time you get this message. My number is 843-002-1245."

Ed sat down in one of the kitchen chairs and ran his hands through his hair. He rubbed his forehead and tried to gather his thoughts. Who was Doctor Hightower and why was he calling? Ed looked at the clock. It was two-thirty in the morning. Call *now? Was he serious?*

Then he remembered. He put his hand on the phone and then removed it as if he had touched something hot. Finally, as his heart pounded in his chest, he carefully punched in the numbers.

Later that night, after Reverend Wilson prayed with him and helped him breathe in slowly and then exhale in a whoosh several times until he could stop hyperventilating, he was able to remember what the doctor said.

"Mr. Campbell, I regret having to tell you this. After giving birth, Patty Jean began hemorrhaging. We did everything we could to save her, but I'm so sorry to say that she is gone. She died at eleven-fifteen last night."

CHAPTER 1
BRYCE CAMERON

PRESENT DAY

Bryce Cameron walked at a fast clip past the throngs of holiday travelers as he searched for gate B-70 at JFK Airport. He'd given up his seat on the earlier flight with the promise that he could fly first class non-stop on a later one. Bryce was a thirty-year-old struggling writer. In his mind, by the time he could afford to fly first class on his own dollar, he would be such an old man, he wouldn't even recognize the difference.

He'd acquired an agent and sold his first novel to a major publisher, but his sudden fame and fortune had fizzled before it began. The only place his novel could be found now was in the mystery section of the used bookstore gathering dust. Out of breath and sweating, he hurried to the United Airlines counter. He handed over his boarding pass and was greeted with a smile.

"Ah, Mr. Cameron, I was hoping I wouldn't have to give up your choice seat to someone else." She smiled warmly at him. Bryce was a handsome man, tall and lean with light brown hair tinged with a hint of red worn a little too long. His forest green eyes were fringed with lashes most women would kill for.

He rewarded her with a smile of his own and in a soft Southern drawl said, "Thank you. I appreciate your holding the seat. I got caught up with something and didn't hear the call for the flight." Held up, he thought. I was desperately trying to imagine something for my next chapter. Something that would set the next book apart so people who read it would ask for more.

He took the boarding pass and made his way onto the plane while murmuring hello to the flight attendant and looking for his much-anticipated seat. He'd never sat in the front rows on a plane before unless it was in one of the puddle jumpers that had only one class of seats available. He'd spent four years at the Naval Academy and another six on active duty. His major in English had not thrilled his father, The Captain, or his mother, the queen of the Officers Wives Club. With a degree in English from Annapolis, he'd spent his time working for the Navy's weekly newspaper and fulfilled his father's wishes, as well as his own. He'd spent much of his naval career in Virginia, except for the time he served in the Middle East as a reporter for the *Navy Times*.

He found his seat and stored his carry-on case in the bin above next to a shiny silver one. He leaned down and looked right into a pair of smiling hazel eyes. An exceptionally pretty young woman with long blonde hair would be his seatmate for the flight to Denver.

"Hi," she said and then turned back to the book she had been reading.

"Hello," he replied and settled down to fasten his seatbelt. Her pleasing, clean scent was more refreshing than the harsh perfume that some women wore. So much for the company of a gorgeous woman, he thought. As soon as the plane was in the air, he took out his laptop and typed the ideas he'd been bouncing around in his head. Several moments later, he heard a book slam against the table tray and an unladylike snort.

Bryce glanced over at the woman, and for the first time noticed the title of the book she'd been reading. "Oh hell," he mumbled. He hoped she hadn't heard him.

To his surprise, she said, "I'm sorry. I didn't mean to disturb you. I... well... I've wasted a few hours of my life I'll never get back."

"Stank pretty bad, did it?"

She looked back down at the book and said, "I've read worse. All and all, it was okay, but the ending was pretty awful."

"Why is that? What was wrong with it?"

"Do you read books, Mister ...?"

"Cameron, Bryce Cameron, and yes, I read books. As a matter of fact, I ..."

"Well," she interrupted, "I don't see the point of reading a book and getting invested in the characters only to arrive at an unhappy ending. Why would anyone want to read a book that doesn't have a happy ending?"

"The critics seem to like it, but nobody else does."

"So, you've read this book?"

"Look on the inside cover."

"What?"

"The inside back cover. Look at it. What do you see?"

She opened the cover and gasped. "Oh no. It's you" She looked away and then back again. "I'm so sorry. I would not have said those things if I'd known you wrote it."

"That's okay. It's an honest criticism. I'm what you would call a one-book wonder. I pitched the idea, got an agent, and got it published. Like I said, the critics liked it, but it didn't sell like they hoped. I've been trying for the past year to come up with something people would like. What would you like, Miss...?"

"Hannah Brody, and I like to feel good after I finish a

book. I want to feel sad that it's over and I won't get to have the characters in my thoughts all day long." She leaned over close to him and whispered, "You can't be doing too bad. You're flying first class."

He burst out laughing and got a frown from the elderly woman sitting across the aisle. He whispered back to her, "Don't tell anyone, but I'm only here by default. The flight before me was full, and they needed the seats. The airline promised me a seat in first class if I'd take the next flight."

This time, Hannah laughed out loud. Her laugh was deep, warm, and rich. She was reprimanded with a harsh look from the same lady. "I don't belong here either," she said. "My ticket was a gift from my parents."

"Nice parents."

"Yeah, they are. I finished my dissertation for my Doctorate in Psychology, and they gave me a week in New York as a graduation present."

"So, you're Doctor Hannah Brody," he said and smiled warmly at her. "I could think of lots of lines to pull out of the air."

"Oh, please don't."

"Seriously, congratulations, that's an impressive accomplishment."

Bryce looked up when the flight attendant stopped and said, "What would you like to drink?"

He turned to Hannah and said, "I believe we should celebrate, don't you? How about a glass of wine?"

Hannah nodded yes and said, "Red wine would be nice."

"Red wine for the lady, and I'll have a beer."

When the drinks arrived, Bryce held up his mug and said, "A toast to you."

"And to you, too," said Hannah. "I've never met anyone that has published a book before. That's an impressive accomplishment. I know several people who have said they wanted to write a book, but no one who has actually done it."

Bryce shifted in his seat. He felt a little uncomfortable with her praise. His father and mother believed writing was a complete waste of his time and weren't surprised when the book hadn't done well, and his girlfriend at the time had lost interest as soon as the promise of fame and fortune disappeared.

"So, Hannah, what's next for you after your big party in New York?"

"It was hardly a party. I met up with some old friends from school. We ate at nice restaurants and saw a couple of plays. I'm on my way to Denver to start a new job at the first of the year."

Bryce looked at Hannah expectantly, waiting for her to continue. When she didn't, he said, "And?"

"I'm going to be teaching at the university, and I plan to write a book, too."

"What will your book be about? Do I have some competition?"

"The Psychological Effects of Genetic and Environmental Conditions," Hannah said with a smug look on her face. "I doubt any of your readers will leave the mystery genre, so I think you're safe."

Bryce looked into Hannah's soft, hazel eyes and noticed the green flecks illuminated by the overhead reading light. The shade of green was not unlike the color of his own eyes. Her hair brushed the side of his arm, and he breathed in her clean, fresh scent. She was stunning, he thought. The flight attendant interrupted before his thoughts could progress to something more personal.

"Sir, we have Mandarin oriental roast chicken or Brazilian beef fillet for lunch today, and which meal may I offer you, ma'am?"

Bryce's stomach rumbled. He didn't realize he was hungry but remembered only grabbing a protein bar before leaving for the airport. He deferred to Hannah, who ordered the chicken, and he did the same. When the meal arrived, they both were like a couple of kids playing dress up.

"This is fantastic," Hannah said as she removed the plastic cover from the dish. The smell of oranges and cinnamon rose in the steam arising from the perfectly browned chicken. "In the past, all I've ever been served on a flight was a bag of pretzels and half a Coke."

"Hey, that's terrific. The last few times I've flown, I didn't even get the pretzels."

Hannah reached for her glass of wine and brought it to her lips just as the plane bounced, sending the red liquid splashing onto her plate. Bryce reached out to steady her and said, "Are you all right?"

"Yes. Wow, what a mess."

The captain's voice boomed from the overhead speaker announcing that the flight had encountered unexpected turbulence and for everyone to make sure their seats belts were fastened.

Well, duh, thought Bryce. The dishes were quickly removed, and Bryce put his tray up and settled down in his seat. He glanced at Hannah and noticed that she did the same. "You don't look too shook up," Bryce said.

"Oh, flying doesn't bother me. My Uncle Bill has his pilot's license, so I've been in planes since I was a little kid. I'm safer here than in my car. The only thing that terrifies me is water."

"Water?"

"I know how to swim and everything, but I don't particularly want to go that way. You know, drown."

"I'd rather not go either way," he said and grinned at Hannah.

When she laughed again in a deep, jovial way, he discovered how much he loved that sound.

"So, what is your worst phobia? Everybody has one?" she said.

"Says the shrink," he smiled at her and winked. "My mother. She scares the shit out of me. Excuse the language."

"Your mother?"

"Oh yeah. My father is an officer in the Navy, and he's a tough taskmaster, but my mother is the one that rules the house."

"Are you close to her?"

"No, but I wish I was."

"How about your dad?"

"Oh, hell no," he said and shifted uncomfortably in his seat. "He's a mean SOB. But that's enough about my hangups."

Bryce leaned back in his seat and closed his eyes. He was tired from lack of sleep because of a late-night conversation with his younger brother, Quinn. Talking about his father with Hannah had brought that conversation front and center again in his mind.

Quinn was crazy and seemed to deliberately do things that he knew would antagonize the old man. Bryce remembered the day Quinn had changed all the rules.

CHAPTER 2
BRYCE CAMERON

BRYCE REMEMBERED **he had not been surprised** when his little brother took off three months after his high school graduation. The old man had been relentless in his criticism of Bryce's choice to take the summer off and his nagging about getting ahead in the world and going to college.

One night in late July, the whole "get a life" speech turned into a raging, screaming match between father and son.

"How can you turn your back on a full ride to the Academy? Do you know how many young men would give their left nut for that chance?"

"You're not hearing me, Dad. I said I wanted to take a year off. Not a lifetime. Only twelve short months."

"Don't tell me what I'm hearing. I'm not a fool. It's now or never, idiot. The U.S. Navy will not wait for you to work off your wanderlust." He raised his fist and took a step toward Quinn.

"Stop," Justine said. "Both of you, stop." Quinn and The Captain glared at each other, and Quinn left, took the stairs two at a time, and slammed the door to his room.

Bryce knew the peace between them would not last long. The tension in the house was palpable. Quinn had been moody and morose since before graduation. Because The Captain was home for the weekend, Bryce decided not to talk to his brother in the house. He texted Quinn and told him to meet him at the end of the driveway.

"What?" Quinn asked as he slid into the passenger seat of Bryce's car.

"What is not the question. The question is why?" He shot his brother a penetrating look. "Why are you walking around like somebody died? What's going on with you?"

Bryce drove to the park and pulled into a parking space. He put the car in neutral and left it running so the air-conditioning could stay on.

Bryce knew his father was riding his brother hard. He also knew if he interfered, things would get much worse. The Captain did not like anyone to question him, and when they did, his already grumpy demeanor became even more unbearable. "Talk to me. Is it the old man? Is he getting you down?"

"Not any more than usual," he murmured satirically.

Bryce was getting exasperated, trying to pull a response out of his brother. "Then what is it? What the hell is going on?"

Quinn's eyes darkened.

Bryce thought he could see the pain in them and wondered if he should back off.

"You wouldn't get it if I told you."

"Well, try me and see. Sometimes I'm not a complete asshole."

That made Quinn smile.

He put his hand on Quinn's shoulder and shook it gently. "Come on, little brother. You can tell me."

"You remember that girl at the diner?" His voice was thick and unsteady.

"Dixie?"

"Yeah. Well, she's gone."

"What do you mean, gone?"

"She quit without notice and moved away. Nobody has a clue where she is, and I have no way of finding her. I don't believe I'll ever see her again."

Bryce let out a long, audible breath. He didn't know what to say. He did not know his brother had been in so much pain.

"How long have you known?"

"Since a few days before graduation."

"Damn, Quinn. I'm sorry. That's a real shame. Is there anything I can do?"

Quinn hesitated. He didn't speak for such a long time, Bryce thought he was going to ignore the question.

"Actually, there is something, but I'm not sure you will agree to do it."

"Well, you'll never know unless you ask me. Shoot!"

Later, Bryce would question if he had done the right thing by helping his little brother plan a trip to Europe. They bought a backpack, stuffed it with all the necessary items, bought a plane ticket, checked his passport, and made sure his cell phone included an international plan.

Bryce wanted to give him a ride to the airport, but Quinn insisted he would grab an Uber and give his father one less thing to yell at Bryce about once he knew that his youngest had flown the coop.

Bryce helped him cart the backpack down the driveway when neither of his parents was home. "You're not going to say goodbye to Mom?"

"Nope. Can't take the drama. I'll call her in the morning so she won't worry."

"Sounds like a good plan. You realize The Captain is going to cut off your credit card and your ATM card. He will cancel them both."

"I have a little money. I've been saving for a while, and I got a big stash for graduation. I'll get a job. I'll be fine."

"There is one thing that Dad was right about. The Navy

will not wait. You are giving up a free education. Will you regret it?"

"Probably. But right now, I can't think straight, and I'm sure as hell not in the mood to be in an institution full of stuffed shirts like Dad who are shouting orders at me."

"Any idea when you're coming back?"

"No. But when I do, I'll be older. I'm not showing my face until the old man can't tell me what to do."

Bryce felt both admiration and anxiety in equal measure for what his brother planned to do.

"Keep in touch and be safe, Quinn," he said and hugged his brother hard.

"Always."

———

Bryce unclasped his hands from the armrests on the plane and crossed them in his lap. All that was old news. Quinn had passed up a full-ride scholarship to the academy to backpack through Europe and then came home to work odd jobs while traveling across the US. Now, Quinn had moved back home to Atlanta and was going to start his own furniture-making business. He had called Bryce the night before to fill him in on the plans.

Who was he to object? He was a struggling author with one published book. So much for the successful Cameron brothers.

"I find family dynamics fascinating," Hannah said, breaking into Bryce's thoughts.

"What?" he said, looking down into her intelligent eyes.

"Your family. Your father and mother. I can't relate. I'm close to my parents, and being an only child, I know I was terribly spoiled. But I enjoyed learning all about dysfunctional families in school."

"I don't know if we're dysfunctional exactly, but we aren't all warm and fuzzy."

"Ah, thus the unhappy ending to your book."

"No, I…" Bryce stopped and considered what she said. "I've never thought about it, but I guess every writer uses his own unique experiences. Perhaps you are correct."

"So, you don't see yourself with a happy ending?"

"Hey," Bryce said, trying to hide his smile. "Are you shrinking me, Doc?"

"Probably. It's an occupational habit," she said and smiled back. "So, tell me a little more about your family. Are you an only child, too?"

"Not hardly. As a matter of fact, I was thinking about Quinn, my brother."

"Sibling rivalry?"

"No, he's six years younger, I was probably more like a parent than a brother since my father was away from home most of the time. He was, well, he is a good kid."

"So, how old is this kid?"

"He's twenty-four going on fifteen. He's smart as a whip and extremely talented. Everything comes easy to him. The problem is, he doesn't seem to have much ambition."

"Why is that? What did he do?"

"It isn't what he did; it's what he didn't do. He had an academic scholarship and blew it off to backpack across Europe and see the world."

"Are you a little envious?"

"No, why?" He stopped and thought about it and then said, "Well, okay, maybe a little," he acknowledged, moving uncomfortably in his seat. "I did what all the Camerons are supposed to do. I went to the Academy and did my time in the Navy. Quinn didn't follow the family plan."

"But you're not in the Navy anymore, are you?"

"No, I did my required time and got out. I wanted to be a writer."

"And you couldn't have been a writer while in the Navy?"

"No, I wanted to write fiction and stop writing about war." Bryce shook his head.

"Geez, you are good." He wanted to get up and walk away, but he was thirty-thousand feet above the earth and there was nowhere to run. "You don't even have to struggle to get people to pour out their guts. I love my brother, and I love my parents. Don't like them very much, but I love them. I did what I was supposed to do, and now I get to live my life the way I want to."

"So, you get to have your happy ending."

Bryce stared dumbfounded at her. He'd never met anyone like her before. She knew him better than he knew himself. "How about another glass of wine? I could use another beer. I need to make my brain numb."

When the drinks arrived, it was Hannah's turn to make the toast. "To you, Bryce."

"Why to me?"

"Because I find you to be an honorable and likable person. I'm pretty sure that you will find the success you are looking for, and I will get to tell everyone I drank wine in the sky with *the* Bryce Cameron. You know, the famous author."

Bryce was touched and found it hard to reply. When he did, it was to say, "So are you from Denver?"

"No, I grew up in the South, too. I'm from North Carolina, but I don't have the sexy accent like you do."

"You think my accent's sexy?"

"Absolutely, and I noticed it gets heavier when you're trying to pick up a girl," she said with a mischievous grin.

Bryce took a long drink of his beer, set the glass down, and ran his finger around the frosty rim. "You think I'm hitting on you?" he said.

"Oh, absolutely, but I don't mind. I've been so busy with school and work that I haven't flirted in a long time."

"What are your plans for tonight after you get to Denver?"

Bryce said as he turned and moved as close to Hannah as his seat belt would allow.

"Well," Hannah said coyly. "I'm going to unpack, take a long hot shower…"

"And?" Bryce said.

"Oh, and then I'll probably call my boyfriend and tell him all about my trip."

Bryce tried to wipe the look of disappointment from his face. He hoped it worked as he said, "Well, ma'am, I was hoping you could show the new guy in town around. I suppose this boyfriend of yours is the jealous type?"

"Probably, but I know for sure since there's never been a reason for him to be. I guess you thought you were going to get lucky tonight. Sorry to disappoint."

That's exactly what Bryce was thinking. He liked this woman a lot. She was pretty, smart, and funny. In the past, it had been his bad luck to find that the beautiful women he encountered were dumb as a stump or had absolutely no sense of humor. Hannah was different. In fact, she was close to perfect.

"So, you haven't said. Are you going to be living in Denver?" Hannah asked.

"Before I answer, let's get this straight. That was a no, right? You won't be showing me around town tonight? Nothing extra-curricular. Simply two sort-of-new friends spending a nice platonic evening?"

Hannah gave an unladylike snort and playfully punched him on the arm. "I like you, Bryce. You make me laugh. Sometimes, I take myself and my job way too seriously, but I'm sorry, as tempting as your offer might be, I'm going to have to pass. In the first place, I'm not available, and in the second place, even if I agreed to show you around, I couldn't. I'm new to Denver too. It would be like the blind leading the blind."

"Well then, the answer is no. I will only be in Denver long

enough to rent a car and then I will drive to Frisco. I've leased a cabin there for the next few months. I'm hoping to get far enough away from distractions to concentrate fully on writing. I've started on my next novel, but I'm having trouble pulling it all together. Maybe if I'm alone, you know, off the grid as they say, I'll get something accomplished. If not, you'll probably find me at the nearby Walmart. I hear they pay above minimum wage."

"You know," she said, pointing at the book she'd stashed in the seat pocket, "the plot was excellent, and the characters were …"

"Less than likable?"

"Well, I wouldn't say that."

"It's okay, other people already have. Seems my characters were well-developed and even intriguing, but they weren't very likable. My best friend told me he didn't know whom to root for since everyone was so despicable. He hoped everyone died in the end."

She threw back her head and let out a great peal of laughter but then sobered, and her tone became sympathetic. "Wow, that was cruel, and you say he's your best friend? Maybe you need to look for a new best bro."

She radiated a vitality that drew him to her like a magnet. She made him feel more alive than he had in a long time.

The flight attendant stopped to pick up the drink glasses and reminded them to put the trays up to prepare for landing. When the captain began speaking, Bryce realized the flight was about to end. He didn't know what to say to Hannah after her revelation about a boyfriend. Was it serious? She used the phrase *at the moment*. Did that mean it wasn't a permanent relationship? Maybe a college romance? What did it matter? He didn't have the time or even the energy to simultaneously jump-start his career and pursue a romance.

An obvious silence loomed between the two travelers, where there had been a friendly camaraderie only moments before. Bryce realized he was responsible and leaned over and said, "I've enjoyed our conversation and thank you for your honest critique of the book. I promise I will take everything you said quite seriously. And if you weren't otherwise engaged, I would love to get to know you better, but I understand."

He helped her with her bag from the overhead storage and was surprised when she remained at his side so they could walk to the baggage claim together. The conversation down the long, crowded corridor was easy and mostly about the perks of being in the one percent who were traveling first class. While they waited for the luggage to circle on the belt, Bryce teased her about being able to pick out which suitcase was hers. In the end, he wasn't even close when she pointed to a plain, dark brown Samsonite.

"I've got to say, that bag doesn't fit your personality at all. I figured you for the bright yellow one over there, or at least a red one." He pulled the luggage off the belt and placed it in front of her.

Hannah smiled and said thank you. Her lips were wide and inviting. He stopped himself from leaning in to kiss her goodbye. "So long, Doc. It was great meeting you," Bryce said. Then he slung his bag over his shoulder and strode briskly away from the baggage carousel. When he turned around to see if she was looking at him, he was delighted to see that she was.

CHAPTER 3
BRYCE CAMERON

BRYCE SQUINTED **at the screen of the GPS on his phone** and sighed when he realized he was losing data reception in the mountains. The drive from Denver had been tiring after his long flight from New York, so he'd stopped at a truck stop on I-70 to get coffee and a semi-warm burrito. The rental agent had led him to believe the cabin was in Frisco, but he'd left the quaint village twenty miles back and was heading into the mountains.

When he pulled over to the side of the road to stretch and get his bearings, he got out of the car and was suddenly ankle-deep in snow. It was freezing outside, but above him, he could see the clear sky filled with twinkling stars. He got back in the front seat, punched in the number for Sky Forest Realtors and wasn't surprised when he reached a recording. The pleasant female voice dictated a number to call in case of an emergency. If not knowing where you were going on a dark mountain road in the middle of nowhere wasn't an emergency, he didn't know what was.

After stating his problem and listening to a man offer sincere apologies for the misunderstanding, he was given new directions to his destination. He glanced at his almost illegible writing, put the car in gear, and slowly headed back up the mountain. He turned onto one dirt road and then another and finally turned again at a rusty water tower. The forest was thicker here, and his headlights had frightened several deer at the side of the road. Thankfully, none had jumped in front of his car. He was exhausted and not ready for a long walk in the snow.

He had seen no signs of civilization for at least four miles and was thinking he might have to turn around when he saw the road up ahead. He guided the car onto the long driveway and saw a rustic log cabin with a large front porch peeking out from between the trees.

Bryce turned off the engine, opened the door, sat, and listened to the silence. He could hear the occasional whistle of the wind blowing softly through the pines, but he heard no barking dogs or sounds of cars traveling down the unpaved road. He was most definitely in the wilderness. Perhaps tomorrow, when it was light, he would travel around the corner and run into a McDonald's. But for tonight, he would live with the fantasy that he was completely alone.

He opened the heavy wooden door and walked into warmth. For an extra two hundred dollars, the Realtor had promised to turn the heat on and stock the kitchen with necessities. He turned on the light and looked at the warm, cozy, great room. He saw the gleaming refrigerator and made his way toward it like one of the living dead. He was starving.

There was a note on the refrigerator door that read: Welcome. Left cold cuts in the fridge along with eggs and milk. Coffee in the pantry. Lucy.

Lucy? Who the hell was Lucy? Then he remembered the receptionist at Sky Forest Realtors. He sure hoped the owners gave her a cut of his two hundred. Seemed like a lot of money for some meat and coffee.

He looked around the kitchen. It had a long bar with three

sturdy stools and a large country sink. There was a gas stove, and a microwave sat on the counter. All the comforts of home.

He opened the pantry and revised his critical thoughts about the Realtors. The shelves were filled with cans of soup, beans, fruit, and vegetables. There were several kinds of cereal and cookies. "Yes! There are cookies," he mumbled. He found a loaf of bread and made a quick sandwich and sat down at the counter. His lips curved into a smile as he looked around the room. He was going to enjoy the next few months.

A fire would be nice, but he was too tired to do anything but find the bedroom and collapse onto the inviting forest-themed quilt of trees, bears, and deer. As he fell asleep, he couldn't get the silly verse out of his head from that movie with Dorothy and the little people: "Lions and tigers and bears, oh, my!"

The sun spread across his pillow the next morning, and Bryce squinted and pulled it over his head. He was having a dream, and he wanted it to continue. It was a tantalizing dream, and the lovely Doc Hannah was a featured player. He couldn't quite remember what they were doing, but it must have been something because he woke up turned on and horny.

Awake now, he saw Hannah's face clearly in his mind, and when she'd walked beside him in the tunnel to baggage claim, he had admired her remarkable figure. She was of medium height, with curves in all the right places. Not stick skinny like most of the girls he'd dated. With her face, body, and brain, she was pretty close to the perfect woman. Too bad it hadn't worked out, but it was probably for the best. He didn't believe she was the kind of woman for casual sex, and that was all he had time for.

He poured himself a cup of coffee and walked out onto the front porch to see what he had missed last night when he arrived in the pitch black. The morning was cold, but perfect. The snow-covered ground looked as if it had been several days since any new accumulation. He looked around for a chair or bench and, finding none, made a mental note to bring a chair out the next time. He reluctantly went back inside, opened his laptop, and sat down to write.

Two hours later, he yawned and stretched and thought about a nap. After looking at what he'd written, he slammed the computer closed in frustration. He got another cup of coffee and a couple of the cookies, something with the fancy name, Milano. He took a bite and decided they weren't half bad, but what was wrong with a good old chocolate chip with lots of nuts? He settled back down at the computer and started again.

He realized one problem was that he didn't like his protagonist. Maybe no one else would either. He hadn't thought much about examining his characters until after his conversation with Hannah. Maybe he needed to overhaul his entire way of thinking. After all, he only had one way to go, and that was up.

He was deep into his second chapter when he heard a car engine and the crunch of tires on the pine needles in the driveway. Annoyed, he pulled open the door to see a short, pudgy woman with dark brown hair cut just below her chin and a round, pretty face.

"Oh, hi," she said excitedly. "I hope I didn't disturb you, but I came by to drop off the car and pick up the rental."

Bryce was confused before he remembered he'd arranged for a long-term rental car that was part of the house lease. The real estate office agreed to pick up the car he had rented in Denver and supply him with an older vehicle he could use to get around in the snow.

"Oh, I'd almost forgotten. I was deep into my work."

The portly young woman stuck out her hand and said, "I'm Lucy. Lucy Rosen. We spoke on the phone a couple of times."

"Yes, I remember. You work at Sky Forest Realty. Please come in, it's cold out there. I'll get the keys."

Bryce came back from the bedroom with the keys in hand and noticed his visitor was standing by the open computer. It was obvious the woman had been snooping since the book page was open and not the screen saver. He quickly moved toward her and said, "I don't like to share my manuscript until I've completed it. I hope you don't mind."

Clearly embarrassed, the woman's face turned beet red. "I'm so sorry," she stammered. "I'm a big fan. I absolutely loved your last book."

"If you did, then you are clearly in the minority."

"I don't understand. The critics gave it a five-star review. I notice things like that," she said as she picked an imaginary piece of lint from her fluffy pink sweater. "And the picture. You look exactly like your picture."

"I hope that's a good thing."

"Oh, yes," she stammered, "a good thing."

"That's kind of you to say, Lucy. I appreciate your picking up the car and for supplying the groceries. You've made my life a lot easier."

"Oh, it's all part of the service. We at Sky Forest like to keep our customers happy." They exchanged keys, and hoping to end the conversation, he walked her to the door.

"If there's anything else you need, be sure to let me know."

"I can't think of a thing, and your kindness is greatly appreciated."

Lucy beamed with delight at his praise and strolled to the car. She waved as she turned the vehicle around and drove off.

Bryce saved the last paragraph and gently closed his computer. He had put in about three hours of solid work, and although not happy with everything, he was mildly pleased with the way the story was flowing. He yawned and stretched and considered taking a nap but took a walk instead.

The afternoon temperature was about twenty-five degrees, but the sky had only mixed clouds and there was minimal wind. He needed to get an idea of exactly where he was and what was out there. He could smell the pine sap in the tall, stately trees.

After about thirty minutes, he had decided he was pretty much on his own when he saw another house off to his left. The short road leading to the property showed no sign of tracks. His nearest neighbor obviously wasn't a winter person. The Realtor had told him most of the people in these mountains only used their homes during the summer. They considered it too remote and cold this time of year. He turned around and headed back toward his house. He thought he might take that nap after all.

Several days later, he had just stepped out of the shower and grabbed a towel when he heard a knock on his door. What the heck? He pulled on a pair of gray sweats and a threadbare T-shirt. He was raking his fingers through his hair when he opened the door to find Lucy standing on the porch holding a bakery box.

"Hi," she said. "I was showing a property a little ways down the road, and I thought I would stop by with breakfast. I remember Simon, that character in your book, had a sweet tooth, so I figured you did too. Aren't most characters based on real life?"

Bryce was dumfounded and at a loss for words. He should invite her in, but he didn't want to. He wanted to get on with his book and his research.

"Lucy, this isn't a good time. I'm up against a deadline." Which wasn't true, but she didn't know that. "This is thoughtful of you, but I'm not a big fan of donuts. Those are donuts in the box, right?"

"Yes, chocolate-filled, the way Simon liked them."

"Lucy, I'm not Simon," he said, talking to her as if she were a five-year-old. "I'm nothing like him. He's a made-up character."

"Oh sure, I know," she mumbled, but he didn't believe her.

She looked so hurt that against his better judgment he said, "Why don't you come in and have a cup of coffee and one of the donuts? But only for a minute because I've got to get back to work."

She sat down at the kitchen table, and he set a mug of steaming coffee and a napkin in front of her. He watched silently as she took a bite of the sugary donut and then wiped the chocolate from her lips. "Delicious. Sure you don't want one? The bakery in town is famous for... well, not exactly famous, but people are always lined up on Saturdays for breakfast."

"I'm sure," he said. He was exasperated and clearly angry with himself. She was only trying to be nice. He sat across from her and watched her eat.

"So, what's this book about? The new one?"

"I'd rather not say. I don't let people look at my work, and I prefer not to discuss my plot with anyone except my editor. But I can tell you it's set in the mountains in the winter."

"So, you're going to make Frisco famous?" She was clearly delighted.

"No, nothing like that. The town and the characters are purely fiction. That's why I came to the mountains, but it didn't have to be Colorado, it could have been anywhere. I have always wanted to visit."

"If you want to look around, you know, take in the scenery, I'd be happy to show you. There's a trail up the peak about ten miles from here and even in the winter, if it's a pretty day, the view is spectacular."

Bryce shook his head no, stood and picked up his empty cup. "I need to get back to work. I appreciate the thought," he said, pointing to the box.

Lucy stood and walked toward the door. She clearly wanted to stay longer, but Bryce was sure he couldn't be civil for another minute. He didn't bother to watch her walk to her car and turned around before he saw the look of longing on the woman's face.

————

The next day, Bryce left the comfort of his warm cabin and made the forty-minute trip into town. The streets were clear of snow and the drive was relatively easy. Two of the amenities he'd taken for granted were access to the Internet and to a phone. Although he wasn't completely without a cell phone signal, it wasn't reliable and couldn't be counted on. He wanted to do some research on the library computers and contact his brother to check on the family.

He was surprised by how large and inviting the building was. A sign on the wall said that the coffee and Wi-Fi were free. He felt like he was back in civilization. Before he got to work or called his brother, he grabbed a copy of the *Denver Post* and sat at a quiet table in the back of the room. Not much was going on in the world. It had been a relatively calm few weeks. He was about to fold up the paper when a photo caught his eye. It was Doc, his Doc from the plane, all dressed up in a fancy gown at some charity function for mental illness. His heart gave a lurch and beat a little faster. The woman definitely affected him and had since the first moment he saw her. He put the article down before reading any further. He wasn't going there.

He placed a call to his brother, Quinn, and was disappointed when he got the voicemail. He left a message and then settled down at the computer to look up the trail Lucy had told him about. The woman annoyed him, but he supposed she meant well, and from the pictures of the mountain, it looked like the setting would fit perfectly into the book. He decided to check it out. He looked up the weather and was pleased to see that a storm was due, but not until late the following night, so he'd have plenty of time in the morning to go on a "field trip."

He slid into his car and was adjusting the rearview mirror when the phone rang. He smiled when he saw his brother's name. "Hey, bro," he said, smiling into the phone.

"Hey, yourself," said Quinn. "How is my wilderness brother?"

"I'm not the one who took off backpacking across the world. I've got running water and electricity."

"I am impressed."

"So how are the folks? Anything I need to know about?"

"Dad's having a cow because you couldn't write at home, and Mom is … well, she's Mom. What can I say?"

"So, same old, same old?"

"Pretty much. How's the book going? Making any progress?"

"Some, but I can't seem to get a handle on where I'm going with it. I'm trying to get the characters right this time."

"You mean people I would actually care about if they croaked?"

"Well, I don't know if I would go that far. I'm doing some steady work. I'm going up to a trail tomorrow to look around for research."

"Isn't it winter up there?"

"Yeah, but one local said it was pretty easy, even this time of year."

"Be careful and keep in touch. You not having email or phone service kind of sucks."

"You know, if there is an emergency, you can contact the real estate office. They'll get word to me. I left the number with the folks."

"What's new with you, little brother?" Bryce said.

"Now that you mention it, there is something you might be interested to know."

"Okay, spill it."

"Well, my boss has been quite good to me lately."

"Good how? Did he give you a raise?"

"My boss is a she."

"Oh," his voice rose in surprise. "So, did she give you a raise?"

"Not exactly, but she did get a rise out of me."

Bryce laughed. His voice was tinged with excitement. "Well, all right! It's about time. I thought you might be turning into a monk."

He said his goodbyes, hung up and started the car. The next time they talked, he would be sure to ask how the furniture-making business was going. He hoped Quinn would not quit his job before he had built up a savings account. Starting a new business was a risky venture, and he wanted his brother to succeed.

———

By the time he reached the plateau, he was winded, and the altitude was forcing him to suck in the thin air. He vowed to start walking or jogging or doing something every day. He hadn't realized he was out of shape, but obviously he was.

The view was spectacular and was well worth the climb. This would make for a great scene in the book. The high mountains were covered in white and the clouds dipping gracefully to embrace them were swollen with snow. It was then that he noticed the wind had increased, and the temperature was falling. He'd worn a warm wool jacket and cap but had neglected to wear gloves or a scarf.

Remembering the weather report he had read yesterday while at the library, he knew a winter storm was predicted, but it wasn't due until after midnight tonight. That should have given him plenty of time to check out the scenery and get back to his warm cabin by early afternoon.

To be safe, he reluctantly turned around and headed back down the path toward the road. The first wet snowflakes brushed his cheeks, and in less than fifteen minutes his visibility was jeopardized. A half-hour later, the trail made by deer and elk was covered in snow.

Unsure now if the direction he was going would lead him off the mountain and back to his car or in perilous circles, he walked carefully, looking for familiar rocks or trees. He looked at his watch again. Time was flying, and he was trying not to panic. Damn, how could he have been so stupid? He should have taken the time to drive far enough to get a good cell signal to check the weather again. He knew better. Nothing was more unpredictable than the weather unless it was a woman.

Better yet, he should have insisted that the cabin he rented have some way he could communicate with the outside world. If he got off this mountain, he would have choice words with the rental company. He clenched his jaw to keep his teeth from chattering and shivered. That was not a good sign. His body was trying to tell him he was getting cold. No shit. He knew he was cold. He pulled his wool cap down farther over his ears and stuck his hands in the pockets of his jacket. His jeans were wet from the snow and clung to his legs.

He refused to freeze to death on the side of a mountain only a few hundred feet from his car. Earlier, on his right, he had seen a large moss-covered boulder which was now covered in snow. Or at least he thought it was the same rock.

He had three choices: stop and try to find shelter, keep going on what he assumed was the path, or lie down and die. Well, he wouldn't do that. And he didn't want to search for shelter. So that left keeping on keeping on. He was sure he recognized the rock, and that had to mean he was on the right trail.

The snow was still as heavy, but the trees were thinning, and he was positive this was the right route. He came out of the forest and was ecstatic when he thought he could see the fine outline of his Subaru through the fat flakes falling from the sky. As he approached, he realized he was safe. The car had four-wheel drive, and the roads wouldn't be icy yet, just snow-packed. Shaking, he reached for the door handle, threw himself into the driver's seat, and jabbed the key into the ignition.

Nothing. Nothing happened. He jiggled the key. Was the battery bad? Frustrated and still freezing, he pulled open the hood and looked at the battery. The cables were all connected, and there was no corrosion or buildup. Bryce tried to start the car again with the same results. It was becoming an exceptionally bad day. It was a good ten miles back to his cabin. Most of it was dirt roads, and the storm didn't look like it was going to let up anytime soon.

Again, he faced a decision. Either stay here and freeze to death or try to make it back home on foot.

Neither one was especially tempting.

CHAPTER 4
BRYCE CAMERON

BRYCE KNEW **the best course of** action was to stay right where he was in the car. However, his instinct as a man was to bundle up and try to walk through the storm to the cabin. Thankfully, he didn't have to make a choice.

A set of dimly glowing headlights moved slowly through the snowflakes toward his vehicle. Some other fool was out trying to get home during Mother Nature's fury. Bryce climbed out of his car and stared at the approaching vehicle. It was a large Ram truck with a snowplow attached. He waved and was rewarded with a blast from the horn.

"Hey," the man said as Bryce leaned into the open window on the passenger side. "What in the blazes are you doing out here in the middle of a snowstorm?"

Bryce wanted to whip off a smartass reply like, "Oh, I thought I'd take in the scenery," but he knew that wouldn't be an appropriate comment. Instead, he said, "My fault. I didn't check the weather when I left this morning and didn't realize the storm had come in early until I was at the top of the peak. By the time I got down, the visibility was next to nothing, and my car wouldn't start." He shrugged and smiled at the man who was staring at him with unsympathetic eyes.

"I'm out clearing the roads. I rarely come out this far since no one lives here, but someone said they saw a car driving around earlier, so I thought I'd check."

"You mean there are other people living up here besides me? I've seen no one since I got here."

"Where's here?" the man said, pushing open the truck door so Bryce could get in.

"About ten miles back the way you came. The log cabin is close to the water tower."

"The Johnson place. I know it. I'll take you there and you can get someone from town to fix your car tomorrow. This should all blow over by morning, but until then it's supposed to dump about a foot of snow."

Bryce shivered, wiped the snow as best he could from his boots and coat, and got in the truck. The warmth encompassed him like a cocoon, and for the first time since the snow began, he realized he was going to be all right.

"Richard Merced," the man said. "I'm the ranger up here."

"Bryce Cameron," he said, holding out his hand, "and I am so glad to see you. I feel like a fool. Everything would have been fine if that damn car had started. I checked the battery and cables. They were okay. The car's a loaner from the real estate office, but it's not that old and is supposed to be equipped for this altitude and weather. That's another bone I have to pick with them."

"What do you mean?"

"The house doesn't have Wi-Fi or TV, much less phone service. I'm completely isolated from civilization with no way to communicate. I didn't think I would mind since I'm a writer and I kind of like the solitude, but not being able to check the weather could have been disastrous."

The ranger gave him a sidelong glance of disbelief. "I don't know why they told you that. That cabin has phone service, and I know they had a dish there for TV. I could see it when I drove by. Can't say as I've paid any attention lately."

Bewildered and speechless, Bryce shook his head. He couldn't understand why they had led him to believe otherwise.

"Place belonged to Kevin Johnson and his wife. I had dinner with them a few times a year. Nice people. They loved to watch Jeopardy, so that's how I know they had a TV. After they died, their kids started renting the place out. I guess they could have taken all that stuff out to save money."

Bryce was fuming by the time he got home but offered Richard a cup of coffee for his trouble. The ranger thanked him but said he'd better get on down the mountain to check on the other residents. He'd promised to send someone up from town tomorrow, or as soon as the roads were clear, to tow the car and give Bryce a lift to the real estate office.

Bryce watched the truck back up the driveway and turn toward town. When he started to open the door, he thought he saw another car's headlights beam through the snow coming from the opposite direction. Damn, he thought. I've been here a month, and I haven't seen another human being except Lucy and today, on the day of the worst snowstorm of the season, I've seen two cars.

The vehicle slowed as it reached the driveway but went on by. It was dark now, and with the snow still coming down, he couldn't be sure, but he could have sworn the car looked like the one Lucy had been driving when she came by with the donuts. What possible reason could she have for being so far from town tonight of all nights?

Bryce walked into his cabin and immediately went to the fireplace. He stopped short when he noticed the two large logs atop kindling and newspaper. The fire was ready to start. He sat back, resting his weight on his legs and was perplexed. Surely, he would have remembered getting the wood out of the box and readying the fire. Besides, he didn't have a news-paper. The last one he'd seen was at the town library, and he hadn't brought it home.

He looked around the room and expected someone to pop out and say, "Surprise." This was beyond creepy. The only person he knew who had a key was Lucy. Angry and irritated as hell, he pulled the wood out of the firebox onto the floor and grabbed the newspaper. It had today's date.

"Damn," he said. He walked through the entire house to make sure it was empty and that nothing was missing. His computer was sitting on the desk, but thanks to Apple, it was password protected.

He glanced into the bedroom at his bed. Years of being in the Navy had taught him to always make the bed. It was still neatly made but had a slight indention on the left side. "That crazy bitch," he growled between gritted teeth. He was sure it was Lucy. What was she, obsessed? Shades of Kathy Bates in *Misery*. He pulled the quilt and all the sheets off the bed and dumped them in the washroom. No way was he sleeping on that bedding.

———

The roads weren't cleared until mid-morning the second day after the storm. The time alone in the cabin with no transportation gave Bryce lots of time to reflect. It wasn't as bad as it could have been. He was certain if Richard hadn't come along that he would have been rescued the next day, or he would have been able to walk home after the snow dissipated. But the whole situation was a powerful punch in the gut.

Then there was the incident with his stalker. He couldn't believe this was happening to him. He wasn't famous. One book does not a celebrity make. He laughed out loud at the circumstances and planned to make Lucy a top priority when he finally went to town.

Growing up with a tough Navy officer for a dad, Bryce was taught to hide his emotions and to always be strong no matter what. Those were traits that were as much a part of him now as breathing, but maybe there was a little bit of room for change. He was as vulnerable as the next guy.

He was looking at thirty-one on his next birthday, and what did he have to show for all those years? Sure, he had an impressive college degree, a halfway decent stint as a reporter, and a critically acclaimed novel that no one wanted to read. He had no wife, no children, and friends he rarely saw. Let's face it; he had no social life at all unless you could count one-night stands. He planned to change that.

———

The man who got out of the wrecker in front of Bryce's cabin looked like he was straight out of Mayberry R.F.D. He was a large man dressed in grease-stained bib overalls and a red checked flannel shirt. His well-worn hat sat on top of a shaggy head of salt and pepper hair. Stitched into the hat was the logo of *Bob's Garage*. All that was needed to make the character real was to greet Bryce with a "howdy." When he didn't, Bryce was a little disappointed.

The man held out his hand and smiled as he said, "Good morning. You must be Mr. Cameron. Richard asked me to come by and tow you to town. Understand your car crapped out on you during the storm. Name's Robert Janis. I own the only garage in town."

"Nice to meet you, Robert. Please call me Bryce."

"So, you wanna show me where the car's at, and I'll jump right on in and see what's going on? Mighty inconvenient time for you to get stuck out in the weather. Good thing Richard came along. It's real easy to lose your sense of direction when the snow's blowing hard."

"Yes," Bryce said, a little embarrassed. He didn't look back on it as one of his finer moments.

"So, what happened? Batteries tend to go bad when it's cold."

"It's not the battery. The car would turn over, but it wouldn't start. I checked the battery and cables. They seemed okay."

"Well, won't know 'til I get it back to the garage. Hop in and you can show me where it is."

———

When Bryce walked into the Sky Forest Real Estate office, he was loaded for bear. He'd just come from Bob's garage, where he'd learned that his car didn't have a bad battery or fuel injector. No, his car had been sabotaged. Someone had taken out one of the fuses, and he had a pretty good idea who had done it. The *why* was a complete mystery.

There was a car outside, so he knew that someone was there, but the office was empty. He paced back and forth and finally called out, "Hey, anybody here?"

A middle-aged man walked out of the back office and greeted Bryce warmly. "Sorry, I didn't know anyone was here. My wife ran out to the post office. She usually hears when we get customers. How can I help you?"

"I'm Bryce Cameron and I…"

"Ah, Mr. Cameron. So nice to finally meet you. I'm John. I spoke with you on the phone the night you arrived. Sorry for the miscommunication on the location of the cabin. How is everything working out for you?"

Bryce frowned and counted to three and then began, "Not so good." He saw the look of concern on the man's face and continued. "It seems I need to file a formal complaint against one of your employees, and if I can prove it I'm also going to file criminal charges."

"Oh, good grief," the man said. "I … I … don't know what to say. Which one? What did they do?"

"Lucy Rosen. She entered my residence without permission, and I believe she vandalized my car." Bryce looked up at the man, whose face had now gone from concern to anger. Shit, just what he needed. He looked like a nice guy, and he hoped they wouldn't come to blows.

"Lucy!" John exclaimed. "Please come back into my office so we can talk. I had to let Ms. Rosen go last week. She didn't show up for work on time and sometimes left in the middle of the day. She couldn't be depended on. I was getting complaints because calls were going unanswered. Are you telling me she's been up at your cabin?"

"Yes. I guess initially to stock the kitchen with food before I arrived. Then she came by on her way to show a property and brought me donuts. While I was out of the room, she opened my computer to look at my manuscript, and then there was the incident with the fireplace."

"I'm sorry, Mr. Cameron, but Lucy didn't show houses. She was our receptionist. She said she took the food because she had a cousin who lived up there, and she was going to make the trip, anyway. I got the key back from her the next day."

John sat down in front of his desk and motioned for Bryce to have a seat in the armchair. "Would you like a cup of coffee? Personally, I need something stronger, but coffee will have to do."

"No but thank you. So where is she now?"

"I don't know for sure. Don't even know where she lives. She came to town last summer and worked at the general store. When the season ended, she was laid off and our receptionist was on maternity leave. I hired her to fill in, and when Molly, that's our old receptionist, decided to stay home permanently, I gave Lucy the full-time job."

"I guess I need to file a report with the police, although like I said, I don't have any proof it was she who broke in or messed with my car."

"I'm sorry, Mr. Cameron. If I'd known what was going on, I'd have put a stop to it. I will have a locksmith out today to change the lock."

"How about the Internet and TV? Can you take care of that, too?"

"What about them? I was under the impression you wanted solitude and didn't want the disruption?"

Bryce looked up at John, smirked and thought, *you've got to be kidding me.* He started to correct the man, but before he could, John said, "Oh, yes, I see."

John steepled his index fingers below his chin and shook his head. "It was Lucy who told me you called and asked that the TV and Internet not be connected. Again, what can I say? This entire situation has been such a disaster. If this gets out, it could ruin us. Please, what can I do to make it right?"

Bryce stood and looked down at the man. "I don't blame you for your employee's deception. Hopefully, I can leave all of this behind and get on with the reason I came to Colorado."

"I understand. I'll call the satellite company right now and have them hook everything up—TV, Internet, and phone. The owner's a friend. This time of year, he's not busy. I'll see if we can get that up and running today, too."

Not quite as angry as he had been before he went in, Bryce left the office. He'd decided to file a complaint with the local police. Even if he didn't have proof, at least it would be on file, and if anything else happened... *damn, I hope nothing else happens. What else could go wrong?*

He'd picked up a few things while he was in town and treated himself to a steak dinner. He thought about eating in one of the restaurants but was hesitant to leave the cabin empty until the locks were changed.

By eight that evening, he had a new key to the cabin and a basketball game on the TV. He thought about calling Quinn now that he had service because he knew his brother would get a kick out of what was going on in his life, but he decided to wait until after dinner. He planned to bundle up and sit out on the front porch and go over the entire last forty-eight hours with his brother. Quinn being Quinn would make him laugh and probably call him some outrageous name.

His cell rang. He picked it up but didn't recognize the number on the caller ID. That would be about right. He hadn't had contact with the outside world, and the first time he did it was a damn telemarketer. He let the call go to voice-mail and went on getting the grill ready and seasoning his steak.

He grabbed a heavy coat, gloves, and cap and moved out onto the front porch. It was a cloudy night, and he was disappointed he couldn't see the stars. That was one of the best things about being out in the middle of nowhere. On a starry night, the sight could be breathtaking.

He slid open his phone, intending to call Quinn, when he saw the message waiting for him. Thinking it could be the Realtor calling or even the police, he listened to the message and gripped the phone so hard it was surprising it didn't break.

"Bryce. I know you're there. I see the lights. I don't know why you've done this to me. I thought we had something special. The police were here. They said terrible things, but I forgive you. I know you're stressed. I'll call you later. Love L."

"Damn, damn, damn," he said and pulled the card out of his shirt pocket with the name and number of the police officer he had spoken with earlier. His previous thoughts echoed in his brain. Something else could happen. It had happened. Not only was this woman crazy, she was looney-bin crazy, and she thought she was in love with him.

He punched in the number and when the policeman answered, he said, "Officer Bonilla, this is Bryce Cameron. I'm afraid there's been another incident with Lucy."

Bryce downed his second glass of Crown and Coke and sat down in front of his computer. He had a nice little buzz, and his creative juices were flowing. He'd been stumped on the composition of the villain's makeup since he began writing. Now, he had a clear vision, and it was a doozy. His fingers flew across the keys.

Several hours later, he was deep into the story. This chapter would introduce the heroine, and he could envision honey-blonde, shoulder-length hair, and beautiful, intelligent hazel eyes. She had a wicked sense of humor, and it was love at first sight for his hero. How could there not be a happy ending?

CHAPTER 5
HANNAH BRODY

HANNAH PUSHED **her hair up inside the warm winter cap** her Great-Aunt Hattie had knitted for her last Christmas. Although it was officially spring on the calendar, she was learning that Denver weather seldom cooperated until June, or at least that's what all the natives said.

Hannah had been so preoccupied with preparing and teaching her university psychology classes and managing her struggling private practice, she had no time for herself. When she noticed her skirts and pants were getting tighter every morning, she could no longer make the excuse that she needed to change dry cleaners. Unfortunately, her sedentary lifestyle was catching up with her. Not that she sat around and watched TV while she ate chocolate chip cookies, but she had eaten way too much fast food because it was easy, and she was busy, and she hadn't put on her running shoes since she'd moved to Denver.

Today she was turning over a new leaf. She'd grimaced as the perky, pony-tailed joggers wearing sexy workout tops ran by with smiles on their faces. Evidently, they didn't mind the cold. Hannah loved to run. Absolutely loved it. She'd been a star softball player in college, and there was nothing like the feeling of slamming the ball into the outfield and dashing for the bases.

She started out at a slow jog and picked up the pace halfway around the park. Her parents had never understood her stamina and competitive drive for sports. They were both from the world of academia. Her father was a physicist and her mother taught history. They'd met at school and had been devoted to each other ever since. Most of the time, Hannah felt like the proverbial fish out of water when she was with them. She'd pursued her psychology degree because it pleased them both that she was following them down the academic path. She'd have been as happy to become a high school softball coach.

Hannah had always been the dutiful daughter. She stayed out of trouble and never gave her parents cause for concern. Although not a brilliant student, she studied hard throughout high school, college, and graduate school. Nothing could beat the look of pride on her father's face when she received her doctorate. She supposed they'd still love her the same if she hadn't been a high achiever, but a tad of niggling doubt lingered in the back of her mind.

Hannah rarely dated, and although she liked men, she was usually uncomfortable around them and shy. She wondered why she'd been so different with the man on the plane. Bryce Cameron was his name. She'd googled him. He was so much better looking in person than on the website. She was surprised that he'd told her the truth about himself and hadn't embellished his story to impress her.

Now, she felt bad that she'd lied to him about having a boyfriend. She wasn't in a relationship and wasn't looking to be. She was a little apprehensive about going to dinner with a stranger, even if he was an extremely handsome one. Too many nut jobs were out there. She saw them every day in her office. And besides, she wasn't good at relationships. They always ended badly or never got started.

Before she realized it, she was back at her condo, gasping for breath and feeling better than she had in months. Although she had no classes on Tuesdays, she had a calendar full of appointments with patients. She wasn't normally so booked, but one of her colleagues was on a month-long sabbatical, and he had asked her to see his more involved clients while he was away. Hurriedly she dressed for work, ready to start a brand-new day.

Her condo was close to the upscale business district known as DTC - short for Denver Tech Center. She had been driving her car instead of walking to work. She told herself that maybe when she had more time she'd try to walk, but today she was almost late because of the morning run.

Somehow, she'd always imagined that her office would be in a quaint little house with a lawn, hedges, and flowers—the office they always showed on TV. Her office was in a ten-story building. Tinted glass windows were set in shiny aluminum frames. She shared the space on the fourth floor with three other psychologists and one psychiatrist. Having an MD in an office next door was necessary since a psychologist could not prescribe medication in Colorado. Sometimes, she coordinated with the patient's family physician.

One female receptionist for the entire office scheduled appointments and handled cancellations. The doctors paid their own portion of the lease and shared the cost of the receptionist's salary. They were also responsible for collecting their own fees. Hannah always felt like a ghoul asking distraught patients to pay in advance, but she had been stiffed twice and was forced to dip into her salary from the university to keep her practice going.

All in all, her new life pleased her. She was starting out on her own, away from family and friends. It was a new adventure, and although she was lonely and missed her parents, she had to admit she liked her freedom.

She loved her parents. They found it hard to show their

affection, but they were always involved in everything she did, and she knew they loved her. Although she didn't think they meant to be cruel, they were always comparing her accomplishments with their own. It was hard growing up and feeling like she didn't quite measure up.

Her parents were generous and unfaltering in their monetary support. She always had the latest computer, phone, and car. They were surprised when she'd accepted the offer for the job in Denver. She had been as well. She always thought she would stay in Chapel Hill and join her parents at the university. But somehow, the idea of being in charge of herself was too good to pass up. She'd even nixed the idea when they had offered to buy her a townhouse. Here she was, three months into her new life and wondering if she'd done the right thing.

The office building was relatively vacant at this time of the morning. She noticed an older woman and a young toddler waiting for the elevator and saw a woman sitting on the bench across the lobby. She was reading a book, and her face was obscured by large, dark glasses. Hannah smiled at the little girl as she waited for the ding of the bell and the elevator door to open.

"Good morning, Pam," Hannah said when she saw the receptionist. Hannah liked the older woman and would often bring her a cup of coffee and a treat from the Dunkin' Donuts shop down the street. She smiled and headed for her office door when she heard Pam calling her.

"Dr. Brody, I hope you don't mind. I let the man into your office. He said you were friends and you wouldn't mind. He's so darn cute. New boyfriend?"

"What? No, I... Who is he?"

"He didn't say. I don't think I even asked. I was too busy looking at his tanned face with those gorgeous green eyes. Did I do something wrong?"

Hannah knew she needed to have a serious talk with Pam.

In a suite of mental health offices, it was dangerous to let an unidentified person roam free. Now wasn't the time for the lecture, but they would talk and soon.

"He's probably one of my colleagues from school. I'm working on my book, and I've set up some interviews, but mostly they've been on campus. Must have gotten our wires crossed." Hannah slowed down and took a breath. Who in the world did she know well enough in Denver that would come unannounced to her office?

She opened her door and stopped. Her hands flew to her cheeks when she saw the smile spread across his face. "Oh my gosh," she said. "It's you. Bryce."

He stood and nodded his head. "That's me. The annoying man you sat next to for three hours."

"Bryce," she stammered. "It's so good to see you. What are you doing in Denver and how in the world did you find me?"

He stood and when he said, "I'm here to see you," she felt her cheeks turn red as a blush crept up her neck.

"I had to do some detective work to find you. You know that sneaky little thing called the Internet?"

Hannah knew all too well. She'd been guilty of the same thing while trying to learn more about him. "I thought you were up in the mountains writing."

"I was and now I'm here."

"Did you finish your book?"

"Not exactly, but mostly. I have the outline done, and I completed chapter twenty last night. I've even got the ending all figured out. Thanks to you."

"Me? What did I do?"

"You, Dr. Brody, inspired me, and I've had a rather interesting few months up in the high country to reflect on everything. I also think I might need some professional advice."

"Bryce. I'm not the right one to help you. We're sort of friends. I don't know if I could be objective, but I will be happy to refer you to one of the other psychologists here. Most of them are okay. One I wouldn't recommend, but that's probably because he always hits on me, so I'm a bit prejudiced." Wow! She was babbling. *Stop it, Hannah. Yes, he's a handsome man, but you've seen better-looking men on campus all the time* .

"Take a breath, Doc," he said as he guided her toward the chair behind her desk. "I've always wondered what it would be like to lie back on the couch and tell all my deepest secrets. I'll bet you could pull them all out of me," he laughed.

"Bryce," she said, clearly flustered. She fiddled with the papers on her desk and looked up to see him stretched out on her rust-brown corduroy sofa. He was dressed in well-worn denim jeans and a charcoal gray, three-button sweater. She tried not to lick her lips. She did love a man in a sweater.

"I told you I can't be your doctor. It…"

"Are you trying to say there is something going on between us? That you like me?"

"You know I like you. What's not to like? You're charming and good looking and funny." She searched his face for a sign and was rewarded by a mischievous grin. "You're yanking my chain, aren't you?"

"A little bit. I'm probably a hopelessly messed-up dude, but so far, I don't believe I need professional help. But I have some research questions, and it just so happens that a shrink can probably answer them. Besides, I missed you."

"You don't know me well enough to miss me."

"How do you know? I've been up there with elk and dangerous man-eating bears, and I was thinking about you."

Hannah didn't know if he was serious or teasing her again. She decided not to encourage him and instead ask him about his research.

"What can I answer for you?" She looked at her watch and saw she had about forty minutes before her first appointment.

"Tell me about stalkers."

"Stalkers? Hmm… that's one mental problem I haven't worked with, but I remember the textbook info." Hannah closed her eyes and thought about it for a moment. "Stalking is a form of mental assault in which the perpetrator repeatedly and disruptively breaks into the life of a victim, usually one with whom they have no relationship. They mistakenly believe that the other person loves them, and they cannot live without them. They refuse to believe that the person they desire is not interested in them and often believe the victim loves them."

Bryce sat up and said, "Can they be dangerous?"

"Yes, most definitely. There are many examples. The most recognizable examples involve Hollywood celebrities, but there are thousands of cases that don't make the headlines because the victim is an everyday, normal person."

"Go on," he said.

"Well, the stalking may start out small and legal. They might make phone calls, send texts or email, and inexpensive gifts. Then, as it escalates, they could engage in vandalism and property damage, and the worst-case scenario involves harming the victim. You know, the *if I can't have you, no one can have you, scene.*"

"So, how can they be stopped?" Bryce asked as he rose from the couch and walked toward the window.

"Unfortunately, they can't unless they commit a crime. The victim can always get a restraining order, but that won't stop the stalker, and it might cause them to become sneakier. Friends and family should be told what is going on and instructed not to give out any personal information. The victim should change their routine. It's harder to stalk someone when you don't know where they are. Hopefully, they will tire of you and move on to someone else. If all else fails, you can always move. Well, I don't mean you specifically, but I assume the character in your book. Usually stalking doesn't end well."

"That was certainly cheery," Bryce said and returned to the couch.

"Was that helpful?"

"Yes, I'm sure I can use that. Moving away seems like an excellent option."

Hannah looked at Bryce and wondered why he would ask questions about this subject. Was this research for his book or something more? She knew it wasn't any of her business, but she was going to ask anyway. "Are we talking about someone you know?"

"Possibly. I'm not trying to be mysterious. I wanted some basic information and an excuse to see you. It isn't anything you need to be concerned about."

"What is the real reason you're in Denver?"

"I've decided to finish the book here in Denver. I was getting cabin fever with nothing to see but snow every day. Also, I needed to be around people. I sent the outline and several chapters of my manuscript to my editor, and she loved it. She seems to think that this one will not only get good critical reviews but will also sell well."

"That's wonderful," Hannah said as she moved around her desk toward Bryce. "I'm so happy for you." She tentatively reached out and was engulfed in his muscular arms for a warm hug. He held her a little too long, but she didn't mind. It felt good to be in someone's arms.

Hannah finally pushed back and looked at her watch again. She only had about ten minutes before her client arrived. She didn't want Bryce to leave. And she wasn't exactly sure what she wanted. Before she could figure it out, he pulled her close again, moved both his hands under her long blonde hair, gently pulled her head toward him, and kissed her squarely on the lips. It was a slow exploratory kiss at first, and then his lips gave way to more passion, and she had to stop herself from swooning. She stepped back and looked at him, waiting for an explanation.

"I've wanted to do that for months. I kicked myself a thousand times for not pursuing you. I've never met anyone like you, Doc. I can't get you out of my mind, and believe me, I've tried. Not wanting to sound like a stalker myself here, but you don't belong with that guy. You belong with me."

"What guy?"

"Your guy. The boyfriend. The reason you wouldn't have dinner with me."

"I didn't have dinner with you because I didn't know you. I was a little apprehensive. I was in a new town. It was all..."

"Too much?"

"Probably."

"Do you love him?"

Before she could answer, Pam buzzed the phone on her desk. "Your appointment is here, Dr. Brody."

Hannah walked over to her desk and grabbed hold of the edge. Her legs were shaking. "Thank you, Pam. I'll be right out."

"I'm sorry," Hannah said, turning to Bryce. "You'll have to go. My patient is waiting." She watched as he moved across the room toward the exit. "Bryce," she said. "There isn't any boyfriend." She couldn't see his face, but she thought she heard a laugh as he walked out the door.

CHAPTER 6
BRYCE CAMERON

OBLIVIOUS TO THE **throngs of people rushing toward the open door,** Bryce walked off the elevator and into the lobby of the medical building. His mind was occupied, and a smile had spread across his face all the way down to his chin. He hoped he didn't look like a complete goof, but he couldn't help it. Doc had just made his day. She didn't have a boyfriend. He didn't know if she had broken up with the man or if the relationship was never that serious. Frankly, he didn't care. All he cared about was that she was eligible, and he was interested.

When he decided to go to her office, he didn't know if he would have the same reaction to her as he did on the plane. And it wasn't the same. This time, it had been a gut-wrenching slam to the chest. He could easily fall in love with this woman, and he hadn't thought about love since his senior year of high school when Penny Baker dumped him for a nerd on the debate team. He'd run into her at his tenth reunion. She hadn't turned out well. She had three kids and an ex-husband, and was bigger than a double-wide trailer. When she started giving him the eye, he ran like hell. It was amazing what sex at seventeen could get you involved in.

When Hannah walked into her office and realized he was there, she blushed from head to toe. That's when he knew he was a goner. He had never seen a more precious sight in his life. He knew it would not be easy. She'd kicked him out when her patient arrived, and although she'd let him hug and kiss her, he could feel her apprehension. He would have to change that.

It was a pretty, sunny day with only a few clouds in the sky. Crisp and cold but not uncomfortable. He could get accustomed to living in the mile-high city. He saw a coffee shop on the corner and headed that way to sit down and work on his plan to seduce Dr. Hannah Brody.

The fragrant aroma of strong coffee and cinnamon rolls tickled his nose. He ordered a coffee and a bagel and smiled back at the pretty, dark-haired barista, who smiled at him warmly and let her hand brush his. Her brown eyes met his with a flirtatious invitation. It was past the morning rush hour, and although most of the tables were still occupied, he was the only person in line. In the past, he might have invited her to join him at his table during her break for a casual hook-up with a pretty girl. That was before he realized the only eyes he wanted to be looking at him were hazel, and they belonged to the most fascinating woman he'd ever met.

He grabbed his tray and a copy of the *Denver Post* someone had left on a table. Moments after he sat down, his phone rang. He'd played phone tag with Quinn most of last night and this morning, so he answered quickly without looking at the screen.

"Hey," he said warmly, with a hint of humor in his voice.

"Bryce, hi, it's great to hear your voice. I thought you might be mad at me, but it doesn't sound like you are."

"Who is this?" he said, but he was afraid he knew who it was. His crazy stalker.

"It's Lucy. You left, and I didn't know where you went. I'm so sorry about upsetting you. I wouldn't have left you out in the snow. I was going to pick you up when I saw you in the truck. I…"

Surprising himself, Bryce calmly hit the end button and disconnected the call. When the phone rang again, he pushed a few settings to block the number. His heart pounded with anger, and he wanted to slam the phone against the table. He looked around, expecting to see her staring at him from across the room, and was relieved when he didn't recognize any of the faces.

Did she know he was in Denver? Had she followed him? He quickly found the number for the police in Frisco and placed a call to the officer he had talked with after the last phone call. He shook his head and thought it was sad when you had to have the direct line to the police listed in your contacts.

A man answered after three rings. "Bonilla," the man said in a gruff, professional voice.

"Officer Bonilla, this is Bryce Cameron. I'm sorry to bother you, but do you have any information about Lucy Rosen? I left Frisco about a week ago and hoped I had left my stalker behind. I'm in Denver, and I just got a call from her."

Silence stretched out over the phone and Bryce was about to ask if they had become disconnected when Bonilla finally responded to the question. "Sorry, Mr. Cameron. We put a BOLO out on her after your initial complaint and thought for sure there would have been a sighting. It's not like the town is a great metropolis. But she has vanished. We did get a report back from the fingerprints she left at your cabin."

"And what did it say?" Bryce asked.

"Well, I was going to get back to you on that. It seems she's done this kind of thing in the past. She had a boyfriend in Tulsa who got a restraining order after they broke up. Seems like she wasn't ready to let go. I'm not sure of all the details, but she was charged with malicious mischief and left town before she had her court appearance."

"And you were going to call and tell me about this when?" Bryce said. He was trying not to raise his voice or lose his temper, but he was angry.

"Things have been busy up here. Since we didn't hear back from you, we, or rather I, assumed she had left you alone. As far as I know, she isn't in Frisco anymore. If she's calling you in Denver, you might want to get the locals involved and maybe change your phone number. I will call you if she is apprehended."

Great help you are. Bryce thanked Bonilla and clicked off the phone. He looked around, expecting to have Lucy pop out at any moment. This whole thing was creepy.

He walked out of the donut shop and squinted at the bright sun. The clouds had disappeared, and although still cool outside, it was going to be a beautiful day. Bright and sunny. He thought about Hannah and how the images he'd had in his head about her these last couple of months weren't even close to reality. She was even better than he remembered. He was going to invite her to dinner. He knew before even asking she was going to say no. But he could be persuasive and charming if he tried. At least his charm had always worked in the past, although none of those women had been as self-assured as Hannah. She had only to look at you to know what made you tick. He chuckled softly. *If I didn't have such good self-esteem, I'd run out of town as fast as I could.*

His phone rang again, and he pulled it out of his pocket and cursed. "Damn," he muttered and shook his head. He didn't recognize the number, but it was a Denver area code.

A woman coming toward him frowned when he suddenly stopped, causing her to almost run into him. "Sorry," he said, "I wasn't paying attention." He hastened off the busy sidewalk and leaned against a building. The call ended, and after a few seconds, he heard the voicemail ding. He listened as the caller's high-pitched, whiny voice sounded in his ear.

"You didn't even let me explain. You are so mean to me. I

was trying to make up and you won't give me a chance. I can't believe you blocked me. I had to get a throwaway phone and that cost me money I don't have. I lost my job because of you. What will I do now? I love you. I know you care about me, too. I could tell when I was at your house and we had coffee and donuts together. It was so special. Please, please, please call me back."

When she sobbed into the phone, Bryce hung up. This woman had serious mental issues. He had nothing to do with her losing her job. She lost her job because she didn't go to work. She had donuts and coffee. He didn't. "Oh, man," he exclaimed out loud. He pressed his finger to the phone and asked Siri where the nearest AT&T store was. He couldn't believe he was going to have to get another phone number. This was a frigging nightmare.

It was after one o'clock when he finished at the phone store and close to two before he went through the list of his primary contacts to text them his new number. He called his mother and was pleased when it went to voicemail. He wanted to avoid the drama a conversation with Justine would involve. He left a brief message about getting crank phone calls and thus the need for a new number. Doc would have a field day if he ever got on her couch and talked about his childhood.

Bryce thought about sitting in the medical building lobby to catch Hannah when she got off the elevator, but immediately nixed that idea. Then he'd be the stalker. Instead, he approached her receptionist and asked if Dr. Brody was with a client and if she was, he could wait. It was late afternoon around four-thirty, and when Pam went into one of the other offices, he checked out the appointment book. He quickly glanced at the calendar and was pleased that Hannah's last appointment was in with her now. He didn't have long to wait. He walked out into the hallway and called Quinn.

"What's going on?" his younger brother asked. "Why the

change in phone numbers? Crank calls? I don't think so. It's that crazy lady, isn't it?"

"Good guess. You must be psychic."

"Nah, after being raised by another crazy lady, you kind of figure things like that out pretty quickly."

"Justine has her moments, but she's not looney tunes like Lucy. Hannah says she could be dangerous."

"Wait a minute. You told the woman you are crushing on that you have a stalker?"

"Of course not," Bryce said as he ran his fingers through his hair and paced up and down the hallway. "I was vague, described my situation, and asked her about stalkers to get her professional opinion."

"And Hannah agrees this stalker is dangerous?"

"Could be. So far, the woman has done nothing but come uninvited into my cabin and call me."

"Are you forgetting that she sabotaged your car and left you stranded in a snowstorm? That sounds dangerous to me," Quinn said and laughed.

"Well, there is that. She apologized, though when she called this morning. Said she didn't mean to leave me out in the snow and was going to pick me up."

"And…?"

"That's when I hung up on her."

"I'm guessing she called you back?"

"Oh, yeah. That's when I got a new phone number. What's going on with you? Still got the long-distance thing with the gal from Sweden. What was her name? Helga something?"

"Hell, bro, that was ages ago. We would chat sometimes on Facebook, but it was nothing serious. Besides, I've been spending time with Lorraine."

"I hear you. But that's only business, right?"

"Well, mostly," Quinn said.

"You haven't been involved with anyone since that Dixie girl. It's not healthy to live like a monk."

Quinn chuckled. "Who says I'm living like a monk? I get around, and besides, I'm busy getting the business started and my shit together. It would be hard to replace Dixie. Anyway, I don't need a serious relationship complicating my life right now, but it's obvious that you do."

Bryce rubbed his hand through his hair again, stopped pacing, and leaned against the wall by the elevator. "What's that supposed to mean?"

"I mean, I can tell you've got a real thing for this Hannah woman. Don't blow it. She sounds like she's way smarter than you."

"I'm sure you're right, and she is way too good for me, but I'm waiting outside her office to ask her to dinner." Bryce looked at his watch and smiled when he saw it was only a couple of minutes until five. "Gotta go, destiny is waiting."

"Hey, Bryce," Quinn said with concern in his voice, "if this Lucy person is dangerous, you need to watch out. I know you think you're invincible, but you bleed the same as us mortals."

"Ha, ha. I promise I'll keep an eye out for her and contact the police if she bothers me again."

————

An hour later, he was in an upscale pizza place, sitting across from Hannah. It was crowded and noisy, but they found a table in the back, away from most of the chatter.

Hannah leaned in and said, "I can't believe you talked me into this. I have class tomorrow, and I've got notes to prepare."

"You must eat, right? So, do I—no reason why we can't eat at the same time and enjoy each other's company. No pressure. You can run out the door if I get too friendly."

"You don't scare me, Bryce. Or at least not in the physical sense. Besides, I looked you up and you are the real deal."

"You googled me?" He moved closer and took her hand. "I thought for sure you'd blow me off after I kissed you in your office."

"But there you were at the end of the day." She laughed, and her eyes twinkled with mischief.

"Have I told you I love your laugh? I remember the first time I heard it on the plane. It's hard to describe, and it's obvious you don't care what the people around you think."

She clasped her hand to her mouth and shook her head. "Oh no, now I've embarrassed you. I'm terribly sorry. My parents hated to take me out in public," she said as she laughed again.

He looked around at the other tables. A few people were paying attention, but most of them were not. "No, I didn't mean it that way. I couldn't care less what people think. You are so completely comfortable with yourself. I find you amazing."

"Wow, I've heard lots of lines before, but that one is especially good."

"Do you think I am trying to get you into bed?"

"Oh yeah, most definitely."

"And are you going to run the other way?"

"Not now. I'm going to have another piece of pizza and a glass of wine. What about you?"

"Doc, I think I may be speechless. I'm going to sit right here with my mouth open and stare at you."

CHAPTER 7
QUINN CAMERON

QUINN SLIPPED **his phone into his pocket** and made his way down the narrow aisle of the lumberyard. He loved the smell of sawdust and wood and felt good about his plans to make and sell custom furniture. He envied his big brother. Presently, he didn't have anyone special in his life, and after knowing a girl like Dixie, he would rather be alone than settle for second best.

It was hot, and he was thirsty. He made his way to the snack bar and pulled a Coke out of the mini-fridge. There was an apple pie sitting on the counter in a plastic container, and when he saw it, he remembered a time several years earlier when pie had been his ticket to talk to Dixie.

———

In the spring of his senior year in high school, Quinn had slid onto the stool at the counter in the Savannah Street Diner in Cabbagetown, removed his ball cap, and run his fingers from the front to the back of his hair. He knew he needed a haircut but wearing it longer than his father approved had always been his special, secret, rebellious pleasure.

"Get you something besides a Coke, sir?"

Quinn looked up into the biggest brown eyes he had ever seen. Fringed with long, black lashes, they sparkled and danced. If asked to describe their color, he would have said they were caramel with dark chocolate swirls.

Quinn swallowed and coughed and tried to get his voice to work. "Pie," he said.

The waitress laughed. "Okay, that's a start. We have five kinds of pie: pecan, apple, peach, coconut, and pumpkin. Can you be more specific?"

He chose the apple pie with ice cream and waited patiently as she took the plate out of the glass container, cut a generous slice, and then went to the cold case to get out the gallon of vanilla bean ice cream.

She wore a green uniform and a white apron. It was the same uniform all the female employees wore while working in the cafe, but on her it looked like a model was pretending to be a waitress.

She had a riot of black curls that spilled down her back, and her wispy bangs framed her lovely, oval face.

Watching her made him nervous. He felt awkward and inept. What if he said something stupid like he usually did? He knew what it felt like to be speechless. He could not think of one thing to say to her except, "Thank you."

"You're welcome, sugar. I hope you enjoy it."

Because she was so busy waiting on people and clearing tables, she never got back to the counter. He took his time finishing off the pie, put a ten-dollar bill under his plate, and left. He hoped she would look his way before he left, but that didn't happen.

Thirty minutes later, when he bounded up the porch steps and into the house, Quinn was still daydreaming about the beautiful waitress. As usual, the fragrant scent of baked goods wafted from the kitchen at the end of the hall.

"Mr. Quinn? That you?"

"It's me, Sophie."

The housekeeper's face broke out into a wide smile as she dusted the flour off her hands and handed him a plate of sandwiches.

He had not even digested the pie that he had eaten earlier, but refusing one of Sophie's meals would hurt her feelings, and he was too fond of her to take that chance. He took half of one sandwich and sat down at the table while she bustled around, getting him a napkin and a glass of milk.

"I knew you'd smell my oatmeal cookies. I could seldom put anything over on you. When you finish, you can have one fresh out of the oven." She laughed and patted his back. "You home for the day?"

Before he could answer, a booming voice made them both jump. "I sure as hell hope not."

Sophie quickly moved back into the kitchen, away from the table, and her smile vanished. He watched her demeanor change from that of a friendly companion to a humble servant.

"Why aren't you in school, boy? Are you slacking off as usual?"

Quinn flinched. He looked up to see Captain Martin Cameron's florid, self-satisfied face mocking him.

Often, his father's caustic words felt like physical blows. He sometimes thought a good right-hand punch would be easier to take than the biting sarcasm. Quinn knew that any reply he gave would only be met with even more verbal abuse, so he stayed silent and took a sip of milk.

"I'm talking to you. You got wax in your ears?"

Quinn swallowed and put the glass down. "This was my half day. I finished up at noon."

"Nobody told me about this," the older man said. "Did you know about this, Sophie?"

"Yes, sir. Mrs. Cameron told me to have lunch ready for Mr. Quinn because he would be home early today."

Quinn wanted to tell his father that it wasn't Sophie's problem. It was his own. If he were more connected to the family, he might know when his wife's or one of his children's schedules changed.

"Well, fine," The Captain said. He turned his harsh gaze toward Sophie. "Tell my wife I'll be home to pick her up at seven sharp. We have plans to attend a cocktail party tonight. I don't want her to forget."

"Yes, sir," Sophie said.

Again, Quinn wondered why poor Sophie had to get involved. Couldn't his parents talk to each other instead of going through the housekeeper? Thank goodness he wasn't expected to be the messenger boy. It was hard enough to be their younger, less-than-perfect son without also being a go-between.

————

Thinking back, Quinn knew his parents had not enjoyed a close and loving relationship, but they seemed to make things work and they had been together for almost thirty years. They had moved around from one naval base to another when the boys were younger. Then, Martin was promoted to captain and stationed at King's Bay Naval Submarine Base in Florida.

One night, Martin told his sons that some of the worst fights the couple had were because his wife, the beautiful and sophisticated Justine Cameron, refused to live in military housing. She felt her boys deserved better schools than the one elementary school on base, and she certainly did not want to hobnob with the other Navy wives to whom she felt superior.

He said he had finally agreed after she promised to commute whenever necessary to help him entertain, and she agreed to make herself available for all the social functions that took place in Atlanta. He would stay in the Officers' Club housing when he was on duty, and they would find a place in Atlanta for Justine and the boys.

Quinn knew they had been lucky to have located a rare find in Ansley Park. It was a lovely, pale yellow, historic Victorian home near Piedmont Park. His mother said she had fallen in love with the two spiral stairways to the upper level. There, four spacious bedrooms, each with its own bathroom, and a master bedroom with a sitting room, were bathed in the eastern sunlight each morning.

"It's perfect for entertaining," Justine had noted. A formal dining room opened onto a screened porch, and the hardwood floors were polished to a high shine. Although she had stopped cooking as soon as they could afford to hire Sophie, she was impressed with the updated kitchen with all new appliances. The private, fenced yard had a three-car garage in the rear.

She had told Martin that she could always drive to the base if he needed her there. They could entertain at the Officers' Club if necessary, but he could invite whomever he wished to the Atlanta house for dinner. She even offered to let them spend the night if they didn't want to make the five-hour drive back to the base. She thought it should work out perfectly for the whole family.

Helpless to object, he had agreed. Martin said he knew the worst thing he could do for his career, which was in full upward motion, would be to get crossways with their mother. He had no desire to get involved in a divorce or child support issue while he was trying to run a huge submarine base.

He didn't say it aloud, but whenever she started in on him with one of her demands and flashed that saccharine smile, his voice said, "Yes, dear," and his mind screamed, "whatever. Please shut the hell up and get off my back."

Quinn was convinced that although his father had a shoulder full of ribbons and medals and a death stare through hooded eyes that struck fear into his men, he had never learned to navigate the stormy waters his pleasingly plump, russet-haired wife could generate like a tropical storm forming in the Atlantic.

————

When Quinn's mother got home, she paused at the kitchen door long enough to make sure that Sophie had followed all her instructions. "Is my dress pressed and ready to wear?"

"Yes, ma'am."

"Did you take out my shoes and buff them?"

"I did. The gray suede ones."

"Did you polish my jewelry?"

Before Sophie could reply, she noticed Quinn, who sat at the outdoor table on the screened porch. Several books lay open and spread out around him. "Oh, hello, son," she said and swooped in to kiss him on his cheek. "Looks like you're taking your mid-terms seriously."

Quinn looked up at her with a quizzical expression. "Mom, mid-terms are a long way off. We've only been in school for a few weeks."

"Is that so? Then what are you doing? I never see you studying."

That's because you're never home. "I usually study in my room, but since it's such a nice day, I wanted to get some fresh air," he said. In fact, he was not studying. He was selecting plans for a woodworking project.

She lifted her head and looked around. The backyard of their home was like a golf course. A green manicured lawn was surrounded by stately oak trees and flower beds overflowing with riots of colorful flowering plants. Their perfume permeated the air.

Quinn thought it a shame that the only time his parents ever enjoyed their yard was when they entertained. They rarely sat in the gazebo or on one of the stone benches that were strategically placed in shady locations.

For a fleeting moment, Quinn thought about walking through the yard with that pretty waitress by his side or sitting beside her on one of the chaise lounges near the pool. An involuntary smile crossed his lips.

"What's got you in such a good mood?" his mother said.

"I'm always in a good mood, Mother. You're usually too busy to notice."

Justine stiffened. "What's that supposed to mean?"

"Don't be sensitive. Nothing disrespectful, I assure you. Simply an observation."

She stood there a moment and then seemed to be satisfied with his explanation. "Oh well, all right then. I've got to rest awhile before I must bathe and dress for dinner."

"What are you making the boys for dinner, Sophie?" she said as she turned her attention to the housekeeper.

"They want some of my baked chicken and rice, so that's what we'll have tonight. Will Mr. Bryce be home late, as usual?"

"Yes, he will. Bryce is tutoring those kids at the community center. He may not be home until around eight."

Quinn wondered at whom her remarks were aimed. He knew exactly what was going on with his older brother because his parents told him and all their friends and acquaintances. And he knew Sophie didn't need all this extra information. She was merely asking what time to have his brother's dinner ready.

———

When Bryce came bursting into the house at eight-forty-five, his energy felt like a magnetic force. Quinn thought his brother must have been born under a lucky star. Everything he touched seemed to sparkle and shine. People loved him, and he loved people. But the paradox was that he didn't need people to make him happy. He had always been secure in himself and was as happy to be in his room writing in one of his spiral notebooks as he was to be amid a crowd at the Academy.

He was a leader but not a bully, a high achiever but not a nerd. He would stop to help an old person across the street on the way to his car and then speed off like he was going to a fire sale.

Their father had made the mistake of trying to pit one son against the other thinking that doing so would create a healthy competition and make Quinn work harder, stand taller, and shape up.

The Captain had wanted both of his sons to follow his lead and join the Navy. Bryce had joined NROTC while still in high school and had no problem wearing a buzz cut. Now, he was in his last year at Annapolis and would soon be ready to begin his Navy career.

Bryce's success could have driven a wedge between the boys and ruined their relationship, but the truth was that Quinn remained his brother's biggest fan. He wasn't jealous, and he wasn't discouraged, but he was realistic and honest about the differences between them.

Trying to walk in his older brother's shoes gave Quinn sore feet and an underachiever's complex, so he walked away instead and started down his own path.

————

"Hey, bro. It's not dark yet. Want to shoot some hoops before we eat dinner?" Bryce's grin was infectious.

"Sure, if you let me win this time."

"Never gonna' happen. It's not good for your character to feed you victories."

The sound of the ball slapping against the driveway

cement and contacting the backboard was music to Quinn's ears. He loved playing basketball with his brother if their old man was not around. Bryce played for fun instead of bragging rights. In fact, Quinn was more athletic and faster with his footwork. Bryce often got lost in his thoughts. Quinn believed if he and his brother took a right-brain vs. left-brain test, they would end up on opposite sides of the spectrum.

"Anything new?" Bryce asked.

"Maybe," Quinn said with a sly grin.

Bryce grabbed the ball and held it out in front of him between his hands. "Come on, spill the beans."

"Well, there's this girl. She's kinda got me tied up in knots." He knocked the ball out of Bryce's hands, and it bounced down the driveway.

"What does that mean? Oh, shit. You didn't get her pregnant, did you? I told you to be careful once you started playing that birds and bees game. It could cost you your future."

Quinn laughed. "I doubt that exchanging a few words with a woman could cause too much harm."

Bryce ran after the ball, brought it back, and stood in front of his brother. "I don't get it. Why are you tied up in knots if you haven't even touched her?"

"Beats me. But I can't think about anything else ever since I saw her this morning."

"Saw her where? At school?"

"Nope. I was over in Cabbagetown at a diner. She works there."

Bryce took a good, hard look at his brother. "You were where?"

"You heard me."

"Why in the hell were you way over there?"

Quinn laughed. "What's it to ya?"

"Come on, Quinn. You know the old man would be

awfully chapped if he knew you were hanging around Cabbagetown. You were supposed to be at school."

"No, I wasn't. We got out early, so I drove over to the Hobby Works to get some more materials. I'm working on a project."

Quinn stood there staring at him as if to say, "And?"

"It's only about a fifteen-minute drive from school. I stopped in at a diner to get a Coke, and this amazing-looking woman offered me some pie." After he said it, he wasn't sure if that was exactly how it had happened, but it was close enough to the truth.

"You mean it's a waitress who's got you all shook up?"

"Yes, she works there. You should see her, Bryce. She looks like Scarlett O'Hara or that actress who played her in the movie. She's amazing."

Bryce put both of his hands on his brother's shoulders. "Listen to me and listen well. Don't even think about going back there and getting something started. Mom and Dad would have a fit if they thought you were getting involved with somebody like that."

Quinn felt as if he had been slapped in the face. A tumble of confused thoughts and feelings assailed him. "They don't have to know anything about it. And you'd better shut your mouth and mind your own business."

The two brothers stared at each other for a second or two as the chill between them grew, and then Quinn stormed into the house and slammed the door in his brother's face.

CHAPTER 8
QUINN CAMERON

QUINN DIDN'T LIKE **to be on the outs with his brother,** but the atmosphere between them remained awkward and strange and Bryce was going back to school tomorrow.

Quinn knew Bryce worked out at the gym when he was home, so that his body fat would not exceed twenty-five percent because that would disqualify him from acceptance. Bryce had already jumped through all the hoops required for entry, but the Navy would take another look at his physical condition before graduation.

Quinn threw on a pair of running shorts and an old T-shirt and took off down the sidewalk toward the park. He loved running on the pathways through Piedmont Park. He enjoyed the sights and the scents of the thirty acres of plants and grass. At times, the running paths were so crowded, it felt like he needed turn signals on his black New Balance running shoes, but in the early morning he had the peace and solitude he so enjoyed.

As his feet pounded, he felt his heart rate increase, and by the end of the run he was dripping wet. When he made his way into the house through the laundry room door, he took off his shirt and threw it on the floor. Then he opened the refrigerator door and stood there letting the cool air rush over the hairs on his chest. He was reaching for a bowl of strawberries when something wet hit him in the back.

"What the …?"

"Will you please get your smelly body out of this kitchen and into the shower?" The voice he heard was one he did not immediately recognize.

He turned around to see his brother with a huge grin on his face. Bryce had his hands on his hips in the exact pose his mother always used with both of her boys when she was scolding them. Bryce continued speaking in a high, falsetto voice. "Wherever are your manners, Quinn? I did not raise you to stand in my kitchen and get your nasty perspiration all over our food." He pinched his nose.

Quinn tried not to smile. He was still a little miffed at his brother, but the whole thing was funny, and in no time, they were both laughing at their mother's expense. It was exactly what she would have said and done, and nobody could imitate her better than Bryce.

Quinn knew he couldn't stay mad at Bryce for long, and the more he thought about it, the more he knew his brother was trying to give him fair warning. His parents would be upset if they knew he was interested in a waitress from Cabbagetown.

He thought about it while he took a shower, thought about it some more while he shaved and dressed, and then continued to think about it as he put the car in first gear and let out the clutch. He wondered what kind of pie he would order this time.

———

The diner was crowded at eleven-thirty in the morning. Customers occupied every stool at the counter, and he found a table near the back and slid into the vinyl-backed chrome chair.

"Something to drink, mister?"

He looked up into the eyes of a woman who had to be at least sixty. Her gray hair was tied back in a loose bun, and the only makeup on her face was a deep red lipstick that also decorated her front teeth.

He swallowed his disappointment. "I'd like a lime Coke please, and an order of fries."

"Ketchup?"

"Pardon?"

"I said, do you want ketchup with those?"

"Uh, sure. I guess so."

When she returned and placed the food in front of him, she studied him for a moment. "You lose something?"

He looked at her blankly.

"I'm asking because you've been looking all around the room ever since you got here. I thought maybe you lost something."

He hoped the rush of blood that had gone to his head did not show on his face. "No, I was looking for someone."

"Oh, I see. Someone meeting you here? Want me to leave the menu?"

"No, thanks."

She turned to leave, and he said in a voice louder than he intended, "There was a waitress here last week. She had black hair. Curly hair."

"And?"

"And she waited on me. I wanted to ask her… that is… tell her something. Is she here?"

"You can see that she isn't. You've inspected the whole place." The older woman poured water into his glass and avoided his eyes. "What is it you want to tell her? I can give her a message."

This time, Quinn knew his face was red. His body felt

feverish. "It's not important. I can come back another time. When will she be here?"

"She doesn't work on weekends."

Quinn felt relieved. He was afraid the woman was going to say she didn't work there any longer. He didn't know how to find her, and he wanted so badly to see her again.

"Can you at least tell me her name?"

"I could, but I won't. Ask her yourself. She'll be here on Monday."

————

The rest of the weekend passed slowly. He did all his homework and spent several hours at the library working on a draft for a term paper that would be due in a few weeks. It wasn't like him to be proactive, and it worried him a little. Good grief, he didn't even know the girl's name yet, and she was already changing his personality. He laughed out loud and then looked around to see if anyone in the silent room heard him.

He got home in time to hear his parents having one of their heated discussions. He rarely learned anything interesting, but his curiosity got the better of him, and he lingered at the base of the stairway to listen.

"So, you're telling me you needed a four-hundred-dollar dress, a two-hundred-dollar pair of shoes, and an eighty-five-dollar purse because we are going to the symphony?"

"Yes, Martin. I needed them, and I bought them. Since I am forced to go to the symphony and sit with all those people you've invited, at least I can look my best."

"It's obvious you need a good dictionary, Justine. There's a big difference between needing something and wanting it. You've got to realize that and rein in your excessive spending. Money does not grow on oak trees. You got that?"

Quinn heard a door slam and then placed his foot on the

first step as his father began his descent. His father brushed past Quinn without as much as a glance as he made his way to the front hallway, where he grabbed his hat and his keys and quickly made his way outside.

There was nothing new in this fight. A similar conversation occurred almost every time his father was in Atlanta. Martin would take inventory of all the new items his wife had purchased and give her hell about it, and she would give him hell right back. He could not remember a time his mother had lost an argument with his father. He sometimes wondered if they fought because they had nothing of interest to say to one another because they led such different, separate lives.

The traffic was heavy after school on Monday as Quinn drove to Cabbagetown. He thought about what he was going to say and rehearsed it aloud as he drove. "Hello, Miss ... uh... I'm sorry, I don't believe I caught your name." That was beyond lame, he thought. "Hi, there. I'm Quinn Cameron. We haven't been introduced yet." Oh brother, that was even worse.

As it turned out, he was tongue-tied again. Her back was to him when he sat down at the counter, and it gave him time to stare at the black curls trailing down to her tiny waist. He took a deep breath while he was waiting, and when she turned around, he let it out in a rush. He knew he sounded more like a winded horse than he did a man.

She took pity on him and ignored his obvious distress. She was chewing her gum and popping it while she poured another cup of coffee for the man sitting on his left. Then she flashed her smile at him, and he felt like he had stuck his finger in a light socket.

"Well, hello there. I thought you might be back today."

He was so surprised he had to take a drink of water

because his tongue was stuck to the roof of his mouth. "Why, uh, why would you think that?"

"Because the pie lady comes in on Mondays. We've got an amazing selection today. We even have a coconut cream pie with whipped cream on top. That one is my absolute favorite. Want a piece?"

He noticed she always rushed through everything she had to say before she paused to take a breath. Her final words were softer and difficult to hear. "Actually, I want a milkshake. What kind do you recommend?"

"I like the cherry one. I always put extra cherries in the ones I make." She blew a pink bubble and popped it. Instead of annoying him, it made him laugh. She was something else.

"Then I'll take your word for it. Bring me one of those, please." For the next few minutes, he watched her move about the room, gathering the ice cream, the milk, and the jar of maraschino cherries. Then she turned to the large silver countertop blender and worked her magic. After a short while, she placed a tall, frosty milkshake in front of him. The top was covered in whipped cream and a striped straw stuck out between the three bright red cherries on top.

He took a sip and groaned. "This is sinfully good."

She laughed, and he heard the tinkling of wind chimes on a breezy night and the melody of a xylophone playing a lilting tune. He knew he had never heard a prettier sound.

She moved dishes aside and wiped the counter with her blue cleaning rag. He didn't know how it happened, and he did not plan it, but when her delicate hand neared his, he covered it with his large, square one and stilled her movement.

She did not remove her hand from his but looked up at him. Her brown eyes registered surprise.

"We haven't been introduced yet. I'm Quinn Cameron. May I know your name?"

She left her hand where it was and flashed her megawatt smile. "You surely can, sugar. I'm Dixie Lee King."

She turned her palm over and clasped his in a gentle handshake.

"I'm happy to know you, Dixie. I swear, you're the prettiest girl I've ever seen." He couldn't stop the words from rushing out of his mouth unbidden and unrehearsed.

She smiled again, and he continued. "Will you go out with me? Please? I will take you wherever you want to go. I want... no... I need to see you again."

She didn't hesitate. "Yes. I'd like that." Her red lips turned up in a smile. "Sure, I will. How about tomorrow night?"

———

Quinn wasn't supposed to stay out late on school nights, so he had to do some fast talking to get permission to leave the house. Somehow, he knew mentioning a girl would be a bad idea. He used the term paper excuse again and said he was going to a friend's house to compare notes and write his rough draft, and his mother fell for it.

He had agreed to meet Dixie at the diner when her shift ended at nine. Dressed in his newest jeans and button-up-the-front shirt, he felt a constant flutter in his stomach until he saw her walk out the door.

She still wore the green uniform, but her jaunty cap was gone, and her hair cascaded around her lovely face and rested below her shoulders.

Quinn could not help but notice how the belt around her tiny waist accentuated her curves and showcased her generous hips and voluminous breasts. He wondered how she could stand up straight and not tip forward. He knew his face was as red as a hot plate, but he could not control the desire he felt every time he looked at her.

"What are we going to do tonight, Quinn? You have a plan?"

"I do. But if you don't like it, I can always change it."

She questioned him with her wide eyes.

"I'd like to go ride bumper cars, but I'm not sure you'd want to do that," he said.

"Where?" Her eyes flashed with excitement.

"Atlanta Park is open until eleven. We could ride awhile and then get a soda." He hesitated a moment. "Or not. The soda I mean. You may be sick of sodas at the end of the day."

She put her fingers over his lips to still his words, then took his hand and squeezed it. "Lead the way."

———

He knew he would always remember that night as one of the best of his life. Dixie was daring and fearless. Her love of speed was exceeded only by her delight in slamming into other cars. Each time he caught a glimpse of her, she was laughing, her white teeth flashing between cherry-red lips.

When they left the park, he helped her into the car and closed the door.

"That was so fun, Quinn. You're a good driver." She giggled. "Too bad, I'm a little bit better."

Quinn smiled and glanced at his watch. It was almost eleven, and he knew his mother would get anxious. She always stayed awake until both of her sons were home.

Dixie took a pack of Fruit Stripe gum out of her purse and offered him a stick. When he declined, she said, "What now, sugar?"

"I need to take you home, Dixie. I can stay out late on the weekend, but my parents are quite strict about being home early on school nights."

"What school do you go to?"

"I'm a senior at Grady High School."

"Isn't that school in Ansley Park?"

"Yes, it is."

"Is that where you live?"

"Yes. How about you? Do you have a curfew?"

She looked at him for a moment and then ignored his question. "Well, if you gotta go, then take me back to the diner."

He was confused. "Don't you want me to drive you home?"

"No, certainly not." Her lips puckered with annoyance.

Her tone was chilly, so he drove the few miles back to Cabbagetown in silence. Quinn didn't know what had changed her from a carefree, laughing girl into the stiff-lipped, cool woman who sat beside him now.

When they arrived, the diner was dark, and only one streetlight illuminated the narrow street. He stopped in front of the building, and she quickly gathered her purse and started to open the car door.

He put his hand on her arm. "Wait. I can't leave you here. Where's your car?"

Her cold eyes sniped at him. "What car?"

"How will you get home from here?"

"I'll walk like I always do." She got out of the car and slammed the door. He opened his door and rushed around to her side.

"Then I'll walk with you."

"It's only a short way. I've done it a million times."

"Well, you won't do it tonight. There's no way I'm leaving you here alone."

A look of tired sadness passed over her face. "Fine then. Have it your way."

———

After a short, five-minute walk, her steps slowed as they got closer to a mobile home park at the end of a long drive. She turned to face him, and he tried to ignore the tears glistening in her brown eyes. "Okay, your duty is done, Sir Galahad. I'm home and safe. You can go now." She pointed to a single-wide trailer about the size of a small UPS delivery truck.

He didn't know what to say or how to make this awkward situation better, so he thanked her for a great time, turned and walked away.

CHAPTER 9
QUINN CAMERON

AFTER THAT NIGHT, **Quinn felt like he had a fever all the time**. He knew their date had ended on an awkward note, but he didn't care. He wanted to see Dixie as soon as possible to reassure her it made no difference to him where she lived.

It took Quinn two visits to the diner to convince Dixie to go out with him again. It would have been so easy to get together if she was free on weekends, but she said she wasn't. He wondered about that but kept his questions to himself.

She wouldn't let him pick her up but agreed to meet him at the movie theater at nine-fifteen on Wednesday night.

Even though Quinn was being creative with his excuses, he knew it was only a matter of time before his mother got wise and gave him grief about his being gone so often on school nights.

He parked the car and made his way to the ticket booth inside the theater. The tantalizing smell of buttered popcorn made him hungry. He was sure they sold the tickets at the food counter to entice people to buy the over-priced items. Anyone with half a brain knew how much it cost to make popcorn.

As soon as Dixie arrived, he bought a large box for each of them and two Cokes. The ticket lines were short, and he was sure it was because the movie they chose had already been playing for two weeks. He let Dixie decide on the film and was surprised that she suggested a modern adventure instead of a chick flick.

After the movie, she allowed him to walk her home, but she stopped him by the rusty mailbox on a post outside her mobile home. There were no lights on inside, so he assumed her parents were not waiting up for her. It made him feel bad knowing that she would enter a dark trailer alone. His protective feelings were growing stronger each time they met.

When he got home, all the downstairs lights in his house were blazing. He thought about entering through the kitchen door but realized it would not make any difference at all. He took a deep breath and walked into the front hall.

"Quinn? Is that you?" His mother's voice was high-pitched and a little shaky.

"It's me, Mom."

She didn't answer, so he went into the living room, hoping she was not as stressed as she sounded. But the first person he saw was not his mother. The Captain was sitting in the large, winged-back chair that the family reserved for him when he was in town. He had a drink in his hand and a stern, twisted smile on his lips.

"So, I guess you've got a good reason for getting home this late on a school night? If not, you'd better invent one as fast as you can."

Quinn stood looking at his father but said nothing.

"The clock is ticking, boy."

His mother stood and moved closer to him as if she intended to offer him her support. "Now, Martin, I told you where he was. He's been putting in extra study time since his finals are coming up. Isn't that right, Quinn?"

Quinn knew it was her feeble attempt at protecting him from his father's wrath. He also knew that it often made things much worse when she tried to run interference for him. Quinn preferred to fight his own battles with his old man. He seldom won, but at least he had his self-respect when it was over.

"I'm later than I intended to be," Quinn said. "I lost track of time. I'm sorry if I worried you."

Martin snorted and then coughed to cover up the first awkward sound. "Nobody's worried, son. Annoyed, unhappy, pissed perhaps, but not worried. You're a big boy now. You can take care of yourself, I'm sure."

Quinn knew better than to take the words as a compliment. He waited for his father to continue. "Apology not accepted."

Quinn continued to stand silently in front of his father. Their eyes were locked on one another, and Quinn would not be the first one to blink.

"Where the hell were you is the question?"

Quinn wanted to blurt out the truth, but he knew it would put his mother in a bad position. She had believed his ridiculous excuses about studying. "I was where I told Mom that I would be."

"And that would be where?" Martin looked at Quinn and then at Justine.

Justine spoke in a low, submissive voice. "He was studying at his friend's house."

"Which friend?"

Justine looked at Quinn for help.

"Larry Nelson," Quinn said.

Martin stood up, walked toward the phone on the end table, picked up the receiver, and pointed it at Quinn and Justine. "So, if I call his house, somebody will still be up to tell me you just left?"

"Probably," Quinn said. "Although his house is about five miles from here, so they may already be in bed by now."

"What's his number?"

"Maybe you should wait until morning, Martin. It's not like anything is going to change between now and then."

Martin stood there and stared at both of them as if waiting for one of them to blink. Quinn clasped his hands in front of him and held his breath so they wouldn't shake. Finally, his father put the phone down and left the room without another word.

———

A long, tense week passed before The Captain went back to the base. Quinn fully expected to get caught in his own web of lies and end up getting punished by being restricted to the house or something worse. He suspected his mother had something to do with distracting his father, so that he would move on to other matters. She had been making all kinds of requests for a new car, a kitchen remodel, and an updated wardrobe.

To ensure he did not get that close to falling into the family fire pit again, Quinn did not go to the diner for a little over a week. Then, on a Wednesday afternoon, he could not stand being away from Dixie a moment longer, so he stopped in after school.

She wasn't there, and the manager said she had called in sick. He had intended to go back, but his father had come home and insisted that the family return with him to the base for a medal ceremony. The trip ended up lasting for days, and when they returned, The Captain remained in Atlanta for the Easter holiday.

Bryce was coming home for Spring Break, and everyone was excited to see him and to spend time with him. Quinn knew he had to stay close to home and not do anything that would make his parents suspicious. He would be out of school in a few weeks, and then he could spend as much time with Dixie as he wished.

He dropped by the diner to find Dixie absent again, so he scribbled a note on a napkin saying that he would be tied up with his brother's visit for a while, but he would see her after Easter. He said that he missed her and hoped to see her again as soon as he could.

———

Bryce insisted the brothers spend a few days of Spring Break together on a brief trip. Quinn grinned from ear to ear when his older brother presented him with a plane ticket to Cancun. It was only a two-and-a-half-hour flight from the Atlanta airport.

At first, they had grand adventures. They swam in the infinity pool, drank at the swim-up bar, and played tennis and mini golf. They flirted with women but stopped short of taking them back to their room. They took a catamaran ride to Isla Mujeres (the Island of Women) and spent the day on the beach. They ate delicious meals and drank whatever and whenever they pleased.

On the third day of the trip, they stayed at the hotel and hung out around the pool area with the swim-up bar. Bryce had lots of practice in putting down mai tais, but Quinn was an amateur at boozing. After a few strong drinks, he started talking, and by late afternoon, he was babbling. Most of the talk was about how their father had always favored Bryce and mistreated his younger son.

"I know you're right, Quinn. I've got excellent vision and hearing. I've always seen how he treats us differently, and God knows you've never been shy about telling me how you feel." He turned over on his stomach on the beach chair and looked his younger brother squarely in the eye. "What I want to know is why you're telling me. What can I do about it, huh? Why don't you take it up with the old man and leave me out of it? I'm sick of the whole poor-me routine, and frankly, I think you're acting like a titty baby."

Quinn stood up and wrapped the beach towel around his waist. He took two steps and lost his balance, sank down in the sand on one knee, and then toppled sideways. When he raised his head, he had sand in his hair and on his face. He locked eyes with Bryce, and then they both burst out laughing.

If Bryce had not put another drink in his little brother's hand, they might have returned to the States with fond memories of bonding while in Mexico. But one drink led to another, and soon words were spilling out of Quinn's mouth as if he were in a confessional booth at the Catholic church.

"She's amazing, Bryce. I can't stand to be away from her for very long."

"You're in lust, little brother."

"Maybe so, but she gets to me like no girl I've ever known before."

"Well, that's not saying much. You haven't exactly been on the make since you hit puberty. How many other girls have you dated, anyway? One? Two?"

"What difference does it make how many girls I've dated? Dixie is special. She's more beautiful and more interesting than any of those Atlanta debutantes Mom introduced to me."

"Those girls were from good families, Quinn. They have money and status. They would make good military wives."

"Then you go out with them. I'm not military, and I never will be."

"Well, if her family lives in Cabbagetown, and she works in a diner, they haven't climbed very far up the social ladder."

"You saying she's not good enough?" Quinn said. His words were slurred.

"I'm saying that you'd better consider what I'm saying before you bring her home to meet the folks."

Bryce ordered some nachos, and the two of them ate hungrily. "For the record, what do you know about Dixie's family?"

Quinn took a bite and wiped away a string of cheese stuck on his chin. He took his time chewing so he could consider his answer. The truth was he knew nothing about Dixie's family. Nothing at all.

———

During the next few weeks, he was caught up in final exams and NROTC parade rehearsals for graduation and frequent visits from his father. He knew he could not take a chance and make lame excuses about studying with a friend without getting nailed. It was over a month before he could make it back to Cabbagetown.

He could smell the freshly roasted coffee beans as soon as he opened the door. Dixie was standing at the counter making coffee and counting out scoops into the machine. Not wanting to make her lose count, he quietly took a seat at the counter to wait for her to finish.

When she closed the lid on the big silver machine, he said, "Hi there."

She jumped as if she had been shot and whirled around to face him. "Don't do that! For heaven's sake. What are you trying to do? Scare me to death?" Her voice was more than merely annoyed. She was furious.

Quinn tried not to be hurt but didn't succeed. "You think saying hello to my girl is something I should avoid? Fine. I can manage that."

Her face fell. She took two steps toward the counter and

took his two hands in hers. "Good grief, Quinn. You startled me. And please don't call me your girl."

"Are you mad at me, Dixie?" He ran his fingers back through his hair. "I'm sorry I haven't seen you for a while. Did you get my note? I wrote one to…"

"I got it," she interrupted. She picked up the green rag, sprayed the counter with a cleaning solution, and began wiping it down. "I'm not mad."

He noticed she was wearing her hair a different way. It was parted on the side, and a long shock of hair hid the left side of her face. He dared not mention it. She was in no mood for observations about her appearance.

She flitted about from customer to customer, refilling their cups and water glasses. He thought she was doing whatever she could to avoid returning to the counter where he sat. Finally, she said, "Are you going to order something?"

He smiled, but she didn't notice because she was not looking at him. "Do I need to?"

"You do if you're going to take up that space much longer. Paying customers are what my boss wants."

He stood up and put a five-dollar bill on the counter. "Okay. Write up a ticket for something cheap and keep the change."

She raised her head to look at him, and he could see a tear glistening in her right eye, but it was too late. Enough already. He was done trying to thaw out the Ice Queen.

———

Finals week was crazy busy. In between his exams, he had to appease his mother by going to a fitting for a new suit. Quinn couldn't understand why he needed to wear a suit under his gown. He was going to sweat like a roasted pig. He knew it would make no difference if he protested or complained. His mother's way was the way it was going to be. No questions asked.

He also had to attend a church service for all graduates whose parents were in the military. His father was in town to strut his stuff and wore his dress white uniform. Although only May, the temperature in Atlanta would be warm for an outdoor ceremony. Captain Martin Cameron visited his favorite barber for a trim with a number two blade. His black hair was thick and would have been wavy if allowed to grow. Quinn had seen photos of a younger version of his father in which he looked kinder and more agreeable. In recent years, his face had only one expression: jaw clenched and eyes narrowed.

Quinn realized his father was not a mean man or even a disagreeable one. He was simply detached and disinterested except where Bryce was concerned. Bryce brought out the human side of his father, the gregarious, garrulous man that Quinn never saw. Quinn knew it was his fault. So far, he simply had done nothing in his life worth talking about, and because it was his choice not to follow in The Captain's footsteps, he was on a completely different path that led away from everything his father held dear.

A week before graduation, Quinn took one of the announcements left in the box of one hundred that his mother had ordered, carefully wrote Dixie Lee King on the envelope, and put it into his backpack.

He was sure Dixie could not attend because it was way across town and held on a weeknight. She would have to work, and he understood that. He wanted to invite her because she was more special to him than any girl he had ever dated, and he wanted her to know that he wanted her to share this milestone in his life. Even if it was more of a symbolic gesture than a realistic one, he felt good about taking the engraved invitation to her.

He parked across the street from the diner, took the envelope out of the backpack, smoothed his hair, and made his way to the door. The welcome blast from the air-conditioning felt good, and he looked around the room, hoping to spot Dixie.

She wasn't there, so he took a seat at the counter and ordered a Coke. He figured she was in the restroom or the kitchen. He sipped on the sweet, cold liquid until the bottle was almost empty. Then he realized she was not coming out at all.

When the busboy passed by with a load of dishes, Quinn stopped him. "Excuse me. Is Dixie here?"

The boy looked at him for a moment as if he had asked an inappropriate question. "No, she ain't."

"What time does her shift start?"

Again, the funny look before he said, "Not sure. I haven't seen her in days."

Quinn went to the cash register stand to talk to the hostess. "Is the manager here?"

"You're looking at her, honey."

"Oh, sorry. I was hoping to talk to Dixie today, but she's not here."

"She hasn't been here in a week. She quit. Turned in her apron and cap and took off. No notice. No consideration at all." She scratched her head and sighed. "Funny, she still had two weeks' pay coming. I know she needs it."

Quinn was too surprised to comment, so he thanked the woman and left. He drove the short distance to the RV park and got out of his car. He had only walked a few steps when he saw the space where the trailer sat. When he got closer he saw the FOR RENT sign in the front window.

He looked around, hoping to find some clue to help him understand where she had gone. He questioned the few people who occupied the nearby mobile homes, but they didn't know her. Some of them had never even seen the girl that lived in that trailer.

Now, even after all this time, Quinn felt a sick, disappointed feeling in the pit of his stomach as he remembered how desperate and confused he had felt when he walked up the three steps and turned the knob on the door. It was locked. Nothing remained but an overflowing trashcan.

CHAPTER 10
QUINN CAMERON

PRESENT DAY

After four years of roaming around Europe alone, Quinn was not surprised to see that the only person waiting for him near the luggage carousel at the Atlanta Airport was his mother. Justine had not aged at all in the years since Quinn had been in Europe. She still looked young and attractive, and men of all ages glanced her way as they walked by. Her red hair, now blended with silver, gave her sophisticated highlights that would be impossible to replicate even in an expensive hair salon. It may have been a cliché, but she was truly only getting better as she aged.

She gave him a warm hug and the scent of Chanel No.5 took him back to his childhood when she would lean over his bed to tuck him in each night and kiss him on the forehead.

He had thought about it many times, and he knew he was lucky to have such a mother. She could not make up for The Captain's cold attitude, but she tried. It wasn't her fault that she went way too far, and her attempts at kindness turned into saccharine gestures.

He hated hearing her call him Quinney Boy in that baby-talk voice of hers, and she never failed to do so around his friends, which made him look like a first-class sissy and a mama's boy. He tried many times to tell her not to be so mawkish, but it didn't help at all. That's who she was; that's who she would always be.

It was difficult to grow up as the younger child between two such opposite and domineering personalities. The old man constantly compared his two sons, and Quinn was always a step behind his nearly perfect older brother. Justine knew that her firstborn son was on the same trajectory as her husband, so she spent her time and effort on her younger boy. Even though Quinn was no longer a baby, she refused to let him walk alone. She wanted to guide every step that he took. She was driving him crazy.

"Well, darling, I am certainly going to work on feeding you well. What did you eat while you were traipsing around overseas? You must not have visited too many good restaurants."

Quinn started to tell her that although he had eaten many wonderful meals, he had lost weight because he had done a lot of walking, but she started in again before he could speak.

"And what happened to good grooming? Have you become a Bohemian as well? I can see that I have my work cut out for me, or should I say you need to have a spa day before the party on Saturday night."

Quinn could have sworn he heard the theme from Jaws beginning to play in his right ear while his mother's voice droned in his left. *Spa day? Party? What the hell?*

———

A week later, he had found his own place and started moving in. He had angered his father and hurt his mother's feelings by refusing to attend any kind of welcome home party and refusing to get his hair cut. His mother had already hired a caterer and invited fifty people, and his father was repulsed by his long hair. His father reacted with anger and threats, and his mother pleaded with him and then cried. Story of his life. He knew he had to start a new chapter.

His new home was an old house in a marginal neighborhood that had an unpainted but structurally sound outbuilding behind it. He knew it would be perfect for his plans to handcraft custom furniture. He had spent most of his time while he was away observing furniture makers and volunteering to do any odd jobs they required so that he could hang around them and observe their skills and techniques.

Now that he was back in Atlanta, he had to find a job and earn enough money to attend classes at one of the best woodworking schools in the area. There were techniques he needed to master before he could compete with some of the craftsmen in Atlanta. He didn't want to be average; he wanted to be one of the best.

He started buying the Atlanta Journal-Constitution and circling jobs for which he thought he might qualify in the classified section. He was learning the hard way that there was not much to be found above minimum wage unless you had a college degree. He could hear his father's voice drumming that thought into his head. No, he had not listened. No, he did not regret giving up the pageantry that was Annapolis. Military life was not for him. Never could be.

One ad sounded promising. He made his way to a large building in the warehouse district and applied for a delivery job. The foreman who took his application took one look at him and snorted.

"Two things we can't have around here, bud—long hair and jewelry. It's a safety issue. Ditch them both and you might have a shot with the boss lady. Otherwise, you're barking up the wrong tree." Then he swept his arms wide to indicate the stacks of two-by-fours and two-by-eight boards and roared with laughter at his own joke.

Quinn grinned at him. It was a good joke, and he couldn't help but be in a good mood around the smell of lumber. "I'll be back in a couple of hours. Will the boss be here then?"

The foreman nodded. "Make it snappy, bud. These jobs go fast. She pays better than most."

Quinn stopped at the first quick-cut shop he could find. Who cared what his hair looked like? It would grow back soon enough. At least he was cutting it for a good reason and not only because The Captain told him to. As for the jewelry, he only had that chain around his neck because his mother had given it to him for graduation. It had become a habit to wear it, but he pulled it over his head and dropped it into the console of the car.

Quinn was back at the lumberyard in less than an hour. He smoothed down the back of his hair, which now reached below his ear lobes, and walked into the warehouse.

He looked around for the foreman, but the place looked deserted. He climbed a steep stairway leading to a landing and saw an office with windows on all four sides. It looked empty also, but then he noticed a woman standing in front of a copy machine. She was tall, slender, and had an amazing, curvaceous body.

He double-tapped on the office door, and when she turned, he had to take a deep breath to calm himself. She had thick, blonde hair that flipped up on her shoulders, blue eyes that regarded him coolly and wore a black jumpsuit that would have looked like a custodian's uniform on anyone else. On her, it looked like she was ready for the red carpet.

"Well, come on in," she said. "Don't just stand there."

When he entered the office, she motioned toward a desk chair that had rollers on it. He sat down, and the chair rolled a little to the right toward her.

"Whoa there, cowboy," she said in a deep, almost masculine voice. "Where you goin' in such a hurry?" Then she laughed, and he could see the laugh lines around her eyes and beginnings of the smoker's lines on her upper lip. She was older than he first thought by at least a decade and a half, but she was still stunning.

"I'm here about the delivery job. Did I come to the right place?" He flashed her his best charming Quinn grin—the one he was famous for in high school. The one that showed his even, white teeth and usually stopped girls in their tracks.

She seemed blind to his charms but sat down behind a desk and picked up a pen. "Qualifications? Education? Goals?"

"Yes, ma'am," he said. "I have all of those. Which one do you want first?"

"You can call me Lorraine or Mrs. Faust. Take your pick. Just drop the ma'am, and we'll get along fine, okay?"

———

The delivery job turned out to be exactly what he was looking for. It paid a dollar above minimum wage, and he got a company truck. The bonus was that he could take any broken scrap lumber home at the end of the week and work on his projects.

Quinn picked up his loads from the dock at the back of the warehouse and had no reason to go into the office except on Friday afternoons. The men all lined up at the base of the stairs and were called into the office individually to get their pay envelopes from Mrs. Faust. They often left with a smile on their face and occasionally he overheard a crude remark, but for the most part they all simply did their jobs, collected their pay, and minded their own business.

He looked forward to seeing her each Friday, and the way she looked at him made him feel better than he had in a long time. She was flirting with him, and he knew it. He knew if she had not been married, he would have flashed that smile of his a little more often. Now, it seemed a pure waste of time.

One afternoon, he collected an especially large order and Marvin, a co-worker, rode with him to help unload the lumber. He was a pleasant enough guy who whistled while he worked, and they finished a few minutes after their shift was over.

"You want to stop for a cold one, Marvin?"

"For sure," he said. "We're off the clock now."

"You pick it," Quinn said. "I'm the new guy."

They ended up at the Green Door Pub, where Marvin assured him the beer was cold and the wings were hot.

After their second round, Marvin started talking. "What's a young guy like you doing delivering lumber? Don't you have better things to do?"

Quinn wasn't sure how to respond. Was this a trick question? He didn't want to say the wrong thing and make it sound like this wasn't much of a job, because after all, it was Marvin's job too.

"It's honest work. It pays okay, and Mrs. Faust is a good boss." He took a drink of his beer and wiped the foam off his lips. "What's not to like?"

"That Lorraine's a looker, isn't she?"

"That she is," Quinn admitted. "Her husband's a lucky guy."

Marvin signaled the bartender for another round. "Not so much," he said and laughed.

Quinn shot him a questioning look.

"The guy's dead," Marvin said. "Heart attack two years

ago. I hear he had a lot of life insurance, so that's when Lorraine went to Italy for six weeks. She always did look pretty good, but when she came back she was somethin' else. Makes the guys drool when she walks by."

––––––––

Quinn wasn't sure why knowing that Lorraine Faust was single had made such a difference in the way he felt each day, but it did. He took extra time each Friday morning to make sure his hair looked good, and he wore aftershave. What the heck was wrong with him, anyway?

Maybe he had been celibate too long. He had not been with anyone since he enjoyed that fling with Helga in Belgium. She had been a tall, blonde Wonder Woman, but she had not been interested in anything but a good time. He managed to fool her for a couple of years, but she left him in the dust when she found out he did not have the means to spoil her with gifts and trinkets.

Lorraine was different. She had more money than she knew what to do with. She could have any guy she wanted. When she sent word for him to come by her office after work on Thursday, he thought he had done something wrong. Geez! Now that his savings account was finally getting healthy, he was probably going to get fired.

She opened the door herself when he knocked and pointed at a chair. "Sit down, Quinn. I need to ask you a serious question." She pulled a bottle of water out of a mini fridge near her desk and offered it to him.

"No, thanks. I'm good," he croaked. *What was wrong with his voice?*

She unscrewed the top of the bottle and took a long drink before setting it on the desk. Then she sat down in her chair and rested her chin on her hand. "You like chicken?"

He wondered if that was a real question. "You mean the kind you eat?"

She laughed and once again he heard that deep smoker's voice. "Yes, that kind."

"Sure, I guess. I'm more of a seafood kind of guy, but chicken's fine, too." He looked at her and grinned. This was turning out to be fun, and for sure, he wasn't in trouble.

———

From then on, whenever Quinn or Lorraine wanted a good laugh, one of them would ask: "You mean the kind you eat?"

That question had led to a fantastic night of adventure and enjoyment for the two of them. Lorraine had asked about the chicken because she wanted Quinn to be her plus one at a Chamber of Commerce formal banquet to be held at the convention center the following weekend.

"I'd like to go, but I'm not sure I have the right clothes," Quinn said.

"Why don't you let me worry about that? You show up at Suave Menswear in Lenox Square. They will fit you from head-to-toe and send me the bill."

"Are you sure?"

"Don't even consider saying no," she said. "Nobody buys formal clothes anymore. They go out of style too quickly. Anyway, it won't cost me much. I gave them a heck of a deal on all the lumber for their shelving and dressing rooms. It's payback time."

His male pride told him to decline, but his best instincts told him to accept her generous invitation. It would be a great opportunity to meet the movers and shakers in town that he would like to know for future reference. Besides that, who in their right mind would turn down an evening with a beautiful woman like Lorraine?

———

They arrived fashionably late in the limo she had sent to pick him up. Lorraine wore a black and silver gown with a folded mermaid tail he had to avoid stepping on all night. His Joseph Abboud Black Peak Lapel Tuxedo was so luxurious it made him want to keep gazing in the mirror and turning to the side to get a better glimpse of the new and improved Quinn Cameron.

His mother had forced him to wear nice suits to the events she compelled him to attend, but he had worn nothing as posh as this. The slim fit coat had a narrow grosgrain lapel, and the sleek flat-front slacks were hemmed to exactly the right length to touch the tops of his shiny, patent leather dress shoes.

His shirt, worn under a purple four-button vest, was a plain front style with a point collar. A deep purple pre-tied tie, along with the plum satin flower pinned to his left lapel, accented the rich lightweight wool fabric of the tux.

Who knew that clothes like this could be comfortable? Maybe he was cut out for the life his mother had always pushed him toward after all. He considered that thought for a moment and then laughed out loud.

It had taken him twenty minutes to get dressed, not counting taking a shower, shaving, and brushing his teeth. He had trouble with the cuff links, so he waited until he was in the car and let Lorraine help him.

"This is a two-person job," he insisted. "I hope you don't mind."

She smiled at him and kissed his cheek. "You look scrumptious. I never realized how good-looking you are until right now."

The rest of the evening, he stood back to watch and learn. She knew exactly what to say to each person she met during the cocktail hour. By the time they sat down at the dining table, he had figured out which people she liked and which ones she didn't. She didn't have any patience for men who fawned over her, and she barely gave some of the haughty women a second glance, sometimes ignoring them as if they had not spoken to her.

A few months later, after he knew her better, he mentioned his observations to her, and she had the perfect explanation. "I learned from the best. My husband did not suffer fools. He showed me from the earliest days of our marriage that certain people were not worth my time or attention. I am an excellent judge of character, Quinn. That's why I'm with you."

"You don't say. I thought you were with me because I have a killer smile and I make a mean martini."

"Well, that too," she said and reached out to touch his hand. "They were seated on the balcony of her home that overlooked a manicured lawn and a lap pool she used twice a day."

They had become friends and then lovers, and Quinn was enjoying her company more than he had any other woman's in a long time. He spent most weekends with her, but she had not suggested that he move in with her, and he was grateful. He liked his house, and he was working on several projects in the outbuilding he now thought of as his workshop.

As far as he knew, none of the other workmen knew anything about their special relationship, and he hoped it would stay that way. She had not given him a raise, nor had she shown him any favoritism. He was happy about that, too. He wanted to be her escort but not become a parasite.

They took a long vacation together in Cabo San Lucas and spent their days snorkeling in placid coves, riding on a catamaran while sighting whales, and eating whatever they wanted from the expansive buffet at the hotel.

Quinn thought she was beautiful and smart and exciting, but something kept him from falling in love with her. He wasn't sure why. It wasn't the difference in their ages, or that she was his boss. She was a dream of a woman, but she wasn't his dream.

And he knew, if he were honest with himself, that he was not hers either. She refused to spend the entire night with him, and she always booked two adjoining rooms when they traveled. It was as if she never let her guard down.

She was affectionate and warm, but she did not let their passionate encounters consume her. There were no declarations of love or longing and no promises of hopes for the future.

Even though he knew he was a lucky man to spend time with such an amazing, beautiful woman, he wanted more. He wanted more than sex. More than a mere companion. He wanted someone who set his blood on fire. He wanted Dixie.

———

Now that he was back in Atlanta, he knew he had to find her, or at least find out where she had gone. He told Lorraine that he was spending the weekend with his parents and planned to backtrack looking for clues.

He breathed a sigh of relief when he pulled up in front of the diner in Cabbagetown. It was still there and the fluorescent, open sign flashed red in the window. What did he expect? To see her standing there pouring coffee?

He sighed with disappointment when he walked into the room and took a seat at the counter. An older waitress was taking an order from the people in the corner booth, but there was no sign of Dixie.

"Something to drink?"

He looked up to see a man who wore pleasant smile and a stained apron. "Coffee, please."

The man turned around and took a white mug from the pile on the counter. He filled it with steaming coffee and set it down in front of Quinn. "Anything to eat?"

"Not yet," Quinn said. "Have you been here a long time?"

"Since I opened the place. I'm Tony, the owner."

"Sir, would you mind if I asked you a couple of questions?"

"Not at all, son. Shoot."

"I remember a waitress that worked here named Dixie. I would like to see her again."

"Me, too," he admitted. "She was a hard worker and a nice girl."

"Do you know where she is?"

"Nope. She came in and quit and didn't give my manager a reason. Never even picked up her pay."

"I went to the trailer park where she lived. I wanted to talk to her parents, but the place was empty."

Tony scratched his head. "There weren't any parents in that trailer, son. Dixie lived alone."

———

Quinn sat there on the stool for a long time, remembering how many times he had let Dixie walk away from him down that dark path toward the trailer. If only he had known she lived alone. *You would have done what? What could you have done? You were still in high school with no money and no plan.*

He knew he could not have helped her much, but he would have tried. She must have been so lonely and so scared. Why would a young woman like that live all by herself? Who would rent to a minor?

The more he thought about it, the more he knew that somebody had to have some answers. He was going to keep asking the hard questions until he found them.

CHAPTER 11
BRYCE CAMERON

MOST OF THE customers had left, and the Italian restaurant was quiet. Hannah finished her second glass of wine and wiped the pizza sauce from her mouth with the cloth napkin. She looked like she was about to suggest they leave, and Bryce took the opportunity to say, "You're yanking my chain aren't you, Doc?"

Her lips turned up in what appeared to be a shy smile, but Bryce knew better. He rubbed the top of her hand with his index finger and waited for her to respond.

"I have no idea what you're talking about."

"Oh, come on. You're killing me here."

"Again, I repeat, I'm completely in the dark."

"You know I like you a lot," he said. "I've been putting out signals all night. I can go anywhere to finish my book, but I'd rather finish it here in Denver."

"And?" she asked.

"And it all depends on you." He was going to make a fool out of himself, but if he didn't put all his cards on the table, he knew he would regret it for the rest of his life. "Do you want me to stay?"

Hannah steepled her fingers against her face and cupped

her chin in her thumbs. She gave him what he thought was her most professional look when she calmly said, "I do."

"Wow, you are one tricky lady. I sketch all my emotions on my face while yours is a blank slate. I guess you have to be like that when you listen to people's problems every day."

"Maybe, but it's probably because it's the way I was raised. My parents are lovely people, but they are… well… I guess the best way to describe them is reserved. I guess if you met them you would say they were aloof or snobby."

"But you don't come across that way. I would describe you as careful, but you're certainly not snobby."

"I am afraid I was quite a chore for them. I was born late in their lives, and I don't honestly know if they knew what to do with me. Do you know how hard it is to be a nerd when all you want to do is to be outside running around and, God forbid, getting sweaty? They bought me lots of books because they were content to sit by the fireplace, and so they thought I would be too. So, in a way, I guess you could say they compromised, and if I had excellent grades, they let me be myself. They didn't stifle me. but they never understood me."

"So why psychology?" Bryce glanced up as the waiter approached the table, and he noticed the room was now empty. "Oops," he laughed. "It appears we have overstayed our welcome. Hold that thought."

———

They walked back toward Hannah's office from the restaurant. It was cold, but they were both dressed for the weather, and it gave Bryce the excuse to put his arm around her and ask if she was warm enough.

He was surprised when she reached up and grasped his hand and said, "Thanks, but I'm used to the cold weather." His heart jumped a beat when she didn't let go.

A few cars passed them, but for the most part, everything was quiet. Hannah broke the silence when she said, "It was something I was drawn to. I'm a social person, and I wanted to understand human behavior. Why were my parents subdued scholars, while in contrast, the next-door neighbors were loud and boisterous? Why I was so different?"

Bryce stopped and turned to look at her. "What?" he said, clearly confused.

"It's the answer to your question as to why I became a psychologist. Also, it would have broken my parents' hearts if I'd become a high school coach."

A group of pine trees filled the courtyard in front of the building. He pulled her toward a wrought-iron bench and onto his lap.

"What are you doing?" she said.

"Getting to know you. What's this about being a coach?"

Hannah scooted off his lap and played with the zipper on her coat for several seconds before she answered. "I told you I liked to be outside. I guess that was an understatement. There wasn't a sport I didn't want to try if it got me in the sun. I settled on softball my junior year in high school and played all the way through college."

"And what did your parents say about that?"

"Oh, they were supportive, but they were academics. I know they couldn't understand why I loved it so much. But they attended my games when they could, their schedules permitting, and didn't belittle me. I decided to get my doctorate to give them back a little of what they had given to me."

"Come to think of it," he said, "I did notice the softball displayed on your desk."

"Game ball. We won our conference my senior year, and I was the MVP."

"So, you were the pitcher. Wow, I am impressed. Do you still play?"

"I didn't have time when I was in grad school, but now I plan to join a team and play this summer? Do you play?"

"Baseball and football in high school, but I'm not in your league."

The wind picked up a little and blew her long hair across her face. Bryce leaned in and tucked it behind her ear and kissed her softly. "I think lady jocks are sexy."

Hannah stiffened and pulled back. Bryce frowned and said, "I'm getting mixed signals here. I'm not pushing, but I thought you might be a little bit interested. Was I wrong?"

"No, but I'm incredibly busy, and I shouldn't have gone to dinner tonight." She shook her finger as she continued, "You are a bad influence on me. I don't have time for this."

"For what?"

"This." She wagged her index finger back and forth between them. "You and me this."

Bryce smiled and felt like a schoolboy. He stood up and pulled Hannah to her feet. "I guess I'd better walk you to your car so I can stay on your good side. I want to do this again."

Bryce noticed that cars sporadically filled the spaces in the parking garage. He listened to the echo of Hannah's bootheels as she walked beside him toward her car. "Pretty deserted, huh?" he said as he glanced down at her face hidden by the shadows. "Do you ever work late?"

"Sometimes, but not this late. It's kind of spooky down here. I guess these people must be dedicated," she said, pointing to the cars.

"Which one is yours? No, better yet, let me guess." He moved his head from side to side and zeroed in on a gray BMW sedan. "That one. The little gray Beemer."

Hannah laughed and tugged his hand, dragging him up the ramp. "Not even close. It's that little Ford Escape SUV next to the little gray Beemer."

They walked along, heedless of the sound of an engine

roaring. Then, they both looked up and were blinded by the headlights of an approaching car. "What the he …" Brett started to say when he realized the car was bearing down on them at a high speed. He pushed Hannah out of the way and dived for the asphalt as the car raced past and pulled out of the garage.

"Are you all right?" he said. Hannah was struggling to get to her feet, and he noticed the blood on her knees and hands.

"I think I'm fine. The coat got most of it. I have a few scrapes and cuts from landing so hard."

"I'm so sorry. I didn't mean to hurt you. I thought for sure that car was going to hit us."

"No, you were right. He certainly wasn't paying any attention. We could have been seriously hurt or killed. What in the world could he have been thinking?"

Yes, what in the world? Bryce hadn't been able to see the driver and only got a look at the taillights as the car drove away.

"Should we call the police?" Hannah asked as she smoothed her coat with her shaking hands.

"I doubt it would do any good, but I would talk to your building security tomorrow. Although I don't know what they could do either."

"Maybe they will have a video."

"Yeah," he laughed. "Like in the movies."

Hannah smiled up at him and said, "You certainly know how to show a girl a good time. It's been an eventful evening."

"It has, hasn't it?"

Hannah unlocked her car and slid into the driver's seat. Bryce looked down into her lovely face and leaned in for a goodnight kiss. She put her hand up to stop him and said, "Where's your car?"

"I walked here from the hotel. It's not far."

"Get in. I'll drop you off. You don't need to be walking

around Denver in the middle of the night. For goodness' sake, you macho man."

He got in beside her, and this time he was successful when he leaned in for a kiss. He slightly exaggerated his Southern drawl. "I would appreciate the ride, ma'am. I'm a few blocks over on Union at the Hampton. I'll be there until I find something more permanent now that I'm going to be staying in town for a while."

Hannah winked, put the car into gear, and drove toward the exit.

CHAPTER 12
HANNAH BRODY

"HANNAH'S A CHICKEN. **Hannah's a chicken, Bwok, Bwok, Bwok, Bwok,**" Jimmy Regis sang. Hannah watched him in the water below her as she held on tightly to the rope that swung over the pond. "Come on, jump."

"Am not a coward," Hannah whispered as she stared down at the murky water. *It's just that I don't know how to swim, and the water is deep.* She bit her lip and fought back tears. She wanted to get along and be one of the gang. Maybe if she told Jimmy he would understand. Teach her to swim. Yeah, as if that would ever happen. A storm was coming in and the wind blew her slender body farther out near the middle of the water hole.

Again, she heard the taunting and then from the bank, the voices of the other kids who had joined the group. Her hands were slippery from sweat and shaking from fear. The water was deep, well over her head, and was fed by a strong current from underground. It was now or never. She let go of the rope and plunged into the water.

———

Hannah woke up gasping for air, her body shaking. She hadn't thought about that terrifying childhood memory in years. It must have been the close call she had tonight that had brought back that horrible incident.

She remembered it was the third day of summer camp. A camp to which she had begged her parents to send her. They'd been reluctant, but she'd pleaded and cried and carried on which was uncharacteristic for her. Finally, her father had flung his glasses down on the desk and relented, or at least as close as he could come to it, when he said, "Ask your mother."

Her mother was usually preoccupied with research for her next paper and rarely listened when she was "in the moment" as she liked to say. So, it was easy for Hannah to slip in the question and get a yes before her mother knew what was happening.

———

Now, all these years later, Hannah shook off the dark thoughts that crowded in and sat on the edge of the bed. The clock radio read six a.m. Already? Where had the night gone? But she knew the answer. She had spent half of it looking at Bryce Cameron over a glass of wine.

He was a fine-looking man and a real charmer. She'd practically let all her inhibitions go, and probably would have toppled right into bed with him if he'd asked, which he hadn't. It was for the best. She was busy. He was busy. Then why had she led him on and let him believe she was interested too?

"Oh, stop it, Hannah," she chided herself. "You like him. Admit it. Let it go where it will go. If it doesn't amount to anything, nothing lost, nothing gained." She looked in the mirror and noticed the dark circles under her eyes. Good Lord, she thought, and now you're talking to yourself. "And, self," she said, poking her finger at the mirror, "get your shit together and get ready for work."

Hannah finished her last lecture of the day. Her Psychology 101 class was an introductory class that all new psychology professors at the university were expected to teach. It was an easy hour and a half and made it possible for her to instruct the graduate students on her true passion: psychology and genetics. The research that the students did in her class gave her invaluable material for her book.

Her class was an elective for most of the BA students, and her classroom could sometimes be filled with two hundred undergrads at a time. The room usually cleared out quickly, and Hannah was surprised to hear someone cough from one of the top rows of the hall and then say, "Hey, Doc, tell me more about my ego."

Hannah waved him off and laughed. "It's way too big for anyone to handle, that's for sure. What are you doing here?"

Bryce jogged down the steps, halted in front of Hannah, and placed his hands on her shoulders. "I wanted to make sure you were okay. You know, after last night and everything."

"You mean because you kissed me?"

"Ha, very funny. No seriously. I was concerned about the tumble you took when I pushed you out of the way. But you look pretty good," he did a wolf whistle and grinned. "So, I guess there's not any permanent damage. What did security say?"

Hannah put her notes in the leather bag on the table beside the podium and slipped it onto her shoulder. She turned back to Bryce and said, "I'm fine. Only a little sore this morning. I thought you'd be busy writing today."

"I am, or rather I was. I couldn't sleep, so I worked most

of last night and until a couple of hours ago." He looked at his watch and then back at Hannah. "It's five o'clock some- where. Have a drink with me and an early dinner. I promise I won't keep you late."

"How did you find me, anyway? Google doesn't have my class schedule."

"No, but Pam does. I think she likes me."

"Pam is already in trouble for letting you in my office yesterday. Now she's giving out my schedule?"

"Hey, don't get mad at her. She only told me you'd be teaching until four today. I did the rest of the investigative work all by myself. You think I missed my calling?"

Hannah looked into his sexy green eyes and couldn't help herself. He was impossible to say no to. Just looking at him gave her a warm, tingly feeling. She hadn't been this attracted to a man in a long time.

————

"I'm liking this idea," Bryce said wiping the foam off his upper lip from the draft beer he'd finished. Pushing the mug aside, he said, "I am way too tired to have any more to drink. Come to think of it, I don't remember having lunch."

Hannah patted her index finger on her pursed lips and took in the man sitting across from her before she spoke. "What idea?"

"Having drinks and dinner together every night. Well, hopefully dinner soon. Did I tell you I'm starving?"

"You may have mentioned it. So, Bryce, where do you think this is going?"

"By this, you mean you and me?"

Hannah leaned in to take his hand when the waitress arrived with their food. She was ready to make the first move, but it could wait.

She dipped a hot french fry in ketchup while her eyes

remained locked with his. Those eyes held a story, and she wanted to hear it. "Why did you go to the Naval Academy?"

If he was surprised by her question and the change in the conversation, he didn't show it. He put his hamburger down and said, "Because that's what all the Cameron men have done since it was founded. I was the oldest son, and it was expected."

"And what did you want?"

"To be honest, I haven't given it a lot of thought. I liked the experience and the camaraderie. I didn't know I wanted to write until my senior year in high school, but I assumed I could do that as well as serve, you know?"

"So, what happened? Why did you get out after six years?"

"Hey, this conversation is getting a little serious here, don't you think?" Bryce ran his fingers through his hair. Hannah could tell he was obviously uncomfortable with the questions.

"We talked about me last night. Now, I want to get to know you." She took a deep breath, and her words rushed out. "If that's what you want too, because if it isn't, we won't need to bother having dinner again. I'm not interested in a fling."

Bryce reached across the table and cupped her face. "I'm a little scared here, Doc. I'm not sure I've ever felt this way before. I'm not sure what you want from me."

"I'm a little scared too," Hannah said as she pulled his hand from her face and kissed it. "This is something new for me, as well."

"I guess you can tell I'm not comfortable talking about myself. Surface stuff, sure, but not the down and dirty. My father is a difficult man. My mother is right out of a Faulkner novel. Old South without the money. It's not complicated. I only did what I was expected to do. I went to school, went into the Navy, went to war and came home."

He stopped, she assumed, to gather his thoughts, and then continued. "I didn't like war so much. I guess I wasn't cut out to see people I was with day and night get blown away, so I got out and wrote a book. End of story."

Hannah knew there was a lot more to the story, but she would not push tonight. "In my opinion, no one is truly cut out to like war, or at least I hope not."

She finished her dinner and sat back against the soft leather cushion of the booth. "I almost died, you know?"

"You, you… what?" Bryce said, clearly at a loss for words.

"I almost drowned when I was twelve. It's usually a distant memory, but I dreamed about it last night. I guess the crazy scare with the car brought back bad memories."

"Hannah, I'm so sorry."

"It's all right. I wanted you to know that it's okay to talk about uncomfortable things. I'm not speaking as a shrink but as a friend."

"Can't we be more than friends?" he asked, his expression open and expectant.

"I'd like that. I've been on a direct path to my goals for the last decade, and I haven't taken the time to have any relationships or at least not serious ones."

"Is that what we're looking at here, Doc, a serious relationship?"

"I'm pretty sure that's what I want, but it depends on you. What do you want?"

Bryce took hold of both of her hands and squeezed. "I want you. Any way I can get you. Whatever it takes." Bryce smiled and motioned for the waitress.

Hannah was nervous and excited as they walked out of the pub with hands clasped together as they headed for their cars.

Bryce stopped abruptly and pulled Hannah behind him. "Why did you stop?" Hannah insisted. "What's going on?"

Then she saw the broken glass sprinkled on the asphalt and gasped when she saw what was left of her little SUV.

"Good Lord, Bryce. Look at my car. It's…"

He gripped her arm and said, "Stay here. Let me take a look first, okay?"

Hannah was too numb to answer and stood silently and watched as he circled her vehicle and got down on the ground to look underneath it. She took a deep, steadying breath and quickly joined him on the ground.

"What are you looking for?" she asked, peering under the frame and looking at his face at the same time.

"I don't know. I wanted to make sure there weren't any surprises waiting for you."

"Surprises?" She stepped carefully to avoid the fragments of glass. She was glad she'd decided she had put on gloves when she noticed that Bryce's hands were bleeding.

"Bryce, look at your hands. You've cut yourself. Get up and let's call the police."

Bryce stood, and Hannah handed him a tissue to wipe off the blood. She stood looking at the carnage and bit her lip. It was a habit she had developed to keep from crying. All the windows had been broken and there were deep gashes sliced through the gray paint. Then she noticed the words carelessly scrawled across the trunk: *bitch and whore*.

"I feel like I'm in a Carrie Underwood song. Why would anyone do this to my car?"

"Do you have any jealous boyfriends?"

"No, I haven't dated anyone since I've been here. I've made a few friends, and I know the psychologists at work. To the best of my knowledge, I don't have any enemies, but it's clear I've pissed off someone."

She watched as Bryce pulled his cell out of his pocket and spoke to the 911 operator. What a nightmare. First the incident last night, and now this. It was possible the two things might not be related, but she wasn't a big believer in coincidence. She smiled weakly at Bryce, and when he ended the call, she waited for him to speak.

"They're sending a car. Shouldn't be more than a few minutes. I'm so sorry about this, Hannah. This isn't how I hoped our night would end."

"I agree, but it isn't your fault," she said and noticed a strange look in his eyes. "Is something wrong? Something you're not telling me?"

She heard the approaching siren and was relieved when she saw the white sedan with flashing lights pull up beside them. She patiently answered the officer's questions and signed all the paperwork so her car could be towed. It didn't appear to have suffered any mechanical damage, but it would be illegal to drive a vehicle without windows. The patrolman had been adamant about that.

They got into Bryce's rental, and she gave him directions to her condo. He was unusually quiet as he drove toward her home. They'd been interrupted when the policeman arrived, and he hadn't answered her questions. What was going on with Bryce? How well did she know him?

He pulled up to a red light and turned to her and said, "Do you have anything to drink at your house? I could use a stiff one, and then we have to talk."

CHAPTER 13
HANNAH BRODY

HANNAH FINISHED PICKING **the tiny glass shards out of Bryce's palms,** applied antibiotic cream, and gave him a small glass of Irish whiskey. She walked back toward the kitchen and returned with a glass of red wine for herself.

Before she could speak, Bryce took a large gulp from his glass and said, "That was good. I wouldn't expect you to be a whiskey girl."

"I'm not. I take it when I have the cramps."

"The what?"

"The cramps. Never mind," she sighed and sat down across from him. "So, what's going on with you? What do you know that I don't know?"

"You won't like it much. I didn't think that you … well I obviously didn't think, or I wouldn't have become involved with you right now. I would never put you in danger."

"What are you talking about?"

"Remember when I came to your office yesterday?"

"I'm not likely to forget it."

Bryce got up and paced around the room, eventually sitting back down and taking Hannah's hand. She didn't resist. She didn't know what he was going to say, but surely it couldn't be that bad.

"You didn't lie to me, did you? You aren't married or worse yet, an ax murderer?"

Bryce laughed, and she was pleased to see the warm smile spread across his face. "No, not married. No girlfriend. And I haven't killed anyone with an ax, not even in my book, but I did kind of lie."

Hannah raised her eyebrows and hoped he would get it out soon. The suspense was killing her. "What? What did you lie about?"

"Stalker. I have a crazy stalker, and evidently she followed me to Denver."

Hannah laughed, practically howling, and ended with an unladylike snort. "You are joking, right?" She looked at his face and realized he wasn't. "You're not joking. You're serious."

He nodded and raked his hand through his hair.

"So, the information you wanted wasn't for your book? It was for you? I don't know what to say. What can I say?" Hannah took a large sip of her wine and said, "How long has this been going on?"

"Since I moved to Frisco. She works for the real estate company, or rather she did. She was fired for being late and disappearing. That's because she was too busy watching me to work. It's a long story.

"Hey, I'm doing research, writer guy. I've got all night. Let's hear this long story. I'm sure I'll find it fascinating." Hannah leaned back to get comfortable on the sofa. She knew she was giving him a hard time, but damn it, some crazy woman had vandalized her car and possibly tried to kill her. She had a right to give him a hard time. He should have told her about the stalker before he asked her out. Now, she was afraid she was in too deep with Bryce. She cared about him and wasn't planning to toss him aside, but she wouldn't tell him that. He needed to suffer a little more. She also chided herself for thinking of the poor mentally ill woman as crazy. But hey, she thought, this is my life and I give myself permission.

"She started showing up unannounced at my cabin with some excuse for being in the area showing a house. At first, I didn't mind, but then it got to be a nuisance. Most of the time, I'd pretend I wasn't home, so she would go away. The last straw was when she left me stranded in a blizzard."

"She what? And don't you tell me it's a long story."

"She messed with my car so it wouldn't start and set things up so she could rescue me, but her plans fell apart when the local ranger helped me out instead. When I found out she'd been in my cabin, I hit the roof. I confronted her boss, who said he'd fired her. He didn't know why she was showing cabins at all because she was a receptionist and never showed rentals."

"Okay," Hannah said warily, knowing he was telling the story way too fast and leaving out a bunch. "So, what happened after that?"

"I called the police, but she had disappeared. Then out of the blue she called my cell the same morning after I came to your office. She was ranting about how she loved me and… I don't know, she said a bunch of crap. I hung up on her and called the police in Frisco. They didn't know anything. Hadn't seen her, but evidently, she has done this kind of thing before with an ex-boyfriend, which I am not. Nothing ever happened between us. The closest I got to her was shaking her hand the first time I met her."

"That was probably enough," Hannah said. "Her reality differs greatly from yours. So, it looks like she's angry now, and she believes you've moved on to someone else. Me. She is escalating, and she is dangerous. It's time to get the Denver PD involved."

"They will just tell me the same thing they did in Frisco.

There isn't anything they can do unless I saw her commit the vandalism or recognized her as the driver of the car that tried to run us down."

"A student in one of my grad classes is a detective. He seems like a nice guy. Maybe I can get him to help us."

Bryce got up and moved closer to Hannah. He knelt and put his hands on her shoulder and looked her in the eye. "I'm so sorry. I'll keep my distance until things can get straightened out."

"Absolutely not. We won't let some mentally ill person dictate how we live our lives. We'll be extra careful until the police catch her." Hannah touched his face and then kissed him softly. "I like you Bryce Cameron. I like you a lot."

Bryce kissed her back deeply and passionately, leaving no doubt how he felt about her too.

———

Hannah was running late. Bryce had stayed until almost midnight. This morning he'd insisted on driving her to see about her car at the repair shop, and then after teaching her class, she had walked into her building about five minutes before her first patient.

"You're late. Mr. Vines is here, and waiting." The flustered receptionist whispered, and pointed to the neatly furnished lobby.

Hannah glanced back at the room and noticed the man sitting between a long-haired biker type and a short, fragile-looking woman. Hannah took a deep breath and calmly said, "No, Pam, I'm not late." Looking down at her watch, she said, "I am right on time." She walked slowly into her office, hoping to avoid giving the impression that she was in a hurry to any of the patients.

Mr. Vines was a fiftyish science teacher who wiped his glasses repeatedly with a clean cloth. In fact, it was the man's obsessive compulsion for cleanliness that brought him to the office. His wife of thirty years had given him an ultimatum. Get a handle on this annoying habit, or else.

Her next patient was a beautiful young woman named Margaret with high levels of anxiety. Pleased with her progress, Hannah had planned to ask the psychiatrist to decrease her medication dosage since she was responding well to treatment. She soon realized that wasn't an option after Margaret told her about having a panic attack when she discovered her in-laws were flying in for a visit. All at once, Hannah realized it was starting out to be a long day.

———

Hannah leaned back in her chair and kicked off her heels as the door closed behind her last patient. She rubbed her forehead where she felt a slight twinge of pain. She was beyond tired from lack of sleep and worry and was annoyed when Pam buzzed her.

"Yes, Pam, what is it? I'm getting ready to pack it in for the day."

"Didn't you check your schedule, Doctor?"

"No. Why?"

"You have a new patient. I put it on the calendar," she said sweetly.

Hannah sighed, checked the Google Calendar on her computer, and bit back a curse. There it was. She had a four-thirty appointment with a Janet Jones. "Has she filled out all the paperwork?"

"Yes, all the background and medical questions, but not the insurance information. She is a cash pay."

"Okay, bring her in while I put my shoes back on." She heard a faint laugh from Pam as she put down the phone.

———

The woman sitting across from her had a pretty face, but she had applied makeup liberally, which detracted from her natural beauty. She was plump but dressed well to disguise it, and her hair was close to the exact shade and style of Hannah's.

Hannah smiled and said, "How can I help you, Ms. Jones?"

"Oh, please call me Janet. I'm sure we are going to be good friends."

Hannah waited a moment and said, "Well, Janet, therapy isn't exactly like that. Although we will talk about many things, including things that you may not have told anyone else, ours will be a professional relationship, not a personal one. It wouldn't be appropriate for us to be friends, and anything you say to me will be held in the strictest confidence."

"So, you can't tell anyone what I say?"

"That is correct, unless you are an immediate danger to yourself or others."

Janet laughed and crossed her legs. "I'm sorry. I'm a little nervous. I've never been in counseling before. This is all so new to me."

"So, what would you like to talk about today? What do you hope to achieve in therapy?"

"Well, I'm an executive at one of the major financial institutions. I got the job right out of college. I guess you could say I am an overachiever. I graduated in three years when I was twenty."

Hannah looked up at Janet and then back down and made a few notes. "Are you happy at your job?"

"I was, but lately I've been struggling with these feelings of being helpless. You know, what if I fail and lose everything?"

"How are you feeling physically? Are you sleeping?"

"No, and I'm tired all the time. I used to be so perky. And

my husband is not at all supportive. In fact, he's seeing someone else. I believe he is cheating on me."

Janet's voice became shrill as she talked about her husband, and Hannah noticed she was becoming extremely agitated. "Why don't you tell me a little more about your work? Do you like it?"

"I did before, but then she came along."

"She?"

"The woman that he's sleeping with."

Hannah tried to steer Janet away from that train of thought, but the more the woman talked, the angrier and more out of control she became. "Janet, you seem to be quite upset. Perhaps we can try some relaxation techniques that will help you get some control over your feelings."

Janet shook her head and smiled sweetly. "I am so sorry. I do that sometimes. He gets me so upset, and I love him so much. Are you in love, Dr. Brody?"

"We aren't talking about me, Janet. Remember, this is a professional relationship."

"You probably can't wait to get out of here and run home. I won't keep you. I'm feeling a little better. Can we do this again?"

"Yes, I would like to help you, Janet. Please come back. You can make an appointment with Pam. If you can, I'd like to see you in a couple of days to see how you're doing. Maybe we could talk about our psychiatrist prescribing some helpful medication for you."

"Medication? Oh, well, I don't know about that, but we will most definitely talk again. I believe you can help me. I'm sure coming to see you will fix almost everything."

CHAPTER 14
HANNAH BRODY

HANNAH TRIED **to remain professional** as she watched Janet Jones walk out of her office. Obviously, the woman needed her help, but she was at a loss to come up with even a hint of a diagnosis.

At first, the patient had shown signs of anxiety with her feelings about losing her job, but then she jumped into a maniac and fixated on her husband. Hannah made a note to speak with Jonathan Scott, the psychiatrist in the office suite. She wanted to have a consultation on what medications he would recommend, and she also made a note to reserve time during her next visit to perform a battery of tests. Hopefully, the results would give her an insight on where to begin.

Hannah stretched and massaged the knot in her neck. She was tired and ready to go home but realized she had no way to get there. Her car was in the shop, and she hadn't had time to get a rental. She could walk. It wasn't that far, but her feet hurt, and it was cold outside. She was feeling extremely sorry for herself when Bryce poked his head into her office.

"Hi, good looking. Are you ready to go? Your ride is here."

Suddenly her mood brightened, and she smiled widely at

the handsome devil in her doorway. He was handsome along with a touch of that bad-boy vibe that women couldn't resist. Or at least she was finding it hard to do so. He had a great sense of humor, and he was smart and easy to be around. So why did she feel a *but* coming on? Oh yeah, he has a stalker who is now targeting you. Well, who said every relationship was perfect?

"Hi back at yah. You must be psychic. I was trying to talk myself into walking home or calling a cab. I would love a ride." She grabbed her coat and felt her entire attitude change. This was a nice ending to a hectic day. "So, what did you do today?"

"Oh, nothing much. I started a fire, killed several people, and then made passionate love to a beautiful woman. You know. Same ol' same ol'."

She looked around the lobby to see if anyone had heard the exchange and then laughed. "You know, if anyone were listening, they'd have the cops waiting for you outside."

"Speaking of," he said, "did you have a chance to talk to your student, the detective?"

"As a matter of fact, I did. He wanted the name of your contact in Frisco, so he could get a copy of the investigation reports."

"I'm not sure you could call it an investigation. I don't think the locals gave it a lot of effort, but I guess they did what they could. If you give me his name and number, I'll call him in the morning."

"Actually, he said he had a little time tonight and for me to call him after I talked to you."

"For you to call?" Bryce said, his voice became stilted.

"Mr. Cameron. Are you jealous?"

"You bet I am. But remember, I've killed today." He took her hand as they stepped off the elevator leading to the parking garage. He squeezed tightly and said, "I'm not taking any chances with you this time."

Hannah looked at the line of cars heading for the exit sign. They were surrounded by people leaving the building, so she felt reasonably safe. She squeezed his hand in return and said, "She probably won't try anything now with so many people around."

Bryce sighed and said, "Hey, Doc, you're the professional here. I haven't got the slightest idea what this looney woman would dare. She's not playing with a full deck, you know."

Hannah looked up at him as they moved toward the car and realized she could probably listen to this man talk in his slow Southern accent all day long.

He caught her looking at him and said, "What? What'd I do?" His green eyes sparkled with mischief.

"Nothing. I enjoy listening to you, that's all."

"Huh?"

"Never mind. It would probably go to your head."

———

They met Detective Jesse Silva at Denny's Restaurant in Englewood a little after six. He was a nice-looking man. Hannah thought he appeared to be in his early to mid-thirties with dark hair and light blue eyes. She'd never considered him as potential date material. She had met many hunky guys in her undergrad and grad classes, but she only admired them.

She wasn't interested in complicating her life by having an affair with a student, but evidently Bryce's thoughts leaned that way since he was frowning and practically foaming at the mouth when she introduced the two men. To his credit, he was polite and shook the other man's hand, and she was pleased that neither man tried to out-macho the other with the childish game of who had the firmest handshake.

Jesse appeared surprised to see Bryce with Hannah, so she nipped any of his romantic thoughts in the bud and took

Bryce's hand affectionately. If Jesse was upset, he didn't show it.

"Good to see you, Dr. Brody. I'm on duty, so I haven't got a lot of time, but I will be happy to help if I can. Did you bring the contact information from Frisco?"

Bryce handed him a slip of paper, and Jesse looked at it and then folded it and put it in his shirt pocket. "Stalkers are the worst, but we can't do anything to stop this woman until she does something that is against the law." He held up his hands and said, "I know, I know. She vandalized your car and more than likely tried to run you both down. But since neither one of you saw her, it would be your word against hers."

"Mr. Cameron…"

"Please call me Bryce."

"Bryce, you probably have grounds to get a restraining order. That won't keep her away if she's truly a crazy, but it will give you legal standing if she comes near you. Since there isn't any proof she has ever been in contact with you, Dr. Brody, I doubt if the judge would grant you one."

Jesse reached for the coffee he'd been drinking and took a sip. "I would suggest you get an excellent security system at your home if you don't already have one, and I would make sure you park your car where there is an attendant or valet."

Hannah frowned and thought, *Why do I have to change my whole life for this woman?* But she kept her mouth shut.

As if reading her mind, Jesse said, "I realize these things are a big imposition on your life, but right at this moment, that is all we can legally do. I will put out a BOLO on her and maybe we will get lucky and can take her in for questioning."

"BOLO?" Hannah said, unsure of the acronym's meaning.

"Be on the lookout," Bryce said. "I think I used that one today."

Hannah patted his hand and said to Jesse, "Bryce is a mystery writer. He's had a busy day with murder and mayhem."

"No kidding. If you ever need a good plot, I've got lots of stories. You wouldn't believe what I see every day."

"Thanks," Bryce said. "If I hit a writer's block, I'll give you a call."

Hannah wasn't sure if he was serious or being sarcastic, but when she saw the smile on his face, she realized he liked Jesse. Hmm, male bonding over a stalker. Who knew? Men were a whole different species.

Jesse got a call and had to leave, but Hannah and Bryce decided to eat at Denny's. It usually had a pretty good menu for a chain restaurant. They got back to the condo about seven-thirty, and he insisted he wanted to check things out to make sure there wouldn't be any surprises.

Hannah didn't try to hide her relief and said so. "Thanks. I've been jumpy since last night. I do have a pretty good alarm system, but you never know."

"Do you have a security camera?"

"No, I didn't think I would need one since this is a condo and there usually are people around. I guess I need to call and get one. Geez, I can't believe this." She saw Bryce's face and immediately bit her lip. "Bryce, I…"

"Hannah, I'm so sorry. This is all my fault. I brought all of this on you. I've completely upended your life."

Hannah grabbed his hands in hers and went up on her tiptoes to kiss him. "Yes, you have certainly done that, but I don't regret meeting you and having you in my life. And before you go all selfless on me and say we shouldn't see each other anymore, it's my decision. Unless you can tell me you're not interested in seeing where this thing between us is going, then I'm not going anywhere."

Bryce leaned into her and kissed her back. It wasn't simple but passionate, and she could feel his tongue mating with hers. He pulled her closer and her breasts pressed into the leather jacket that he hadn't had a chance to remove. Her body tingled with anticipation and yearning. It had been a long time since she'd felt this way about a man.

She deepened the kiss to let him know what she wanted and practically purred when one of his hands skimmed down her back and rested on her hip while the other one began to unbutton her blouse slowly and seductively. She moaned and pulled his face down, bringing his lips to her breasts as the silky material slipped off her shoulders.

Maybe it was too soon. Maybe she should put the brakes on before they went too far, but she wanted this. Needed this. The doorbell chimed, bringing her back to reality, and she broke off the embrace. Bryce tried to pull her closer, and she almost gave in, but before she could settle into his arms, the bell echoed through the living room again.

She had her hand on the knob and paused when she heard him say, "Don't. Don't open the door without looking. You don't know who it might be."

Feeling foolish, she pulled back the curtains on the long front window close to the door but saw no one. "There's no one there," she whispered and then wondered why she was trying to be quiet.

Bryce came up behind her, and she could feel his breath warm on her face as she leaned back into him. "Look," he said. "There's a package. It was probably a UPS delivery. Are you expecting something?"

Hannah thought for a moment and then laughed. Her heartbeat was returning to normal, along with her common sense. "I did order some makeup from Macy's. I haven't had time to go to the store, and it's so much easier to buy stuff online if the shipping's free."

She reached down for the package and drew her hand back when Bryce yelled, "Wait!"

She stopped, stood up, and turned back to look at him just as the world exploded and blasted her back through the doorway.

CHAPTER 15
HANNAH BRODY

HANNAH WINCED **as the ER nurse placed gauze on the wounds** on her lower legs and thighs. Her head throbbed, and her body ached all over. All things considered, she'd been lucky, or at least that's what the doctor said.

"You're very lucky, Ms. Brody," she remembered him saying. "The burns are mostly superficial except for these on your upper thigh. You have also sustained some pretty nasty cuts from the flying debris that will need a few stitches. We need to keep a close watch on you the rest of the evening. The CT scan showed nothing, but since the EMTs said you were knocked out for several minutes, you may have a concussion."

The doctor quickly moved on to other patients after telling her she would be spending the night and left her with Nurse Ratched. She guessed that wasn't quite fair. The woman had said she was sorry every time Hannah moaned in pain, causing her to clench her teeth together to keep from crying. She was feeling cranky and worried about Bryce. She hadn't seen him since the explosion, and when she asked about him, all the nurse would say was that he was being treated for his injuries.

A short while later, she looked up and was relieved to see Bryce's handsome face. It was marred now by splotches of red that reminded her of a bad sunburn. She knew they would turn dark purple in a couple of days. He also had a couple of lacerations, but she didn't see any stitches. She started to speak, but he quickly shushed her by putting his finger across his lips and pointing to the nurse's back.

Hannah smiled widely and at the moment didn't care. She spoke loudly so he could hear. "Nurse, my boy…"

"Brother, her brother is here," Bryce interrupted. "The lady at the desk said since I'm immediate family, I could check on my sister."

The nurse looked up, grunted, and continued with the bandages. "Come in. I'm almost done here."

"Bryce, are you all right? Your poor face."

"I'm fine. And thank the Lord you're okay, too."

"If you hadn't stopped me from touching that package, I could have lost my hand or worse yet been hit right in the face. You probably saved my life."

"The police don't believe it was meant to kill anyone. It was a box of high-powered fireworks that was set off by remote control. She waited until you came out to set it off."

"She?"

"We know who did this. It couldn't be anyone else. I called Jesse. He and a couple of other cops are outside waiting to talk with you as soon as you're done here."

"The doctor says I have to spend the night. That I might have a concussion." She was frightened and didn't like the feeling. "I can't stay here. I have to go to work. I don't have patients today, but I've got class. Get me out of this place," she pleaded.

Bryce tenderly touched her face and said, "I'll talk to the doctor. See what I can do. I'm sure he will release you if I tell him you won't be alone tonight. I'll be with you all the way.

You won't be alone until they catch her. She's gone too far this time. Now, the police must do something."

As if summoned, Jesse walked into the narrow treatment room with a uniformed officer by his side.

"What is this, show and tell?" the nurse said.

"Sorry for the intrusion, but we need to talk to Dr. Brody while everything is still fresh in her mind."

"Come on in. I'm done here." She coughed, frowned, and made air quotes with her fingers. "She and her 'brother' are all yours." Then she smiled and left the room.

"Brother?" asked Jesse.

"That's the only way they would let me in. Had to be next of kin. Why'd they let you in?"

Jesse grinned and took out a pocket-sized notebook. "Did you see who left the package on the doorstep?"

"No, it was dark, and I was in a hurry. If Bryce hadn't stopped me I would have picked it up."

"We have good news. You should be able to go back home anytime now. The techs are done, and the feds are satisfied it wasn't terrorism. Looks like they took a couple of prints from what was left of the device. We'll compare them to the prints taken in Oklahoma when Lucy was arrested there."

Hannah sighed. She pulled the hospital gown tightly closed and moved to the side of the bed. "Will that help you catch her?"

"The fingerprints themselves, no, but knowing who set off the device will move apprehending her to a top priority for the department. The next time she could decide to do something in a crowded place."

"The next time?" Hannah said. She was getting angry and refused to be a victim. "I want to go home now." She looked at Jesse and said, "You'll contact me as soon as you know anything?"

"Yes, I will. What are your plans?"

"I plan to cancel my classes for today. What time is it anyway?"

"Close to six thirty in the morning," Bryce said.

"I'm going to go home and go to sleep. Hopefully, when I wake up, you'll call me and tell me you have her in custody, and you are going to lock her up and throw away the key." She smiled and thought, if I let this get to me it would take over my life.

"Ah, if it were only that simple," Jesse said. "This is Officer Kage. He'll take you home and will be outside your condo today. Hopefully, that will give you some peace of mind and you can get some rest. We don't have the resources to give you protection beyond today."

"I'll be there," said Bryce. "I know what Lucy looks like. She won't get anywhere near Hannah again."

"I'll request a picture from Oklahoma. I'll try to get it to you within the next couple of days. I've already checked with the Colorado DMV, and it looks like she never got a license in this state."

"Thank you, Jesse. Will I see you in class next week?"

"Does this mean I'll get an A?"

It hurt to laugh, but Hannah did anyway. "It's a sure thing."

When they were alone, Bryce said, "That guy likes you."

She took Bryce's hand and said, "And I like him too, but not in the same way I like you. It's kind of cute that you're jealous. It does wonders for my self-esteem, which is a little deflated at the moment."

———

Exhausted, Hannah slept until five o'clock that evening. It was already getting dark when she peered through the blinds of her bedroom window and shivered. The wind howled, and the bushes scratched on the bricks outside. She heard a noise coming from the living room. She put on her old terrycloth robe and made her way gingerly down the hall. Bryce looked up when she walked in.

"Hey," he said. How are you feeling?"

"Like I was the donkey at a child's birthday party. She glimpsed herself in the mirror over the couch and groaned. "Oh, good Lord. My hair. I look like a cave lady."

Bryce laughed and kissed her softly on the lips. You look beautiful, as usual. Look at me. I think I fell asleep on the beach and a lobster took up residence on my face.

Hannah laughed and sat down limply in the easy chair. "I guess I kinda underestimated my recovery time. I was sure I'd be able to bounce right back. I know I need rest, but I don't want to take time off. That would mean she's winning."

She followed Bryce into the kitchen and ate a small bowl of chicken soup he'd brought home from Panera. She didn't realize she was hungry until she took her first sip. It tasted delicious and warmed her up from the inside out.

"Any word from Jesse?"

"No, and I don't know if that's good or bad. The police car left about an hour ago, but everything is locked up nice and tight for the night. I parked my car in your garage, so we are set."

"You don't have to stay."

"Yeah, I kinda do. Remember, I said I'm not leaving until she's caught. You have a comfortable couch. I took a nice long nap on it this afternoon."

"So, what did you do all day?"

"Since the patrol car was outside, I went back to my hotel, got my stuff, and checked out. I don't have much, and I hope you don't mind, but I put everything over in the corner. The rest of the day, I worked on the book."

She'd never lived with a man before. The thought should have scared her, but it didn't. She didn't exactly know what she felt, but it wasn't fear. Was this the first step toward a commitment? She'd never done that before either. Granted, these were extraordinary circumstances. She looked up and saw the question in Bryce's eyes.

"Are you okay? I'm not trying to pressure you into anything you're not ready for, but I don't want you out of my sight while Looney Lucy is on the loose. This is only temporary."

Did she want that? They'd only known each other for a few days, even though they'd met months before. How long did it take to fall for someone? There weren't any manuals or guidebooks to tell you. But Hannah knew. She'd known from the first time she'd looked into his beautiful green eyes. He was the one.

"Looney Lucy. That would be funny if it weren't so pitiful. I'm finding it hard to remain professional where she is concerned." She finished her soup, gave Bryce a peck on the check and shuffled back to bed.

———

It was a good forty-eight hours before she felt human again. That afternoon, Hannah found Bryce in the kitchen and watched him as he placed pasta in boiling water and added a pinch of salt. He was wearing a threadbare gray T-shirt with Cameron stenciled across the back and a pair of gym shorts. She'd never seen him looking so relaxed. "I didn't know you could cook," she said.

Startled, he turned around and then smiled. "How are you feeling?"

"So much better," she said. "I think I have officially slept my life away, but it was worth it. I think I'm going to live now. What about you?"

"I'm fine. I thought I'd fix us some dinner and was going to wake you in about thirty minutes."

"Can I help?"

"Nope. This is my treat. Sit right there at the table and relax. "I learned to cook out of necessity, but I'm afraid I'm limited to what I can make. Spaghetti and bacon and eggs are about the extent of it. Thankfully, you had both on hand."

Instead of sitting down, Hannah went to Bryce and tentatively kissed him. Bryce pulled back and took both of her hands. "What is this all about?"

"As a psychologist, I guess I could say it is the subconscious need to reaffirm that I'm alive. After all, someone tried to kill me twice this week. But, as a woman, I know that is an excuse. We started something the other night that we didn't get to finish."

"Hannah, you're hurt and vulnerable. I would be taking advantage of you."

She moved closer until their bodies were touching and kissed him again, this time with passion. "Yes, please do." She reached around him and turned off the burner. "I've got a soft comfortable bed right down the hall. I'd love to show it to you."

His eyes were dark with desire as she pulled him down onto the cool sheets. The room was dark with only a soft glow from the outside street lamp.

Hannah's hands moved down his back and pulled at the old shirt, and with his help, she took it off. Bryce's fingers moved up her body until he found her naked breasts and he moaned, "You're killing me."

"I wasn't planning to seduce you when I woke up, but I saw you standing in my kitchen, and you looked so... I don't know... so normal. Like all the bad stuff hadn't happened, and then you said you moved your stuff over here, and I just knew."

"Knew what?"

"Ah, Bryce, I think I'm falling in love with you."

"I think I'm falling crazy in love with you, too."

"I want you to make love to me. I really, really do." She

moved closer and felt him pressing into her and then reached down to stroke him. Bryce's lips found hers in a deep, crushing kiss and she moaned when his fingers played with the lacy trim of her panties. His fingers found her, and she moved wildly and arched her back.

"Bryce please, I can't wait. I want you inside me now."

"I'm not prepared. I wasn't expecting to… geez, I don't have a condom."

"I'm on the pill, and you've been living in the wilderness with the bears."

They discarded the last of their clothing, and his hands pulled her body under him. He stroked her back and kissed her breasts. Desire and need engulfed her as they came together with a fierce passion.—a renewal of life. There would be time for gentle lovemaking later. She planned to make this an endless night.

————

Hannah rolled over and watched Bryce sleep as the first rays of the morning sun spread across the bed. He was a beautiful man. All long and sinewy. His hair was curled slightly around his ears. The reddish hue contrasted with the stark white of the pillow. He had a thin scar on his upper thigh and a longer one close to his knee. She reached out to touch him, and he opened his eyes.

"Good morning, beautiful."

"I could get used to that. I'm not beautiful, but I love to hear you say it."

He reached up and pulled her down for a kiss. "I need a shower and some breakfast. We didn't make it back for the spaghetti."

"But," she laughed. "We have bacon and eggs."

She watched him walk naked across the room into the bathroom. Yes, she could definitely get used to this.

———

"Morning, Pam," Hannah said as she walked across the lobby toward her door.

"Dr. Brody. Are you all right? I was so worried."

"I'm fine. Only a few cuts and scrapes. Some superficial burns, but nothing serious."

"What happened? The doctors said you were in an accident and would be out for a few days. I'm so glad you're back."

"It was someone playing a prank with firecrackers, and I got in the way. But I'm fine. Do I have a busy day?"

"I rescheduled the appointments you missed for next week, and you have your usual clients today. Later this morning, You'll see that new woman, Janet Jones."

Hannah wanted to moan, but she put her professional face on for Pam. She didn't want to mess with that drama today, but the woman had real issues and needed help.

Ms. Jones arrived in a mood. She paced the room and refused to sit. After about five minutes, Hannah gently persuaded her to stop pacing, and she finally relented and took a seat.

"You seem truly upset today. Did something happen?"

Janet looked like someone had run over her puppy and began to cry. "I'm at my wits' end. I don't know what to do. He's supposed to love me, not her." She pounded her ample breasts and sniffed. "I've done everything for him. What has she done?"

Hannah took a calming breath and tried to separate fact from fiction. "Janet, do you know for a fact that your husband is cheating on you?"

"Yes, I do. He was at her house, and they were kissing. I'm sure they were doing it too."

"Did you talk to your husband? Ask for an explanation?"

"Well no. I can't go near him."

"Does it upset you when you get close to him?"

Janet looked at her like she was the stupidest person in the universe. "No, it doesn't upset me. I love being with him. He doesn't want me near him."

"It seems like a lot has happened in the past few days. When you were here earlier, you suspected he was seeing someone else. Now you're certain. Are things worse at your job?"

"You know they are. I got fired, you know that." Janet jumped to her feet and paced around the room again. She was wearing a large floor-length coat and kept pulling her hand in and out of the pocket. "You think I don't know, don't you? Well, I do. I know everything."

Hannah was becoming alarmed and thought she needed to put an end to the session. Janet Jones was reaching a breakdown and might need hospitalization. "Janet, why don't you have a seat? I'll get you a glass of water and we can discuss some options that you have."

"Why are you still here anyway, Dr. Brody," Janet said in a sing-song voice. "You're supposed to go away. Leave him alone."

Was Janet transferring the anger she had for her husband's lover to her? This was unusual, and Hannah was afraid things were getting out of hand. She knew she needed to end the session. "Janet, we've talked enough today. I can see you are upset. Perhaps you'd feel better if I called someone else to help you."

Hannah's phone chimed with a text. She glanced down and saw it was from Jesse. It was a headshot of Looney Lucy. She realized she didn't know her last name, but it didn't matter since right now the woman in the picture was standing across the room from her and holding a gun.

Hannah took a deep, calming breath and said, "Lucy, I'm sure you don't want to hurt anyone. Please put the gun down. Bryce will be extremely angry if you hurt me."

"You don't get to say his name. He belongs to me, not you. We were fine until you messed with him. He loves me."

"I'm sure you are correct. I'm sure he loves you, and I don't mean anything to him. So, there isn't any reason to hurt me or anyone else."

"I want him back." Lucy cried, and the gun shook with every sob.

"Let me call him and have him come and talk with you. I'm sure you'll be able to work things out and see that everything is simply a big misunderstanding."

Hannah reached down for her phone and touched Bryce's name just as she heard Lucy yell. "No. You're trying to trick me. If you're gone, then he will love me again."

Hannah realized she was getting nowhere and this woman was going to shoot her. She didn't have a weapon. She'd never learned how to shoot, and her letter opener was in her desk drawer. Her eye was drawn to the softball sitting in the open case. She had been a pretty accurate pitcher back in college.

"Lucy," Hannah said softly. "Do you like softball?"

"What? Softball? What are you talking about? Stand still and let me think."

Hannah reached in and pulled out the ball. "I played softball in college, and I was pretty good. Want to see?"

Before Lucy could react, Hannah threw the ball with a force and skill she'd used in school when her pitches had sometimes reached 75 miles an hour. It was a square hit right between Lucy's eyes.

The other woman hit the floor without a murmur.

CHAPTER 16
BRYCE CAMERON

BRYCE ANSWERED HIS PHONE. He was pleased to see Hannah's number. He'd been thinking about her all morning but was trying not to crowd her and give her time to soak in everything that had happened last night. It was easy for him to drop everything and call, but Hannah had an important job helping people with their mental issues, and he needed to take her schedule into consideration. He was trying so hard not to be a selfish jerk. He was extremely proud of everything she had accomplished and wanted her to know that her career was important to him, too.

He was expecting to hear her sexy hello but was surprised when he only heard noise in the background. Had she accidentally called him? He listened closely and held on to the phone with a death grip when he recognized the high-pitched, erratic voice he hoped to never hear again. Lucy. Somehow, that crazy woman was with Doc, and it sounded like she was completely losing it.

He didn't want to break the contact with Hannah. It was her only lifeline, and she must have called him, knowing he would hear the conversation and realize that she was in trouble. Fortunately, Hannah's condo had a landline. He called

911 and reported what he knew, and then called the number he had for Jesse Silva.

By the time he reached his car, there was nothing but silence coming from the phone, and then thankfully he heard Hannah say, "Bryce, I'm all right. I need to hang up and call the police. I'm fine."

"I already called them. They're on the way and I'm right behind them. What happened?"

"I guess you could say I threw the best pitch of my life."

———

By the time the EMTs arrived, a groggy, incoherent Lucy moaned and looked with confusion around the disheveled office. When she saw Bryce, she attempted a smile, and he knew he should feel sorry for the woman, but somehow he couldn't muster any sympathy. She had pointed a gun at Hannah, and for all anyone knew, if Hannah hadn't brained Lucy with a softball, Lucy would have shot her and severely wounded or killed her.

Jesse had arrived shortly after Bryce. After taking a brief statement, he asked Hannah to come to the precinct in the afternoon for an in-depth interview. He suggested that in the meantime, she should go home and take a couple of days off.

"Not gonna happen. Lucy has interfered with my life enough. I have patients to see who shouldn't be inconvenienced."

"What now?" Bryce asked.

"She won't be getting out of jail anytime soon. The techs found her prints on what was left of the explosives at your house. With that charge, and the threat to Dr. Brody's life today, I doubt if the judge will give her bail. More than likely, he will request a mental competency evaluation."

Bryce laughed and looked at Hannah. "I guess you could attest to how sane she is."

"I'm glad I'm not the one that has to do it. I guess the reason I couldn't come up with a diagnosis was because she actually was mentally ill while she was pretending to be mentally ill. The whole idea makes my head hurt. I'm glad she regained consciousness, and I didn't kill her."

"For your sake, I'm glad she will be okay," Bryce said.

"I'll see you later this afternoon, Dr. Brody, and we will need a formal statement from you too, Bryce, about the phone call you received."

He'd rather be in bed with a naked Hannah than at a police station. All he wanted to do right now was hold on to her and never let her go. She could have died today, and it would have been all his fault.

He looked at Hannah and saw her studying him with her therapist's eyes. "What?" he said.

"You're blaming yourself, aren't you?" she said.

"What are you, psychic or something?"

"Doesn't take a psychic to know how your mind works." Hannah inched close to Bryce, and he felt her head rest against his shoulder as she whispered, "It's not your fault."

He kissed the top of her head and could smell the subtle floral scent of her shampoo. When she began to tremble, he knew she would not want her colleagues to see her lose control. He kicked the office door shut and held her while she cried.

———

Hannah seemed determined not to let the incident with Lucy affect her, which was another reason Bryce was crazy about her. She didn't miss a beat and continued meeting with her clients and teaching. At first, Bryce was afraid that it might impact their relationship, and it had, but in a positive way. The last few weeks had been perfect.

Now was as good a time as any to see exactly where they

were headed, he thought. She'd just walked in the door from a busy day at the university when Bryce came out of the kitchen with two glasses and a bottle of wine.

Hannah smiled and said, "So, what's the occasion?"

"I believe a celebration is in order. The book is done and is in the hands of my editor. She seems to think it won't take a lot of rewrites, so it looks like it will be out in about six months."

"Oh, that's fantastic. I'm so thrilled for you, but I had hoped to read it before it was published." He heard the disappointment in her voice.

"And I want you to read it. That's why," he said as he placed the bottle and glasses on the coffee table and picked up his printed manuscript from the couch, "I have this very special unedited draft for you."

She grinned like a child, took the book greedily, sat down and read the title. "*Burnt Toast?*" she asked. "Your book is called *Burnt Toast?*"

"Yeah, it kinda describes the state of mind my main character is in at the beginning. Read it. See if you agree. Besides, the publishers will probably change it anyway."

Bryce watched her closely as she flipped over the first page to what he knew was the dedication.

To Doc, who makes me believe in happy endings.

He knew when she had read it because she turned her face up to his with unshed tears glistening in her eyes. "Bryce, I don't know what to say, Thank you. That's ... I..."

Bryce sat down beside her and pulled her close. "I love you Doc Brody. You are the best thing that has ever happened to me."

"I'm pretty sure you're the best thing that's ever happened to me, too." She laughed and threw her arms around his neck hugging him tightly.

———

Bryce was pretty much walking on air. His book was completed. He had already drafted the outline for the next one, and he was living with Doc. Nothing was ever formally stated, but he had smoothly moved right into her life as well as her home.

He'd returned the rental car because he didn't need one since he spent most of his day writing and anything he needed was within walking distance. When he moved to New York, he'd left his car with his brother. Then, because he knew Quinn didn't have the money to buy a car of his own when he first got back from Europe, Bryce left it there in Atlanta. Between the money he'd earned from his first novel and the salary he'd banked from his time in the Navy, he wasn't rich, but he was doing okay.

In their last conversation, Quinn said his cash flow was improving, and he could buy a second-hand truck. He said he felt bad about keeping Bryce's car. Bryce wanted to go pick it up, but he didn't want to leave Hannah even for a minute. He shook his head and thought, *man, you've got it bad*.

The object of his desire opened the door several minutes later with a big smile on her face. "Hey," she said.

"Hey yourself." Bryce walked toward the door and gave her a scorching kiss. "I won't ever tire of doing that," he said. "You look delicious."

"You fibber you, but don't stop. I like it."

"So, what are you so happy about?"

"You know the book I told you I was writing when we first met?" Hannah said.

"The one about psychological effects of the environment and genetics?"

Hannah plopped her large satchel on the table by the door and continued toward the kitchen. Then she stopped, and turned to him with an astonished look on her face. "You remembered?"

"I certainly did. I remember everything about that flight and you."

"Well, while I was writing my dissertation, I published an article on the subject in a psychological journal, and today I got a letter from a researcher who wants to discuss my ideas."

"Sit down," he said. "Tell me all about it. What does he want?"

She pulled the letter out of her satchel and handed it to him. "Here, read it and see what you think."

Bryce opened the expensive-looking embossed envelope and pulled out the letter. He scratched his chin as he read it and frowned at the illegible signature. "Who is this guy, anyway?"

"He's a psychiatrist who established a research center outside of Savannah about ten years ago. I don't know exactly what he does. I googled him after I read the letter to see if he was legit."

"And?"

"He is, but the institute seems to be shrouded in mystery. Few people are allowed inside. It sounds like there is some hush-hush government stuff going on, and if I go, they have to do a background check on me. Should I call him?"

"Now that sounds like the makings of an excellent plot for a book," he said as he wiggled his fingers and made spooky noises.

Hannah frowned at him. "Bryce," she said and stamped her foot, "be serious."

"Okay, okay. Sorry, but I couldn't help it. It sounds like a Vincent Price movie. The letter says he wants you to go there to meet with him. Is that something you are interested in doing?" He smiled at her, trying to give her the most encouraging vibes he could.

"I think I am."

"Then you should do it."

"Do you want me to go?"

Hell no, he thought. He didn't want her to go to some mysterious research center where they probably turned people into real-life zombies like characters in *The Walking Dead*. Maybe they were even inventing a virus there.

"Bryce! Are you listening to me?"

"Again sorry. My imagination is getting the better of me. I want you to go if you want to go. I'll even tag along if you want me to."

"But what about your work?"

"Come on, Doc. I can write anywhere. Besides, I was thinking earlier today that I needed to get back to Atlanta to pick up my Jeep and see my family. It's been a while, and I want them to meet you."

CHAPTER 17
HANNAH BRODY

UNITED AIRLINES FLIGHT **7124 touched down in Atlanta** at five-thirty-three. The flight had been a nightmare, and Hannah clutched Bryce's hand for dear life. About an hour before landing, the plane encountered a trough of rough air and the turbulence was so severe, that the fasten seat belt light never went off. Hannah was usually comfortable in a plane because she had flown many times with her Uncle Bill, but she had never experienced anything like this.

Before the flight attendants could collect the cups and cans, the plane fell rapidly, and cell phones, iPads, paperback books, and drinks flew upward amid fearful screams. A mother snatched her infant from mid-air, and a female flight attendant smashed headfirst into the ceiling and then back down, where she crumpled to the floor.

Bryce and Hannah watched in horror as the other attendants carefully helped the poor woman back to the rear galley. Her head was bleeding, and she was pale and unsteady.

Within moments, there was an announcement from the captain asking for anyone with medical training to make their way to the back of the plane.

Then the pilot's voice cautioned all passengers to stay seated with seat belts fastened. Hannah sat on her phone and secured her purse by putting her leg through the straps.

For the next hour, it felt more like they were riding on a bucking bronco than flying in a plane. Hannah's stomach would settle and then they would bounce again, and her stomach would lurch. Now she knew what the expression *white knuckled* meant. Her right hand gripped the arm of the seat, and her left hand held on to Bryce. She had both feet firmly planted on the floor and tried to remain relaxed so that each violent bump would not jar her neck.

Bryce, she would tell everyone later, was a rock. If he was frightened, he didn't show it. He held her hand and reassured her in a calm voice that she was safe if she had her seat belt fastened.

"No jet has ever flipped upside down because of turbulence in the history of aviation," he said. "It's uncomfortable, and it's nerve-racking, but we're okay. Hang on, sweetheart. We'll be landing soon."

When they finally landed, everyone was told to remain in their seats until an emergency medical team could come in and examine the flight attendant. After about fifteen minutes, they had her on a backboard with a neck stabilizer in place and carried her off the plane.

Everyone quickly deplaned and made their way down the jetway. Most of the passengers were subdued. Some were still trembling. As they made their way to the luggage area, Hannah began to relax. She could see that Bryce was scanning the crowd. They had agreed to meet his brother there, and she could tell that he was excited.

Bryce reached for the blue and white suitcase that had a yellow belt tied around it and was pulling it off the luggage carousel when a large hand slapped him on the back.

Hannah saw him turn to see his younger brother's big grin. Quinn showed his entire rack of perfectly straight white teeth when he smiled. Hannah thought it was a smile that few could resist returning.

"There you are. I knew you wouldn't make us walk to the house," Bryce said and pulled his brother into a big hug. He didn't notice the second suitcase as it moved past them on the conveyor belt. Hannah thought a reunion with his brother was more important than pointing out that the bag was moving away from them at a rapid pace.

Bryce stepped back, the luggage forgotten, and introduced Quinn to Hannah. "Hannah, this is my little brother, and Quinn, this is the woman of my dreams."

A couple standing near them snickered at his sentiment, but she loved it and loved that he wasn't afraid to show his feelings in public. Before she could extend her hand towards Quinn, he took two steps in her direction. "May I?" he said to them both, and without waiting for an answer, he took Hannah into his arms and gave her a gentle hug.

"Anyone my brother loves is somebody special in my book. It's great to meet you, Hannah. I've never heard my brother say anything like that before, so it must be true."

———

After a fifty-minute drive from the airport to Ansley Park, Quinn pulled up into a half-moon driveway in front of an imposing white structure.

"Home sweet home," Quinn said.

Bryce laughed, and Hannah was sure it was a private joke between the brothers.

"Are you armed for battle, big brother?" Quinn said.

"Locked and loaded. Let's do this," Bryce said.

"Wait a minute," Hannah said. Her voice was light with amusement. "What can I expect inside that door?" She pointed toward the front of the house.

"You'll be fine, honey," Bryce said. "They'll love you. It's the two of us that need to worry."

When the door opened, a woman with mounds of red curls piled on top of her head glided toward them. "You're here," she said. Her blue eyes sparkled with pleasure. She reached for Hannah's hand and pulled her inside. "Come here and let me have a good look at you in the light."

Hannah felt like a bug pinned in an insect box as the older woman inspected her from head to toe.

"My, my, you're a beauty, aren't you?"

"She certainly is."

The booming male voice caught Hannah by surprise. Then she saw the tall man descending the steps. His posture was so erect that he appeared to have a string tied from his head to the ceiling as he marched in quick step toward them.

Bryce stepped forward to make the introduction. "Mother, Captain, may I present Miss Hannah Brody."

"Miss? Why would you insult her like that? I'll address her properly and call her Doctor Brody," The Captain said.

"Oh, no, please," Hannah insisted. "Call me Hannah."

"Hannah it is," said Justine. "Now come with me, dear, and later I'll show you where you can freshen up. Plane trips can leave a person looking so rumpled."

Hannah looked down at her wrinkled linen pants and felt dowdy. How skillful this woman was at making others feel bad. She had not even greeted her son whom she had not seen in months. In fact, neither of her sons had received so much as a glance except for issuing orders about the luggage.

"Take Hannah's things up to the blue room," Justine said without turning around as she guided Hannah into the expansive living room.

The furniture looked comfortable and expensive, Hannah thought. She also took noted of the grand piano near the heavily draped windows.

"Your piano is beautiful," Hannah said. "Who plays?"

Silence filled the room and stretched out into an embarrassingly long few moments. Finally, Justine coughed politely and said, "Well actually, dear, no one does. I bought the piano hoping that one of my boys would show some interest in music."

"But we were a great disappointment," said Quinn, who had come into the room after taking the luggage upstairs.

"Oh, Quinney Boy, you know that's not true. Your talents lie elsewhere, that's all."

"You could have fooled me," The Captain said. "The question is, Justine, why do we still have a piano that takes up half the room?"

A red blush crept up from Justine's creamy white neck to her face. "You know why. I keep it for entertainment at parties." She ran her hand over the smooth shiny surface of the black piano.

The Captain snorted but dropped the subject and turned his attention to Hannah. "What may I offer you to drink, my dear?"

"Nothing for me," Hannah said. "Do you want something, Bryce? Are you thirsty, Quinn? You had to wait a long time for us at the airport."

Neither man wanted anything, and she wasn't surprised. She wondered if their parents would have offered them anything at all if she had not done so. What was wrong with these people? How could they have produced a man as fine as Bryce? He was as kind and loving as anyone she had ever known. The contrast was glaring.

And what the heck was that Quinney Boy business all about? Quinn was a grown man and his mother talked baby talk to him most of the time. That was embarrassing and not at all healthy. This family would make an interesting case study in her next book.

CHAPTER 18
QUINN CAMERON

QUINN LIKED **his brother's girlfriend.** She was smart, beautiful, and kind. The two brothers and Hannah had left the house as soon as dinner ended and headed for a tavern a few miles away.

They had barely settled into the semi-circular booth before Hannah started talking a mile a minute. Although under most circumstances, Quinn would have found her questions intrusive, he knew she was asking because she cared about him.

"How do you dodge all the daggers your father throws at you, Quinn? How do you remain so calm?" Her eyebrows raised inquiringly.

"So, you picked up on that, did you?" he said in an amused tone.

All three of them laughed, but Quinn knew she was being serious. It was probably a professional question, as well as one of curiosity.

"I didn't follow the rules. I never have, so he'd rather I'd simply get lost." Quinn picked up his beer and took a sip, then wiped the foam from his lips with the back of his hand. "I stopped hearing him years ago. Everything comes across as blah-blah-blah. It's a blessing that comes with age."

She tilted her head and looked at him expectantly. "Because?"

"Because he's impotent. He can't hurt me now. He can't punish me or restrict me. I have my own life, my own money, and I don't need anything from him. In short, the emperor has no clothes."

She looked into his green eyes as her soothing voice probed further. "But it still hurts."

He paused a moment to consider how he felt. "Sometimes, but I brought it on myself. I didn't follow the rules. I still don't."

The waiter appeared, and they ordered another round. "This is my last one, boys," Hannah said. "I'm leaving early in the morning for Savannah."

"How far is it, anyway?" Quinn said.

"About three and a half hours if the traffic is light," Bryce said. It's a straight shot down Interstate 16. My Jeep is comfortable and easy to drive."

"It's all ready to go," Quinn said. I changed the oil and checked the belts and tires before you two got here."

"Thanks, brother. You're the best."

"You'll get no argument about that from me," Quinn said and turned his smile up a notch. Then he reached across the table to grab the ticket.

———

The next day, Bryce waited outside the house for Quinn to pick him up. They had decided to spend time together until Hannah returned.

"You have any plans?" Quinn asked. He didn't want to mess up his brother's trip. He had not seen Bryce in way too long.

"No plans. I'm open to anything."

"Great! I have us booked at the Foxy Lady Club at four o'clock today."

Bryce was momentarily speechless in his surprise. Finally, he said, "You what?"

"Seems to me you're getting serious. I thought you needed one last fling." Teasing laughter was in his eyes.

Bryce clasped his brother's knee and squeezed. "Damned if you didn't have me going there for a while."

"Or we could have a burger at Grindhouse later today. They're still the best burgers under ten dollars in the entire city."

"Hmmm," Bryce said. "Let me ponder this a bit. It's either burgers or broads."

"I know you, Bryce. It's no contest."

They grinned at each other and rode along in companionable silence for a while.

———

"I hope you're taking me to see your shop," Bryce said.

"I am. We're almost there. You'll be the first person in the family to visit." He bit down hard on his lower lip.

"Did you invite them?"

"Once. The Captain said he was too busy, and Justine wrinkled her nose. Sawdust bothers her sinuses." His voice held a contempt that forbade any further argument.

Bryce clenched his jaw, turned to look out the window and rigidly held his emotions in check.

———

"Here we are," Quinn said a short while later and pointed toward a large structure that had seen better days. Set into the wooden walls were old-fashioned, six-pane, weathered, wood-framed windows. The only thing modern about the structure was the front door. It was a steel garage door that Quinn opened remotely from the visor in his truck.

Bryce didn't know what to say, so he let Quinn take the lead. "The original doors were so beautiful, a week after I moved in, I sold them for fifteen-hundred dollars. If I wanted to, I could take the walls down one-by-one and sell all the wood. It would bring me a hefty sum. Problem is, I don't have the time or the money to build a whole new frame. It's what's going on inside that's going to make me money."

They got out of the truck and walked into the structure. The smell of sawdust and freshly cut lumber was pleasant and reminded Bryce of the pine forest he had recently left in Colorado.

He could see stacks of cut lumber of all shapes and sizes stacked against the wall. Another wall held a huge pegboard on which various tools hung neatly arranged by size. In the center of the room was a long worktable, a saw, a sewing machine, and an old metal desk. The chair next to the desk was something to behold. The arms and back were carved in intricate patterns, and the cushions were thick and colorful.

"Where did you get that chair?" Bryce asked.

"Seriously?" Quinn said.

"You made that?" An arched eyebrow showed his humorous surprise. His voice squeaked a bit. "The cushions, too?"

"Yep. Top to bottom. It's a QC original."

"When did you learn to use a sewing machine?"

"When I was in Europe. That's what I was doing, Bryce. I learned a little about a whole lot of stuff. Furniture makers usually know something about upholstering too. If not, they farm that part out, and it often costs too much. They have to do it themselves if they want to make a profit."

Bryce ran his hand over the smooth wood on the back of the chair, turned it around to face him, and sat down. "It's comfortable, too."

"Yep. Memory foam. I have it cut to size."

"How are your sales going?"

Quinn laughed. "Well, they were great for a while. Lorraine was helping me advertise on social media, and she has lots of friends with deep pockets."

"And now?"

"Well, since our romance has slowed down, she's kinda slacked off a bit. I don't blame her. After all, it wasn't a paid position. She was simply doing me a favor."

"Slowed down? Not to be nosy, but are you still sleeping with her?"

"Occasionally, but not every night like we were in the beginning."

"Are the two of you okay, or are there hard feelings?"

"None on my end. She's a terrific woman. The problem is we don't travel in the same circles, and our age difference was beginning to show."

"How so?"

"Well, she wanted fine dining, and I wanted a bowl of chili with Fritos. She wanted a bottle of expensive wine, and I wanted to split a six-pack of beer. I listened to Keith Urban, and she liked Miles Davis."

"I get it."

"Yeah. We could never agree on which channel to watch on TV."

"Now that's a deal breaker," Bryce said.

"Damn straight," Quinn agreed.

———

Quinn showed his brother around the shop and then they got back into the truck, and he pushed the remote to close the garage door.

"It's a great workshop, Quinn. Where do you live?"

Quinn backed out of the driveway and pointed at a rather

shabby house on the left side of the car. "Right there, but there's nothing much to see inside. It only has one bedroom, but all I need is a coffee pot, a bathroom, and a comfortable bed. I don't spend much time there at all."

"Because you're out in the shop?"

"Yes, and I'm still working for Lorraine, and I'm going to furniture design classes two nights a week."

"I always knew you were lazy just like The Captain said you were."

Quinn laughed and flashed a look filled with pride at his brother.

"So, you want to meet Lorraine?" Quinn said.

"Sure, if you want me to."

"You're more her type than I am, so be sure and tell her up front about Hannah or she'll put the moves on you, and we'll all be embarrassed."

Bryce thought he was joking but soon found out it was true. Lorraine took one look at Bryce and started batting her eyelashes so hard it looked like she might take flight. He liked her, though, and he appreciated everything she had done to help his little brother. It appeared she would be a good friend to him even though their romance had cooled.

When they left, she promised to read Bryce's books and said to let her know when the four of them could go out to dinner. She said she would love to meet Hannah.

"So, any progress in locating Dixie?" Bryce said when they got back into the truck.

Quinn pulled the seat belt across his chest, snapped it into place, and nodded toward Bryce to do the same. Then he turned the key in the ignition and waited while the carburetor coughed and finally fed fuel to the motor. He turned his head to the right, looked over his shoulder, and backed out of the driveway. "Not much."

"What do you know?"

"I know she left a week before my graduation. When I went to the RV park where she lived, her trailer was empty."

"Did you ask any questions?"

"Who would I ask? I was a high school kid. Nobody was going to talk to me."

"Well, you're a man now, and if we go together and look official, maybe somebody will have something to say."

Quinn scratched his chin as if he had an imaginary beard. "Seriously?"

"Worth a try."

"Yeah, but people in trailer parks are usually transient."

"Or they're still there because they can't afford to live anywhere else."

Quinn made a U-turn as soon as he could and headed toward Cabbagetown.

They reached the trailer park around midday, and people were up and about. One man was mowing the sketchy lawn in front of his double-wide, a woman was sweeping her porch, and a lanky greyhound stood on the steps. Its eyes were a light yellow and his legs were long and powerful.

The trailer that Dixie had occupied was gone and in its place was a nineteen-foot Airstream that had seen better days.

Quinn and Bryce got out of the car, and out of habit, Quinn pushed the lock twice until the horn honked. Bryce shot him a look that could have said, "Way to go, Bro. Make them all hate us from the get-go."

The man stopped his lawn mower and turned to look in their direction. The dog moved closer to the woman, and she rested her hand on the tall animal's head.

"Let's try our luck with the woman first," Bryce said.

Quinn nodded, and they moved forward toward the steps to the porch.

"Good morning," Bryce said. "We are looking for someone who lived here a few years ago. Wondering if you could help us?"

"Nope. I've only been here for three months." She tossed her head to the right. "Ask Mort. He's been here a while. He can't move that big house of his very often. Me, I'm portable." She laughed.

Quinn thought she would have been attractive if she had combed her hair and fixed her teeth. "Thank you, ma'am," Quinn said.

They walked a few yards down the paved drive until they stood outside the four-foot-fence that surrounded the double-wide. The lawn mower was now silent and the man she called Mort watched them with suspicion.

"What do you boys want?" he said. "You selling some-thing? If you are, I'm not buying."

"No, sir," Bryce said. "We are looking for information about a young woman who lived here a few years back."

"Are you the law?" he said. His voice was louder now. "I want nothing to do with the law."

"No, sir," Bryce insisted. "We aren't. We are looking for an old friend that we lost touch with a long time ago."

He glared at them for a long time before he said, "Who is this girl?"

Quinn took the lead. "Her name is Dixie Lee King. She's hard to miss. She has curly black hair, and she lived in an eighteen-foot trailer right there where that Airstream sits now."

Mort glanced in the direction that Quinn pointed. "That trailer's been there as long as I've been here," he said, "and I never saw anybody that looked like that."

Quinn felt the disappointment slam into him, and he found it hard to breathe. He took a few steps back and was turning toward the truck when the older man said. "Have you talked to Mable? She's managed the place for decades. If anybody knows, she will."

The brothers jumped back into the truck and rode to the end of the driveway where a single-wide mobile home sat. It was skirted and had a porch all the way around it. The path leading up to the house was bedecked with flowers on both sides, and the whole place looked inviting and neat.

Quinn tapped on the door, but no one answered. Then Bryce knocked so loudly the screen door rattled. "She may have a hearing issue."

"Well, if she didn't before, she does now," Quinn said as he grinned at Bryce. He had forgotten how much he loved the assertive, outgoing nature of his big brother.

"What in the world?" a woman said. She had a low voice, scratchy but clear. She put her hand on the door latch but did not open it. "May I help you boys?"

"I hope so," Quinn said. "Are you the manager?"

"I am. And I don't recognize either of you, so state your business fast before I take *Baby* out of my pocket. My hand's not as steady as it once was, but it's steady enough."

"I used to date a beautiful girl that lived in this park. Her name is Dixie Lee King. I lost track of her a week or so before I graduated from high school, but I've never been able to forget her. If you can help me get in touch, I'd be forever grateful. All I want is a phone number or to have her call me. Here's my number." Quinn held out his card.

"Or she could call me," Bryce said. "I am Quinn's older brother, and I can vouch for him. He's a good guy, and he only wants to say hello. Here's my card too."

Both men stood with their arms outstretched, but she did not open the door. "We don't mean her any harm, Bryce said. We would simply like to know that she's okay."

There was no movement from inside.

"Well, thank you, ma'am. We will leave our cards here on the porch for you in case you can help us."

They had reached the end of the path when Quinn heard her say, "What in the hell took you so long?"

He started to turn around, but Bryce stopped him. "Keep walking, brother. She's not having a good day."

———

They got back in the truck and Quinn said. "She knows something."

"Yes, I'm sure she does. But she won't tell us anything today. Maybe we frightened her. You'll have to try again, and you should come alone next time. We probably look like two undertakers trying to sell her a plot. Let's go get that burger. I'm starving."

Over burgers, fries, and chocolate milkshakes, the two brothers caught each other up on the news in their lives. They had always been on different journeys, traveling on different paths, yet they had never lost each other. Now, as adults free of their parents' manipulation, Bryce was sure they never would.

CHAPTER 19
HANNAH BRODY

HANNAH LEFT EARLY **that morning for her appointment** with Dr. Dreschler outside of Savannah. Bryce offered to drive her, but she'd wanted him to stay and visit with his parents and brother. There was an underlying tension within the family, and she thought it would be good for them to air their dirty laundry without an outsider in their midst. She remembered all the conversations she'd had with Bryce about his family and laughed to herself when she realized they were all true.

Justine Cameron was a character right out of a Tennessee Williams play. She hadn't decided yet which character in a Southern tragedy she could assign to their father but was pretty sure she would come up with a name before the trip was over. Now, she completely understood why his sons called him The Captain.

Black clouds floated in the morning sky with the promise of impending rain. Live oak trees with their limbs draped in Spanish moss lined the highway. Hannah was born and raised in the South but hadn't appreciated its beauty at the time. Now, coming back, she was awash with memories of her childhood, her parents, and especially her Uncle Bill. He was so unlike her intellectual parents. A lifelong bachelor, he had visited frequently and enthralled Hannah with his globe-trotting exploits and adventures. He'd always said, "Hey, you and me, Hannah Banana. They found us under a rock."

It had been months since she'd seen her mother and father and years since she'd seen her uncle. She missed him and didn't understand why, as she'd grown older, his visits had become less frequent, and her mother had refused to discuss what was obviously a rift. Hannah saw him twice when she was an undergraduate and was pleasantly surprised when he'd called with congratulations when she'd received her doctorate. He'd started the conversation with the humorous quip, "What's up, Doc?" Strange that Bryce used that same nickname. She planned to see if they could make a detour on the way home. She wanted to mend fences.

Hannah called the number of the institute she'd entered into her contacts the night before. She'd told Dr. Dreschler's secretary that she would call when she got into town.

A pleasant Southern voice answered, "Institute for Psychological Research, Dr. Dreschler's office."

"Ms. Elliot, this is Hannah Brody. I will be approaching the outskirts of Savannah in a few moments. According to the GPS on my phone, I should be there in about twenty minutes."

"Oh, Dr. Brody. So glad you phoned. I received a phone call from Dr. Dreschler, and he won't be in today. His wife, the poor thing, has been extremely ill."

"I'm so sorry to hear that, but I've driven over three hours to meet with him."

"Oh, you misunderstood me, my dear. He didn't cancel the meeting. So sorry if you thought that. Oh no, he wants you to meet with him at his residence. If you have a pen and paper, I can give you that address."

Hannah pulled off the highway and quickly plotted the new address into the GPS on her phone. She was trying not to be agitated, but she was a planner and didn't do well with sudden change. She'd been nervous about the interview and now more anxiety was creeping in. She closed her eyes, took a deep breath, and remembered what Bryce had said earlier that morning. "Just remember, Doc, he asked to see you and not the other way around. Nothing to be nervous about. You'll wow him, I'm sure."

By the time she reached the residence, her anxiety had calmed down, and she finally felt in control again. She turned the car into a long driveway and saw a large, dark, wooden home with distinctive gables and a tall, slender, red brick chimney. The house looked old and probably dated back to the middle eighteen hundreds. Heavy foliage covered the front and a wash of color from numerous rose bushes lined the brick walkway, which led to four steep steps and a magnificent wooden door.

She couldn't help it. Hannah put her hand to her mouth to suppress a giggle. She took a quick picture and sent it along with a text to Bryce. *Can you spell creepy?*

It was a warm spring morning and Hannah dressed in comfortable beige linen pants, a lavender silk blouse and a black blazer. Her long, blonde hair was pulled up off her neck and secured with a large comb that matched her blouse. She wanted to make a good impression. She wasn't exactly sure what she wanted to get out of this meeting but hoped for recognition of her work and funding for her research.

A handsome man, at least twenty years her senior, with dark hair streaked with silver, a prominent silver mustache, and a Coppertone tan, answered the door. His smile showed perfect teeth in his tanned face. Wow, she thought. I bet his classes are always full of sweet young coeds.

"Dr. Brody, I am so happy to meet you," he said in what she thought was a European accent. He took her hand and stared into her eyes for so long it verged on being rude. She eased her hand out of his and took a step back.

"I am so sorry. But, for a moment, you reminded me of someone. My wife, before … well before the accident."

"I am so sorry to hear about her illness. If I'd known, we could have scheduled our meeting for another time."

"She has been ill for some time. Several months ago, she was in a horrific car accident. I'm afraid it left her in a minimally conscious state, but she is making improvements every day, and before long we expect she will be her old self again. Today, she was having a particularly bad day, and I wanted to be here when her therapist arrived. Everything is back to normal now. I hope you didn't mind coming to the house. We can go into my study and talk. Would you like some coffee?"

"Oh no! But thank you. I'm quite curious about why you wanted to talk to me."

"Your research for your dissertation was brilliant. I was impressed by your premise of the link between personality and genes. I have had that premise, as have so many others for years, but you had a fresh take on it. I was especially intrigued by your hypothesis concerning oxytocin." He laughed and stoked his mustache. "In layman's language, its better known as the love hormone. I am working on a synthetic hormone to mimic it. It will revolutionize how we humans view romantic relationships."

"I'm afraid my research is only in the early draft stage. And I'm not a scientist. All I have is a theory. It is up to other people in the field to make my premise a reality," Hannah said and shifted uneasily in her chair. She was not comfortable with praise. "But surely you don't think you can create feelings between two people with a drug?"

"Oh no, nothing like that. It would be used in the treatment of antisocial behaviors to stimulate feelings of empathy in those individuals lacking that characteristic."

"So, you believe, as I do that the hormone would help in the treatment of sociopaths? But I am astonished that you are close to an actual drug therapy."

"Well, yes, very close and very promising. I wanted to discuss the possibility of you joining the Institute. We would offer an excellent salary and benefits." He wrote a figure down on the back of a business card and placed it in front of her.

To her credit, Hannah didn't gasp at the amount, but she felt like it. "This offer is generous of you, but I'm afraid I couldn't possibly accept. I am under contract with the university in Denver and then there's my private practice. Perhaps it is something I could consider next year."

"No," he snapped. "That won't work."

Hannah watched as he took a deep breath, smiled, and then continued. "I mean, I wanted you to teach classes on the subject and work with my graduate assistants. A year would put... well, it will hamper my plans, but if you would consider it next year, perhaps we could work something out."

"What do you mean?"

"Perhaps you would be amenable to giving guest lectures to my colleagues and to my sponsors? I have seminars set up all over the country. If you're not interested in that, then I'm afraid I will have to look at the other candidates on my list."

Hannah was speechless. She was being offered a once-in-a-lifetime opportunity and was turning it down. Well, not turning it down exactly, simply honoring her present commitments. A year wasn't *that* long was it? "I understand if you need to fill the position. I'm not saying *never*. I just can't commit right now. As far as the guest lectures, the idea intrigues me, but I will need to consider it. Can I let you know by tomorrow?"

"Yes, tomorrow will be fine." He handed her his business card and said, "My private number is on the back. I will wait to hear from you before I schedule any more interviews." He walked her to the door and Hannah could see him standing on his front porch staring at her intently as she turned the Jeep around in the large driveway.

Something about the man was off. She decided it was the arrogant attitude that so many other brilliant individuals possessed. Such people could not see the world the same way the common folk did. To a strange degree, her parents possessed some of those traits. She was glad, as her Uncle Bill had said, she was found under a rock.

She called Bryce immediately after the interview and told him about the offer. As she expected, he was supportive and excited for her. If the move was something she wanted to do, then when her contract in Denver was up they could move to Savannah, and if she wanted to give guest lectures in the meantime, that was fine too.

Hannah was not surprised by his response. It was what she expected and one of the many reasons she had fallen hopelessly in love with him.

CHAPTER 20
HANNAH BRODY

HANNAH PULLED **into the circular driveway of the big house** and waved when she saw Bryce sitting on the front porch. She got out of the car and hurried to his side to give him a hug. His strong arms encircled her, and she looked up into his clear green eyes and handsome face.

"You were waiting for me?"

"I was. I calculated the time it would take you to drive here after you texted me that you were leaving Savannah. I guess my math was pretty good."

"I guess it was. I'm happy to be back. Where is everyone?"

"Justine is at the salon. She likes to call it that, and The Captain is somewhere around."

"You know," Hannah said as she grabbed his hand and walked toward the door, "if I were a psychologist or something, I would read a lot into what you call your parents. Not your typical mom and dad names."

"Yeah?" he raised his eyebrow in a question. "Does that mean I could use some time on your couch?"

"Oh, definitely it means that."

"I missed you," Bryce said and pulled her in for a long, satisfying kiss.

"I've only been gone a few hours. What will you do if I decide to accept the offer? I know I said on the phone we would talk about it later, but right now I want to take my shoes off and have a glass of wine."

"I know there's a bottle around here somewhere, and if you decide to accept the offer, then we will adjust, or rather I will, but I will still miss you."

Hannah punched him in the arm and squeezed his hand. "You're just about perfect," she said. "Do you know that?"

"What do you mean, just about?" They both laughed and walked into the house arm-in-arm.

———

Because the spring semester at the university had ended, Hannah had most of the summer off before she needed to return to teach in late August. She'd scaled back on most of her private patients to spend more time on her research project. Today's meeting with Dr. Dreschler fueled her desire to finish her research and publish her book. She hoped to get tenure in a few years and unfortunately the old saying was true: for academia it was publish or perish.

Her parents were well respected in their chosen fields. Her father was a physicist and her mother was a history professor with an emphasis on medieval and early studies. After being in the same room with them, she sometimes felt her IQ slipped by twenty points. They had both published numerous articles in academic journals and written textbooks.

Hannah looked down into the dark burgundy liquid swirling around in the cut crystal wine glass Bryce had taken out of the immense hutch in the dining room.

"Hey, did you find a bug in your wine?" Bryce teased.

"No, I'm sorry. I was remembering my conversation today with Dreschler, and then my thoughts wandered even further to my parents and how successful they are. I want to make them proud, and if I accept the offer, it will help me toward my end goal."

She watched Bryce's face as he studied her before he spoke, "I don't know your parents, but they would be crazy not to be proud of you."

"Would it be okay with you if we took a couple of days away from this visit with your parents to fly to North Carolina? I want you to meet my mom and dad, and I especially want you to meet my Uncle Bill."

"Doc, I don't know how you've managed to last here this long. My parents can be a bit much. I would love to go visit your folks."

"Oh no, I didn't mean to imply that I wanted to get away from here. It's just that I don't know when we will have a chance again."

"I'll see if we can leave tomorrow. Believe me, we'll be getting out in the nick of time. If we are still here on Sunday, we will be expected to dress for dinner."

"You're kidding, right?"

"Not on your life. See all those fancy things in the cabinet?" he pointed at the wine glasses. "We were taught which fork to use and how to make polite conversation. Justine wanted her boys to move flawlessly through Southern society. Unfortunately, it didn't take. Quinn and I are a great disappointment."

Hannah belted out a delightful peal of laughter. "Oh Bryce. That is priceless and almost worth being here to see it. Almost."

———

Hannah gathered the pages of Bryce's novel and stuffed them into her large leather bag. She had been trying to finish his book ever since he'd given it to her. She'd started reading on the plane trip to Atlanta but didn't have an opportunity to even take it out of her bag once they got to his parents' house. She was nearing the end, but still had several chapters to go.

"Uh oh, you're still plodding through it. That can't be a good sign," Bryce said as he moved into the aisle of the plane, allowing Hannah to squeeze in front of him.

"Oh, Bryce, it's good. I mean that. I can't wait to finish it. I'm almost positive I know who did it, but then maybe not. Am I going to like the ending?"

"I certainly hope you like the ending. I can't wait to see what your reaction will be."

———

Mildred and Robert Brody were waiting at the luggage carousel for Hannah and Bryce. Hannah waved exuberantly when she saw them. Mildred was a tall, striking woman, her height reaching almost six feet. She had short-cropped silver hair and was a sharp contrast to her husband. Robert was a good three inches shorter, with a slight stature and thinning, mousy brown hair. They were an odd match but appeared extraordinarily happy during their forty years of marriage. Hannah wondered what Bryce's reaction would be. She'd always taken them in stride, but seeing them now through Bryce's eyes, she noticed little things.

Her mother's posture accentuated her lean frame. Hannah instinctively straightened as she remembered her mother's daily dictate, "Keep your head up, abdominals in, and shoulders back, Hannah. Good posture will keep you healthy."

Her father was a fidgeter. He seldom sat still for any length of time, and when he did, his feet or hands were in constant motion as well as his mind. Hannah had sadly not inherited her mother's propensity for good posture, and thankfully not her father's attention disorder.

Looking at the two of them standing together in the distance, she noticed, for the first time, how old they looked. She'd always known her parents were not as young as those of her friends, but when she'd asked why they'd waited so long to have her, all her mother would say was they hadn't wanted children when they were first married. She'd asked her mother if she'd had a difficult time getting pregnant and was told in her mother's blunt way, "Yes, Hannah. After all, I was almost forty-three years old when you were born."

Hannah smiled, embraced her mother and father warmly, and turned to introduce Bryce. They were aware she was living with Bryce and had neither condoned nor condemned the arrangement. For all their liberal leaning, her parents were both old-fashioned when it came to sex, and she wasn't sure where she and Bryce would be sleeping tonight.

She needn't have worried about Bryce. He got along with everyone and soon had her mother charmed and her father chatting away like they were old friends. He'd even talked him into a round of golf after her father explained the physics of the game. Something about swinging speed and free rotation of the wrists. Her father was eager to demonstrate the science.

Hannah joined her mother in the kitchen where she was busy making a healthy salad with all the things Bryce would hate, including alfalfa sprouts, raw squash, and cauliflower. The one time Hannah had put sprouts on a sandwich for him, he'd jokingly accused her of confusing him with a horse. She was glad he and her father had escaped.

"Hi, Mom. Can I help?" Hannah asked as she washed her hands. She looked out the kitchen window over the sink to the familiar backyard. The grass was cut, and the flower beds were bursting with colorful early summer blossoms. Her father took pride in keeping the yards in pristine condition. "The yard looks fantastic, as usual."

"Yes, Robert is obsessed with making sure it is perfect. I wish he would have a gardener do it. He has been having trouble with his back, and he's not as young as he once was. You realize your father will be seventy in a few months."

"Are you all talking about retirement anytime soon?"

"Yes, remember I told you that a few months ago. These next two semesters I will teach only three classes and your father has decided to scale back too."

Hannah didn't recall a conversation with her mother about that. To avoid an argument, she said, "I don't remember. I guess I was preoccupied with my move and didn't pay attention. I'm glad you guys will take it easy. You're both in good health, aren't you?"

"Oh yes, we're fine. Your father has his high blood pressure, but it's controlled, and you know me, I have the constitution of an ox."

It was a saying Hannah had heard all her life. While Hannah had frequent bouts with whatever virus was going around and allergies to everything, her mother remained unscathed.

"I like your young man, Hannah. He has good manners and treats you quite well. I know you are living together. Are you planning on making it permanent?"

"We haven't discussed that part of our relationship yet. We're happy with the way things are right now." Hannah reached over her mother and grabbed a plump red cherry tomato and popped in her mouth.

"Hannah," her mother scolded, "where are your manners? I taught you better than that. For goodness' sake, living in the Wild West has made you just plain rude. So why are you here?"

Hannah felt her heart sink and sat down at the table. " I'm sorry that I'm a disappointment. Aren't you happy to see me, Mom?"

"You know I am, but you've changed so much. You're been so different since you've been on your own, and besides, you said you couldn't get away until later this summer."

"My plans changed. I interviewed for a job in Savannah and Bryce's parents live in Atlanta, so we made the trip together. Since we were this close, and I had the time, I wanted to see you."

"What kind of job? Aren't you happy with your position in Denver? If you're not, your father and I could put a good word in for you here in Chapel Hill."

"No, it's not that. I love my practice in Denver. I was offered an opportunity to work for a private institute in Savannah. I have commitments in Denver for the next year, but I'm seriously considering taking the offer when my contract ends. In the meantime, I may travel occasionally while giving lectures. I'm not sure. Bryce and I haven't talked about it yet."

"You can't let a man make your decision for you, Hannah, you …"

"Mom, Bryce is supportive of everything I do. He wouldn't try to sway me one way or the other, but it is a big decision, and we are a couple. I would at least like to have his input before I decide."

Her mother made a dismissive noise and turned back to the salad giving it a hasty toss. She knew her parents were disappointed when she moved over seventeen hundred miles away. She'd attended college and grad school at the University of North Carolina and Duke, which was practically in their backyard. The move to Colorado was a scary venture but it was the best decision she'd ever made. Hannah needed to be on her own, and besides, she would never have met Bryce if she hadn't been on that plane to Denver.

"I need to tell you, Mom, that I plan to see Uncle Bill while I am here. I don't know what happened between you two, but I miss him, and I want to see him."

Her mother's face took on that look, the one that said, *I don't approve, but I can't stop you.* Hannah got up and hugged her mother's stiffening body. "I wish you would tell me what is wrong. Maybe I can fix it."

"Hannah, I will not discuss my brother with you. If you need to see him, then so be it. I'm not hungry anymore." Her mother covered the salad bowl, placed it in the refrigerator, and left the room.

———

The next morning, Hannah arranged to have breakfast with her uncle on the way to the airport. The last conversation with her mother had put a damper on the visit, and that evening Mildred had gone to bed early claiming a headache. Her father was his usual self and oblivious to what was going on around him. Sometimes he reminded Hannah of the movie character in *The Absent-Minded Professor*. She loved both of her parents fiercely, even if she didn't understand them and they didn't understand her. She knew they loved her, but she'd often wondered why they'd ever decided to have a child.

Her Uncle Bill was tall and slender like her mother, but the strands of hair touching the collar of his shirt were still ink-black with only a few strands of gray. When Hannah was younger, she'd thought he was handsome and mysterious. For a time, she'd convinced herself he was a spy because he was always traveling all over the world. Then, much to her disappointment, her mother told her to stop her fantasies. Her uncle worked for an oil company. To this day Hannah didn't know if she believed her or not.

"Hannah Banana," her uncle said and embraced her in a bear hug. "I have missed you, girl. You look good. Real good. And this must be Bryce," he said extending his hand. The two men exchanged greetings and sat down at a booth in a back section of the Waffle House.

"Breakfast is on me. Don't know about you guys, but I'm

starving. I've been in Calcutta and believe you me you can't get good bacon and eggs there."

"What were you doing there?" Hannah asked as she unfolded the menu.

"Oh, you know, this and that."

This and that was her uncle's standard reply to questions about his job. No wonder she'd been sure he was a spy for the CIA. She looked at Bryce and he raised his eyebrows as if to say, *I see what you mean,*

"So, Dr. Brody," her uncle said in his loud booming voice, "what are you doing in North Carolina?"

"I had an appointment in Savannah and Bryce needed to get his car, and … well it's a long story. Since I was in this neck of the woods, so to speak, I took the opportunity to see Mom and Dad. Unfortunately, Mom and I didn't part on the best of terms."

"Your momma can be obstinate when she doesn't get her way. What did you do now?" he said and looked up when the waitress approached.

Hannah waited until they ordered and took a sip of hot coffee before she answered. "I wanted to know what had come between you two. She refuses to tell me and I…" she set the coffee down and it sloshed onto the table. "I want things to be the way they used to be."

"Things change, little girl. You know that, especially being in the field you're in. People change. I love my sister, and she loves me, but we simply do not agree on one certain thing, so she decided it was best if I didn't come around."

"What thing? Why? Is it because of me? What are you not telling me?" Hannah looked across the table into her uncle's eyes, and if she hadn't known him so well, she would have missed it. But it was there, just a flicker, but she saw it. It was her. Their estrangement was her fault.

"That's for your momma to tell. You 'll have to ask her."

Frustrated, Hannah turned to Bryce for help. He looked helplessly at her and shrugged.

"She won't tell me anything. She gets upset and refuses to talk to me," Hannah said.

"So, here comes our breakfast. Like I said, I'm starving."

Hannah could tell the subject was closed, and she knew it would be hopeless to pursue it. If her uncle didn't want to tell her, he wouldn't, and no manner of pleading would change his mind. In this way, he was exactly like her mother.

"So, Bryce, what do you do? You don't look like a professor to me, but what do I know? My sister was always the brains in the family."

"I'm a writer. Fiction."

"Anything I might have read?"

"I doubt it. It wasn't around for long."

"Bryce is being modest. The critics loved it. *The Perfect Lie.* That's the title."

"Yes, I remember that book. I did read it. Well, I'll be. You're Bryce Cameron."

"You don't have to be polite," Bryce said and grimaced. "It stank."

"No, not at all. I liked the book. Great characters. Great ending."

"You liked it?" Bryce said ,clearly amazed.

"Oh yes, I liked it. Like I said, great writing. Great story. What's not to like?"

Bryce beamed and turned to look at Hannah. She patted him on the shoulder and said, "See? I said you would like my uncle."

They settled into their seats for the short flight back to Atlanta. Hannah was upset by the conversations with her mother and then with her uncle. Something was going on and now she knew it involved her, but what could it possibly be? It made no sense.

Hannah took the pages of Bryce's manuscript out of her bag, hoping to go somewhere else with her mind for a while, and started to read. She wasn't kidding when she told him it was good. He was a fantastic writer, and she was thoroughly engrossed in it. She could see him looking at her out of the corner of her eye. He was like a little kid waiting for Christmas.

The flight attendant came by and before she could answer, Bryce ordered for both of them. Two glasses of wine. Okay, she thought, why not? After all, it was almost noon and assuredly five o'clock somewhere.

Hannah turned over the next-to-the-last page and finished. She had a lump in her throat. The ending was brilliant, and it was a happy one. Below the last line of the last paragraph was *The End*, written in Bryce's handwriting. And then he wrote, *Well, not quite yet please turn the page.*

She tilted her head up to see his reaction, but for once he wasn't looking at her and appeared to be engrossed in the airline's magazine. She turned the page and read:

I know you were made for me, and I think you know I was made for you. We were meant to be. I'm crazy in love with you. Marry me, Doc.

CHAPTER 21

HANNAH BRODY

BRYCE AND HANNAH **had just walked in the front door** when Justine swooped down the stairway. "I'm so happy to see you," she said. "You have both been on my mind night and day."

"Why is that, Mom?" Bryce said.

"Well, because I simply don't know if I can trust that people who take long airplane flights are going to get home safely. I don't trust any of those commercial pilots. You could have ended up in the ocean."

Bryce rolled his eyes so that only Hannah could see and ignored his mother's words.

Hannah wondered if Justine cast ridiculous comments like that into the wind because she was so hungry for conversation or if she simply enjoyed hearing her own voice. In Hannah's opinion, at least two-thirds of the things Justine said were not based in reality. She would make an interesting case study.

"Come in now, my big guy, and bring your lady. Sit down, both of you, and I'll make you a drink," Justine said. "What would you like? I have hard lemonade, white and red wine, and all kinds of liquor. Name your poison."

"I'll have water with lemon, please," Hannah said.

"Me too," Bryce said.

Justine looked at them both in confusion. "Well, yes, we have water, but it's way back in the kitchen. We don't keep it in the bar."

"No problem," Bryce said. "I'll get it."

After Bryce left the room, Justine turned to Hannah and lowered her voice. "Does Bryce have a drinking problem?"

Hannah met her accusing eyes without flinching. Instead of answering the question, she said, "Why would you ask me something like that?"

Justine forced her lips to part in a curved, stiff smile. "Well, isn't it obvious?"

Hannah waited in silence.

"It's the cocktail hour. In the South, you only refuse a cocktail if you just got out of rehab."

There was nothing in the world that Hannah could say that would make a difference. Something was wrong with this woman, and she felt sorry for the two men who called her Mother.

———

Later that evening, they all sat down around the mahogany dining room table. The heavy upholstered chairs were at least a decade out of fashion. The Captain was a few minutes late, and sat at the head of the table, and Justine sat on the opposite end. Hannah and Bryce sat beside one another, and Quinn took the seat across from them.

The conversation was light, and without incident until Hannah asked Justine to pass the potatoes. When she reached for the bowl, her diamond ring flashed in the reflected light of the chandelier.

"What in heaven's name is this?" Justine said and grabbed Hannah's hand in hers.

Hannah was momentarily speechless in her surprise, but then looked at Bryce, and he nodded. "It's my engagement ring. I've only had it a few hours."

"And you were going to tell us when?" The Captain said. His eyes were filled with contempt.

Hannah pulled her hand away from Justine and turned to Bryce. She was going to answer, but Bryce beat her to it.

"After dinner tonight was the plan."

"Why all the secrecy?" The Captain insisted.

"Not a secret, Captain. But it is our news to share on our timetable."

"Well, I say congratulations to you both," Quinn said. "I was hoping he would ask you soon. In my opinion, he's one smart man. Welcome to the family."

He raised his water glass and waited until everyone did the same. They clinked glasses, and everyone started poking at the food on their plates once again.

The Captain said he was tired and left before dessert was served. After he left the room, it was as if the tension followed him, and everyone relaxed and enjoyed their food.

Hannah assumed he had gone to his study to google her and find out what her credentials were. Once again, she felt a pang of sympathy for the brothers who had endured his behavior for decades.

The next morning, breakfast was served on the veranda near the beautiful rose garden behind the house. There was a buffet spread with practically any breakfast food a person could want.

Bryce had slept in, but Hannah was hungry and made her way through the expansive downstairs rooms to the back of the house.

As soon as Justine saw her, the chatter began—so much

for a peaceful cup of coffee and the local newspaper. Hannah had never been a morning person, and keeping up with Justine's twists and turns in conversation made her head hurt.

"You know I am famous around here as a wedding planner, don't you? Everyone calls me when their kids are ready to get married, and I take care of everything."

Hannah smiled with what she hoped was polite interest.

"You are going to get married in Atlanta, aren't you? Will your parents be here for the wedding?"

Hannah blew on her coffee and then took a sip. "I haven't had time to talk to them yet."

"Why not? You just got back from there, didn't you? Why didn't you tell them? You mean I was the first to know? Goodness me, that makes me so proud. Don't worry, I won't tell your mother. Bless her heart! She might get terribly upset."

Hannah took another bite and chewed on her toast so that she would not have to respond. Which of the rapid-fire questions would she answer, anyway? Best to say nothing at all.

Bryce appeared at exactly the right moment and Hannah watched as Justine transferred her attention to him. The way she behaved reminded Hannah of an older woman who was trying to look and sound pretty for a younger man. Nothing she did was inappropriate, but her behavior made her look like a fool. Surely Bryce and Quinn were both embarrassed by her mannerisms. But then, maybe not. To them, she had always behaved exactly in this way, so it was nothing out of the ordinary.

———

After breakfast, Hannah and Bryce went for a long walk along a trail in Ansley Park. The entire area was filled with elegant old homes. Holding each other's hand, they made their way through winding streets. The picturesque trail meandered beside streams, and they saw many historic churches.

"Did my mother drive you insane with her questions?" He pulled her close to his side.

"No, but she is insistent that she be our wedding planner."

"How do you feel about that?" His eyebrows raised inquiringly.

"Frankly," she said, "that would be fine with me."

"It would?"

"I don't know why, but I have never been one of those women who daydreamed about her wedding or wedding dress." She stopped walking for a moment, turned into his arms, and faced him. She looked up at him before she said, "I was one of those women who fantasized about who my husband would be. What he would look like and what he would say and do."

Bryce leaned down and kissed her, and she was shocked at her eager response to the touch of his lips.

"I don't care who plans our wedding, Bryce. I just want to be your wife. I've never wanted anything more."

———

Hannah called her parents and told them about the surprise proposal and invited them to the wedding, which she and Bryce had decided would be in two weeks in Atlanta. She couldn't be away from her practice any longer than that.

"Two weeks?" Justine shrieked after they told her. "Well, it was nice of you to give me such a generous time frame in which to get everything arranged." Her voice was heavy with sarcasm.

"Remember whose idea it was for you to plan the wedding," Bryce warned. "Nobody asked you to jump in head first."

Hannah put her hand on Bryce's arm. "We don't want a

big wedding, Justine. I'm confident that together we will manage everything quite well."

"You must know that two weeks is not long enough to have a dress custom-made."

"I do know that. I plan to find one that I like at a local bridal shop or department store. I'm sure there will be many to choose from."

"And you, Bryce. How will you ever be fitted for a tuxedo in time?" She sat down on the sofa and fanned herself with a magazine.

"I'm wearing a dark blue suit, Mom."

"Well, do you have one?"

"No. I'm renting one for me and one for Quinn."

"Renting? Oh, good grief. Don't tell anyone that. What about your father?"

"He can wear whatever he wants," Bryce said. "I'll pay for it."

"Well, you know your father," Justine said. "He'll want to wear his dress uniform."

"Fine, then. That's settled."

———

If Hannah thought having her future mother-in-law arrange her wedding would free her up to spend time with Bryce, she was wrong. Justine had something for her to do every day. They had to taste the cakes, choose the flowers, go to the print shop, and have the invitations printed. It was too late to mail them, so Justine planned to have them hand-delivered to her special friends.

Justine decided at the last minute to have the wedding and the reception in the garden behind the house. Her cell phone was attached to her ear as she arranged for tents, chairs, tables, a caterer, and a musician.

Hannah was exhausted from watching her future mother-in-law flit around like a neurotic butterfly from task to task.

"Oh, heavens," Justine said as she swooped into the dining room where Bryce and Hannah were having a light lunch.

"What now?" Bryce said. Hannah gave Bryce a look, and he added, "I mean, what's wrong? How can we help?"

"Well, I'm not sure who is going to perform the ceremony. Do you want a minister? I don't even know what religion you are, Hannah." She pulled out a chair and sank into it. "I forgot to ask if you are Protestant or Catholic. Oh, please tell me you are not Catholic. There's not enough time for Bryce to convert before the wedding. You could marry him anyway, but you might be ex-communicated or whatever they do these days to bad Catholics. You're not a serious Catholic, are you, Hannah?"

Hannah took a drink of her water to avoid answering until she could modulate her voice. She could not believe how the older woman's mind worked. She had no filter and no regard for other people's feelings or beliefs.

"Actually, I'm not Catholic at all. The church my parents attended was non-denominational. You could come and worship without worrying about a label. When I have more time, I am going to find a church like that in Denver. Bryce can come with me if he likes, but it's not mandatory."

"Well, thank goodness for that," Justine said. "I can ask Reverend McKinney if he will do it?" She turned towards Hannah to explain. "We have attended his church for many years. We are major contributors, so I'm sure he will consent."

"That will be..." Bryce began.

"Oh, no," Justine interrupted, "what if it's too short notice?"

"Then we'll go to Plan B. Call him now and see what he says," Bryce said.

"Okay, sweetie boy. You always know how to calm me down. Be right back."

After she left the room, Bryce and Hannah looked at each other and burst out laughing. "Don't expect me to call you 'sweetie boy.' If you get too excited and need to be calmed, I'm going to turn the hose on you."

Bryce stood, gave her a seductive smile, and gently pulled her up into his arms. "Is that so?" he said playfully, whispering in her ear. "Let's go upstairs and test that theory."

Somehow, they survived the wedding planner's crazy, mixed-up preparations, and everything worked out, including the weather. Mildred and Robert attended the wedding, but they didn't stay long enough to cause a scene or get crossways with Justine or The Captain. Uncle Bill sent his regrets along with a generous check and a note. He said he wanted to avoid a scene with Mildred that might put a damper on Hannah's special day.

At four o'clock, Hannah walked across the perfectly manicured lawn on a path strewn with rose petals and into Bryce's arms. They had written simple vows and spoken them from their hearts.

"I will cherish you for all of my life," Bryce promised.

"And I will love you with all of my heart for as long as I live," Hannah said.

"And I pronounce you husband and wife," the minister said, and they turned to hear the applause of their guests and begin their lives together.

CHAPTER 22
BRYCE CAMERON

BRYCE'S **first summer in the Rockies was amazing.** He sat out on the patio of their townhouse enjoying the beautiful, eighty-one-degree June day. After living most of his life in the sultry South, the cool, arid climate of Denver was like being in heaven. Married life was pretty damn terrific too. Every day with Doc was an adventure, and every night was X-rated.

He took a sip of his coffee and looked up as Hannah walked out of the patio door. She was dressed for work in a soft gray suit and a silky lilac blouse, her favorite color. "Hello, beautiful," he said and got up to kiss her goodbye.

"Hi, hon. I've got to go over my notes after I see my last patient today to get ready for my trip tomorrow. It should be a fly-out and fly-back event weather permitting, but I won't be too late."

"You're enjoying presenting those seminars for the institute, aren't you?" Bryce said and settled back in his comfortable chair.

"I like everything about it but…"

"But?" he teased.

"Being away from you. I don't like that at all."

"Ditto," he said and smiled over his coffee cup.

"So, who are you killing off today and how? Is it something gory?"

"Blood thirsty little thing, aren't you? Nobody is getting killed today. It's too pretty a day for that. Instead, I have a very steamy love scene in mind, and if I get writer's block I will probably have to do some research tonight."

Hannah laughed and blew him a kiss as she walked toward the gate and said, "I'm counting on it."

Bryce looked at his watch and realized it was close to eleven. He saved the chapter he was working on and closed the lid on the computer. It was a productive morning, and he was pleased with the progress on the book.

He had plans to meet Jesse Silva for lunch. After the initial bout of jealousy Bryce experienced when the two men first met, he now considered Jesse a friend. A former Marine who had served in Iraq and Afghanistan, Jesse had been raised in a military household the same as Bryce. Well, not exactly the same. Evidently, Jesse's dad was a cool dude and the two of them were close.

Bryce wished he felt the same way about The Captain, although the old man did seem to love Hannah. She had a way with him that he and Quinn never did. The Captain admitted she was like the daughter he wished he'd had. Justine liked her too. What was not to like? The woman was perfect. Bryce had even agreed in a moment of weakness to spend Christmas in Atlanta. Go figure. Life was good.

———

He met Jesse at a pub about halfway between both residences. He ordered a sandwich and a mug of stout beer. Jesse was working later that afternoon, so he had to settle for a glass of iced tea. Bryce thought about teasing him but decided that wasn't quite fair. Some people had to work for a living. Bryce got to play all day long with his imagination.

Their friendship had begun when Bryce called him to ask about a specific police procedure he needed to use in his book. Jesse was glad to help and even seemed excited. Now, it was a regular thing to meet and bounce ideas off the detective to see if they were plausible. If a plot point was too far out there, Jesse had no trouble telling Bryce he was full of it.

"Hey, before we get started, I wanted to let you and Hannah know you should hear from the DA's office anytime now."

"I assume this is about Lucy. Are they taking her to trial this soon?" Bryce asked.

"No, she flunked her psych eval. They are putting her in the state mental hospital in Pueblo until she is fit to stand trial."

Bryce frowned and said, "So, what is this? The first step to letting that crazy psycho off by reason of insanity so she can come after Hannah again?"

Jesse shrugged. "I honestly don't know. Colorado's law allows for an insanity defense if the defendant was incapable of distinguishing right from wrong or if she has a medical condition that would do that."

"Well, she is definitely a psychopath. Hope that doesn't count," Bryce said and set his mug down on the table with a loud thump. "So how come you found out about this?"

"I make it a point to keep tabs on how the case is going. And they will give me answers," he smiled weakly and said, "before they will give them to you. Sorry, that's how the system works."

"I appreciate the heads-up. Hannah is leaving tomorrow for a lecture, and I'm not going to spoil tonight with this news. I'll let her know when she gets back."

Jesse finished his tea and signaled the waitress. "You ready to order?"

They placed their orders, and Bryce sat silently while studying Jesse. Finally, he asked the question he'd wanted to ask since the two men became friends. "You have a thing for Hannah, don't you?"

"Had," Jesse said, "past tense." He didn't seem at all surprised by the question. "If you hadn't been in the picture, I would have given it all I had to get her to go out with me. But after I saw the two of you together, I knew I didn't have a chance. But I admire her and I'm fond of her. If you ever treat her wrong, I'll kick your ass."

"Duly noted," Bryce said as the waitress set their plates down, "duly noted." Bryce took a bite of his sandwich and realized that Jesse was unusually quiet. "What's going on? I didn't intend to cross the line."

"Oh, hell no, it's not that. I guess I'm a little distracted. I'll finish up my Master's degree at the end of the summer, and I suppose I haven't said anything because I didn't want to get my hopes up."

"About what?" Bryce said, clearly intrigued.

"I applied to the FBI about six months ago. They usually want accountants, not law enforcement, but with my Master's in psychology, I thought, what the heck?"

"A G-Man, huh? Wow, I'm impressed."

"I have my interview this week."

"You're an ace cop. You'll do great. This is fantastic. I'll be able to get all kinds of ideas and live vicariously through you."

"The job is not quite as exciting as it is in the movies."

"Or in books? "Bryce smiled.

"Yeah, as in your books."

"I wish you luck, man. Let us know how it goes."

"So, what do you need to pick my brain about today? And please make the cop a good-looking stud."

The two friends passed the rest of the hour talking about what-ifs for Bryce's new novel.

———

Bryce pulled into the parking spot and was presently surprised to see that Doc's car was there. She was home. Way early. At first, he was ecstatic and then on second thought, he began to worry. Something was wrong. She had patients, and she said she was staying later to look at her notes. He bounded out of the car and up the steps at a dead run. He tried to stay calm, but with the news about Lucy going to the nut farm, he was wary.

By the time he reached the front door, he got himself under control. He opened it and called out. "Doc? Hey, Doc, you're home early. Everything okay?" His heart was still racing, but he was relieved when she answered.

"Yeah, everything is fine. I wanted to come home and see you. Why don't you come in here and help me with something?"

Bryce walked into the bedroom and stopped. Standing by the bed stood Hannah, wearing a black teddy. Her lush blonde hair hung loosely around her shoulders. He swallowed hard and took a deep breath. "Oh, wow," he said, "you look fantastic."

"You know, we haven't had a real honeymoon. I had to get back to work, and I've been spending most of my free time now either working on my lecture notes or away giving lectures. You've been extremely patient."

"I don't feel neglected, Doc. I'm proud of you and what you do. It's your dream to get your research recognized."

"It was my dream. Now I have two dreams, and one of them is you. Our life together. Our future."

Bryce walked slowly to her, placed his hands gently on her shoulders, and pulled her close. He whispered in her ear, "You know I'm a sucker for skimpy, lacy things."

"I know," she whispered back. "And remember that little something I needed for you to help me with."

"Yes," he said, his breath against her ear.

"Well, I can't seem to take it off all by myself. Could you help me?"

"Oh yeah. I think I can," he said as he slipped the thin straps down her shoulders, freeing her breasts to fall into his hands.

"Is that better?"

"Oh, yes," she moaned. "Much."

He kissed each breast and moved down to her belly, pulled the teddy off and let the lacy material fall to the floor. He buried his face between her legs, felt her quiver, and heard her moan again. He moved back up her body and kissed her lips gently at first, and then became more demanding. When she returned the kiss, he tenderly laid her on the bed.

She moved her hands to remove his shirt, and he quickly finished the rest. Their bodies were now skin to skin, and he took in the fragrance that was only hers, the scent of lilacs. What had he done before this woman? He didn't know. He only knew that he was nothing without her. She gave his life meaning and substance. She built him up when he was down and loved him unconditionally. He'd never had that kind of love with anyone else. He knew as long as he lived, he would never want anyone else the way he wanted his Doc.

"I love you," he murmured, and he moved into her as their bodies became one.

He felt her tighten around him as he thrust into her and heard her whisper, "I will always love you, too."

———

Later, he lay across the bed with Hannah tucked snuggly against him. He blew kisses in her ear and she laughed. Oh, Lord, he loved her laugh. Sometimes it was subtle like now, but usually it was loud and boisterous and completely uninhibited. "Hey," he said. "I'm trying to be all romantic here and you're laughing."

Hannah turned and faced him, and he felt her trace his lips with her fingers. "You know the first thing I noticed about you?"

"Aside from my fabulous good looks?"

"Yeah, aside from that," she snickered. "The fact that you didn't take yourself too seriously. When I said horrible things about your book, you were so gracious."

"Well, facts are facts. It kinda stank."

"No, it didn't. I read the reviews. The critics were very kind."

"I have learned from my mistakes, thanks to a beautiful shrink that I met a while back. She set me straight."

"She sure did," she said and kissed him passionately.

"You know, you're playing with fire."

"I know," she said as she rolled over onto his body.

———

Bryce woke up when he heard the first lines from *Carry on My Wayward Son*, the ringtone on his phone for Quinn. He thought about letting it go to voicemail, but when he looked at the beside clock, he realized it was still early. He and Hannah had fallen asleep after an afternoon of lovemaking. It was a fantastic afternoon.

"Hey, Bro, what's up?" Bryce said as he tiptoed out of the bedroom.

"You won't believe it, but I may have a lead."

"Lead? Lead on what?"

"Dixie, man. A lead on Dixie."

CHAPTER 23
QUINN CAMERON

QUINN TEXTED **his brother** a few minutes before he pulled into the driveway. His whole day would improve if he avoided Justine's morning routine of cooing and fussing and calling him Quinney Boy.

He was grateful that Bryce had flown back to Atlanta to help with the search for Dixie. Grateful, but not surprised. Bryce had always been on his side.

"Dude, I'm glad to see you, but you didn't have to spend all those bucks on a plane ticket."

"I had plenty of free miles. I've been flipping that airline card out quite a bit lately. Besides, Hannah is so busy she won't even miss me for a couple of days."

"I'm sorry you had to stay here with Dudley-Do-Right and his lady. I only have the one bed and my accommodations are a little untidy, to say the least. Did you eat yet?"

Bryce shook his head. "Nope. You?"

"Good, because we're heading for the diner, and we might have better luck with the old man if we order."

"What old man?"

"Tony, remember, the owner?"

"I thought he didn't know anything."

"I thought so too, but then I got a call from the old lady at the trailer park. She suggested that Tony knows more than he's saying. He had been like an uncle to Dixie, and he probably helped her get set up in a new job."

They hadn't finished their bowls of chili when Tony walked in. He didn't notice them while he unzipped his gray Members Only jacket, hung it on the hook, and unlocked the door to his office. Then his eyes scanned the counter, and he spotted them.

"Crap," he said loudly enough that he had to apologize to the roomful of customers. Then he walked over and filled their water glasses. "Now what?"

"We wanted to talk to you again," Quinn said. "We had a talk with Mable at the trailer park, and she said the person who knows the most about Dixie is you."

He slammed the water pitcher down on the counter. "Follow me. We'll talk in the back."

When they entered the office, he indicated two folding chairs, and they sat down. He sank into a worn leather chair. "Exactly what's your interest in all of this? I need to know."

"I hope to see her again and find out what happened. We were dating a few years ago and getting serious and then she vanished. I haven't been able to get her out of my mind."

"And you? What's your story?" The older man looked at Bryce.

"He's my brother. I'm his wingman. I've never met Dixie."

Tony reached into a jar, took a Tootsie Pop, and unrolled the paper. "Want one?" he offered.

Both men refused and waited patiently while Tony rolled the candy around in his mouth and made sucking noises. "I don't know much, but I have a theory."

"What do you mean," Quinn said.

"One day she came to work with a new hairdo. I think it's because she was hiding bruises on her face." He slurped on the candy again for a while and then continued. "I asked her if she was all right and she blew me off. Acted like I was getting nosy. But once when she leaned across the counter, her hair fell away from her face, and I saw the purple bruises on her cheek and her temple."

Quinn was confused. "I thought you said she lived alone."

"She did, as far as I know."

"Then what happened to her? Who could have hit her?"

"Beats me, son. She left the next day, and I never saw her again."

"So, you can't help me, can you?"

"Well, maybe I can, a little." His teeth had found the chocolate Tootsie Roll in the center of the sucker, and he bit into it and chewed until it was gone.

Bryce gave his brother a warning look. Be patient. Wait.

"How?" Quinn insisted.

"I got a call from a guy up in northwest Atlanta who manages an Applebee's. He said he needed a reference for a girl who worked for me. Said her name was Dixie."

"When?" Quinn said. His voice shook with excitement.

"Hmm," Tony said. "Seems like that was a couple of years ago. Could be a false alarm. She's probably moved on by now. The tips wouldn't be so good in that neighborhood."

"I want to check it out, anyway. Can you give me the address?"

Tony reached across the desk and scribbled on a scrap of paper. Bryce and Quinn thanked him and left.

After they walked out of his office, he placed a call. "Two men were here a while ago asking questions about Dixie. What do you want me to do?"

————

Bryce kept urging Quinn to slow down as they drove to the other side of the city. "A speeding ticket won't help your situation much. It's been two years. What are the chances that she will still be there?"

"Probably slim to none, but someone may point us in another direction. It's the first lead I've had, and I'm glad to get it."

He pulled into the parking lot at Applebee's. It looked bright and clean and inviting. Several big screen televisions were positioned around the bar. At the reception desk, a young man greeted them with a big smile. "How many?"

"We need to speak to the manager," Quinn said.

The youngster looked worried. "You do? What's wrong?"

"Nothing's wrong," Quinn said. "Is the manager here?"

"Well, sure she is, but we're supposed to handle problems by ourselves before we go and bother her. May I help you?" He folded his arms across his chest.

Quinn took a deep breath. "Yes, you certainly may." There was an icy edge of irony in his voice. "You can get your skinny butt back to the office and tell your manager that I want to talk to her. Now!"

A few moments later, a woman wearing a uniform and a wrinkled apron made her way to the front of the restaurant. Her face and her posture said she was annoyed, or maybe she was tired.

"Yeah? You wanted to see me?"

Bryce stepped forward and held out his hand. "We're sorry to disturb you, ma'am, but we have a few questions about an employee of yours, and we knew it would be better to talk to the boss."

She paused, looked at his hand, and then shook it. "I'm Lorena Wilson, and you are?"

"I'm Bryce Cameron, and this is my brother Quinn."

"Brothers, huh? Not cops?"

Quinn wondered if the woman was more than tired. Maybe she was also a little dense. The two brothers were dressed in shorts and golf shirts. It was obvious they were not armed, and since when did cops casually drop into an Apple-bee's and not identify themselves? Maybe she thought they were undercover agents. He almost laughed out loud at that.

"No, ma'am," Bryce continued with his polite young man routine, "not cops."

"Well, spill it. What do you want? I have a pile of receipts in the back that are not adding up. I'm kind of busy today, so make it quick."

"We are looking for a young woman who worked here about two years ago. She may still work here now for all we know. Her name is Dixie Lee King. She has black curly hair and golden-brown eyes." Bryce continued to take the lead.

"Why?" Lorena Wilson said.

"Excuse me?" Quinn said.

"Why are you looking for her? Did she do something wrong? Why don't you know where she is?"

"No, no. Nothing wrong. Quite the opposite. We are trying to locate her because she has come into some money, and we want to make sure she gets it," Bryce said.

What the hell? Quinn's eyebrows shot up in surprise, and then he quickly got himself under control before the woman saw him. He took a business card out of his pocket and handed it to the woman. "Here's my contact information."

"Oh goodness, that's amazing," Lorena said. "It's a rags-to-riches story. Is it a lot of money?"

"So, she's here?" Quinn said in as reasonable a voice as he could manage.

"I didn't say that. I said it's amazing that a waitress has come into some money. Doesn't happen often. Too bad she's not here. I don't know her. Maybe she was before my time. Two years you say? That would mean she worked for Sal Lewis."

"Is he the former manager?" Quinn said.

"Was," she said. "He died last year. Lung cancer."

By the time they finished talking to everyone who

worked at the diner, Quinn had a headache and was in a foul mood. The ride back to his parents' house was quiet. There wasn't much to say. He had no idea what to do next. He had reached a dead end this time, and a pain squeezed his heart.

———

At first, after Bryce returned to Denver, Quinn did not take his daily calls. Quinn would respond with a text and say that he was tied up now and would get back to him soon. But he didn't. He was too miserable to be good company to anyone.

He worked long hours at the lumberyard and volunteered to take shifts for some of the other employees to keep himself busy. One evening around seven o'clock, he was putting away his tools and cleaning up his area when he looked up to see Lorraine standing a few feet in front of him. She was wearing a slim, leather skirt, a white low-cut peasant blouse, and high-top boots.

He let out an admiring whistle. "Whoa, lady, you look fantastic. Are you shooting an ad today?"

Her laugh was deep, warm, and rich. "Aren't you a flatterer?" she said. She was clearly pleased with his reaction. "I am happy to see you are still here. I've missed seeing you around."

"Oh, I've been here every day. I've been out on the delivery truck most of the time. Business is booming, isn't it?"

"You bet it is. They are building that new arena, and it takes a lot of lumber. Good for me. Good for you," she said. Her smile was warm.

"You going somewhere? You look great."

"I'm going anywhere you want to take me tonight," she said. Her eyes sparkled with flirtatious light.

Quinn laughed. "Do I look like somebody who's dressed to go out?"

"No, but after you shower and shave, you'll be a brand-new man. I can wait."

"Lorraine, I don't think so... I... uh..." He didn't know how to tell her that the last thing he wanted was to spend the evening with her friends and be paraded around as her boy toy. Then, before he could finish the thought, he felt terrible. Lorraine was a wonderful woman. He would be lucky to spend an evening with her.

She turned a vivid scarlet and the look she gave him made him feel like a first-class heel. Her pride had been seriously bruised by his behavior.

Too late he said, "Give me an hour. I'll go home and come back to pick you up."

"Don't do me any favors, Quinn. I've never had to beg a man to take me out, and I sure as hell don't plan to start now. Consider my invitation rescinded."

"Lorraine, let me explain. I've had a few bad days in a row."

"Well, let's hope tomorrow is a better one for you." The silence between them became unbearable, but he didn't know what to say.

"Don't be mad. I didn't mean to hurt your feelings."

"My feelings are perfectly fine, but there's one thing you should know, Quinn. Our personal relationship is over. Done. Finis."

She was as good as her word. Although he saw her when he picked up his paycheck and when she walked past him in the warehouse, their relationship never again crossed into the realm of personal. They were strictly boss and employee. He was sorry, but he felt a sense of relief. It was hard to pretend to care when he really didn't.

On Saturday, Quinn worked late into the night in his workshop. A young couple had told him about an old barn that was falling apart on their grandfather's farm. He spent several days reclaiming the wood from the walls and paid a very reasonable price because the couple had commissioned him to craft a dining room table as a gift for their grandfather's eighty-fifth birthday.

By the time he crossed the driveway to the house to get ready for bed, he was exhausted. He went into the bathroom and shed his dusty clothes. Clad only in his boxers, he slathered toothpaste on the brush and cleaned his teeth. He continued brushing as he walked into the kitchen to get a glass of water.

He almost missed seeing the blinking light on the answering machine. Only people who had his business card called that number. He talked to friends and family on his cell phone. He knew the business could probably wait until tomorrow, but his curiosity got the better of him. Maybe it would be the big job he kept hoping would pay off the loan on his equipment.

He pushed the play button on the machine and nearly choked on the toothpaste in his mouth when he heard the message.

"Quinn, hi, it's Dixie." Her voice was velvet-edged and strong. "I need to talk to you. Call me back when you can, will you?"

CHAPTER 24
QUINN CAMERON

QUINN RINSED **his mouth and washed his hands.** He had a moment of panic when he realized Dixie had not left her number. His thoughts ran amok. *Maybe I should push star sixty-nine. Maybe she'll call back.* He ran his hands through his hair and paced around the room. Then he remembered that her number would be safely stored on the caller ID built into the desk phone.

After carefully writing the number on an index card, he took a drink of water to clear his throat and called her back. He didn't care if he was calling too late. He did not plan to waste another minute.

The phone rang once, twice, three times in succession, and his stomach did a flip-flop. On the fourth ring, the answering machine picked up, and he heard her voice. Her soft Southern accent made him smile.

"Hi, it's Dixie. Leave your number and ..."

Suddenly, he heard a click and a bang and then, "Hello? Hello? This is Dixie. I'm here."

For a moment, he couldn't speak. The words forming in his mind would confuse her. All he wanted to say was *I love you. I've missed you so. Where have you been?*

Instead, he said, "Dixie? It's me, Quinn."

"Oh my, is it you?" she said. "How did you find me? How are you, Quinn? What's going on with you?"

He could tell by the tears in her voice that she was emotional but was trying to be casual. "Dixie, I need to see you. I have so much to tell you. Where are you? When can I pick you up?"

"Quinn, I thought I would never see you again," she said. Her voice sounded soft and sad.

"It's a miracle we found each other. I kept poking at the people at the diner until we finally got a clue. I can't wait much longer. I need to see you."

"I'm free tomorrow afternoon. I work the morning shift."

"Where? At Applebee's?"

"No, not there. I work at a laundry on Thursdays. Until noon. Then, I'm free."

"Just give me an address, and I'll be there."

———

The next morning, Quinn looked at himself in the mirror and frowned. What if he had aged badly, and she didn't find him attractive anymore? He saw a frown line the size of the Grand Canyon between his eyes. His five o'clock shadow now showed around three p.m. His hands were rough from working with lumber all day, and he couldn't remember if he'd worn cologne all those years ago. *Had he? Should he?* He shaved carefully, splashed a little aftershave on his neck and hoped for the best.

Before he left, he sprayed Febreze in the cab of his truck to eliminate the odor of tuna sandwiches, Fritos and Nutter Butter Bars that usually resided in a paper sack on the front seat each day until he could come back and eat lunch.

He set off early in heavy traffic on the long drive to the

north side of Atlanta. He wanted to be early and catch a glimpse of her first before she saw him. Was she as lovely as he remembered, or had his imagination conjured up a fantasy woman with silky, black curls and eyes the color of honey? Sometimes he awoke from dreams of her and doubted that she had ever existed except in his imagination.

He parked around the corner from the front door, shaded his eyes with his hand, and peeked in the expansive windows that lined the front of the twenty-four-hour laundry.

For a few moments, he felt uneasy. What if she had changed her mind? What if she was gone again?

He didn't have to worry for long. Dixie glided around the huge room as if she were wearing ice skates. She stopped at a long metal table. With her back to the window, she pulled clothes from a tall mound of clean laundry and folded each piece carefully. Focused on her task at hand, she didn't look up, and it gave Quinn time to observe her.

She had changed some. The young girl's prettiness had changed to a grown woman's beauty. Her wild, curly black hair was the same, although several inches longer. Her body had matured. Her hips were wider and her breasts fuller. He wasn't sure how she could be any lovelier than he remembered, but she was.

Feeling like a voyeur, he turned away and made his way back to the truck. Then, at eleven-fifty-five, he pulled into a parking space in front of the building. He got out of the pickup and waited outside the door. He wasn't certain who else was inside and did not want to embarrass her.

When she came out, she smiled shyly at first, and then a smile of enchantment touched her lips. They looked into each other's eyes and smiled in earnest.

Later, he could not recall who made the first move, but all at once she was safely in the circle of his arms, and he knew she was exactly where she belonged.

She lived in a clean, nicely furnished one-bedroom apartment, and they spent the afternoon sitting near one another on the soft, brown sofa. Quinn kept looking at her, trying to believe that she was actually there. He would reach for her hand, intertwine his fingers between hers and hold on tightly.

"How did you find me?" she insisted.

"My brother and I did a little investigative work. We started at the diner and got nowhere. Then we went to the trailer park and talked to Mable, who sent us back to Tony, and he mentioned Applebee's."

"I know. He called Lorena and told her to tell me that two guys were asking about me. I thought it might be you but wasn't sure who the second guy was. I told Lorena not to give me up, until I was sure it was you that was looking for me."

"And now that I'm here, do you feel like talking about what happened? I don't want to rush you..." Quinn began.

"You first," Dixie said. "What happened after high school?"

"Well, I came to the diner to give you an invitation to graduation, and I found out you were gone. Without a word. Poof! Up in smoke." His expression clouded in anger. Until that moment, he hadn't realized how mad he had been all these intervening years.

She cowered and looked down. Suddenly, she appeared smaller and more delicate than she had been moments before. Tears gathered in her eyes and her expression showed him how uneasy he had made her.

At once, he hated himself for being such a bully. Here she was after all this time, and he was berating her and being abusive. When had he become The Captain's son? This was not at all how he wanted their reunion to be.

He moved closer to her and gently lifted her chin. "Look at me, Dixie. I am so sorry, so terribly sorry I spoke to you that way. I guess I've been kind of mad at you all along, but I never knew it until now."

The tears spilled down her face and fell on his wrist. When she tried to speak, her voice wavered. "I don't blame you for being mad. I left you without a word, but Quinn—"

"Shhh," he said. "You don't have to explain yourself to me. I know you had a good reason. I wish I could justify why I treated you so badly just now, but I can't. I can't explain it even to myself, but I swear it won't ever happen again. I'm not mad at you, honey, and I'm so happy to see you, to be near you again." His eyes darkened with emotion, and he took her gently into his arms and held her close until she relaxed and tightened her hold around him.

He knew then, without having to be told, that she had been hurt, and it would take time for her to trust again. Whatever had made her run away without looking back was something she was still recovering from, and he needed to give her time and space.

That evening, they went out to a local pizza place she frequented. The red oilcloth checkered table coverings, the white napkins, and the shakers of crushed red pepper and Parmesan cheese gave the place an authentic Italian atmosphere, and the food smelled amazing.

They ordered calzones with saucers of marinara sauce for dipping. When they discovered that they both liked the same wine, they ordered a bottle of Pinot Noir to split.

"A friend of mine used to work here," Dixie said. "We would often get free leftover pizza and eat it together while we studied. It's a good thing my textbooks were well used," she said with laughter in her voice, "because they were smudged with red sauce after I got through with them."

Quinn took a deep breath, took a sip of wine, and then another deep breath. *What in the hell was wrong with him?* He wanted to ask her exactly who this friend was and if they had been a couple. He was jealous of every moment he had not spent with Dixie. This time, he checked his emotional outbreak before it happened. His jaws tightened on the calzone, and he chewed it slowly while waiting for her to continue.

"Lynette is the best study partner I've ever had. Most of the women in my class would rather gossip than get down to business. I don't have any time to waste. I am going to school on a Pell Grant, and they do not have any patience for people whose grades are in the tank."

Quinn's grin stretched across his face. "You're going to college?"

She grinned right back. "Don't look so surprised. Did you think I was going to serve pie the rest of my life?"

He started to reply, but she wasn't finished.

"I have to do it right now. I have no choice. They only gave me five thousand, seventy-five dollars a semester. That doesn't go far enough, and I need extra money for my apartment and food. So I'll work two jobs until I finish up. I am almost finished with all my coursework. After I take the exam to get my license, I'll be ready to go to work."

"What's your major?"

"Nursing. I'm going to be an LVN in pediatrics. I want to help children."

Quinn was so proud of her he felt like the buttons on his chambray shirt were going to burst. "Well, that's amazing, Dixie. Any little person would feel better the moment they saw you."

She ducked her head slightly and gazed up at him through her eyelashes. "What about a big person? How does he feel about me?"

"He feels damn lucky to be anywhere near you." He leaned across the table and his lips came coaxingly down on hers. Her lips were warm and sweet on his, and suddenly he wanted more. So much more.

He put a twenty-dollar bill on the table and stood up. "Let's get out of here, sweetheart. I need to be alone with you."

She didn't hesitate and took his hand and led him toward the door.

CHAPTER 25
QUINN CAMERON

WHEN THEY AWOKE **the next morning wrapped in each other's arms**, Quinn felt like he had died and gone to Heaven. Her black hair spilled across the pillow and onto his chest. She had insisted on keeping the lights off when they undressed and got into bed. He wasn't worried about her shyness. They had time, and he would be patient.

He did not try to hide the fact that he was watching her. Something pulled her attention to him, and she looked up into his eyes and smiled.

"Good morning, love," she said. "Did you sleep well?" She sat up straight in bed. "This mattress isn't the best, but it's all I have right now."

"The mattress is fine," he said. "I could sleep on the floor if I were next to your beautiful self."

"Well, I'm hungry, and I have to be at work by ten."

"I'll take you out for breakfast. Where would you like to go?"

She moved to the bathroom and closed the door behind her. "My usual is toast and coffee. Shall I make you some?"

"Sure."

He heard the water running in the sink and got out of

bed and pulled on his jeans. He had not undressed completely the night before because she came to bed in pajamas that went all the way up to her neck and all the way down to her ankles. It was exceedingly clear that they were going to take things slowly, and that was all right with him. It had to be.

She had to work until six o'clock and her night class started at seven, so he drove back to his shop to get some work done and told her he would be back around nine-thirty or ten.

She was waiting for him when he got back to her place and it occurred to him to ask, "Where's your car?"

She laughed, but it wasn't bitter. "Car? Are you nuts? I ride the bus or walk. It's way too expensive to own a car right now."

He felt terrible. Why did he have to keep putting his foot in his mouth all the time? She had already eaten, but she fixed him a peanut butter and jelly sandwich and poured him a glass of milk. In no time, they were deep in conversation again.

She had so many questions about his travels in Europe, and it was fun to tell her. He carefully chose the adventures he thought she would have enjoyed and edited out the few women who had spent time in his bed. They meant nothing to him, but he wasn't sure she would believe it. He didn't want to say anything that might make her distrust him.

She tried to hide the yawns that came in waves, but he could see how tired she was. "Do you want me to stay, honey, or would you rather that I go home and let you catch up on your rest?"

"Stay with me, Quinn." There was a gentle softness in her voice. "I need to sleep, and if you're here, I won't have to dream about you."

They lay intertwined and shared intimate kisses and whispers, but he could tell that she wasn't ready for more. He had waited this long; he would not ruin things now by acting like a licentious goat.

When daylight came, his heart sank. "Do you have to go to work, Dixie?" He cupped her chin and searched her upturned face. "I've only just found you, and I'm afraid you will disappear on me again." There was a note of pleading in his voice.

The heavy lashes that shadowed her cheeks flew up, and she met his accusing eyes without flinching. "I won't," she said simply. "I swear I won't."

For the next few days, Quinn was waiting for her at the end of every shift. They went out to dinner or picked up takeout food and then went back to her apartment. Quinn sensed her hesitation about making love. Each time he tried to do anything beyond kissing her, an unwelcome tension arose between them.

One night, they lay beside each other on a quilt on the carpeted floor watching a re-run of *Friends* on Netflix. He was trying to calm himself after she had nearly driven him crazy with her kisses and soft, feathery touches. He wanted her so badly it caused a physical pain.

To his surprise, she took his hand and moved it under the waistband of her shorts.

"Feel that," she said.

He wasn't sure what she meant, but he felt a horizontal ridge of hard flesh below her navel. Was it a scar? "Honey, what happened to you?" he asked. His voice was gentle, with no hint of accusation.

"I had a hysterectomy," she said.

He was astonished as he watched the play of emotions on her face. Sadness, anger, and then sadness again washed over her features. Her eyes told him everything she felt.

He lifted a wayward strand of black hair and tucked it behind her ear. "I'm sorry, Dixie girl. I'm so sorry." He could smell the scent of strawberries in her shampoo. Everything about her was so lovely and so sad.

She gulped hard as hot tears slipped down her cheeks. "I didn't want to do it, but my organs were so damaged, the doctor said I was going to bleed to death if I didn't."

She turned into his arms and held on tight. He held her as sobs wracked her body. "I wanted to have babies. I always dreamed of babies."

Quinn didn't know what to say to make it better, so he tightened his arms around her and waited for her to cry it out. He wanted her to explain. He had a million questions, but all he said was, "Hush now, baby. It's okay. I'm here. It's okay."

———

One night, while they lay in bed, Quinn stroked her hair. Her head fit the space between his shoulder and his chest perfectly. He knew he could not go on this way much longer. She needed to free herself of whatever was holding her back before they could become a couple.

"Dixie?"

"Yes?"

"You know I love you, right?"

"I do know it, and I love you too. I should tell you more often. I have loved you since the night you insisted on walking me home from the diner. You made me feel special."

"So," he said carefully, "you won't think I'm being pushy if I ask you about something that has been bothering me?"

She withdrew from his arms and moved to the right and propped her head on her hand. "Okay, I guess not."

"Well," he inhaled and then blew out his breath, tickling the tendrils of her hair, "I thought we were falling in love. I'd never been as happy in my life as I was with you, and then you were gone. I need to know what I did wrong to make you leave me without a word." His heart started beating errati-cally. He was terrified beyond measure, she would get out of the bed and leave again. Then what would he do?

Her expression grew still and serious, but he saw no sign of anger. She sat up straight and sat cross-legged on the bed beside him. She reached for his hand and gripped it. "Promise me you will not throw on your clothes and run from me until you have given my words time to sink in. It's not a pretty story, Quinn."

A flicker of apprehension coursed through him and he, too, sat up in the bed and tried to look confident and support-ive. "I promise. I'm not going anywhere."

Her eyes flooded with tears, and then she sniffed and took a deep breath and began. It was as if she had gone back in time. Everything about her body language changed and the confident woman she was now became a frightened young girl again. Her voice became a broken whisper.

"I didn't have a car back then either," she said. "I got a ride to school with another girl who lived in a big double-wide, but I had to walk to work and walk home. I rented that little trailer near the diner so I could be near where I worked."

She stopped talking and looked at him. He didn't know how she wanted him to respond, so he simply said, "Go on, honey, you're doing fine."

"It was dark on that walk. Well, you remember, don't you?"

He nodded. The memory was clear. At the time, it had worried him, and he hated remembering it even now.

"Well, I was on the way home. It was about eleven o'clock. We'd had a big crowd that night. The high school kids had come by for a late dinner after graduation rehearsal. I don't know why they picked that night. Maybe they had been drinking all day. I didn't know them. They were strangers to me. Couldn't pick them out of a line-up even though I tried."

Her words flowed now like rushing water in a mountain

stream running downhill. Nothing was going to stop her from telling this story. He sat still as a statue, hoping not to interrupt her momentum.

Her voice cracked, but she continued. "Three of them. There were three. They slugged me in the face, stuck a filthy rag in my mouth, and dragged me over behind the bushes. It was dark. No moon at all. One of them held my hands over my head and one of them pulled my legs apart and the third one raped me."

She took both his hands in hers and squeezed. "I fought them, I kicked, I bucked, and I nearly choked to death trying to scream. Couldn't do it. No chance at all."

Tears were streaming down her face now, blinding her eyes and distorting her voice. "Then they traded positions and took turns. One of them went back for seconds. By that time, I was completely limp. I had no fight left in me."

Quinn could not stand seeing her this way. His eyes filled with tears. Taking a chance, he pulled her into his arms and rubbed small, gentle circles on her back.

"That was my mistake, I guess. I stopped fighting."

He held her closer and whispered into her ear. "You made no mistakes, Dixie. You were so brave. You did the best you could. You were a gentle woman assaulted by three large, vicious animals. If I ever find them, I will kill them."

"No, please. Don't say that. I have finally reached a peaceful place in my life, and I have moved on. What they did to me altered the course of my life forever, but they did not ruin me. I am going to be a nurse and help children like me. I will seek children who need me, and I will help them."

"What about your parents?" he asked. He had wanted to ask this question for so many years.

"Dead," she said without emotion. "Killed in a car accident when I was sixteen. It was their fault, so there was no insurance money. They were drunk and took out a whole family."

"And you? Didn't you have anywhere to go?"

"I have an uncle. Lives on a houseboat on the Chatta-hoochee."

"Did he offer to take you in?"

"He had no way to locate me. I made sure of that. He's a drunk and a pervert. I didn't feel safe with him even as a child. My parents didn't believe me when I told them some of the things he tried to do, so I made sure we were never alone."

Quinn wanted to tell her how sorry he was about the terrible, unfortunate circumstances she had dealt with in her life, but anything he said would not come out right. He wanted her to feel his love, not his pity. All he said was, "Shh, baby. It's okay. I'm here."

She let the rest of her story out in drips and spurts as if too much at one time could drown her. Clearly, she was damaged and hurt. Sometimes, he wished he could call Hannah and ask her for advice, but he felt that would betray Dixie's confidence and invade her privacy.

He knew how to repair furniture and fill in a crack or a seam, but what did a carpenter know about mending hearts? Not a damn thing.

The next night, she was better. It was as if she had fallen through thin ice and discovered that the water was not as cold as she expected it to be. He thought she had realized that she could survive the ordeal she had been through.

She took her time in the bathroom before coming to bed. He was getting his pillow settled and preparing to turn off the light when she opened the door. In the soft light from the bedroom lamp, he could see that she was wearing a short gown. He could see through the thin material, and it looked like she had nothing else on.

Before he could be sure, she moved into the bed beside him. Gathering her into his arms, he held her snugly. She did not move away and lifted her face up to his, inviting him to kiss her.

His heart was hammering foolishly. Was this an invitation? Was she ready to make love? He had to know. "Are you sure, Dixie? Do you want me to ...?"

His last words were smothered on her lips as he felt her lips touch his like a whisper. As he roused her passion, his own grew stronger. His hands explored the soft lines of her back, her waist, and her hips and she responded in kind.

He reached across her, intending to turn off the lamp, but she stopped him. "Leave it on, sweetheart. I've been waiting a lifetime for this night."

CHAPTER 26
BRYCE CAMERON

"HEY," **Bryce said, looking up from his computer.** "Packing all done?"

Hannah crossed the room and leaned down to give him a kiss. "Yep, all done."

"I'm sorry I can't leave with you tomorrow, Doc. Even though you're not saying it, I know that you're nervous. Well, not nervous, but apprehensive maybe."

"Know me that well, do you?"

"I know you don't like water and being on a cruise ship surrounded by water isn't your idea of a fantastic vacation, even if it is for only two days."

"I will have to put on my big girl panties and make the most of it. Besides, you'll join me in St. Thomas when the ship stops there, and I don't have to get back on. We can fly home after we have enjoyed a real honeymoon."

"Whose crazy idea was it anyway to have a cruise filled with shrinks? I don't know why you couldn't have given your presentation on dry land."

Hannah shrugged and smiled. "It is what it is. It's about time I got over my phobia. The institute felt this idea would attract a large group of medical professionals, and it has. The cruise is fully booked."

"I can always tell my publisher that I have a prior commitment. I don't have to go to New York tomorrow." He got up and pulled Hannah into his arms. "Mmm, you smell wonderful and look even better. What's the occasion?"

"You must go to New York. You need to get everything in place for your book tour. Your book is coming out next week. The occasion is that we need to spend some time together tonight. I thought we could walk down and get something to eat and maybe have a little wine. Have an early vacation meal."

"That sounds tempting. But I get to pick the restaurant. Do I get to have dessert?"

"As a matter of fact, you do. I have something in mind with whipped cream after we get home tonight."

Bryce laughed and leaned down for an intimate kiss and a promise of things to come.

————

The waiter brought the house special, a pizza loaded with mushrooms, sausage, and pepperoni, and oozing with melted cheese. Bryce leaned back and watched Hannah pull an ample piece from the platter and bite into the gooey, thick crust.

"What?" she said, looking at him through squinted eyes.

He reached across his plate and picked out his own perfect slice. Taking a bite, he wrapped the sticky strings of cheese around his finger. Hannah was still giving him the eye when she said, "You're not so graceful yourself there, fellow."

Bryce finished the bite and said, "I absolutely adore you, Mrs. Cameron."

"What, you love me because of my bad manners? My

mother's not looking over my shoulder, and I happen to love pizza. And don't think I didn't notice that you picked this place because of our first date. I was on my best behavior then. I wanted to impress you. I even ate my pizza with a fork."

"You did not. You didn't even like me," he said as he wiped a dab of sauce that clung to her lip with his index finger. "But I liked you. I thought all night long about how it would be between the two of us. All I got was a goodnight kiss, and you know I wanted more. So now you're telling me since we're an old married couple, you can let it all hang out?"

Bryce laughed and took in the beautiful lines of her face. Her complexion was unusually dark for her having blond hair, and she had a tiny mole at the corner of her full mouth, a mouth that was always smiling. All her features were a contradiction, but when put together they were bewitching. He knew this was true because from the time he'd looked down into her hazel eyes, he'd been under her spell.

"You betcha," she said and took a sip of her wine. You know I kind of adore you too."

"Just kinda?"

"Bryce," she said, setting down her wine and grabbing his hand. "I'm so happy it's scary. I listen to people's troubles all day long and wonder how I got so lucky. To find you and to be so content. I am truly blessed. Do you know what I've been thinking?"

"No, what?" he asked. He knew with absolute certainty he'd give her anything she wanted. Except give her up. He would never do that willingly.

"We've talked about moving to Georgia at the end of next semester so I can work at the institute. There's something else I'd like us to consider seriously," She moved her hands nervously and bit her lip. "I know we just got married and everything is so new, but I want to have a baby. I don't want to wait until my career is established. Not like my parents did. I want us both to be young enough to enjoy our children."

Bryce considered her question before he responded. They had not talked about having children, and he assumed it would be one of those things for the future. Now that he thought about it, he couldn't think of any reason to say no.

"I know you would be a fantastic mother. I'm not sure what kind of a father I would be, but I would have to be better than The Captain. I've learned all the things not to do. Aren't you psychologists always saying that we either repeat what our parents did, or we do the exact opposite? Please, Lord, let me be the exact opposite."

"Bryce, you are an honorable, generous, and caring man. You will be a great father. We will be great parents."

"Well then, I guess it's settled." He picked up his wine glass and said, "To the future little Cameron." They clinked glasses and laughed together. He couldn't wait to get started.

"I guess we will need to plan all kinds of romantic things for our trip."

"Like what?" he said, wiggling his eyebrows.

"Well, yes definitely that," she whispered, "but also lying on the beach and watching the surf and drinking those cute little concoctions with oranges and lemons and umbrellas."

"Oh yeah, that's manly."

"I won't tell if you won't." She punched him on the arm and grinned. "Okay, I'll drink the fruity stuff and you can stick to beer."

"Thank you. Men everywhere commend you for your insight. What do you have planned for tomorrow?"

"The ship leaves at four in the afternoon. The plane gets in at noon, so that should give me plenty of time to get on board and settled. I will call you when I get to my room. Then, I'm going to listen to a relaxation tape and pretend that I'm not traveling at turtle speed on an ocean."

They finished their pizza, and Bryce paid the check. He

took a final gulp of his wine and set the glass on the red checkered tablecloth. He wasn't ready for the evening to end. It was silly because he knew he would see Hannah in two days, but he was still tempted to postpone his trip and leave with her tomorrow. He shook off the feeling he had and stood to help her out of her chair.

They walked home holding hands, acting like the newlyweds they were. Bryce couldn't ever remember being happier unless it was yesterday or the day before. Life couldn't get any better. He was writing feverishly with ideas flowing freely. It was all because of the woman beside him. Doc was right. This was scary. He shivered, but it wasn't from the cool fall night. His late grandmother would have said someone just walked over his grave.

CHAPTER 27
HANNAH CAMERON

HANNAH PLACED **her cosmetic bag on the bathroom counter** and watched helplessly as a glass jar filled with rose-colored blush smashed onto the floor, painting the tile and much of her bare feet a bright pink. "Damn," she said, reaching down to clean up the mess. She stuck her feet in the shower and was drying them off when she heard the soft knock on her cabin door.

Who in the world could that be? She didn't know anyone on board. For a moment, she had the crazy thought that Bryce had canceled his trip and was here to surprise her. Her heart racing, she dashed across the room and jerked open the door with a huge grin on her face.

Her hopes were dashed, and her face fell in disappointment when she saw Hans Dreschler standing in the hall. "Dr. Dreschler, what are you doing here? I wasn't expecting to see you." She looked up and down the corridor for anyone that might be with him. "I didn't see your name on the program, so I assumed you wouldn't be on board."

"Oh, it was a last-minute decision. I didn't tell anyone I would be here," he said. "Were you expecting someone?" Hannah shook her head no and tried to hide her dismay.

Hans brushed his fingers across his mustache and continued. "I wanted to let you know the institute has had nothing but positive feedback from your lectures. I also wanted to invite you to dinner to discuss your future."

"My future?" Hannah asked with a frown. "I don't understand."

"Your employment, my dear. When you join the institute next summer."

Hannah felt silly standing in the doorway while talking and realized she should invite him in, but she was uneasy about having a man in her room who wasn't her husband. Good grief. I'm too old-fashioned, she thought. Then her good manners prevailed, and she said, "Would you like to come in?"

"Yes, thank you." He was a large man and took up most of the space in the cabin. Hannah pointed to the built-in sofa and said, "Please sit down. I was putting my things away. Sorry for the mess." She looked around at her open suitcase and clothes strewn across the bed. Thank goodness she'd already put up her underwear.

"I can wait if you want to change," Hans said. Hannah watched his eyes roam around the room and take in her open suitcase and papers stacked on the coffee table. She felt the same discomfort she'd had when she'd first met the man but decided European men were probably different from Americans.

"I can't offer you anything to drink," she said, pointing to the unstocked mini bar. I wasn't planning on having any guests. She hoped he would get her meaning without being insulted.

"No, that is fine. We can get something to drink before dinner."

"I'm sorry, Dr. Dreschler, I didn't mean to give you the impression I was going to have dinner with you. I ate a late lunch after the plane landed, and I'm going to relax tonight.

After I give my husband a call, I'm going to bed early. I have a long day tomorrow." No way was she going to encourage him. Even if she had been single, he was way too old for her and gave her the creeps.

She wasn't sure from his expression if he was angry, but he didn't seem to be pleased. "Ah yes, I heard you had recently married. I suppose congratulations are in order. I didn't realize that you were engaged when we talked in Savannah."

"I wasn't then. It happened later. Is that a problem?"

"No. It's only that in the past with my other female proteges, I've found that once they got married, then came babies and well, you know, the work suffers."

He would be upset if she told him she'd had a conversation with Bryce about babies last night. Then she decided it was none of his business and maybe she'd have to rethink her priorities. Her family would come first.

"My husband, Bryce, was going to join me on the voyage but had to go to New York to meet with his public relations people. He's an author, and his new book will be released soon."

Hannah didn't know why she needed to explain Bryce's absence, but she felt she should. She also felt like she was in elementary school and was trying to explain her behavior to Mrs. Woodberry, her tyrannical Spanish teacher. She hated Mrs. Woodberry. After she cleared her throat she said, "He'll be joining me day after tomorrow when we stop in St Thomas."

Hans rose and said, "Well then, I'll be going. Maybe we can get together later when your husband arrives. Day after tomorrow, you said?"

"Yes, but we don't plan to finish the cruise. My last presentation ends at five tomorrow, so I'll be getting off the next morning. We are going to explore the island and have an extended stay before we fly home."

"I'm sure I'll meet him at a later time."

Before he reached the door, Hannah said, "I'm sorry, I should have asked. How is your wife doing?"

"My wife is doing well. She is in Europe now getting some additional therapy. She has made miraculous strides, and I'm happy to say she will be back by my side very soon. I can't tell you how much I have missed her."

Hannah chided herself for her previous thoughts. Maybe the man wasn't trying to put the moves on her and was simply being polite. He obviously loved his wife. She leaned against the door after he left and sighed. She wanted Bryce. She picked up her phone and called him.

The phone rang several times, and she was ready to leave a message when he finally answered. Breathlessly he said, "Hey, babe. I was in the shower. Wish you were here. New York is a fascinating place. Would be even better with you."

"Are you going out?"

"Nah, I just got back from the gym here at the hotel. Paula, the publicist, asked me to dinner with several of the staff, but I begged off. I plan to have room service, watch a little news, and go to bed. What about you?"

"I got an invitation to go to dinner too, but I'm not going anywhere. I guess you and I are in the same funk. I'm going to prepare for tomorrow and get some sleep. When I heard the knock on my cabin door, I thought it might be you."

"Oh, babe, I'm sorry. See? I should have rescheduled this meeting. I can cancel and leave first thing in the morning."

"You're silly. You'd have to sit around until the next day when we dock. I can wait, but I miss you so much. I don't know what's wrong with me. I lived my adult life taking care of myself, but…"

"I feel the same way. Like we're two parts of a coin," he murmured.

"You romantic you."

"That's me. So, should I be jealous of this invitation?"

"No, he has a wife he adores."

"What difference does that make? You're a little naïve, Doc. There isn't a man alive who wouldn't be interested in you. If you were here, I could nibble on your neck and show you."

The talk turned kinky and after several minutes, Bryce told her he was going back to take another shower, this time a cold one, and she laughed and said she had boring lecture notes to review.

———

Hannah was on her third and last lecture for the day on *The Possibilities of Synthetic Hormones in the Treatment of Certain Psychological Pathologies*. She'd been pleased to see Dreschler sitting in the audience for her first lecture, puzzled when he attended her second, and now she was apprehensive when she noticed him in the back of the room again.

The first time, she assumed he was interested in seeing her presentation style because, after all, he had contracted with her to give lectures for his institute. But he surely knew all about the content of the lecture since he'd read her rather lengthy dissertation. Now, when she looked out into the faces of the men and women, it disturbed her to see him sitting among them.

She lost her train of thought and looked at her PowerPoint presentation to regain some composure, and when she looked up again, he was gone. Hannah breathed a sigh of relief and continued with her lecture.

She was gathering up her handouts and shutting down the projector when she heard a voice calling her name. She'd neglected to turn on the overhead lights, and the dim light coming from the corridor cast a shadow across the open doorway. She couldn't see his face, but she recognized the accented voice.

"Dr. Dreschler, you startled me. Please turn on the lights," she said. "I saw you sitting in on all my lectures today. Is there a problem?"

He came across the room and gripped her hands. "No, my dear, no problem. You were magnificent. I was in awe."

Hannah frowned and pulled her hands free. "I don't see how. You've read my paper, and I said nothing new today. I would have expected my lecture to bore you."

"Not in the least. You are a beautiful woman and men will always enjoy listening to you." He leaned close and Hannah could smell alcohol on his breath.

She turned and put all her notes and handouts into her briefcase and said, "Dr. Dreschler, you are making me extremely uncomfortable. I wish you would only interact with me professionally. I am married, and even if I weren't, I'm not attracted to you in that way."

"Perhaps I misread your interest. It looked as if you were talking only to me all day. Come have dinner with me. I promise to be on my best behavior. I've opened a bottle of Chateau Margaux 2009. I assure you, the glass I had was exquisite."

"I don't even know what that means. If I inadvertently gave you any idea that I was interested in a relationship, I apologize. I'm not interested. I love my husband. I'm happy, which is more than I can say about you. I thought you missed your wife."

"I love my Juliette, but she isn't here. It's only for the night. As the French would say, *liaison amoureuse*. I came on this little cruise so I could be with you."

"I don't understand French, and I don't understand you. Is this why you gave me the job? You're hoping to hop into bed with me. Well, no thank you, Dr. Dreschler. I am not interested. I will be sending in my letter to terminate our association." She pushed past him and headed for the door.

"That would be a mistake, Hannah. I have much influence

in the profession. I would hate to see your research mocked as a sham. It would only take one word from me to make that happen."

"You're threatening me? If I don't sleep with you, you'll ruin me? Well, go ahead and try." Hannah slammed the door and stalked down the hall. How dare that egotistical jerk try to intimidate me, She couldn't wait to talk to Bryce and to get off this ship.

CHAPTER 28
BRYCE CAMERON

BRYCE CAUGHT **the earliest available flight to Miami out of La Guardia,** and then he planned to hop on a commuter plane for St. Thomas. Hannah hadn't called last night, which was unusual. They talked every day. He hadn't been worried at first because he knew she may have finished late or have become involved in conversations with colleagues.

He called her this morning as soon as he woke up and left a message, and then twice more before he had to turn off his phone on the plane. He was concerned. It wasn't like Hannah.

When the plane landed, and he could take his phone off airplane mode, it blew up with five phone calls and messages from numbers he did not recognize, but nothing from Hannah. He listened to a man's deep, gruff voice and felt all the blood rush from his head.

"Mr. Cameron, this is Lieutenant James Kearny with the United States Coast Guard. Please call me back immediately." The next message was similar, and the final message was that officers from the Coast Guard would meet his plane in Miami.

When Bryce walked out, he saw three men with bright white uniforms standing a few feet outside the jetway scanning the passengers. Bryce's mouth was dry, but his palms were sweating. He walked up to the men and said, "I'm Bryce Cameron. What is going on? What's happened to Hannah?"

The larger of the two men said, "If you'll please follow us, we'll go someplace where we can talk."

This must be the man who had left the message, Bryce thought. He recognized the deep, gravelly voice. "I don't want to go somewhere and talk. I want to talk right now. Where is Hannah? What has happened? You're Lt. Kearny, right? The one that called me?"

"Yes, I'm Lt. Kearny and ..." he rubbed his hands across his face and said, "we don't know. It appears that sometime last evening your wife disappeared from the ship."

Bryce needed to sit down before his legs collapsed beneath him. Feeling for the hard, plastic chair behind him he awkwardly took a seat. "No, that can't be correct. What do you mean she disappeared?"

"We believe she fell overboard."

He stood up and pushed his hands deep into his pockets. "No, that's not possible. Hannah is afraid of water. She would never have gone anywhere close to a rail."

"She was expected for breakfast this morning with some of the other presenters. When she didn't show up, someone went to look for her. Her personal effects were still in her room. The cruise ship's security detail conducted a complete search of all the staterooms, but she was not on board."

Bryce felt like he was going to be sick. He hadn't felt this helpless since he was in Afghanistan, trying to keep the guy beside him from bleeding to death. His first reaction was denial. "I don't believe you. I'm sorry. There must be a mistake. She probably got off and didn't tell anyone. Hannah... wouldn't..."

The older man shook his head. "All passengers are electronically logged out when they leave the ship. There is no record of Dr. Brody leaving. The Coast Guard began searching the waters as soon as we were notified. Sometimes, passengers have too much to drink and get careless, or perhaps they are despondent…"

Bryce interrupted him with a resounding, "No, not Doc. She wouldn't do that. And she doesn't get drunk or even tipsy." Bryce rocked back and forth on his heels, trying to create a positive scenario in his mind. "There are surveillance cameras everywhere. Surely they'll show that she didn't jump."

"Unfortunately, there was a malfunction, and the cameras didn't record last evening. The crew wasn't aware of the glitch until the ship's captain asked to see the tapes."

"I don't believe this." Bryce ran his hands through his hair as tears flooded his eyes. "Doc," he whispered and looked up into the solemn eyes of the lieutenant.

———

A few hours later, Bryce looked around Hannah's cabin on the ship. There was no sign of a struggle, and a black suit and red blouse she had probably worn the day before hung in the closet. Her robe, the ratty, ugly, baby blue one, was hanging on the back of the bathroom door. He often teased her about it, but she said she'd had it since high school, and she liked it. Why spend the money on a new one? He grasped it with both hands and buried his face in the soft cotton while breathing in the scent of her. "Oh, God," he cried. "You can't be dead. What am I going to do without you?"

He looked up when he heard voices and was amazed when he saw his brother walking into the room along with their father. "Quinn? Dad?"

Surprisingly, his father engulfed him in a firm embrace. An inconceivable act from this man.

"What are you doing here?" he asked, looking over his father's shoulder at his brother.

The Captain stepped back, and it appeared he was trying to regain his composure. It was the first time Bryce had ever seen his father at a loss for words. He cleared his throat and turned toward Quinn. "Your brother called me after he spoke with you, and we were able to get on a transport immediately."

Bewildered, Bryce said, "How?"

"I have a few connections with the Navy. I spoke with the Coast Guard, and I have the coordinates for the ship's path. Considering the currents and wind factors, I have a pretty good estimate of where Hannah could be. I've got a helicopter on standby, and we can leave immediately to search for her." Looking up at Bryce, he said, "I assume that is what you would like to do?"

"Dad, I don't know what to say. I..." Bryce tried to hold himself together. He'd never cried in front of The Captain. Not even as a little boy. It simply wasn't done. He pinched the bridge of his nose and took a deep breath. "Is there a chance that we can find her?"

"I don't deal in chances. If she's there, we will find her," his father said in his no-nonsense voice. This was the man Bryce knew best. The take charge, take no prisoners, military officer. This was the man he needed, and, in-spite-of all the man's faults, he loved.

The rich blue of the choppy ocean waves was transformed into murky gray as the bright orange sun sunk into the line where sky met water. Bryce's eyes stung as he rubbed them, weary from the day's exhaustive search of the bleak, endless ocean. Hannah wasn't there, and he realized she'd never been there. The odds of finding her alive and floating in the ocean were miniscule, if not impossible. His father, a practical and unemotional man, had offered his eldest son the only means of comfort he knew how to give.

Bryce leaned forward and looked at his father sitting in the seat next to the pilot. The Captain's eyes met his, and he saw the truth in those eyes and in those of his brother Quinn who was seated beside him in the back. This had been a fool's mission to ease Bryce's pain. He would always know that he had done everything in his power to find her, and that his family loved him and would always stand with him. Tears rushed to his eyes as he gathered his emotions and said, "She's gone, Dad. Let's go back."

CHAPTER 29
BRYCE CAMERON

BRYCE COULD SMELL THE COFFEE, **but it left no taste on his tongue.** In fact, the only breakfast food he had kept down since that fateful phone call was a handful of orange slices. Somehow, citrus fooled his taste buds enough that he could swallow without gagging.

When his phone rang, he considered not answering it but decided on the fourth ring to pick it up. He didn't recognize the number on the caller ID. When he spoke, it came out as a whispered croak. "Hello."

"That you, Bryce?" The voice boomed and shattered the silence that had filled the kitchen of his townhome. Bryce wasn't sure who was calling, but whoever it was spoke too loudly. It hurt his head.

"Who else would it be?" he said. He sounded grumpier than he intended.

"Oh, it is you. Silly me. I wasn't sure if you would be home."

Bryce almost said, "Where else would I be," but reconsidered. This guy sounded friendly.

"Not to seem rude, but who is this?" Bryce asked.

"Oh, damn. I'm sorry. This is Bill Allen speaking."

Silence.

"Uncle Bill to you."

All at once, Bryce could picture the man. His most striking feature was his jet-black hair salted with a few strands of gray. He had an athletic build and an infectious smile. Bryce had liked him at once when they first met.

"Oh, hello, Uncle Bill. I'm sorry I didn't recognize your voice or your number."

"Well, why would you? I've never called you before, now have I?"

Bryce didn't know what to say. He wasn't up to taking part in light banter.

"I thought I would call to see how you're doing. I know you and my sister and brother-in-law are at odds right now, and I thought you could use an ally in the family."

That was putting it mildly, Bryce thought. Hannah's parents were furious with him. He sank onto one of the bar stools at the breakfast counter. "Then, you agree with me? About not having a funeral?"

"Well, let's put it this way. I agree it is up to you and only you to make that decision."

"What is your opinion?" Bryce said. He wanted to know, because sometimes he felt as if he were being selfish. He clarified that there would be no funeral because there was no body to bury, and there would be no memorial service because no one had yet convinced him that she was dead. She was gone, no doubt, but he could not bring himself to believe that she would never return. Not yet.

"I think that as her husband and next-of-kin only you can make that decision."

"You said that already."

"I did. That's how I feel."

"What would you do if you were me?"

"Hell, son. I have no idea. She was my favorite and only niece. I loved her something fierce, but how I feel can't touch how you're feeling right now. I won't judge you, and I didn't call you to give you any trouble. I wanted to say hello and let you know if you ever want to call me … maybe to talk about her, I'll be here. Or if you're especially lonesome, you let me know and I'll fly up there and see you."

Those last words were just too kind and too much for Bryce to handle. Tears ran down his face as he disconnected the call.

———

Going anywhere proved to be a challenge for Bryce. Leaving the house meant taking several steps that he had neglected for the last few months. After he took a shower, he looked in the mirror at the man he had become. His unshaven face did not look handsome like those actors on TV who let their five o'clock shadow grow for a couple of days. He looked unkempt. He looked miserable.

After lathering his face and shaving, he decided it was time to get a haircut. He dressed in comfortable chinos and a button-down shirt that he left untucked because that's the way Hannah liked him to look. He had quickly discovered that he could not return to any of the places that they had frequented together. People asked about Hannah.

"Where's your lovely wife? Going solo today?"

He couldn't invent a good answer, so he simply found a new supermarket, a new barber, and eventually, when all his clothes were dirty, a new dry cleaner shop. Then, he sat in the car and tried to figure out if going to these new places meant he was closing out the Hannah chapter of his life. If so, then the life he wanted to live was over.

Then there were the days he got angry. Angry with Hannah for leaving him and going on the cruise and even more furious with himself for not being truthful and asking her to stay. He was even irrationally angry with Doctor

Dreschler or inviting her to speak while she was still a newly-wed. The man should have been more considerate.

But mostly he was miserably sad, anguished, and without hope for any kind of happy life without his beautiful Hannah. Bryce didn't know what he would do with the timeshare condo they owned in Vail. They had bought it hoping to learn to ski, and if that didn't work out, they had planned to sit in the clubhouse before a roaring fire while drinking hot chocolate and watch other people glide down the slopes.

———

On Thursday, he awoke from a nightmare. Hannah was reaching out to him. Her hair was wet, and she was crying. He woke up gasping for air, and it took a long time for him to calm down and fully awaken. When his phone rang, he jumped. He reached for it and saw *Denver Police Department* flash on the caller ID.

"Hello?"

"Bryce, it's Jesse Silva."

Bryce sat up straight and listened intently. "Yes, how are you, Jesse? Do you have news?"

"I wanted you to know that I checked on Lucy like you asked me to."

"And?"

"She got loose for a few days, but they found her, and she is safely back in custody at the mental hospital."

"When? When did this happen?"

"It was right before Hannah disappeared."

"Have you questioned her? Does she know where Hannah might be?" Bryce's hopes soared.

He could hear Jesse's voice soften. "She's not involved. She doesn't know anything."

"How can you be sure?"

"Because she didn't leave Colorado. She was nowhere near that ship."

"And you know that because?"

"Because she went to her sister's house, and her sister said she was never out of her sight. The whole thing only lasted a few hours. Her sister couldn't wait to get rid of her. She called the hospital herself and turned Lucy in."

———

An hour later, Bryce sat on a bench in the park near his house and took deep, calming breaths. As the month of October marched to a close, daylight since the month began had shortened by over an hour. For the most part, the days were warm and sunny, but the smells and sights of fall were everywhere. The hummingbirds that buzzed around the feeder on the back deck were gone for the year, and the Canadian geese would soon start their journey south. Winter sometimes arrived like the switch of a light bulb and snow clouds would gather in the Rockies.

He still wasn't sure he could stay here through the winter. Thoughts of how they had met on the plane, his time in the mountain cabin in the snow, and then how he went to Hannah's office and their relationship began flooded his mind. Now, when his chest hurt and his pulse raced, he was sure a doctor would say it was indigestion or a panic attack, but he knew better. He could feel his heart breaking.

CHAPTER 30
BRYCE CAMERON

WHEN THE PHONE RANG, **Bryce closed the lid on his Mac** and reached for the phone. Sometimes distractions made him cross when he was working, but he always liked to hear his brother's ringtone. Quinn wasn't much for conversation, so when he called, it was a special treat to talk to him.

"Bryce, it's good to hear your voice. How are you?"

"Fine."

There were a few moments of empty air before Quinn said, "How are you really?"

"What do you think?" Bryce knew his voice sounded sad and tired, but he couldn't help it. Then he tried to cheer things up a notch. "Brother of mine," Bryce said, "what has she done this time?"

"Who? Nothing. Why would you say that."

"Because if it's in the middle of the day when you call me, it's usually because Mom made you mad, and you want moral support for calling her names in your head."

Quinn laughed. Bryce could hear the relief in his voice. "Funny you should say that," he said. "I actually do need your support."

"You broke? Spend all your money on Dixie Lee?"

"No, you jerk. I don't need money, but I have some big news."

"Tell me."

"Well, you know that Dixie and I have been together for a while now, and things are going great. In fact, they are going so well we have moved in together."

"That doesn't surprise me. You've waited a long time to find her, and I'm sure you don't want to waste any time getting on with your lives."

"She's only got a few weeks of school left, and then she's moving to my place. She's already got a job offer at Children's Healthcare. I'm building an apartment on the top floor of the shop."

"That's great news. Will her commute to work be a problem?"

"Nope. Short drive. I can take her and pick her up, until we get her a car."

"Well, that's great news, brother. So, what did you mean about needing my support?"

Bryce was silent for a moment.

"You still there?"

"Yes, I was trying to figure out the best way to tell Justine and The Captain."

Bryce scratched his head and thought for a second. "Well, why not take them to an expensive, posh restaurant to tell them? You know how Justine hates to make a scene in public. We can't predict what they will say, but at least there won't be any raising of voices and slamming of doors."

"Now that's a good idea."

"Are you sure Dixie can handle two hard asses like our parents?"

"She's handled way worse than anything they could dish out. She's a survivor."

"Okay. Tell me when, and I'll be there. You can pick me up at the airport and the three of us will go to the restaurant together. Anyway, I want to meet Dixie before they do. I've heard about her for so many years, I hope she lives up to the hype."

"Oh, she will. You have no idea."

Bryce wondered what his brother meant but would not dare to ask. He couldn't wait to get back to Atlanta. Being in Denver without Hannah was getting harder on him every day.

───────

When Quinn pulled up in front of the passenger loading area at the airport, Bryce opened the back door and tossed in his duffel bag. He hadn't packed much and didn't intend to stay any longer than it took to help his brother introduce his girl-friend to their difficult parents. He started to slide in when Quinn said, "Sit up here with me."

"Where's the lovely lady?" he said as he sat down in the passenger seat beside his brother.

"She's working the day shift today at the hospital, but you will meet her soon. I have to pick her up in an hour."

"So, what bothers you about this dinner?" Bryce said.

"I'm sure our parents will show their true colors and act like two elitist jerks. Anything different would astonish me."

"Is Dixie prepared?"

"That's just it. I don't know whether it would be better to tell her what to expect or to let it unfold. Or, if the timing was perfect you..." He stopped talking and smiled a crooked, little-boy smile.

"Oh, you want me to do it, huh? Make me the bad guy."

"Not the bad guy, but you could reinforce what I have already told her about Justine and The Captain. It sounds so whiny when I talk about it. Sometimes I'm afraid that Dixie thinks I am making the unhappy events in my childhood sound worse than they actually were."

Bryce did not comment. Anything he said could be taken the wrong way. He sometimes thought Quinn had let things get under his skin that were not as damaging as his brother thought they were. But then, what did he know? Until recently, he had remained on the straight and narrow path his parents envisioned, and it had still been difficult at times. He would not judge his brother. Especially not now that Quinn was finally doing what he wanted to do and had found the lost love of his life.

———

By the end of the afternoon, Bryce was completely enchanted with Dixie Lee King. She was not only beautiful and charming but also so down-to-earth and friendly. She would make a wonderful addition to their family. It broke his heart to think that she would never get to know Hannah. He knew the two women, who were worlds apart in experiences, would have found common ground and bonded instantly. His parents were another matter altogether.

"FYI," Bryce began carefully, "our parents are not the easiest of people to warm up to. Quinn and I have been around them for years, and they still don't like us much."

Dixie's eyes grew openly amused. "You and Quinn are both trying to prepare me for an uncomfortable evening, aren't you?"

"Well, yes. We don't want you to think that our parents' deplorable behavior will have anything to do with you. They are difficult with everyone."

"Please don't worry," she said. "They don't have to approve of me. Quinn has assured me he will still love me, even if they don't find me worthy."

Bryce coughed. "You said that, Quinn? You said she might not be worthy?"

"No, I did not," Quinn said. "You made that up, Dixie."

"Those were not your words, sweetheart, but that was surely your meaning."

Silence filled the room for a few minutes until Quinn said, "Well, we'd better get going. If we get caught in traffic, we'll be late and get off to a bad start."

"I won't be but a minute," Dixie said.

When she left the room, Bryce turned to his brother. "You are going to scare her off. For Pete's sake, the folks aren't that bad."

"We'll see about that, won't we, big brother?"

———

Quinn and Dixie walked slightly ahead of Bryce on the walkway in front of the vast tan and beige brick building with white southern columns that was one of Atlanta's most prestigious country clubs. The Captain had come from money. Old money. And early in their marriage, Justine had insisted they join "the club."

They walked into the building and down the long staircase. Their steps echoed against the marble floors. At the bottom, Quinn pulled Dixie toward the exquisitely carved wooden doors that led to one of the private dining halls reserved for weddings and other social functions. The doors had always enthralled Quinn. Bryce thought that perhaps his brother's love of woodworking had probably begun right here. He doubted Justine would appreciate the irony.

He noticed that tonight the room was hosting a banquet for the presentation of the award for Distinguished Scientific Contributions to Clinical Psychology. His heart lurched, and he turned away, almost bumping into an older woman who was clearly annoyed by the intrusion. He didn't know it was possible for someone to get her nose that high in the air. He smiled and waited for his brother.

Bryce had hated most of the pretentious club members but

had been the dutiful son and accompanied his mother to Friday night dinners when The Captain was away. Quinn, on the other hand, had rebelled and often had refused to go. His little brother spent most of his youth grounded or restricted to his room. Now, it seemed he was balking at convention again.

Bryce thought Dixie was a beautiful young woman with curly black hair, brown eyes, and a curvy figure. A figure that was vastly different from the slim stick figures of most of the young debutants that frequented the club. She was dressed in a simple, flowered, peasant dress that cinched at her tiny waist, accentuating her hourglass figure. If she was nervous, she didn't show it.

Quinn ,on the other hand, seemed to be a bundle of nerves. Bryce knew it mattered a great deal to him for his parents to accept Dixie. Bryce didn't know if Quinn had deliberately looked for someone who was the exact opposite of his mother, but Bryce knew that he always had. As soon as he met Hannah, he knew there was no pretense, and what you saw was what you got.

Tonight would be an interesting evening, and he knew if The Captain or Justine were rude to Dixie he would intervene. It was a prospect that didn't appeal to him, because the last time he'd seen his father, they had parted on good terms. The last time was the day he knew he'd lost Doc.

The maître d greeted them warmly and showed them to their table. It was tucked discreetly in the back surrounded by the club's wine collection, but with a full view of the entire dining room. The Captain rose as they approached, but Justine remained seated and offered her cheek for her sons to kiss.

She was dressed in a high-necked, elegant, black sleeveless dress accented with a braided gold chain. Sparkling diamonds practically dripped from her fingers and her ears. She looked like money, and Bryce knew that was the impression she wanted to make. *Oh brother*, he thought.

"Quinney Boy," she cooed. "This must be the young woman you've been telling us about?"

"Yes, ma'am. This is Dixie Lee King." He turned and took Dixie's hand and said, "Dixie this is my mother, Justine, and my father, Captain Cameron." His expression was clearly one of pride and anticipation.

"I am pleased to meet you both," Dixie said in a soft, unsure voice.

Everyone took a seat, and Bryce purposely put himself across from Justine. Dixie didn't need "Mommie Dearest" staring at her all night.

"So, Dixie, what a perfectly lovely name. It's so Southern. You're a regular Scarlett O'Hara with your curly black hair and that cute little dress. I was telling my friend Mavis just the other day. Girls these days. They simply don't know what fashion is anymore. You'd be amazed at what a little hair straightener and a simple dress can do."

"Mother," Bryce mouthed while kicking her shoe under the table. He turned to look at Quinn's reaction, and it wasn't good.

The Captain, it seemed, came to the rescue. "I'm hungry, and I'm sure Dixie isn't interested in your opinions on fashion. Most kids these days aren't."

"Dixie and I aren't kids, Dad," Quinn said gruffly. "We…"

"All right, all right. Enough said. I know you're not kids." The Captain ordered wine, and everyone began to study the menu.

Justine broke the silence when she said, "Bryce, I'm so happy to see you. You look so thin. Are you taking care of yourself? So, what is the big occasion that you wanted to get us out to celebrate? You've completely ignored my calls, and all I ever get is an occasional text. I worry about you."

"I'm doing fine. This isn't about me. It's about Quinn and Dixie. They have some news."

"Oh, sweet Lord," Justine sputtered. Looking accusingly at Dixie, she said, "You're not pregnant are you?"

Dixie flushed bright red but did not respond.

"No mother," Quinn said, clearly angry. "Dixie is not pregnant, but if she was it would be a cause for celebration."

"Oh, well, yes, but it's just that…"

"It's just what, Mother?"

Bryce put down his menu and said, "Quinn and Dixie have moved in together, and when he called to tell me the good news, I suggested we all get together so you could meet the lovely woman he has fallen in love with."

"Oh," Justine said, looking like she had sucked a lemon.

Quinn started to rise from his chair, but Dixie put her hand gently on his arm, and he sat back down and took a sip of his wine.

The Captain nodded toward the waiter and ordered another bottle of wine and the Seared George's Bank Sea Scallops. He looked around the table and insisted everyone else do the same.

The restaurant was usually quiet during the week and the lack of conversation at their table was especially obvious. Bryce set his fork down and looked past his mother. He had a direct view of the lobby and the large curved staircase leading to the outside. He'd noticed several men and women walking up the staircase. When the door to the ballroom opened, he sometimes heard the applause that he assumed was for the recipients of the awards that were being given out. It reminded him of Hannah, and so when he heard the laughter, it didn't surprise him. It seemed she was always with him. But tonight, even more so than usual.

Then he heard the laughter again. It wasn't his imagination. Only one person he knew had that laugh. He pushed his plate back and stood up, listening intently.

"Bryce," Justine said, "what is it? What's wrong?"

"Quiet," he said. A woman with shoulder-length blonde

hair, wearing a long, flowing blue dress, walked across the lobby, and started up the stairs. She turned to speak to someone beside her, and Bryce saw her face. He caught his breath as tears filled his eyes and his heart raced. In his rush, he pushed his chair out of the way, and it fell backward and crashed onto the polished floor.

Justine nervously looked around the room. "Bryce, stop it. You're making a scene."

The Captain stood now and said in his commanding voice, "Sit down, son. What is the matter with you?"

Bryce's thoughts ran wild as he ignored them both and stepped around the table acting like a crazy man and hurried across the room, dodging waiters and tables. His eyes hadn't tricked him. It was her. *Oh, God! It was her. Oh please, please, please don't let me lose her.*

He bounded up the stairs and out into the cool evening and caught a glimpse of the beautiful blonde getting into a black limousine. He raced toward the car and managed to touch the back fender as it sped away down the wide street. In his anguish, he yelled her name into the starless night as he ran down the street and watched the red taillights turn the corner.

"Doc," he cried into the cold night air and turned around to see his brother coming toward him with open arms.

CHAPTER 31
BRYCE CAMERON

BRYCE PULLED AWAY **from his brother and sat on a stone bench** that was tucked under one of the trees lining the driveway in front of the country club. His mind raced in a million directions, and he felt like beating his fists against his head and screaming. He'd just seen Hannah, hadn't he?

He looked up and saw the bewildered expression on Justine's face as she rushed toward him. The Captain stood staunchly outside of the door talking with the valet and Bryce couldn't imagine what he was thinking.

"Bryce, what in the world is the matter with you?" his mother said. "You went running out of the restaurant like you'd seen a ghost."

Bryce wanted to laugh. That's exactly what he had seen. But this ghost was a living, breathing woman who looked exactly like Hannah. Ignoring his mother's questions, he stood and walked back toward the main entry.

"Bryce, where are you going? Your father has already paid the bill. We need to leave before someone sees us." He ignored his mother and kept walking. He had only one thought on his mind, He must find out who she was and where to find her.

"Quinn, stop your brother." Justine shot a desperate look at him and then pointed at Bryce. "He's acting like a crazy person."

Dixie put her hand gently on Quinn's arm and asked, "What's happening?"

"Bryce thought he saw Hannah, but we know that's ridiculous. Hannah is dead."

"Evidently, your brother doesn't think so, and he needs you to support him. Go with him. Help him," she said in a soft whisper.

"Dixie," he said, exasperation clearly in his tone. "It will be an exercise in futility. I need to help him move on, not encourage him."

"Did you ever give up on me?" Tears glistened in her eyes.

"No, I didn't, but…"

"But?"

He grabbed her, kissed her hard, and said, "Dixie, I love you, and you know I can't deny you anything. Will you be okay here with her?" he indicated his mother with his eyes.

"Sure. She has a pretty good bark, but I'm sure she won't bite me. Or at least not here in front of the Country Club," she whispered.

————

There were only a few people still lingering in the ballroom when Bryce walked up to an overweight man dressed in a black tuxedo. The man's face was flushed, and his eyes were glazed. He was finishing a glass of Champagne and looking around for another.

"I'm sorry to bother you, but were you a guest at the awards ceremony tonight?" Bryce said.

"Yes, I'm Doctor Benjamin Reed." His words were slurred. Have we met before?"

"Bryce, Bryce Cameron and no, we haven't. I'm not a psychologist. I was wondering if you could help me?"

"Be happy to. Call my office. I'm sure I have a card here somewhere with the number." He pulled out his wallet before Bryce could stop him.

"Oh, no. I don't mean that kind of help, although after tonight I probably need it. I was wondering who attended this…" he looked around and raised his hands and said, "this thing."

"This thing is the most prestigious award you can receive from your colleagues in this region. Tonight, we gave that award to Hans Dreschler. He's a pompous prick, but he is brilliant. He has developed…"

Bryce interrupted him. "Dreschler? The Dreschler from that place in Savannah?" He looked up and saw Quinn coming warily toward him.

"Yes, he's the one. Why? Do you know him?"

"I'm looking for a woman who was here. She was dressed in a light blue dress, long blonde hair, pretty."

"Aren't we all looking for someone like that?" the man winked and belched.

"My brother is serious, mister," Quinn said as he joined the two men. "Was a woman like that here?"

Bryce wanted to hug his brother. He didn't realize how much he needed some support until he saw Quinn. "She's about five-foot-seven and is a psychologist."

The man pursed his lips and sighed. "Sounds like Dreschler's wife. She's not one of us, though. She runs some charity or something in Savannah. This is the first time I've seen her in a while. Rumor has it she was in a car accident. What's this all about?"

Bryce ignored the question and walked swiftly away, with Quinn trailing him. He didn't know what any of this meant, but he was going to get answers. How could Dreschler be married to someone that looked exactly like Hannah?

"Who's Dreschler?" Quinn said, panting as he kept up with Bryce.

"The doctor that owns the fancy psychological institute in Savannah. You know, the one Hannah did the presentations for."

"What presentations?"

Bryce stopped and stared at Quinn. "Remember I told you she was going all over the place doing lectures based on her research for grad school? That's why she was on that damn ship. She hated the ocean."

"Okay, so? This guy is married to a woman that looks a lot like Hannah?"

"No, not a lot like Hannah. She could be Hannah."

"Bryce," his brother said slowly with sympathy, "you know it can't be Hannah. You only saw her from a distance. You can't be sure."

"She laughs exactly like Doc. I know you think I'm crazy, but no one laughs like her." Bryce turned and started up the long staircase leading to the outside.

"Okay, okay, let's say you're right, and this woman is Hannah's doppelganger. What do you plan to do about it?"

"I'm going to find out who she is and why she looks exactly like my wife." He pulled his phone out of his pocket and scrolled until he found Bill Allen's name. He touched the name and saw the curiosity in Quinn's expression. "I'm calling Hannah's uncle. If the CIA can't help, I don't know who can."

"CIA?" Quinn said with wonder. "Her uncle is in the CIA? You didn't tell me her uncle was a secret agent."

Bryce smiled for the first time all night. He'd tell Quinn the truth later, but right now the look on his brother's face was priceless.

Bill picked up on the first ring and Bryce said, "Bill, it's Bryce Cameron."

"Bryce, good to hear from you. How have you been?"

"I'm okay. I'm here in Atlanta visiting my parents and my brother. Bill, I know this is going to sound strange, but I saw Hannah tonight. Same hair, same face, same laugh. I'm not crazy. I know it was her."

There was dead silence and then Bill said, "Boy, I need you to come to Chapel Hill. There's something you need to know."

"Why do I have to come there?" Bryce raised his voice and gritted his teeth. "Just tell me now."

"I can't. I made a promise, but if you come, I will take you to someone who can."

———

Bryce sat in the neatly furnished living room of Mildred and Robert Brody's home. The one and only time he had been here was when he and Hannah had visited. The room was filled with reminders of her. A picture of a smiling Hannah in a cap and gown between her parents, a picture of a younger Hannah in what must have been a high school picture, and then one golden-haired child wearing a uniform and holding a bat. It hurt to see her, so he turned away.

Bryce glanced at Mildred and saw that she was staring at him with eyes filled with distrust, and her voice held an angry challenge when she said, "What are you doing here Bryce? I didn't expect to see you again, especially after you refused to attend Hannah's memorial. Can you imagine how it looked to my friends when my daughter's husband did not bother to attend her service? And now, here you are here with Bill, of all people. Will you please tell me why?"

"I'm pretty sure you know why, Mildred," Bill said as his sad eyes rested on his sister.

"I have no idea. And can't this wait until later? Robert will be home soon."

"Probably not," Bill said. "This is between you and Bryce. I'm pretty sure none of it was Robert's idea."

Bryce looked at Bill and then back at Mildred. "Would one of you tell me what is going on? I want to know why I saw a woman tonight that could have been Hannah. May, in fact, have been Hannah. Bill believes you can give me some answers." Bryce stood up and walked restlessly around the room and stopped by the wide, picture window facing the front lawn.

The look on Mildred's face turned from anger to what he could only describe as fear. Fear of what, he wondered.

"You better tell him, or I will," Bill said. His voice was uncompromising, yet oddly gentle.

Mildred wrung her hands, and tears pooled in her eyes. Her face was ashen. "Hannah was adopted as an infant. She didn't know it. We never told her."

Bryce was shocked, but not overly so. That would explain the deep divide between her parents' personalities and Doc's. "And?" he asked.

"She was a twin... an identical twin. It's probable that's who you saw."

Bryce sat down and exhaled and rubbed his hands through his hair. "Why the secrecy? Why not tell her the truth?"

The response from Mildred was only silence.

"You let her go her whole life, never knowing that she had a sister?" He ran his fingers back through his hair. "How could you be so selfish?"

Mildred had the good sense to look away from his riveting gaze.

Bryce turned to look at Bill and said, "You knew this?"

"Yes, that was the basis of the estrangement between us. When Hannah started high school, I tried to persuade Mildred to tell her. I knew Hannah was mature enough to handle the fact that she was adopted. Mildred refused because she was afraid there might be consequences if Hannah ever tried to find her biological parents."

"Consequences? What consequences?"

"Tell him."

"It's none of his business."

"It certainly is my business. My wife disappeared, and now you tell me she has an identical twin that she never knew about? What part of that is not my business?"

Mildred began to cry softly. The emotion coming from this cold woman was surprising to Bryce.

"I didn't want children when we married, and I thought that was what Robert wanted too. We were happy. He had his career, and I had mine. We were tenured, and our life was all planned. But then, when we were approaching our forties, he got involved with a grad student. It ended when I found out, but the dalliance had made him realize he wanted more, and he decided he wanted a child. We fought, and he was going to leave me. I tried to get pregnant, but I couldn't conceive, so we decided to adopt. Adoption of an infant is nearly impossible, so we went through… uh… different channels."

"So, you mean the adoption was from the black market?"

"Not exactly that," Mildred said, wringing her hands again as she looked around the room. "It was all handled through a lawyer and a medical professional who had connections. I handed them fifty thousand dollars, and they gave me a baby. I found out from the nurse that there were two identical babies, but the other one was promised to another family." She sighed. "I knew it was for the best. I could never have handled two."

"Does Robert know any of this?" Bill said. "I've always wondered."

"You know Robert. He didn't ask many questions. I told him about the twins and about only one of them being available for adoption. He thought it a shame that they would be separated, but he was happy to have a daughter."

"Why would the birth mother agree to let her twins go to two different families?" Bill said. Bryce could see that Bill had always wanted to know the answers to these questions but had held his peace until now.

"I don't know. Robert and I never discussed it again, and we both agreed that it would be best if Hannah believed we were her natural parents. We went on a sabbatical to England for several months on the pretext of historical research, and when we came home with Hannah, we told everyone she was ours."

Bryce looked at Bill and shook his head. He didn't know what to believe. He only knew that he had to find Hannah's twin sister.

CHAPTER 32
BRYCE CAMERON

BRYCE FOUGHT **the urge to scream obscenities at Mildred Brody.** How dare the woman keep such a monstrous secret from Hannah? What kind of person does not reveal to her adopted daughter that she has an identical twin?

No wonder Hannah went into the mental health field. Some part of her must have felt empty. She must have felt a void in her life after spending all those months in the womb with her sister. At least, that's what he thought she would have felt.

He hated that Hannah may have died without ever knowing that she had a birth family out there somewhere. And what about her parents? Who were they? But even more than all these angry thoughts, he felt sad that he had to admit that Hannah might really be gone.

After a long, uncomfortable conversation, Bill had finally forced his sister to admit that she had never told her husband the whole truth.

"Did Robert go with you to get the child from the hospital?" Bill said.

Mildred stood abruptly and walked to the window. She pulled the curtain back and looked out toward the driveway.

"No, I didn't want to take a chance on anything going wrong. We had all our travel papers in order, so he left for Europe a week before I did."

"So," Bryce said, "you picked the baby up from the hospital by yourself?"

"I didn't go to the hospital," Mildred said. Her voice sounded tired.

They waited for her to continue and exchanged a glance.

"I drove to Charleston."

"Charleston?" Bill said. "Neither of you mentioned that before."

"Robert doesn't know. He thinks I went to UNC Hospital. Actually, I went to the Catholic Mercy Home in Charleston. That's where I picked up Hannah."

Bill stood and put his hands on his hips. "Mildred, what are you talking about? You're not Catholic."

"Exactly. That's why I lied to Robert. He doesn't know it was a private adoption."

"Didn't you both have to sign the paperwork? The birth certificate?" Bryce said.

"Yes, but he didn't even read it. He realized he had a choice. Either I got this baby girl, or our marriage was over. He didn't ask questions, and he got out of the country so I could do it however I wanted to without him being involved."

"But the money? Where did you get the money?" Bill asked. "Wouldn't Robert know about that?"

"I sold the jewelry our mother left me and cashed in some stock. It wasn't Robert's place to tell me how to spend it, and he damn well knew it. He'd already spent plenty of our money on that girl."

Bill's cheeks puffed up, and he blew out air in a whoosh. He sat back down, clearly defeated.

Bryce wasn't even close to finished with Mildred. He needed more information from her, so he changed his tone.

"Do you still have those papers?" he asked carefully. He was so afraid she had destroyed them after Hannah's death.

"Well, yes," she said. "Why?"

"I would like to have them," Bryce said gently. "That is, if you don't mind. I could always make copies and give you back the originals."

She thought for a moment and then stood. "I'll get them. They're of no use to me now. I've lost my daughter, and no papers will bring her back to me."

He could hear her sobbing as drawers opened and closed in the bedroom. His anger morphed into compassion. He knew what it was like to want something so badly you would do anything, go anywhere, break any rules to get it.

———

It was getting late in the day. Bryce planned to get some sleep at a Holiday Inn Express, eat a good breakfast, and then leave for Charleston first thing in the morning.

"Want some company?" Bill said.

Bryce considered it. He knew he didn't. He wanted to make the drive and mull over everything he had learned and daydream about Hannah, but he liked Bill, and he couldn't be rude.

"Don't worry," Bill said. "I'll pay my own way. I want answers as badly as you do. I've been living with this secret for years, and I feel terrible for keeping it."

"Well, don't," Bryce said. "Feel terrible, I mean. You had your sister to deal with. And yes, I would like your company. It's a long drive, and I'd appreciate somebody having my back when we face those nuns. I'm not Catholic, but I've always been afraid of those women. What do you suppose is under those robes that makes little kids behave so well?"

Bill burst out laughing. "Well, great! Let's get some rest and hit the road in the morning."

———

Bryce studied the papers over breakfast and handed them to Bill to read in the car. From what he could see, the birth mother's name was Patty Jean Campbell, and the father was listed as unknown.

"This is kind of strange, Bryce," said Bill. There's a signature here, but it isn't Patty Jean Campbell's. I can't read it very well, but it looks like it reads, Sister Marsha Flannery."

"I didn't see a lawyer's signature there, did you?"

Bill looked over the papers and then said, "Nope."

"I also don't see a notary's seal. Do you suppose it was ever notarized?"

"I doubt it. Unless there's a page missing."

"All I can see is that the child weighed four pounds and fifteen ounces at birth. She was eighteen and a half inches long."

"She was awfully tiny," said Bryce.

"Indeed she was. I'm surprised they let Mildred take her home at that weight."

"I think we are going to have quite a few surprises when we get there, Bill."

———

Bryce was right. The former home for unwed mothers was now a convent. Bill shook the gate, but it was locked, so he rang the bell.

A tall woman in a long black skirt, white blouse, and black vest met them at the front gate after they rang the bell several times. "Goodness, have patience," she chided. "I'll be there directly," she said as she hustled across the yard kicking up dust in her wake. Bryce noted that the hem of her dark skirt was dirty. It appeared that she spent lots of time outdoors.

She ushered them in through the heavy oak door at the

front of the building and into a large room with oversized furniture. It looked like the sofas, chairs, and tables had been custom-made.

"Aren't they amazing?" she said. "Take a seat. They are all comfortable, too. Sister Louisa has two brothers who fashioned all this furniture for us many years ago. It is well worn, but we wouldn't replace it for anything."

"It matches the room," Bryce said, trying to be polite. He had a million questions and couldn't wait to ask them, but this lady could not be rushed.

"Now," she said. "Can I offer you some tea or coffee?"

"No, thank you." Bryce sat forward in the chair and crossed his hands over his knees. "Do you mind if I ask you some questions?"

"I was wondering when you were going to get down to business. We seldom have visitors here and rarely have unannounced guests. I was quite surprised to see you."

"May I know your name?" Bryce said.

"I am Sister Patricia Showery, and you are?"

"I'm Bryce Cameron and this is Bill Allen. We understand this is a home for unwed mothers, and we have come to ask questions about my wife's birth. She was born here twenty-six years ago."

"You are partially correct. This was formerly a home for girls who needed a place to have their babies, but it has not been so for many years. This is a convent now. Twelve of us live here. The younger sisters work in the garden, tend the chickens, keep the grounds landscaped and clean the building. The older sisters, now retired, have earned the privilege of having time to rest and reflect on their religious life."

Bryce and Bill exchanged looks. "Were you here when the mothers and babies lived here?"

"No," she said. "I am one of the sisters who manages the upkeep of this convent. We sell eggs, jam, baked goods, and do several other things in the community. Two or three of the

270 CHARLENE TESS & & JUDI THOMPSON

older sisters have been here for many years. They don't have to work anymore. They have time to read and pray and spend their final years in repose. Their work is done."

"Could we talk to one of those older nuns?" Bill said. "You know, one of the retired ones?"

Sister Patricia smiled. "We are called sisters now, Mr. Allen. And I'm not sure if that's possible. I will certainly ask and see if they will talk with you. Most of them don't like to talk at all. They spend their time in silent prayer and reflection."

The three of them sat facing each other silently for a few moments. Bryce could feel the heat rising, and he was sure his neck would turn red at any moment and give him away. He was agitated and impatient. He had driven a long way and waited a long time to have a conversation with one of these women. What was the big deal?

"Well, would you ask them please?"

"I will. If you come back tomorrow, I will give you an answer, and if any of them are willing, you can have your visit at that time."

He started to say something, but Bill interrupted. "That sounds like a good idea, Sister Patricia. Thank you. What time should we come back?"

"Ten o'clock after morning prayers would work for me."

———

Bill put his hand on Bryce's arm and practically shoved him out of the room and across the yard to the car. When they got inside and slammed the doors, Bryce said, "What the hell was that? Did you see how that woman was stalling? She knows something."

"Knows what?" Bill said. "Come on, Bryce. Whatever happened over a quarter of a century ago is not her fault. We need to get some information on our own and then talk to the older sisters tomorrow."

"So, what do you propose we do?"

"I can't believe that a hotshot writer like you is asking me what to do. Let's get to a library and look in the morgue for old newspaper stories. Then we'll comb the Internet and see what we can find out about the Catholic Mercy Home in Charleston."

By the end of the day, they had learned more than they ever expected. A series of newspaper articles revealed that a network of illegal adoptions had operated out of the unwed mothers' home for many years. Catholic families who were shamed by the immoral behavior of their daughters sent them there to give birth, and then the sisters were to find suitable homes for the babies. No one figured out for the longest time that the babies were being sold for exorbitant sums of money. The mothers of the children didn't know about the money. They were told that their living and hospital expenses were paid by the adoptive parents, but no one knew about the lucrative baby deals that were being arranged.

In fact, according to the newspaper articles, one woman, Sister Bobbie Shook, was the brains and the perpetrator of the whole illegal operation. She was compared to the infamous Georgia Tann, although this South Carolina hospital's adoption scandal was small potatoes compared to the intricate web spun by the child trafficker who operated the Tennessee Children's Home Society in Memphis, Tennessee.

According to one source that Bryce found on the Web, one sister had discovered what was happening and turned in Bobbie Shook, who went to prison and died there. The doctor who delivered the babies became a rich man and was planning to leave the country, but he too was arrested and sent to prison.

"Look at this," Bryce said excitedly. "This Doctor Hightower might still be alive. There's no mention of him dying."

"Let's find out. Let's call the prison," Bryce said.

After waiting on what seemed like an endless hold while listening to bad music, getting the runaround, and talking to three clueless, rude people, Bryce finally got the answer he wanted.

Doctor Hightower was indeed incarcerated in a correctional institution in Bishopville, South Carolina. He had received a life sentence due to the deaths of several of the young women while in his care.

"What are we waiting for?" Bill said. "Get your phone and let's go."

CHAPTER 33
BRYCE CAMERON

BRYCE HOPED **he would never have to visit anyone in prison** ever again in his lifetime. He hated the loud clanging sounds of the metal gates opening and closing, and the smell of urine, disinfectant, and fear. Most of all, he hated to see the soulless looks of despair in the eyes of everyone he met, including the armed guards.

After the muscular guard searched him and lectured him about rules for visitors, he led Bryce into an airless room that smelled of sweat. A thick glass window separated him from the prisoner he had come to visit, and a black, corded telephone rested on the wall beside the window.

Two guards led Hightower into the room on the other side of the glass and removed his handcuffs. Then, they left the room and locked the door behind them. The man didn't look like a criminal and certainly not a murderer. He was short, had few if any muscles, and a full head of gray hair cut short.

Bryce saw no outward stereotypical signs like tattoos or any mannerisms that would indicate that he was a man to fear. In fact, he looked pathetic and vulnerable. His hand shook as he picked up the receiver.

"Who are you, young man? I haven't had a visitor in

months. My grandson visits when he can, but not often. He's a busy doctor."

Bryce could hear the pride in the older man's voice, along with the loneliness. "My name is Bryce Cameron. After some research, I have discovered that you were the doctor who delivered my wife twenty-six years ago at the Catholic Mercy Home in Charleston."

"Probably was. I delivered lots of babies there. No way to know for sure."

"Oh, I'm pretty sure there is. Her mother's name was Patty Jean Campbell. Patty Jean died giving birth to twin girls. She was only sixteen at the time."

He leaned back and closed his eyes. It was a long time before he spoke. "Yes, I remember. I had to make the phone call to tell her father that she died giving birth. It was a hard thing to do. The father was devastated."

"What happened?" Bryce insisted. "Didn't you know she was having twins?"

Hightower snorted. "Certainly, I knew that. What are you implying? That I'm some quack? I could hear two strong heartbeats, and she was as big as a house. But they didn't call me until it was too late to save her. She delivered five weeks early and had been in labor for hours. She had been losing blood the whole time. By the time I got there, it was all I could do to save the babies."

"You remember the twins?"

"Yes. They were tiny, each weighed under five pounds, but they were healthy and strong. Good thing they were female. Male preemies sometimes aren't as strong and might not have made it through such a long, complicated birth."

"Do you know what happened to them?"

"Sure. They were both adopted right away. Bobbie Shook had planned their adoptions months in advance. She found a different family for each of them. She'd make more money that way. Nobody wanted to pay double, and it would be rare for a couple to adopt two newborns at one time."

"Any idea where they went?"

"No. That wasn't any of my concern. Bobbie Shook took care of all the adoptions."

"Do you know Patty's father's name or where she came from?"

"His name was Campbell, same as hers. They gave me his phone number, that's all. What's going on, Mr. Cameron? Why all the questions, and why ask me?"

Bryce could see the cold indifference in the doctor's eyes. He had not cared then, and he didn't care now. "You wouldn't believe me if I told you," Bryce said as he dropped the phone on the table and left the room.

———

On the two-hour drive back to Charleston, Bryce tried to fill Bill in on what he had learned from Doctor Hightower. "You know, at first I felt a twinge of sympathy for the old man. He looked frail and didn't seem like a murderer. But the more he talked, the more I could see that he didn't care one whit about those girls at the home. He was there for the paycheck."

"That's a damn shame," said Bill.

"I thought a doctor took an oath to do no harm and to care about their patients, but this guy had a cold heart. I'll bet he never took the time to have a conversation with those girls. He knew nothing about Patty Jean. She must have been terrified of giving birth to twins. Isn't a doctor supposed to make his patients feel safe?" said Bryce.

"Well, it looks like he got what was coming to him. I don't feel sorry for him at all," Bill said.

———

The next morning, after coffee and a hearty breakfast at the hotel, Bryce and Bill drove back to the convent. This time the gates were open, and they drove up to the front of the building and parked.

Sister Patricia answered the door, welcomed them, and showed them to the sofa in the large living room. "I asked all three of the sisters who were here all those years ago if they would speak to you. One of them is having trouble with her memory and another is nervous about talking about the past, but Sister Flannery said she would join us in a few minutes. "I'm going to get you a plate of cookies and a pot of tea. Sister likes her sweets, and the tea will relax her. I'll be right back."

Bill kicked Bryce's foot and said in a stage whisper, "That's the name on the birth certificate."

Bryce frowned, nodded, moved a few inches away from Bill, and rubbed his foot. The name had not escaped his attention, and he girded himself with resolve. He had so many questions to ask this woman, and her answers could help him know what direction to travel next.

She was a tall, thin woman with a regal demeanor, and she wore a dark skirt and white blouse. If no one had told him, he would never have taken her for a nun. He stood at once but wasn't sure if he should hold out his hand. She made no indication they should shake hands, so he waited until she sat and then did the same. Bill bobbed up and down like a jack-in-the-box. He seemed terribly ill at ease around the Catholic sisters.

"I'm happy to meet you, Sister Flannery," Bryce said. My name is Bryce Cameron, and this is my wife's uncle, Bill Allen."

"A pleasure," she said quietly. "We seldom receive visitors, and you are most welcome."

Sister Patricia fussed around them and poured each of them a cup of tea after asking whether they took milk or sugar or both. She passed the cookie plate around and then made her way to the other side of the room and took a seat in one of the big chairs.

"What do you need to ask me, Mr. Cameron? Don't be shy."

Bryce took a swallow of tea, put down the cup and began. "Were you present the night that Patty Jean Campbell delivered her twin girls?"

A flicker of pain flashed in the old woman's eyes. "Yes, I was there. It was terrible to watch her suffer. The girl was so weak. She never got to hold her babies. She was probably unaware that she had two little girls."

"Were the girls born healthy?"

"Oh, yes. They were tiny, but you could hear their cries all over the house. Their lungs were well-developed, and they were strong and pink. Beautiful girls. Absolutely beautiful in every way." She smiled as she remembered.

"So, they were identical?"

"Most assuredly. No one could tell them apart. They had the same face, the same tiny noses and ears, and their hair was an identical shade of blonde. Everyone remarked about how impossible it was to distinguish them from one another. We called them Angel A and Angel B. We tied a ribbon around Angel A's ankle so we would know them apart at feeding time."

"Well," Bryce said, "either Baby A or Baby B grew up to be my beautiful wife, Hannah. I absolutely adored her."

"What happened?" she said, her eyes blinking in confusion.

"It's a long, sad story, so I'll skip the details, but she died. I am lost without her."

"I am so sorry, young man. I will pray for your heart to heal."

"Thank you," Bryce said and fought back tears.

"So, you are here because you want to know everything you can about your wife's past?"

"No, not exactly. The truth is, I saw a woman that looked exactly like Hannah. I thought it was her. Then, I found out she has an identical twin. I am looking for that twin. I need to talk to her. It is very important to me."

"I'm sure it is."

"Do you know who adopted her?"

She smoothed her skirt and placed her saucer on her knees. "I wish I could help you, Bryce. The only thing I know is that after Patty Jean died, I signed the birth certificates so that the babies could be adopted. Patty Jean talked about her father often. Ed Campbell was his name. He was her only parent, and they were close. I told Doctor Hightower how to reach Patty Jean's father in Greensboro, North Carolina, to tell him about Patty Jean and the babies. He made that phone call, not me."

"And what happened to the babies?"

"Again, I'm not sure. The adoption process was not part of my job. I took care of the pregnant girls, and I tried to give them love and comfort. I got close to all of them, but often I did not even see their babies except for a few moments after they were born. The infants were taken to the third floor and their new parents picked them up there."

"So, you don't know what happened to Patty Jean's twins?"

"I'm sorry, no."

———

In the car on the way back to the hotel, Bryce turned to Bill. "Are you up for one more road trip? I want to find Ed Campbell and see what else we can find out."

"I'm already on it. I looked it up on the Google map. Greensboro is a little over four hours from here on I95. Take a left up here at the next intersection."

"You mean you're not too tired to do it today?"

"Do I look tired to you? Well, I'm not. I could use some lunch, though. I'm not a tea and cookies fella."

Bryce chuckled. He could see why Hannah had loved her Uncle Bill so much. The guy was a gem.

After a barbecue sandwich and a cup of coffee, they were on the highway and talking strategies. "I guess we should have made some phone calls before jumping in the car and heading out," Bill said.

Bryce smiled. "I totally agree. That's why I looked him up in the online white pages and got a phone number, called him, and got an address. He's expecting us late in the afternoon. I didn't tell him the truth about why we were coming. I thought I'd save that information until we are face to face."

"Well, damn and double damn. Aren't you the smart one? When did you do that?"

"When we went back to the hotel to get our bags, I thought we might need a plan. It can save a lot of time and trouble if you know where you're going before you leave." Bill laughed and picked up his iPhone again to check their progress on the map.

Greensboro, North Carolina, was more picturesque than Bryce expected it to be. Covered bridges poised over streams, vast green open spaces with flowering trees and bushes, and a mixture of modern buildings and quaint structures made the drive enjoyable.

He had given Bill the address and the male, British voice on his GPS led them directly to the front door of a house in an old part of the city. The house wasn't large, but it appeared well-tended. The grass was cut and edged, and the flower beds were bursting with colorful blooms.

Ed Campbell opened the door and stepped out onto the front porch before they could get out of the car. He pulled a pocket watch out of the pocket of his pants, looked at it, and then replaced it quickly. "You made good time," he said. "It's not a bad drive if you aren't in the rush hour traffic." He held out his hand and shook with both of them.

"Nice to meet you, Mr. Campbell. I'm Bill Allen."

"Likewise," said Ed.

"And I'm the one you spoke to on the phone. Bryce Cameron, sir. Nice to meet you."

Ed took a step backward, held the screen with his shoulder, and pushed the door open. "Well, come in. Come in."

He motioned to the sofa and two well-worn wing chairs. Bryce could see a stairway to the left and an archway in the back that most likely led to the kitchen. The room was clean, but out-of-date and dark.

Bryce knew there was no way to soft-pedal the news he was about to bring, so he said it plain. "Bill and I wanted to meet you, Mr. Campbell and …"

"Ed, call me Ed."

"Ed, we have learned that your daughter Patty Jean got pregnant at sixteen and went to the Catholic Mercy Home in Charleston. Before I go on, is that correct?"

Ed fingered the crease in his pants and put his hands on his knees as if bracing for a collision. "That's a fact. A sad one, but a fact. You see, Patty's mother died when she was ten years old, and we never had a woman in our life again. I didn't know how to take care of a pregnant teenager and a baby."

Bryce could see that the man felt guilty, and that was not his intention. He would not judge a man who had lost everything. He knew how that felt, and it was beyond imagining.

"We are so sorry for your loss, Ed. It must have been terrible to lose your wife when your daughter was so young, and then to lose your daughter at sixteen. We hope it's not too painful to talk about," said Bryce.

"I'm okay," Ed said. "It's been a long time, and I am used to being alone. I don't like it, but I have no choice."

"I know that feeling," said Bill. "Eating alone, now that's

the worst. I hate it. I always have the TV on... you know... for the noise."

Ed smiled. "I hear you. Sounds like all of us old loners are in the same club."

Bryce waited to see if Bill would take offense at being called *old*, but there was no reaction.

"That phone call you got from Doctor Hightower must have been hard," said Bill.

"It was. I could hardly grasp the horrible news that I had lost my daughter and my grandbaby all in one night. It was a girl too. A baby girl."

Bill gave Bryce a sideways glance of utter disbelief. Before Bryce could say anything, Bill blurted out, "Baby? Oh, no. Your daughter had twins, and they didn't die."

———

It took quite some time to fill Ed Campbell in on all the details of their visit to the home and to the prison. They shared everything with him they had learned about his daughter and what happened to her in Charleston. He had been relieved to learn that the director of the Catholic Mercy Home had died in prison and that the heartless doctor was still serving time there.

"That bastard lied to me. He told me that when a baby died at the home, they took care of everything. I didn't even ask what that meant. I didn't want to know. He arranged for Patty Jean's ashes to be shipped to me, so I didn't have to go to Charleston. She's right over there," he said and pointed to a stoneware urn that sat on the fireplace mantel. "That's all I have left of her," he said. He was fighting tears.

"But the twins ..." he said. "What happened to the twins?"

"Well, that's where we come into the picture," Bryce said. "One of those beautiful girls was my wife, Hannah. She was adopted by Bill's sister and her husband. Bill was Hannah's favorite uncle. They were always close."

"And were the girls close? Where's the other one?"

"Hannah never knew she had a twin sister. No one told her. I found out only after she died."

This time, he could not control his emotions. He put his head into his hands and a sob escaped. "That's so sad," he said. "Why does everything have to be so sad?"

CHAPTER 34
BRYCE CAMERON

IT WAS RAINING **when Bryce's plane touched down** on the runway in Atlanta. It had been a busy and emotional few days and he was exhausted. Quinn had invited him to stay with him and Dixie, but Bryce didn't feel like talking.

He had learned things about Hannah's past that she should have known. She should have been told that she had a grandfather who would have loved her if only he had known of her existence. And she had an identical twin whom he was pretty sure he'd seen at the country club.

Bryce was wrestling with the fact that Hannah was gone and trying to accept that the woman he had seen wasn't his wife. As much as he wanted it to be his Doc, he knew it wasn't her.

But he wanted answers, and he intended to get them. What kind of sick game was Hans Dreschler playing? Why would the man hire Hannah, a woman who looked exactly like his own wife?

Bryce took a cab to the first halfway decent hotel he saw that was close to the airport. After he texted Quinn to let him know he was back in town, he face planted onto the king-sized bed and fell into a deep sleep.

It had been several weeks since he had awakened from a dream in a sweaty panic while trying to find Hannah as she cried out to him in a ferocious, dark sea. Now, when he awoke, his eyes immediately popped open, but his heart wasn't beating out of his chest. He was calm and had an almost serene feeling. It was as if Doc were right here in the room with him. He sat up looking at the clock. It was four forty-five and already he could hear the early morning traffic.

"Help me here, Doc. I don't know what to do or where to go. I miss you so much. Am I crazy and like Don Quixote simply tilting at windmills?" There was no answer from the dark room as he headed for the shower.

A short while later, he re-packed his duffel bag with his few clothes and necessities, rented a car, and decided to drive to Savannah. He wanted to confront Dreschler and get to the bottom of the mystery. He still didn't have a plan and was hoping his years of discipline from the academy and then in the service would restrain him from punching the man in the face. Maybe Dreschler wasn't directly responsible for Hannah's death, but he was a contributor. Hannah should never have been on that ship.

He pulled up to a stoplight and closed his eyes while he imagined the overwhelming fear she must have experienced as the water engulfed her. He beat his hand on the steering wheel and said in a strangled voice, "Why? Why were you by the rail?"

It had rained all night and there was still a fine mist this morning as he pulled onto the highway toward Savannah. It made the drive slow and gave him plenty of time to gather his thoughts and consider what he had learned.

Bryce planned to arrive at the psychological institute unannounced. He had received a sympathy card from the institute a week after Hannah's disappearance, and it made him so angry at the time he tossed it into the trash. If he wanted to get answers, he knew he should not confront

Dreschler in a combative way. Didn't his mother always say, "You catch more flies with honey?" He would remain calm and thought Hannah would have been proud of him.

Bryce wanted to make sure he looked presentable when he met Dreschler since this would be the first time they had met face to face. After he checked into the Hyatt Regency, he changed from his shorts and T-shirt into a pair of brown Dockers and a dark green pullover sweater. Hannah had bought the sweater for him because it matched the color of his eyes. He thought it was silly at the time, and now he cherished it.

The building was not what he expected. It was a three-story, aesthetically pleasing, beige concrete structure with dark windows flanking the wings of the building. When he pulled off the main road, he noticed the guard shack, and then remembered when Hannah had first talked about the place. She told him it was hard to get into. He needed a cover story, and his prior experience as a reporter hopefully would open the gates.

His first break came when the guard turned out to be a woman and the second was when he learned she was a fan. After his simple explanation about doing research for a book and having an appointment with Dreschler, she let him pass.

The reception area was painted a soft blue. Plush carpeting blanketed the floor and skylights filled the room with light. A glass-enclosed area to his right looked like a large sunroom filled with green vegetation. A pretty redhead wearing a headset sat behind a mahogany desk and smiled when he walked in.

"May I help you, sir?"

Bryce turned on his best Southern charm and said, "I certainly hope so, ma'am. I'm Bryce Cameron. I was at a reception for Dr. Dreschler a few days ago, and I wonder if he would have a moment to speak to me? He said to stop by if I was in the neighborhood and we could talk."

Her phone rang, and she put up her finger to indicate she was taking the call, so he took that opportunity to look around. That's when he saw the portrait. She was younger, and her hair was more platinum than honey blonde, but it was Hannah, or at least it could have been Hannah except for the smile. The woman in the painting seemed wistful. Her lips turned up in a half smile. Bryce couldn't pull his gaze away.

The young woman came up behind him and said, "She's beautiful, isn't she?"

"She..." Bryce finally found his voice to speak.

"The doctor's wife. Juliette Dreschler. It was so terrible about what happened to her?"

"I'm sorry, I don't know the details. What happened? I saw her at the dinner with the doctor. She looked fine."

"Oh yes, she is now. It was truly a miracle when she woke up." The phone rang, and she turned to go back to her desk.

"Ms ...?"

"Jennifer," she said, "my name's Jennifer."

"Jennifer, how long ago did the accident happen?"

"Over a year. I've got to get this, and the doctor is in a meeting all afternoon. But I can give you an appointment when I finish this call."

Bryce wanted to pump her for more information on Dreschler's wife. Hannah had mentioned something about the man's wife being sick, and that was the reason they met at his home rather than at the institute. She also might have told him about a car accident, but if she did, he probably wasn't paying attention. At that time in their relationship, he was totally absorbed in asking her to marry him and most of his thoughts had been on the anticipation of the moment she finished his book. He smiled when he remembered how long it had taken her to do it. He was on pins and needles for days.

He took another long look at the painting and walked

back to the desk. Jennifer was off the phone and was clicking on her computer keyboard.

"I don't have any openings until early next week. Will that work for you?"

"Oh, I'm sorry, but no. I'm not from Savannah, and I'm only in town until tomorrow. I don't suppose you could fit me in then?" he asked.

"Well, I shouldn't, but maybe right after lunch. He usually asks me to leave about fifteen minutes free."

"Perfect." Bryce turned and motioned toward the portrait of Juliette. "I understand she isn't a psychologist."

"Well, not exactly. Rumor has it she was studying in Paris for her undergrad in psychology when they met. Nancy, that's the doctor's secretary, says it was love at first sight. They married in France, and when he decided to open the institute they did it here in Savannah. Juliette grew up in the South, and she wanted to come home."

"So, what does she do?" He saw the frown on Jennifer's face and thought maybe he'd asked too many questions, but the young woman flipped her hair back and took a sip from a Diet Coke can.

"She does charity work for the Children's Mental Health Association. She arranges many fundraisers and a charity ball every year. I was invited to it by one of the doctors two years ago." Bryce watched her shudder, and then she said, "He was a real creep, but the ball was phenomenal. Last year, everything was low-key because of her, well, you know, her accident."

"So, she's good now?"

"Seems to be. Although she doesn't talk much anymore. She visits the garden often and even gives tours introducing children to the native plants of the South. As a matter of fact, she should be here today. Dr. Dreschler is extremely protective of her and doesn't permit visitors to speak to her. I'm sure you understand. Her health and all."

Bryce thanked her for the information and said he would see her tomorrow for his appointment and then turned toward the exit.

The door opened, and a group of five men and two women entered the lobby. When they reached the desk, Jennifer seemed to be overwhelmed, and Bryce took that opportunity to slip into the sunroom. He wanted to get a peek at Hannah's twin.

When he opened the heavy glass door, he noticed the immediate change in temperature. The room was warm, almost tropical, and there was green foliage everywhere. He saw her seated on the far side of the room. Her hair was pulled up, and she was wearing glasses. He noticed she was reading a book, but from the distance he couldn't make out the title. Bryce didn't want to frighten her, but he wanted to talk to this woman who was Hannah but wasn't.

He cleared his throat, and she looked up but didn't appear to be alarmed. "Hello," she said, putting down the book.

He swallowed, but he felt like he had cotton in his mouth. Suddenly, he didn't know what to say or how to say it. His voice was rougher than he intended when he said, "You're Juliette?"

"Yes," she said with a quizzical expression. "Have we met? I'm sorry I seem to have lots of holes in my memory, and I have a hard time with names." She picked up the book. On the cover was the picture of a brain and the title *Your Memory*. "Thus, the book," she said.

Bryce chuckled and said, "I have that problem with people I met only yesterday."

"So, I'm in good company then. "And you are ...?" She let the last word trail off as she smiled up at him.

"Bryce Cameron. I came to talk to your husband, but he's busy and I saw the garden and wanted a look." She raised an eyebrow, indicating that she didn't believe him but said nothing.

"All right, that isn't exactly the truth."

"Should I be afraid of you?"

"Oh no. I'm sorry, no. I didn't mean to scare you," he said as he took a seat on the edge of a brick planter. "I did come to see your husband, but then after I saw the picture of you ... and Jennifer said you were here, I wanted to see you." He knew he was mumbling and talking too fast and most likely sounded like an idiot, but Lord, talking to her was the same as talking to Hannah.

"Mr. Cameron, are you all right?"

"No," he shook his head. "No, I'm not. My wife Hannah died only a few months ago, and I came here because ... well because I think you are her sister."

Juliette didn't seem surprised as she looked around the greenhouse. Her eyes glanced toward the door and then back at Bryce. "I usually stop for tea at least once or twice a week at Gryphon's. Do you know it?"

"No, I'm not from Savannah, but I can find it."

"It's a little restaurant on Bull Street in the Historic District. I'll meet you there at four o'clock this afternoon."

CHAPTER 35
JULIETTE DRESCHLER

JULIETTE SAT **in the back of the café and watched the door**. Every time it opened, she felt the chill of the late afternoon. She'd purposely arrived early because she wanted to gather her thoughts before the mysterious man arrived and had assured her driver that he didn't need to escort her inside. The leash that Hans kept on her was beginning to chafe. He'd assured her he was worried about her health, but at times she felt like a prisoner.

She looked around the little café with its walls lined with shelves or books and intimate tables with crisp, white linen tablecloths and was almost certain that Bryce Cameron had never been inside a tea house before. She was equally certain that he could and would fit in anywhere.

The door opened again, and he walked in. Her heart lurched, and she didn't know why. He intrigued her, and she was attracted to him. She was married to a man nearly twice her age, and she never felt there was a piece missing until she saw Bryce.

He smiled, waved, and crossed the room to her table. Taking a seat across from her, he said, "I wasn't sure if you would be here."

"Why? I said I would, and it was my idea."

"I know, but you don't know me, and I told you I'm married to your sister. That must have seemed strange. I'd be a little wary."

"It doesn't come as a surprise, or at least the fact that I am adopted doesn't. I've always known, but I had no idea I had siblings."

"A sister," he said sadly. "Her name is Hannah, and she looks exactly like you."

"An identical twin. I don't know what to say except that it's wonderful news." She stopped and looked up into his sharp green eyes and said, "I guess not quite so wonderful. You said she died. And yet, you still talk about her in the present tense." She watched him shift uncomfortably in his chair and run his fingers through his hair. A nervous habit, she thought. It was endearing that he was nervous.

"I guess I still haven't come to terms with it. I expect her to walk into a room at any minute, or when the phone rings, I think it will be her. She drowned in the ocean, and her... well... we never found her."

Juliette reached across the table and took his hand. Then, after realizing what she'd done, she quickly pulled it back and said, "I'm so sorry. You must have loved her very much."

He nodded but didn't reply, and the silence grew uncomfortable.

"I was in a coma for several months, and as I told you earlier, my memory is in bits and pieces. I remember my early life, where I grew up, and my parents. I remember meeting Hans and marrying him, but it's like I'm watching a movie, and the characters are familiar, but I don't know them. I guess my strongest memories are of my husband, who has been very kind to me, and I will never leave him."

Suddenly, Juliette became uncomfortable. Grimacing from a splitting headache, she rubbed her forehead. She noticed the concern on Bryce's face and said, "Oh, it's nothing to worry about. The doctors said I might have headaches and maybe even become disoriented, but I assure you I'm fine."

"The last thing I want to do is upset you. I suppose it was selfish of me to spring all this on you. I should have called and set up an appointment with both you and your husband," Bryce said.

"I assure you this would not interest Hans. My mother tells me I was looking into finding my birth parents before my accident, but Hans was against it. He was afraid I would be rejected or wouldn't like what I found out. I've thought about resuming the search, but everything has been so over-whelming since I woke up. Life has been an adjustment."

"You look fantastic. I mean," he paused, clearly embar-rassed. "I mean, you don't look like you were ever in an acci-dent. When I saw you the other night, I didn't see signs of any physical problems."

"Wait," she said, putting up her hand, "you saw me?"

"Yes, at the awards dinner in Atlanta."

The waitress stopped at their table and put a mug of coffee in front of Bryce and a miniature teapot and cup by Juliette, along with two scones and bowls of cream and jam. Juliette thanked her and said to Bryce, "I hope you don't mind. I took the liberty of ordering before you got here. You don't look like an afternoon tea man, so I requested coffee. If you don't like scones, I'm pretty sure my driver will eat the second one."

"I don't know that I've ever eaten a scone, but if it's got sugar in it, I'm sure I'll like it."

"I found this café by accident, and I love the place. My mother assures me I was a girly girl and we used to have tea parties frequently. She's in Florida, and I don't see her or my father often. Hans says we weren't close, but I don't have any bad memories of them."

She took a sip of her tea and said, "Let's get back to that night in Atlanta. I'm pretty sure if I'd seen you there, I would have remembered you. You're a psychologist then?"

"Good Lord, no. I don't mean that in a bad way. I wouldn't have the patience to delve into the inner workings of someone's mind. I was having dinner at the club with my parents and brother when I saw you. It took my breath away. It still does. You look so much like my wife."

"I can't imagine what that was like for you. I wish I could have known her. Tell me about her."

"Doc was ... I called her Doc because she was a psychologist. She was amazing. Smart, funny, sexy, and always so nice. She didn't know she was adopted. Her parents never told her. If she'd known, I'm sure she would have been looking for her birth parents like you are."

He stopped suddenly, and Juliette waited for him to continue.

"But you don't know, do you?"

"Know what?" Juliette hoped it wasn't something horrible. Perhaps her birth mother didn't want to meet her, or worse yet, that she had abandoned them.

"Your mother died giving birth to you, and your grandfather never knew that you or your sister survived. He didn't know that Patty had given birth to twins."

Juliette let the name echo inside her head. Her mother's name was Patty, and she had a grandfather. "What about my father?"

"Ed said Patty got pregnant when she was only sixteen, and he didn't know what to do with her. Patty's mother was dead, so he decided to let the nuns care for her in an unwed mother's home until the baby was born. He said Patty was adamant she wouldn't give up her baby, but all along he knew she would have to no matter how much it hurt."

Juliette laughed. "Good heavens. I didn't know those places still existed. A warm feeling engulfed her. Her mother had loved her, wanted her. "And my father?"

"Ed doesn't know what happened to your father. He was a local boy who took off when Patty told him she was pregnant and never came back. Ed never tried to find him, but if you want to pursue it, I'm sure Ed will give you his name and any information he has. Your grandfather's name is Edward Campbell, and he lives in Greensboro, North Carolina. I'll give you his number, so you can get in touch with him if you want to. He would probably love to talk to you."

Did she? Did she want to delve into her past? Most days, she felt like she was only half alive. Her life was scripted. She lived in a lovely old mansion and was deeply involved with her charity work, but she felt with her new lease on life there should be more. All of Hans's friends said it was a miracle she was alive. All of Hans's friends. Where were her friends? Her head ached again. She poured another cup of tea and asked Bryce if he wanted more coffee.

"I need to show you something," Bryce said and pulled his phone out of his pocket. He showed Juliette a picture of a smiling woman who had her face, her eyes, her hair. "That's Hannah," he said.

"She could be me." Juliette found it hard to believe that there had been another person in the world who was identical to her. "I wish I had known her."

"There is a reason I came to Savannah. I wanted to meet you, but I also wanted to talk to your husband. There's something I don't think you know. Your husband hired Hannah to work for the institute and to give lectures throughout the country. He met her, and he knew she looked exactly like you. He didn't tell her."

Juliette's cup fell into the saucer and tea splashed on her hand and onto the white tablecloth. Her head was pounding now, and she thought she was going to be sick. It made no sense. Why would he do that? "I don't understand. Maybe he never met her. Hans is not directly involved with the hiring."

Bryce's voice was sharp and clipped when he said, "He met her. She came to Savannah for the interview. It was when you were sick, and he interviewed her in your home."

Juliette took another sip of the now tepid tea and tried to stay calm. She looked at the man across the table whose face was filled with pain and said, "I don't understand why he wouldn't tell her about me."

"I don't either, but I came to Savannah to find out."

Juliette pondered the decision she was about to make. It would mean going up against her husband, and Hans did not like to be crossed. She knew that about him but wasn't sure how she knew. He'd been nothing but kind to her. Hadn't he? A thought echoed in her mind. *My husband has been very kind to me, and I will never leave him.*

"Bryce," she blurted out before she could stop herself. "Come over to the house tonight at seven and we'll get to the bottom of this. I've got to go now. My driver will come in any minute to make sure that there is nothing wrong."

Juliette made her way toward the exit but turned around to look at Bryce one more time before she opened the door. He was sipping his coffee and looking at her with a strange expression on his face. She wasn't sure what she'd put into motion, but she knew that it felt right.

CHAPTER 36
JULIETTE DRESCHLER

JULIETTE BREATHED DEEPLY **to calm herself** on the way home from the café. It didn't help that Lenny kept looking at her in the rearview mirror. Hans hired him to be her driver, and the man had been her constant companion for the last several months.

Hans told her she was prone to seizures since the accident, and it would be dangerous for her to be behind the wheel. He'd won the argument when he'd chided her about all the innocent people she could hurt if she passed out while on the road. She didn't remember ever having a seizure, but then she didn't remember a lot of things. Sometimes her headaches got so bad that when she closed her eyes and opened them again, hours had passed.

Lenny didn't look like a chauffeur. He looked more like muscle for the mob. His head was shaved, and his neck was larger than her thigh. He stood tall, close to six four. Surprisingly, he didn't scare her, and his demeanor was in direct contrast to his size. He was calm, polite, and seemed nice. Juliette knew Hans had hired the man to be her keeper. It made her uncomfortable to know he felt she was incapable of taking care of herself.

She looked out the window at the gray, wintry sky and sighed. The weather was as depressing as the knowledge that Hans was keeping secrets. Theirs was a complicated relationship, and not being able to remember most of their life together made it more difficult. At times, she was almost overwhelmed by her feelings for him, and then at other times, she couldn't stand to have him near her.

The idea that he had knowingly hired her identical twin and not told her was... well it was simply intolerable. If only he had told her about the woman who looked exactly like her, she might have been able to meet Hannah and become a part of her life.

Damn, her head hurt. She reached into her purse and took one of the pills the doctor had prescribed. She hated being dependent on the medication. Most days, she tried to go it alone, but today had been an unusually bad day. By the time she got home, the pain would hopefully be gone, and she could relax and get ready for the evening.

Juliette and Hans had just sat down at the dining table when the doorbell rang. At first it startled her, and then she remembered. She jumped up from the table carelessly tossing her once elegantly folded napkin across her plate and rushed toward the door.

"Juliette." Hans stood looking angry. "Where are you going? The housekeeper will get it. Come back and sit down."

Juliette stopped and turned to look at him. "I forgot. I invited someone for dinner."

"What? Who?" he said and moved toward her in a few long strides.

"You'll see," she said as she flung open the door.

Bryce stood there, and the two men locked eyes. Juliette could tell from the expression on Hans's face that he recognized Bryce immediately.

"What's the meaning of this?" Hans said and scowled at Bryce.

"Juliette thought it would be a good idea for us to meet and talk about a few things over a nice dinner. You know, interesting things about my wife, Hannah, and her twin sister." Bryce followed Juliette into the dining room, and looking back at Hans, he said, "It looks like you were going to start without me."

"It's true, isn't it?" Juliette said. "You knew his wife was my sister."

Han's voice was soothing as he answered Juliette. "No, darling. I assure you I didn't know she was related to you, and I honestly didn't know that she looked like you until I met her. You were in a coma at the time, and I wasn't myself. My only thought was to protect you."

Juliette studied her husband. She couldn't recall ever seeing him this unhinged. She knew he thought she would never find out, and if not for Bryce, she supposed she wouldn't have.

Hans raised his voice as he approached Bryce and said, "This is all your fault. How dare you come to my home and upset my wife? How did you find her, anyway? Never mind, it doesn't matter," he said and reached out to grab Bryce's arm. "I want you to leave now."

Bryce shrugged out of the older man's grip. The look on his face made it clear it was not going to happen twice. "I had no intention of upsetting Juliette, but I deserve some answers."

"You deserve nothing, and if you do not leave, I will call my security."

"Hans, stop it. I invited Bryce to dinner. He's my guest, so please speak to him with courtesy. You are the one who is upsetting me." Juliette sat down at the table, trying to gain in control of the situation. Hans acted like he hated Bryce and for no good reason.

She motioned to the chairs at the table and said, "Sit

down, both of you. Hans, I don't understand why you are so angry with Bryce."

"He's angry because I found out," Bryce said and remained standing near the table.

Juliette saw the fear on Hans's face when he said, "Found out what?"

"That Juliette looks just like Hannah. Why didn't you feel it was necessary to talk to me after my wife died? Didn't you think I had a right to know?"

The fear in Hans's face quickly vanished. Juliette didn't know what Hans thought Bryce was going to say, but evidently it wasn't the answer he expected.

"I apologize, Mr. Cameron," Hans said. "I didn't think with Hannah's passing that it would matter. I didn't know that Juliette had a sister until you told me tonight. I was amazed at the resemblance. But darling," he said and turned to Juliette, "it was only a physical resemblance. She was nothing like you."

"What do you mean she was nothing like Juliette?" Bryce looked down directly into her eyes. "You are her right down to the way you laugh. I hope you have a good life. Live it well for Hannah."

Juliette followed Bryce to the door and watched him walk down the driveway to his car. Then, she returned to the table where Hans was already seated and drinking a glass of wine. "Dinner is cold," he said. "It has been a disturbing evening for you, my dear. I am sorry."

"Why didn't you tell me about Hannah and the reason you hired her?"

"What do you mean?"

"Oh, come on, Hans. It couldn't have been a coincidence that you hired a psychologist who looked exactly like your comatose wife. What exactly did you have planned?"

Hans got up and pulled Juliette to her feet. "Darling," he said as he pulled her close for a kiss, "you're jealous."

She pushed him away and said, "No, Hans, I am disgusted. I'm going up to bed. Alone."

"Juliette," he said in his commanding, authoritative voice. "Do you remember?"

"Yes, Hans. You have been very kind to me, and I will never leave you."

———

Several hours later, after calling Bryce to meet her, Juliette stood in the lobby of the Hyatt waiting for Bryce to come downstairs while she pondered the second reckless decision she had made today. She needed to see Bryce, to apologize, and to ask him more questions. All she knew was that she needed to see him.

When the elevator doors opened and he rushed out, she caught her breath. His hair was mused, and he was wearing a loose shirt, sweats, and no shoes.

When he saw her, he smiled. "Juliette! What are you doing here? Are you all right?"

She quickly pushed him back into the elevator, and as the doors closed, she watched as he punched in the number to his floor. When they got to the room, he opened the minibar, took out two Cokes, and located a bottle of Crown Royal in his suitcase. "I don't know if you want a drink, but I need one."

Juliette nodded and swallowed. "I don't know why I'm here. I wanted to talk to someone who doesn't feel sorry for me. All of Hans's friends look at me like I'm broken." Bryce put ice in the glasses, followed by Crown and Coke, and handed her one. She took the drink and sat down on the edge of the bed.

"What about your friends?" he said, taking a seat beside her.

"I don't believe I have any. They all seem to have deserted me."

He took a sip of his drink. "You must be lonely."

"Yes, I am. I wanted to visit my parents, but Hans said it would upset me. I'm not sure why it would. He believes everything that comes along will upset me."

"How did you come to marry a man like Hans?"

"What do you mean?"

"He's twice your age and from a different country."

Juliette rolled the glass between her palms, the condensation wetting her hands. She glanced at Bryce and gathered her thoughts. "We met in France. I was a student studying there for a semester, and he was a dashing professor. All the female students were enamored of Hans, but he chose me. We married there, and I understand my parents were quite upset."

"You understand?"

Juliette stood and walked to the window where she could see the lights from the swimming pool shining below. "As I told you at the café, my memories are sketchy. Some things I remember clearly and others not so much. I often must rely on what other people tell me."

She turned around but didn't return to the bed. "I never finished my degree. I regret that. I hadn't decided if I wanted to major in psychology or business, so I could go to work for my father, but after I married Hans, I don't know, I guess I decided that being a wife and being involved in the community was enough. What do you do Bryce?"

"I'm a writer."

"How wonderful. I envy anyone with artistic talent. I'm afraid I have none. Not that I would remember, but is it anything I might have read?"

"I've written two novels. The most recent was a best seller, but the first one, I'm afraid, was not very memorable. I am currently writing another one, but since Hannah's death, I'm afraid my progress is slow."

"I'm sorry. I didn't mean to bring up painful memories. Can you tell me what happened to your wife?"

"That's the thing. I don't know. She was on board a cruise ship. It was one of those theme ships and the hundreds of passengers were psychologists. Your husband hired her to be a speaker at the conference. Then she didn't call me, and she always called every night."

"Bryce, it's okay. You don't have to tell me. I…"

"No, I need to talk about it…. about her. Sometime that night, the ship's captain thinks she fell overboard."

"They think? They don't know?"

"No. People saw her all that day and saw her going to her cabin that evening, but she didn't meet her colleagues for breakfast the next morning. There is no evidence of foul play and no record of her leaving the ship. She just disappeared."

Juliette couldn't stand the anguish in his voice and moved closer intending to comfort him. Bryce reached up and touched the tendrils of her hair that had come loose and said, "You almost died, too. Tell me about your accident. What happened?"

She didn't pull away and leaned in closer. Close enough to feel his breath on her cheek. "I don't remember. I wish I did. My mother insists that I was traveling to Florida to see them. That I was unhappy in my marriage. But I don't remember any of that, and Hans says my mother is bitter because she didn't approve of the marriage and is now telling lies."

"Do you believe him?"

Juliette put her head against his shoulder and squeezed her eyes shut. Her head began to throb, and she murmured, "My husband has been very kind to me, and I will never leave him."

Bryce put one finger under her chin and lifted her face to his. "You realize that is the second time today that you have said those same words to me. Why?"

"I don't know why I say it. I don't even know if I believe

it. I feel drawn to you, Bryce, and it scares me." She could smell the fresh, lemony fragrance of his cologne, and she wanted to move even closer into the warmth of his arms.

"It scares me too," he said and gently kissed her lips. She immediately pulled away, and before she could say anything, Bryce stood up and spoke. "I'm so sorry Juliette. I shouldn't have touched you. Please forgive me. You should go home."

CHAPTER 37
JULIETTE DRESCHLER

JULIETTE STOOD **in the garden and waited until she saw Hans's car leave** before she made the call. She looked around for Lenny but didn't see him, so she felt reasonably safe. She nervously counted the number of times the phone rang and considered leaving a message when he finally answered.

"Hello?"

"Bryce, it's Juliette. I hope I'm not disturbing you."

"No, I was packing and getting ready to go downstairs. Is everything okay?"

Her heart plunged, and she had no explanation for the sudden loss she felt knowing he would be leaving. "You're going back to Atlanta?"

"No, I'm turning in the rental and flying home to Denver. There's no reason to go back to Atlanta. I can only take so much of my parents, and my brother has his own life."

"Oh, I see. You must be eager to get back to your routine."

"No, but it is probably best for you if I go. I acted inappropriately last night, and I'm truly sorry."

It wasn't as if she was cheating on her husband. She'd done nothing wrong. "I called to let you know that I've decided to go to Florida to visit my parents. I need to put some pieces of my memory back together. I want to thank you for helping me make that decision."

"I don't understand. I didn't do anything."

"You listened to me and made me question my life. I can't explain it, but I find it so easy to talk to you. Can I ask you a favor?"

"Yes, anything."

"This Saturday is the annual Charity Ball for the Children's Mental Health Association. I'd like you to be there as my guest."

It took several seconds for Bryce to answer. Finally, he said. "Are you sure that's wise?"

"No, but it's going to be my first big appearance since my accident, and I'm a little scared. I don't know why, but you make me feel safe."

"Safe? What are you afraid of? Is your husband upset about last night? He didn't threaten you, did he?"

"Oh no, of course not. He is very kind ...," she stopped herself before she finished the sentence and simply said, "No, he didn't know I left last night, and I didn't see him this morning." She waited for an answer and finally said, "You'll come then?"

"I tell you what. I'll stay in town for a few more days, and we'll talk when you get back from your trip. I can keep myself busy working on my book here in Savannah, as well as back in Denver. It will make my agent extremely happy."

Juliette laughed, thanked him, and said she would call him later in the week. The next call was to her mother to let her know she was coming for a quick visit.

———

Hans had not been happy with her decision to fly to Florida. He said he was concerned about a relapse and insisted that

Lenny accompany her. He told her to continue taking her medications to prevent possible seizures and control her headaches. She found it difficult to go against any of his wishes, but this time, she was determined. Their conversation led to a terrible fight. She couldn't remember ever fighting with him before.

"And exactly what will you do for money? I can close your credit card accounts with one keystroke. Then what will you do, huh?" His contemptuous tone sparked her anger.

"I will ask my mother for money. She has plenty, and I'm sure she would not be stingy about sharing it with me. You cannot keep me a prisoner here if I don't want to stay." She lifted her chin and showed no sign of relenting.

Finally, he must have realized that he could not dissuade her, and gave in. The fight had given her one of the worst headaches she could remember, and a contrite Hans gently put her to bed after placing two of the pills in her hand and kissing her on the forehead. She'd watched him sit by her bed until she closed her eyes.

When she'd booked her flight online, she'd made sure she was not seated next to Lenny. The man was nice enough, but he made her uncomfortable, and she knew he was spying on her as well as ensuring her safety.

Juliette walked briskly through the Orlando airport terminal, She was eager to see her parents, but also apprehensive. She felt like she hardly knew them, and what she did know wasn't good. Janice and Conway Aldridge were waiting for her by the baggage claim. Although she had carried her luggage onto the plane, Juliette thought this would be an easy place to meet.

Her mother engulfed her in a perfumed hug, and Juliette saw tears in her eyes. Janice Aldridge was a pretty woman with red hair, a round face, and sky-blue eyes. The hug felt good, and Juliette returned it warmly. She turned to look at her father, who, although in his late fifties, still had a full head of hair that had turned steel gray. She didn't know if it had ever been another color. Why didn't she know? Why didn't she know lots of things?

"Baby Girl," her father said. "Are you all right? You look so lost."

"Daddy," she said and hugged him. "I'm so glad to see you. I would have come sooner, but I know things are strained between us."

Her father frowned, and with a grave expression, looked at her mother. Janice ran her hand down the side of Juliette's face and said, "We'll have lots of time to talk about everything while you're here. Maybe we can explain a few things."

Lenny cleared his throat and Juliette jumped, having forgotten that he was there. "Oh sorry, this is Lenny Raines. He is my shadow," she said irritably. "Hans wants to make sure I'm safe. He worries about me."

"I'll bet he does," Conway said. Juliette didn't miss the sarcasm in his tone. Conway held out his hand. "Lenny, it's good to meet you. Will you be staying with us?"

"No," Juliette said quickly, before Lenny could answer. "I've made reservations for him at the Hilton."

"Oh, nonsense," Conway said. "We have plenty of room. Lenny is welcome to stay at our place."

It seemed her parents were conspiring against her, too. She smiled timidly and followed them to the car.

Her parents lived in a three-bedroom thirty-seven-hundred square foot condominium in a revitalized neighborhood outside of downtown Orlando. Conway had made a fortune in real estate and was now semi-retired. Janice had been a stay-at-home mom after they adopted Juliette and was involved in running a foundation to provide college educations for the underprivileged. Juliette supposed that was why she had also become involved in charity.

The next day, she and her mother were sitting out on the balcony overlooking the park while enjoying a quiet lunch.

Her father had surprised her by insisting that she and her mother have a chat while he showed Lenny around downtown. She didn't understand that at all. Why would her father want to be best buds with Lenny?

"Juliette, is something bothering you?" Janice said.

"Yes, I don't understand his sudden interest in my keeper. He doesn't even know Lenny."

"Oh, honey, you know how your dad is. He loves people, and he probably feels grateful that Lenny is taking such good care of you."

"I don't need someone to take care of me."

Her mother patted her hand and sighed. "We know that, but your father worries. We almost lost you, and we couldn't take it if anything else happened."

"Mom, what did happen to me? Why don't we get along? What did I do?"

Tears pooled in her mother's eyes, and she suddenly burst into tears. "Oh, Julie dear, you haven't done anything wrong. We love you dearly. It was you that hasn't wanted to see us. You said everything was so confusing to you, and you needed some space."

"I said that?"

"Yes, a couple of weeks after you came out of your coma. We were devastated, but Hans said we needed to honor your wishes, and well… we've been waiting for you to make the first move. We were hoping you would remember your childhood."

"I know you didn't want me to marry Hans, and that it's caused tension between us. Surely now, after all these years, you've accepted that he is my husband, and I will never leave him."

"It's true we weren't pleased when you decided to marry Hans so soon after meeting him. You were so young and naïve. We wanted you to wait a few months. But after you married him, we accepted it. He seemed charming, and you obviously were happy until you weren't."

"What does that mean?"

"You called us the morning of your accident. You said you were coming home and that you would tell us everything when you got here. I could tell you were terribly upset. It was raining, and you wanted to concentrate on your driving, so we didn't talk anymore. The next thing we knew, you were in the hospital."

"I'm so sorry, Mom. I want things to be like they were before. I want you and Dad to tell me all about my childhood, especially the things I don't remember. I want to have my family again."

"We want that too, sweetheart. We loved you from the moment we held you. Our tiny baby girl."

"Was I a twin?"

"A twin? Why would you ask me that?"

"Because I saw a picture of a woman that looked exactly like me."

"I honestly don't know. If you had a twin, the agency didn't tell us. We would have adopted both of you had we known."

Juliette hugged her mother, and they were both crying when Conway and Lenny walked out onto the terrace.

———

The two-day visit flew by and suddenly Juliette was sitting on a plane heading back to Savannah, after promising her parents they would talk to each other often, and she would visit regularly. She'd taken the opportunity while out shopping to stop at a used bookstore and pick up a copy of Bryce's first book. She couldn't wait to talk to him about it, and if she were being truly honest with herself, she couldn't wait to see him again. Several times she had been tempted to call him, but she knew it wouldn't be appropriate. She was hoping he had kept his word and not left Savannah.

She glanced back at Lenny, who was sitting across the aisle and one row back from her. He appeared to be sleeping, but she couldn't be sure and didn't want to be caught staring. She still couldn't wrap her head around the bromance between Lenny and her father. What was Lenny up to?

CHAPTER 38
BRYCE CAMERON

BRYCE STOOD **in the dressing room of the Men's Warehouse** while getting fitted for a tux. He hadn't worn one since his senior prom. His wedding to Hannah had not been a formal affair, no matter how much Justine tried to make it one. He'd worn a blue suit and Hannah had been a vision in a simple, sleeveless white dress.

He was trying not to let guilt slip into his thoughts while he anticipated seeing Juliette. His rational brain told him Juliette wasn't Hannah, but his heart had a hard time seeing the difference. Would it be so wrong to fall for someone exactly like Hannah? Would it be so wrong to become involved with a married woman?

Although he knew he was setting himself up for a tremendous fall, this was the happiest he had been in months. He would have only the one evening. He'd go back to Denver afterward and let her get on with her life.

Juliette had been so excited when she called. She was so happy that she had mended fences with her parents and had learned more about her childhood and more about herself. There was no way Bryce could tell her he wouldn't go to the Charity Ball. He couldn't stand to disappoint her.

She told him she was reading his book. When he asked her what she thought, she said she was reserving judgment until she finished it and would let him know when she saw him Saturday. It was three long days until Saturday.

———

Bryce walked into the ballroom at the Westin Savannah, gave the woman at the table his name, and picked up the invitation Juliette left for him. He made his way into the crowded room filled with banquet tables and the city's most prominent citizens, who were dressed to the nines. If Justine had known where he was, she would have been ecstatic.

He weaved his way through the tables looking for his place card to find his seat for the evening as the orchestra played an old Sinatra song, *I've Got You Under My Skin*. He looked across the room and that's when he saw her.

Juliette looked like a princess. She was dressed in a simple, low-cut pleated lilac gown, and her hair was pulled up with tendrils of her golden curls spilling down onto her cheeks. Bryce couldn't take his eyes off of her. He looked down when a petite elderly lady pulled on his sleeve and said, "Son, you have the same look I had when I first saw my Jamey."

"Pardon?" he said, clearly bewildered.

"Juliette. She's something, isn't she? Sit down by me. Juliette asked me to keep a lookout for you. You are Bryce, aren't you? I haven't seen another unaccompanied, handsome young man walk in."

"You know her?" Bryce said and sat down, not sure what to make of the brazen lady with the white hair.

"You bet I know her. I paid her five hundred dollars for my ticket to sit here and eat rubber chicken. She and my granddaughter are friends. She pretends she knows me, but I tell you the girl's not the same since her accident, what with her sketchy memory and all."

"My name's Annie O'Hare, and I'll be eighty-five next month, so I don't tiptoe around things anymore. Life is way too short, or in my case it's been long, but who knows, I could go to sleep tonight, and it could be, you know, lights out."

Bryce laughed. He liked this lady, and maybe she could give him some insight into Juliette and her marriage. "Yes, I'm Bryce, and it's nice to meet you, Mrs. O'Hare."

"Call me Annie."

"Okay, Annie. You'd said she's changed. How? What's different?"

"It's the little things. She used to be the life of the party, and now she's way too quiet. Cindy, that's my granddaughter, had to practically beg her to host this event. Juliette said that being out in public around so many people gave her a headache because she spent much of her time trying to put names with faces."

Annie picked up the glass of white wine that was near her plate and took a healthy sip. "How do you know her? I'm surprised her husband let you get within ten feet of her. A young guy like you." She winked and patted him on the arm.

"I don't know her well. I only met her about a week ago. She has a lot of things in common with my late wife. We struck up a friendship of sorts."

"So, you're a widower. I'm so sorry. I lost Jamey about five years ago. We were married for sixty years."

Bryce didn't know what to say. He and Hannah had only been together less than a year, but it seemed like a lifetime. He started to murmur an appropriate sympathetic response but stopped when the lights dimmed, and a distinguished man introduced himself to the audience as Dr. Somers. After thanking Juliette for her tireless efforts in setting up the charity event, he invited everyone to enjoy the delicious meal prepared by the chef, a glass of wine, and a little dancing.

Bryce noticed Hans stood next to Juliette with his arm possessively encircling her waist. He watched as Juliette stepped away and joined a conversation with another man and woman. Hans didn't seem happy, but Bryce realized there was nothing the man could do without causing a scene in front of a hundred people.

Bryce nibbled on his meal while keeping a constant watch on Juliette. When she began dancing with a short, stocky man, and Hans seemed to be nowhere in sight, he made his move.

"Be careful, Bryce," Annie said. "Dreschler has a reputation as being overprotective and jealous of his young wife."

"Thank you, Annie. I enjoyed our conversation and meeting you. I'll be fine."

The dance ended, and the orchestra began to play *The Way You Look Tonight*. Bryce walked up and inserted himself between Juliette and the other man. "May I have his dance, Ms. Dreschler?"

Juliette startled, and then smiled. "Bryce, I'm so happy you came. I wasn't sure if you would but seeing you here … well it's nice."

He pulled her into his arms and took a step forward while keeping time with the music. "They're playing this song for you. You look beautiful, Juliette." He leaned in and was overcome with emotion when he smelled her perfume. It was the same lilac scent that Hannah always wore, and her dress was Hannah's favorite shade of purple. He closed his eyes and enjoyed the moment, knowing it would end as soon as the music stopped.

"You're a good dancer, Mr. Cameron," she said playfully.

"You bet I am. Those Thursday afternoons in Miss Elizabeth's dance classes paid off."

"You took dance lessons?" she said clearly amused.

"Until The Captain found out and put a stop to it. My mother was furious, but I was ecstatic."

"How old were you?"

"Ten or eleven. Old enough to be completely humiliated. I was always the dutiful son. I can't tell you how many fights I got into to defend my manhood. But it wasn't all bad. At least now, I don't have two left feet."

The song ended and while everyone was still on the dance floor, he pulled her out into the hallway away from the crowd and the noise. He wanted to talk to her and to ask her a million questions. She was so much like Hannah.

"I read *The Perfect Lie*," she said. "I liked it for the most part. The characters were well defined …"

"I feel there is a *but* coming," he said, teasing her.

"Well, yes, but why would anyone want to read a book that doesn't have a happy ending?"

Bryce was stunned and didn't know what to say. He was shocked and his face showed it. Juliette looked crestfallen, and he quickly tried to reassure her and explain his reaction. Then, from behind him, he heard Hans's angry voice.

"I think you have monopolized my wife long enough. Come along, Juliette, you need to attend to your hostess duties." Juliette smiled sadly at Bryce before taking Hans's arm to return to the ballroom.

Bryce watched her walk away as impossible thoughts flew through his mind. Maybe she was so much like Hannah because she was Hannah. He needed to talk to someone who wouldn't call him crazy. Would Quinn understand? Energized with his irrational theory, he left the hotel and headed for Atlanta.

CHAPTER 39
BRYCE CAMERON

BRYCE LISTENED **to the phone ring four times** and was about to press the end button when he heard, "Hello, hello. Don't hang up, Bryce. Quinn's not here. This is Dixie."

The sound of her youthful, lilting voice put Bryce in a better mood. He made a mental note to tell his brother that after getting to know Dixie, he now understood why Quinn couldn't let her go. She was worth the search and the wait.

"Did that brother of mine go off and leave his cell behind again?"

"Well, yes, as a matter of fact. The only way he would remember it would be if I'd tie a string around it and attach it to his wrist. He's not much of a phone man, but he's a pretty good guy in every other respect."

She laughed in a soft, pleasing way. It was nothing like the deep, rich laugh Hannah would belt out when she was amused, but hearing Dixie's happy tone made him feel better.

"Are you all right, Bryce? Do you need to talk to Quinn? I could take the phone out to the shop."

"There's no need to bother. I wanted to run something by him, but it may be too foolish to even talk about."

"Try it out on me," she said.

He thought about it for a moment before responding. "Well, okay, I will. But you must promise if I start sounding like I need a straitjacket, you'll stop me."

"Done deal," she said. "Shoot."

"Well, I know you haven't met my wife, but if you had, you would understand everything I am saying right now. She wasn't a person you could forget, and there will never be anyone in the world like her. The way she walked, the way she smiled, the way she laughed, All her mannerisms were so uniquely her."

"Go on," Dixie said.

"That's how I found her twin, you know. That night when we were all at the restaurant, I heard her laugh. Nobody laughs like Hannah. It's a belly laugh that's contagious. It was impossible not to laugh with her even if you didn't have a clue what was funny. People sometimes turned around to stare at us as if she was being rude and then they would have to smile because she was obviously so tickled about something."

"She sounds like someone everyone would love to know."

Bryce's words rushed on as if she had not spoken. "I'm not sure how I know, or why I know, but I am becoming more and more convinced that Juliette is not my wife's sister. She is my wife. She's Hannah."

"Have you considered that it may be your heart and not your head that is leading you to this belief?"

"Yes, that's when I begin to doubt myself. I also realize Hannah and Juliette might have similar mannerisms because they are identical twins."

Dixie cleared her throat. "Now, let's consider that one. That might be true if they had been raised by the same family in the same environment, but didn't you say they were separated at birth? They might look alike, but why would they behave the same? Doesn't sound like that theory will hold water."

"You're right," Bryce said. "So, you don't think I've lost it?"

"I think you owe it to yourself to get more information. Quinn told me Juliette's husband was responsible for Hannah being on that ship. Something about that isn't right. I'm a firm believer that if something seems like a coincidence, it probably isn't."

———

When Quinn returned his call, Bryce's voice must have revealed how miserable he felt because Quinn insisted he come by their place for a while. Quinn and Dixie welcomed him into their comfortable apartment and offered him a drink.

"No, nothing for me. I'm driving, and I'm depressed. Both of those are a recipe for disaster."

"What's going on, Bryce?" Dixie sounded genuinely concerned. "Are you making any progress?"

"Come on now, honey," Quinn said, and his dark eyebrows slanted in a frown. "Maybe he wants to take a night off from wallowing in his misery."

"No, I don't," said Bryce. "Dixie understands that this feeling I have isn't going away. Talking about it helps."

"Well, okay then," Quinn said. "Sorry if I put my foot in it. I'll back off."

He sounded so childish and hurt. Bryce and Dixie looked at each other, and then at Quinn and all three of them laughed.

Bryce spent the next hour or so filling them in on every detail that had been keeping him up at night. They asked an occasional question but mostly listened intently as he laid out all the evidence that he thought pointed to the fact that Juliette was, in fact, Hannah.

"So, how could this even be possible?" Quinn said. "How

could Juliette not know that she was her own sister? Is she faking it? Why would she?"

"I am afraid that something is wrong with her mind," Bryce said. "She has horrible headaches all the time and is always rubbing her forehead. She admitted her memory is faulty. Many of the things she believes to be memories are conversations she's had with her parents and Dreschler."

He expected them to disagree, but they waited for him to continue.

"You know, what got me wondering was something she said the other night at the dance."

"What did she say?" Dixie said.

"She wanted to know why anyone would want to read a book that doesn't have a happy ending."

Dixie waited for him to go on. She and Quinn exchanged a curious glance. Finally, Quinn said, "I don't get it. What did she mean?"

"That didn't make much sense, did it?" Bryce ran his fingers back through his hair. "The day I met Hannah on the way to Denver, before she found out I had written the novel she brought with her on the plane, she said those same exact words to me."

"About the happy ending? You mean exactly the same words?" Quinn said.

"Yes. She doesn't like to read novels unless they have a happy ending." He knew he was speaking in the present tense, but he couldn't stop himself. She was still a part of his present and not his past.

Dixie took a seat on the ottoman at the foot of Bryce's chair and took both of his hands in hers. Bryce welcomed her touch, both soft and warm. "Here's my opinion, Bryce. That's way too revealing to ignore. It's like a puzzle piece that fits exactly into the right slot. You have to pursue this. You've got to turn over some more rocks. There's a scorpion under there somewhere."

———

Armed with Dixie's faith in his strong feeling about Hannah being alive, Bryce made the three-and-a-half-hour drive to Savannah, hoping to find Juliette at the institute. It was early afternoon before he saw her get out of a big, black car and make her way into the building. He waited a few minutes and then tried to make himself as invisible as possible while making his way to the solarium.

She was sitting on a bench and wearing a wide-brimmed sun hat. Her long blonde hair fanned across her thin shoulders, and he noticed how delicate and fragile she looked. He had no desire to upset her and was turning to leave when she said, "Bryce, is that you?" She was shielding her eyes from the sun.

"Hello, Juliette. I didn't want to disturb you, but I wanted to say hello."

"That's nice," she said and patted a place on the bench beside her. "Maybe Hans was wrong."

"Pardon?" he said as he sat down. "Wrong about what?"

"Hans said the only reason you are paying any attention to me is because I look like your dead wife." She clasped her hand over her mouth. "Oh, forgive me, please. That was so harsh. Those were his words, not mine, and I should not have repeated them."

Bryce hoped the wounded look had left his face before he spoke. "That may have been partially true," he said. "But then we danced, and I held you in my arms. Now, I'd like to get to know you, Juliette." There was a nearly imperceptible note of pleading in his voice.

Her face flushed pink. She took off her hat. "I'd like to know you better too, but I feel guilty about betraying my husband. He's been very kind to me, and I will never leave him."

Bryce gently took her hand and looked her in the eye. "Do

you realize that you have repeated that same phrase to me word for word on three different occasions? It sounds rehearsed."

"I have?" she said. "I don't know why I say it. I have no idea."

Bryce wanted to stay and ask more questions, but Juliette kept rubbing her forehead and finally said she had to go home and lie down.

He left her with a promise that they would talk again soon.

CHAPTER 40
DIXIE LEE KING

DIXIE KNEW **she was taking a big chance.** She put gas in the car and headed for Savannah, knowing that Quinn would be mad at her, but he would get over it. It was Bryce she was worried about. What if she made things worse for him? He might never speak to her again. Even as she made her way into the huge building that housed the Institute for Psychological Research, she knew nothing was going to stop her from talking to Juliette.

She had heard Bryce talk about meeting Juliette in the sunroom, and it didn't take her long to find it. A group of people were touring the building, and she walked behind them until they passed the closed French doors, behind which the docent said was the sunroom.

Dixie slipped inside and made her way down the narrow pathway between potted trees and plants. She had almost given up hope when she heard a woman's voice. The beautiful blonde was talking to a gardener about replacing some of the flowering plants. Dixie knew this was Juliette Dreschler. She had seen a photo of Hannah that Bryce had shown her, and the likeness was remarkable.

"Oh, hello," Juliette said when she saw Dixie. "Were you looking for me?"

"Yes. I was hoping to find you here. Is there somewhere we could talk privately?"

"About?" Juliette seemed wary and hesitant.

"About Bryce Cameron," she said. "I am Dixie Lee King, his brother's girlfriend, or perhaps even more than that. Has he spoken of Quinn?"

"Well, yes, indeed he has. He thinks the world of Quinn. I almost feel as if I know him, but that's impossible."

Dixie smiled. "I know we are strangers, but sometimes an outside look at things makes things clearer."

"We can talk right here," Juliette said. "No one will disturb us, and my husband is out of town until tomorrow. Not that he would bother us, anyway. He rarely minds if I talk to other women, but he hates it when I talk to strange men. Which I never do anyway, for heaven's sake." Juliette clamped her lips closed as if she had only then realized that she was babbling.

"That's great," Dixie said. "Shall we sit over here?" She indicated a rattan loveseat with flowered cushions.

"Would you like something to drink?" Juliette said. "I'm parched. It gets warm in here after lunch."

"Please. Water is fine for me."

Juliette walked to an intercom near the door, spoke into it for a moment, and then returned. In no time, a young woman brought two bottles of water and two cups filled with ice.

Dixie poured the water into the cup, took a long drink, and then began. "Bryce tells me you don't remember much about your childhood. Is that very hard for you?"

"Yes. It's almost as if I am reading a story that someone told me. The events are all arranged in order, but there are no sights, smells, or sounds that return to me. You know what I mean? If you think about a delicious ice cream cone, you can probably remember how cold it was on your tongue and how sweet it tasted, but I can't."

"Are those events always the same? Do the details ever change?"

"No, they don't. They are always the same. Is that unusual?"

"Not so much unusual as unnatural. I know when I look back on my childhood and my past, some things are painful, so I can't remember them clearly. I think my mind is protecting me from too much information."

Juliette smiled. "TMI, huh? I feel that way all the time. Hans is always filling me in on events I can't remember. He tells me the most intricate details of whatever event he is describing. Sometimes I want to scream at him and say, enough, I've heard enough. My head hurts, and I can't listen to you anymore."

"Juliette, I'm a nurse, and although I have much to learn about patients who have come out of a coma, I am familiar with some of the challenges you are facing. Bryce said you have debilitating headaches, and that your memory is impaired. I'm wondering if you remember where you were when you came out of your coma?"

"Where I was?" Juliette pondered the question.

"Were you still in the hospital?"

"No, my husband said he thought I would get better care at home. He hired a private nursing staff to be with me around the clock."

"Do you remember being in pain when you awakened?"

"Only for a brief time. Hans made sure they gave me pain medication whenever I needed it. He was quite attentive."

Dixie shook the ice around in the cup and took another swallow of her water. "Were you confused when you awoke?"

"Confused? What do you mean?"

"Did you know where you were and who you were?"

Juliette thought for a moment. "I remember opening my eyes and seeing the nurse. She told me I was going to be all right and said she would get my husband. Hans came into the bedroom and then …"

"And then?" Dixie prompted.

"I was a little confused at first. I remember asking him who he was, and I remember how angry he became." She closed her eyes as if trying to replay a movie. "He said he was my husband, Hans Dreschler, and I should never ask him that again. I was so tired. I went back to sleep." She clasped her hands in her lap and then looked up at Dixie. "You know, that's the first time I've thought of that. You are the first person who has ever asked me how it felt when I came out of the coma."

"I'm sorry, Juliette. I hope you aren't upset with me."

"Not at all. It is so refreshing to have a conversation with someone who wants to know how I feel."

Dixie nodded.

"So, what does this mean?" Juliette said. Tears had formed in her eyes, and she was trembling. "You are frightening me."

"I'm sorry. It may mean nothing. I don't want to scare you. But there are so many questions and so few answers."

"What do you expect me to do?"

Dixie rested her hand on Juliette's arm. "Nothing at all. I just want you to consider that perhaps the memories you have are not memories at all. They are scenes in a script that Hans wrote, and you are required to act them out. If you question him, he gets angry. Don't do anything, Juliette, but keep thinking about your past. If a memory surfaces that doesn't fit into the past Hans has created for you, examine it and try to bring it to the forefront."

Juliette stood and walked a few paces away and then returned to sit beside Dixie. "You know, I have had dreams. Erotic dreams in which I am making love to a handsome, sexy man. I can't see his face, but I know I love him, and that he loves me. It isn't Hans. We have never had a relationship like that. Do you think …?"

"I don't know what to think. Maybe those are memories, not dreams. Try to bring those dreams into your waking hours. Try to remember that man and maybe you will figure out who he is. Do you remember …?"

Juliette interrupted her. "My husband has been very kind to me, and I will never leave him."

Surprised, Dixie heard the sing-song rote expression in her voice, and she saw the strange, glassy look in Juliette's eyes.

"You only need to think about it, Juliette. You don't have to tell anyone."

"Hans doesn't like it when I question him."

"Then don't. And whatever you do, keep this to yourself. I am going to talk to Bryce and Quinn and tell them what we have discussed. Do you have a cell phone?"

Juliette put her hand in her pocket and brought out an iPhone.

"What's your number?"

Juliette told her, and Dixie typed it into her contacts. "I will call you now, so my number will be in the missed calls on your cell phone. If you ever need us, we are only a phone call away."

When she left the solarium, Dixie thought she had never seen anyone look so lost and alone. Her heart went out to the beautiful woman, whoever she was.

CHAPTER 41
DIXIE LEE KING

DIXIE FOUND **Quinn in his workshop.** She loved the strong lingering scent of the wood chips. Freshly cut wood took her back to some happy memories spent in the forest when she was a very young child. She waited by the door until the sound of the table saw ceased. Quinn wiped his brow with the red rag he always kept in his back pocket and looked up.

"Hello, beautiful. I didn't see you standing there. Where've you been all day? I never even got to say good morning to you since you left so early."

"I just got back from Savannah. There was something I had to do."

"Where?"

"Savannah. I might as well tell you that I went to see Juliette."

His jaw clenched, and his eyes slightly narrowed. "And you thought that was a good idea because ...?"

She could see that he was not happy with her, and she didn't want this to turn into an argument. She didn't know how to handle him yet. Should she be flippant? Repentant?

Contrite? Well, hell, she thought. I'm not any of those things. I'm simply telling the truth, and he can take it or leave it.

"I hoped that she would be more comfortable talking to another woman. Bryce is so miserable, honey. He's family and family is everything. We must find a way to help him, even if it means butting into his business."

She glanced at Quinn for a sign of objection, but he merely stood there and let out a long, audible breath. She hoped that was his way of relenting.

"And after I talked to her," she rushed on, "it was obvious that Denmark is rotting."

Quinn was silent for a moment, and then he burst out laughing.

"Don't laugh. I read the Cliff's Notes version to get through English Lit."

He crossed the space between them and took her in his arms. "How can I stay mad at you, Dixie? I don't think Shakespeare would be happy to hear how you slaughtered his words, but to me, you are most delightful."

She tilted up her chin, and his lips slowly descended to meet hers. She loved the way he took his time when he kissed her, as if it were the most important part of his day.

"So, we're in agreement?" she said.

"About what?" He looked confused.

"About helping your brother get Hannah back."

"I'm not sure what you mean. Hannah is dead. Shouldn't we be trying to help him accept that she's gone?"

"I need to tell you everything, but I want Bryce to hear it, too. Will you call him? Tell him to drive back here and come over for supper tonight, and I'll fill you both in at once on what I learned. He doesn't need to be in Savannah all by himself right now."

———

Bryce looked thinner and sadder than he did the last time Dixie saw him. He ate very little and then flopped into a chair in the living room and stared at the TV. Some lame sitcom was on and the laugh track annoyed Dixie and jangled her nerves. She picked up the remote, turned off the set, and then sat down across from Bryce. He looked up at her as if to say, "What did you do that for?"

"Bryce," she began, "I hope you won't be upset with me when I tell you about my day."

His eyes showed a spark of interest.

"I drove to Savannah and spent some time with Juliette."

Bryce looked at her and then turned to glance at Quinn, who had come into the room and stood behind Dixie with his hands on her shoulders.

Bryce swallowed and then muttered in a feeble voice. "No, I'm not upset. Why?"

"Well, I thought you might think that I overstepped…"

"I don't," he interrupted, "but why did you go to see Juliette?"

Dixie looked him right in the eyes and said, "Because I had to find out if you were on the right track or if you were so desperate to get your lovely Hannah back, you were inventing things and distorting reality."

Bryce didn't say anything, and his eyes darkened as he met her gaze.

"Now, don't be upset with her, Bryce," Quinn said. "She was only doing it to help you."

"I'm not upset. Not at all. I'm grateful that somebody understands how I feel and is willing to help me. I don't know what to say except thank you, Dixie."

For the next few minutes, she took Bryce and Quinn step-by-step through her conversation with Juliette. Hearing it again, as she spoke it aloud, made her even more convinced that something wasn't right about Hans and Juliette's relationship.

"Have you noticed," Dixie said, "when she starts talking about Hans she kind of stares off into space and recites this speech? It sounds like lines from a play."

"I did notice. It's so weird, and it has happened several times when she is with me. She says her husband is very good to her and she will never leave him," Bryce said.

"Yes, that's it. I think he hypnotized her or brainwashed her or something. The only memories she has are the ones he has fed her."

"Wow," Quinn said. "You two are freaking me out. You think this woman is Hannah and not her twin sister? How is that possible?"

"I don't know," Bryce said. "But I'm damned sure going to find out."

Bryce and Dixie exchanged a determined look.

The next few days were busy ones. Bryce decided to go to Florida where the headquarters of the cruise line was located. He had more questions and wanted more answers than he got the first time. Dixie wanted to go with him, and Quinn refused to let the two of them have all the fun, as he put it. They booked a round-trip flight for the two days Dixie was not working and flew into the Miami airport.

Bryce thought an unannounced visit would be best in case there was a conspiracy afoot. Quinn said he was crazy and had been reading too many crime novels. Dixie compromised and said they should make an appointment to be sure someone in authority would be there to help them, but they should not give their real names in case Hans Dreschler was a stockholder in the cruise line.

When they called the Dream Cruise Line headquarters, they had to listen to several prompts to find the one they needed. There was a complaint department, a missing or damaged items department, a specialty foods department, a special occasion cruise department, a wedding cruise department, and a photography department.

"That's it," Bryce said. "They take photos the whole time you're on the ship. Maybe somebody took a photo that would help us."

———

When they arrived, an employee took them to a large room in the back of the suite of offices. Photographs lined the walls and the bulletin boards. This was one of the busiest departments in the corporation. Portraits sold at premium prices, and the travelers usually bought them as souvenirs of their vacation.

"How may I help you?" a pretty young woman asked. "Are you here to pick up your photos?"

"No," Bryce said. "But we would like to look through some of your sample books so we can decide which package we are going to purchase when we go on our cruise."

"You can certainly do that," she said. "Take a seat over there at the table, and I'll get a book for you. Or would you like two?"

Quinn held up three fingers. "We're all going. Won't that be fun?"

Bryce and Dixie both stifled grins and looked away.

Not sure what they were looking for, the three of them begin slowly turning the pages in the albums. People dressed in their finery stood at the bottom of a curving staircase and smiled into the camera. Forty-five minutes later, all of them gave up.

"There's nothing here," said Dixie. "What were we expecting to find?"

When the woman came back into the room, she said, "Would you like a price list?"

"Yes, thank you," said Dixie, not wanting to arouse suspicion. "Are there any other photos we could see?"

"Well, there's an entire wall of candid shots from the cruise that people didn't buy while on the ship. We sold those for a dollar each, and we keep them online for several months in case someone wants to take a second look." She smiled sweetly. "Come this way."

They turned a corner and saw an expansive white wall spread out in front of them. It was covered with three-by-five and four-by-six snapshots of people involved in various activities. Some were eating, some playing ping-pong, others dancing, or lying by the pool.

The three of them walked along, looking up and down and running their finger lightly across the prints.

"Wait a minute," Quinn said. He pointed at a group of photos featuring people in business suits instead of shorts and casual attire. "Didn't you say it was a business trip for Hannah?"

"Yes," Bryce said.

Moments after he said that Dixie's eyes widened in astonishment. "Look at this, will you?" She pointed at a photo in which a man and a woman stood facing each other while having a conversation.

"It looks exactly like Hannah," Quinn said. "And who's that man?"

"It is Hannah," Bryce confirmed. "She is wearing her lilac business suit. She said it gave her luck." His eyes misted, but he cleared his throat, and his voice was strong. "And that is Hans Dreschler. That son-of-a-bitch never told me he was on that cruise."

CHAPTER 42
BRYCE CAMERON

AFTER EVERYTHING HE HAD LEARNED, **Bryce couldn't leave the woman** whom he believed to be his wife with Hans Dreschler. He didn't know how Dreschler had done it or even why he had, but somehow, he had replaced Juliette with Hannah.

Bryce knew it sounded insane. He couldn't go to the police. What would he say? I think this man's wife isn't really his wife, but she's my dead wife instead. It didn't sound plausible even to him, but he believed it with all his heart, and he planned to get Hannah back.

He didn't know if he could convince Juliette to believe him. He'd followed her for the past two days and finally was able to speak to her alone when Lenny dropped her off at the café where they'd met once before. When he walked in, she was sitting in the same spot in the back of the room. As he approached her table, she looked up. She didn't seem alarmed, but she didn't smile and looked resolute.

"Hi, can I sit down?"

Juliette motioned for him to take a seat. He could tell she was nervous from the way she kept running her finger around the rim of her teacup.

"Can we talk?" he said.

"Bryce, I don't know. I'm scared. Hans has said terrible things about you, and he believes you are trying to destroy our marriage. I'm not that kind of woman. I made a commitment to him. I don't know why I married him, but I did. He says we love each other passionately, and were happy before my accident."

"What would you say if I told you that was true? I am trying to take you away from your husband because I'm in love with you, and I have been since the first time I saw you on that plane to Denver."

"What are you saying? I've never been to Denver."

"Yes, you have. You just don't remember. I met Hannah on that flight. I met you."

"Bryce, you know what you're saying can't be true. I am Juliette Dreschler, and I just met you recently. Hans told me not to trust you, and you're not giving me any reason to."

"Okay, tell me if I'm wrong. Your favorite color is lilac, favorite movie is *Casablanca*, and you don't like broccoli, but you love cauliflower."

Her mouth curved into an unconscious smile. "That Hannah and I have similar tastes doesn't mean anything. I looked it up and lots of identical twins raised apart like the same things."

"Oh, yeah, and here's the kicker. You're deathly afraid of water, and you have tiny little scars on your legs that you got the night a wacko stalker tried to blow you up."

Juliette gasped and put her hand to her mouth.

"I'm right, aren't I?"

Her eyes filled with tears, and she rubbed her forehead. She reached in her purse for her pills and Bryce grabbed her hand to stop her. "Don't take that. I don't know what it is, but I've got a pretty good idea it's not a painkiller."

Her eyes filled with confusion.

"What's the first thing you remember when you woke up from the coma?"

"I don't know. My head hurt and … I don't know. Stop it, Bryce. This is extremely upsetting for me. I need to take my medicine. I need to go home and lie down."

"Do you trust me?" Bryce said in a soothing voice.

"Yes, I do. I don't know why. I love being with you, and when you're gone, I miss you. I've been miserable these last few days, but I knew it would be wrong to call you, to see you."

"Because?" he asked.

Tears were streaming down her face when she said, "Because I'm married, and Hans is very kind to me, and I …"

"Stop it." Bryce reached across the table and pulled her close. "Don't tell me you will never leave him. Don't you see? Those are words he put into your mind. Whenever anyone challenges your feelings for him, that is your pat answer. It's always word-for-word the same."

Bryce looked around the café. No one seemed to be paying attention to their conversation. He only hoped that her driver wouldn't come looking for her. If he couldn't convince her now that she was Hannah, he might never be able to. "Besides the pills for your headaches, what other medications does he give you?"

"Vitamins and a protein shake every morning and something to help me sleep. I sometimes have nightmares."

"I want you to promise me something."

"I don't know if I can."

"Promise me you won't take those pills that are in your purse anymore, and tonight you won't take anything to help you sleep. Also, don't take your vitamins or the protein drink in the morning."

Juliette nodded in agreement and wiped her eyes with the napkin.

"And I want you to promise not to tell Hans. I have no

proof, but I think he is drugging you to keep you compliant and to keep you from remembering your other life. And hell if I know how that is possible."

She remained quiet and had a lost look on her face. "I want to believe you, but then I don't. If what you say is true, then I have been living with a monster. A cruel and cunning monster who has manipulated me and destroyed my life."

Bryce watched her catch her breath and saw a horrifying look spread across her face. Her words made his blood run cold. "If I'm Hannah, what has he done with Juliette?"

CHAPTER 43
JULIETTE DRESCHLER

"MRS. DRESCHLER, DID SOMETHING HAPPEN?" Lenny said as he helped her into the back seat of the Lincoln.

Juliette pulled her compact from her purse and looked at her face. It was splotched, and her eyes were puffy. "I got some bad and surprising news about someone while I was inside. I'm afraid I'm not handling it very well. I'll be okay, but I need to get home."

"I'm sorry. Do you want me to call your husband at work?"

"No, that won't be necessary. I'll talk to him tonight but thank you."

"Are you getting one of your headaches again?"

Juliette didn't want Lenny to know that she did indeed have a mother of a headache. If Hans knew, he would insist that she take her medication, and Bryce believed the pills did more than reduce the pain. "No, I'm fine. I don't need to take anything."

She leaned back in the seat and closed her eyes while hearing Bryce's voice repeatedly in her head. She didn't feel like Juliette, but then she didn't feel like Hannah either. She didn't think she had any of Hannah's memories. At least her mind wasn't a complete blank. She remembered meeting Hans. It was very romantic. Their first date had been in a cozy bistro in France. She'd had pizza and red wine.

She sat up straight in her seat and shook her head. No, that wasn't right. It wasn't pizza, It was Gougére that puffy cheesy pastry, and the wine wasn't red it was white. She remembered Hans's words describing that night, but did she remember the actual event? And why did she have a memory of pizza and wine and laughter?

She clamped her teeth together to keep from moaning out loud. She needed to get home and go to bed, so that hopefully her head would quit throbbing. She'd promised Bryce she wouldn't take the pills, but she didn't know if she could keep her word.

After she got home, she stood under a hot shower until the water turned cold. She put on her warmest pair of pajamas and spread out her yoga mat on the bedroom floor. She let her mind relax, and after about ten minutes of deep breathing exercises, her headache was minimized, and she felt calm enough to sleep.

She was easing under the covers when she heard Hans's voice. "Juliette," he called from downstairs. "Where are you?"

She settled her head into the pillow and closed her eyes. Before Hans entered the room, she relaxed her muscles and took slow, rhythmic breaths, hoping that he would think she was asleep. She heard him approach the bed, and after a few seconds, he closed the door silently as he left.

She lay in the dark while trying not to think about anything. She'd told Bryce she would call him if she remembered something but that he needed to give her some space. She wanted to believe him, even if the possibility of his theory terrified her. After tossing and turning for what seemed like hours, she finally fell asleep.

———

She felt groggy the next morning, but she didn't have a headache. She found the housekeeper in the kitchen, pulling dishes out of the dishwasher and putting them away.

"Good morning, Mrs. Jackson. I'm sorry I missed what I'm sure was a delicious meal last night. I wasn't feeling well, so I went right up to bed."

"I'm so sorry you weren't feeling well, ma'am. I hope it's not that virus that's going around. My oldest son was sick most of last weekend with it."

"I hope so too," Juliette said. "I'll make sure I get plenty of rest."

Hans stood in the doorway, staring at her. "You certainly went to bed early last night, my love. I was hoping we could enjoy a nice meal together since I've been away for the last couple of nights." He opened the refrigerator and pulled out a bottle that looked like a strawberry shake. It was almost empty, and Juliette noticed him smile when he put it on the counter.

"I see you've been giving her the protein drink every morning. Thank you, Mrs. Jackson. I knew I could count on you to take care of my wife."

"Hans," Juliette said, glancing at the housekeeper. "I don't need anyone to take care of me. I'm fine. I don't know why you fuss over me, and I don't need anyone to drive me around. I haven't had any seizures. I'm sure it's perfectly safe."

Hans poured the liquid into a glass and handed it to her. "Humor me please, my Juliette, for a little while longer. I've noticed some things that have worried me, so the doctor has prescribed an injection of your medication. I'll be picking it up today and then I'm sure you will feel like your old self again."

"Hans, no. I don't want that."

"Mrs. Jackson, will you excuse my wife and me for a moment?"

"Yes sir, Dr. Dreschler. I'll go upstairs and get started there."

"Why don't you take some time for yourself this afternoon? I plan on coming home early to take my beautiful wife out to dinner. I heard you say that your son has been sick. I'm sure you'd like to be home to take care of him."

The woman nodded and quickly left the kitchen, looking back at Juliette with concern.

"Here," he said and put the drink in her hand. "This will give you much-needed energy until I can get back this afternoon. I think it's about time we got to know each other again. We'll spend a passionate evening together like we used to do."

Juliette let the glass slip from her hands and it smashed onto the tile floor and the pink shake splashed all over Hans's trousers. "Juliette, what is the matter with you? How could you be so clumsy? I don't have time to mix another drink for you. I must change so I'll get to my meeting on time."

Juliette pasted a contrite look on her face said in her sweetest voice, "I don't know what happened. I've made such a mess. I'll get Mrs. Jackson to pick it up right away before someone gets cut."

She watched Hans stalk out of the kitchen and breathed a sigh of relief. So far, she'd skipped her evening and morning medications, but she would have to think of a plan to avoid the next medical assault he had planned for tonight.

After Hans left, she went upstairs to change into her yoga pants. Apart from deep breathing, she was ridiculously inept with the different yoga poses, but Hans said she enjoyed it, so she persisted in trying until she could become proficient.

Outside her bedroom window, the sun was shining, and it looked like it was going to be a beautiful, unusually warm day. On a sudden whim, she put on her tennis shoes, yelled where she was going to Mrs. Jackson, and took off in a run down the long driveway leading to the main shady, tree-lined street. It felt exhilarating and invigorating. She heard the crowd yelling as she ran around the bases. She could hear her team chanting, "Go Hannah Go, Go Hannah Go."

She stopped running, gasped for breath, and looked around. There weren't any cars on the street or pedestrians chanting as she ran by. Suddenly, she felt lightheaded, but as quickly as the memory surfaced, it disappeared again. She tried to bring it back because it meant something, but as hard as she tried, it was futile. It was gone. It was like waking up from a lovely dream but being unable to recall the details in the morning light.

Hans was true to his word and arrived home promptly at five-thirty. Juliette watched him get out of his car and speak briefly to Lenny. The other man nodded twice and went back into the garage. She didn't know what Lenny did when he wasn't driving her around. She'd never thought about it before, and she hadn't cared. Why did she care now? It made little sense that he was paid a good salary to do nothing. She wondered what he did for Hans,

When he entered the house, Hans was smiling and carrying a leather case. He put the case down on his office desk as Juliette watched him silently from the door. She supposed he sensed her presence, and he turned. She stepped back, suddenly afraid. This was all wrong. She wasn't supposed to be here. She belonged somewhere else. She didn't know where, and she didn't know how she knew, but she did.

"What is it, my love, my beautiful Juliette?" He walked up to her and gently cupped her chin.

She shuddered, and she knew he felt it because his eyes turned hard and cruel. "You used to like it when I touched you. You liked it quite a lot. You will again. You'll see."

"Hans, there is something missing. It's not you. It's me. You've been very kind to me and …"

"And what?" He seemed to anticipate her answer.

"I know you want me to say I'll never leave you, but I can't. I simply can't say that. I think it would be best if we separated for a while. I will move out. Maybe I'll stay with my parents. I'm going to go up and pack a few things and have Lenny take me to the airport."

She turned to go, but Hans grabbed her arm forcefully and bellowed, "No! You will not leave me! I cannot live without you. You are my perfect woman. I have made you, and you will love me."

"Hans, you're talking crazy. You can't make someone love you, and you can't make me stay with you."

"It's that man, isn't it? I knew when I saw him that night I should have told Lenny to get rid of him. He's made you remember, hasn't he? I needed to be patient. I couldn't give you too much, or I could have destroyed your personality totally. You could have been a shell just like my Juliette."

"Your Juliette. What are you saying?" Her voice was breathless. "Then it's true, isn't it? I am Hannah. Bryce's dead wife?"

"I love you. Don't you understand? You were leaving me and going home exactly like you're planning to do now. You're my life and have been ever since I saw you that first time, standing by the fountain in Paris. I knew I had to have you."

"I've never been to Paris, have I?"

"It doesn't matter. I can give you those memories. Don't you see? You are one and the same. A perfect copy of my beloved."

"What did you do with her? Did you kill her?"

"No," a look of horror crossed his face. "I would never. Her head injury was severe, and I tried to keep her with me, but after I saw the picture of you she found in a psychological journal, I knew it was divine intervention."

"She knew about me?"

"I assume. I found the article about your groundbreaking

research in her luggage after the accident. It was as if she were giving me permission."

"To what? Replace her?"

"Yes. There you were, and it was fate that you happened to be a psychologist. We were meant for each other."

"Where is she, Hans? What have you done with her?"

"She's in a coma. A team of doctors tells me she will never awaken. I have placed her in a nursing home in Switzerland. I trust the staff there. It is costing me a fortune, but she is being cared for with the respect she deserves." He stood up. His fists were clenched, and he raised them toward the ceiling. "It's not fair. I loved her, and I needed her. She was no use to me in a vegetative state. Then, I saw you. Her perfect twin, and I knew what I had to do."

The oddest thought came to Hannah's mind, and she almost said it out loud. *Bryce's stalker had been crazy, but Lucy couldn't hold a candle to Hans.* She clung to it, not wanting it to slip away. It was a memory. Her memory and not Juliette's.

———

In a calm voice, she said, "I'm going to walk out the door now, Hans. Please let me go." For a moment, she thought he was going to comply, but then he pulled a gun out of his desk drawer.

"I don't like guns," he insisted. "They are loud and messy, but if I have to, I will shoot you. I won't kill you, my dear, but I will stop you. Sit down, Juliette."

"If we are going to play your game, at least call me by my real name and tell me how you did this to me. How have you made me forget everything?"

"The forgetting part was relatively easy. A cocktail of the right drugs given to you daily took care of that. And the feelings? Well, they are the product of my synthetic oxytocin hormone. I told you it was the love hormone, but I doubt if

344   CHARLENE TESS & & JUDI THOMPSON

you remember. And finally, a little hypnosis took care of the rest. My only flaw was in determining the correct dosage of the drugs and the need to give them to you daily. I have been working day and night on my serum, and I believe it will now have permanent effects."

———

Hannah sat in the high-backed, antique leather chair and looked around Hans's office. Why hadn't she ever noticed the dark and foreboding brown, intricately carved fireplace, and dark burgundy curtains? It looked like something out of a Gothic novel. Perhaps she'd never noticed because she had never actually been in this room before. She wasn't sure.

She was beginning to panic. She didn't want to lose herself. She didn't want to become someone else. She was confused about who she was and only had tiny bits of her memory, but she knew she didn't want to spend her life with Hans Dreschler. She wanted to spend it with Bryce. She didn't want to be Juliette who was weak and could be managed easily. Juliette had allowed her husband to control every aspect of her life. Hannah knew in that way she was nothing like her twin sister.

Why did she tell Bryce to give her space? Why did she insist they wait a few days to see if what he said was true and her memories were false? She feared she wouldn't see him again before it was too late. Then, once again, she would have no memory of him, but this time it would be forever.

She started to rise from the chair but sat back down when she saw the gun's barrel pointed at her knee. She looked up into the half-crazed eyes of a man she didn't know at all and tried to figure a way out. Maybe Mrs. Jackson had forgotten something and would come back, although the thought of Hans injuring or killing that sweet woman was incomprehensible.

"Hans," she said softly, hoping to appeal to some part of his brain that was rational. "You know this can't work. I have reunited with my, or rather, Juliette's parents. They are expecting me to call. If I don't, they will become suspicious. Then there's Bryce. He will never accept that I suddenly don't know who he is. You have to see the flaws in your plan."

"I kept Juliette away from them before. There is no reason to believe I can't do it again. After all, I am your husband, and I have complete control over you. I will simply tell them you've had a relapse and that you do not wish to see them. It will be easy to convince you they don't care about you."

"But what about Bryce? He won't just go away."

"Yes, he will. He has been very distraught over losing his wife. No one will be shocked when he takes his own life."

"You would murder him?"

"I will do what needs to be done. You are my wife. You belong to me, and he cannot have you."

"I'm not an object that can be owned. I don't love you, Hans. I don't want to live with you, and no matter what you do with my memories, that will not change."

"No, no, you're wrong." He pulled a large roll of duct tape out of his bag and threw it toward her. "Wrap this around your feet and then tape your right arm to the chair."

When she didn't comply, he pressed the gun forcibly into her thigh. "Remember, I am a doctor, and I know how to inflict pain without causing immediate death."

After she secured her legs and arm with the tape, Hans pinned her other arm to the chair. She bucked, tried to bite him, and screamed until she was hoarse. He slapped her angrily across her face and blood poured from her nose.

"You made me do that. I didn't want to mar your beauty."

Hannah didn't know if she had ever hated anyone before in her life, but she hated this man. She spat in his face and was relieved when he moved away from her and wiped his eyes with his shirtsleeve.

She fought him again when he pressed the duct tape across her mouth and tried not to cry. Her entire world was going to end and there was nothing she could do to stop it. Then she heard a noise and saw Lenny standing in the doorway with a gun of his own.

"What are you doing, Dr. Dreschler?" Lenny said. The look of shock on his face convinced her he was not part of Dreschler's plan.

Hans didn't seem to be upset by Lenny's sudden appearance. He laughed and looked back at her. "Lenny, I told you when I hired you that there would be certain things you might find distasteful. After I checked you out, I knew you were the right man for the job. Armed robbery, attempted murder. Evidently, you had a misspent youth. But the best part was being in violation of your parole. I believe the state of Florida would love to have you back. I hired you so I could know every move my wife made, and as promised, you have been a valued employee."

"Thank you, sir. I tried to do my best. But I'm afraid I fell short." He pointed his gun at a surprised Hans and said, "I don't work for you, Dr. Dreschler. I work for Juliette's father. He was concerned after his daughter's accident and felt her life might be in danger."

Hans shook his head and said, "It seems we are at an impasse."

"No, sir. We're not. Put your gun down now, and I won't have to kill you."

"My former employee didn't get hit by a car and die, did he?" Hans said.

"No sir, he did not. He was extradited to Texas, where he is standing trial for aggravated assault and murder. The background check you did on him was real, but I'm afraid mine was all made up."

"How?"

"I'm a very resourceful fellow. Please step away from Juliette."

Hannah's heart leaped, and then she noticed the shadow behind Lenny. Oh, thank God, she thought. It was Mrs. Jackson.

The quiet unassuming woman quickly slammed a brass statue across the back of Lenny's head, and he fell limply onto the floor.

CHAPTER 44
BRYCE CAMERON

BRYCE PACED BACK **and forth across his hotel room** with his cell phone in his hand. He wanted to call Juliette but talked himself out of it. Finally, he threw the phone back on the bed in frustration. He said he wouldn't push, and he would give her time, but with every hour that passed, his anxiety increased. He didn't trust Hans.

When he gave in and called her, the phone went immediately to voicemail. Disappointed, he poured himself a drink, switched on the TV, and plopped on the bed with his head against the wall. He began calling her repeatedly, but each call went straight to voicemail.

What would it hurt if he just drove down the street? He didn't have to go down her driveway because he could see the house from the road. He could just make sure everything looked okay. He put down the drink, grabbed his jacket and left the hotel.

There were no lights on in the front windows. The Lincoln and Hans's car were probably in the garage, but there was a small, compact Chevy parked in the circular drive. Someone was there.

He made the only decision he could make and pulled in

behind the other vehicle and walked up on the porch He knocked forcibly on the front door but heard nothing coming from inside. He waited and then knocked again. Hans finally opened the door a narrow crack. He looked disheveled, and his eyes shone with hatred when he looked at Bryce.

"I need to see Juliette," Bryce said.

"I don't care what you need, you can't see her. She's gone to bed. This past week has been too much for her, and I fear she's had a setback. I think you are to blame. From now on, you will leave her alone, and I will call the police, and have you arrested for trespassing if you ever come on my property again. Stay away from my wife."

Bryce got back in his car and slowly drove toward the main street. In the rearview mirror, he could see Hans glaring at him. Bryce was in panic mode and was uncertain what to do. He wanted to call the police, but again he had no proof of any crime.

He parked his car on the street and walked silently back down the long driveway while keeping in the shadows of the trees. He climbed over the brick wall into the backyard and eased around the corner onto the patio by the large pool.

He could see ornamental French doors leading into a dining room. Bryce pulled on the handles only to find them locked. Next, he crept across the back of the house, trying each window until he found one unlocked in what he believed to be a bathroom. After opening the window and easing himself inside, he listened but heard only silence. He made his way noiselessly down the hall, and almost tripped over the body of a man lying in a doorway. It was Lenny, Juliette's chauffeur. His pulse was weak, but he was still alive.

Knowing he now had a reason to call the police, he quickly dialed 911 and whispered the address. The operator said to stay on the line, but he knew any noise would surely put Juliette's life in danger. He disconnected and put the phone on silent.

Then, Bryce heard Hans's taunting voice coming from the basement, and his eyes widened in horror as he peered into the room and took in the scene. It was something out of a Sci-Fi Channel movie. Juliette was strapped to a surgical bed with an IV drip running into her arm. Her eyes were closed, and she seemed to be asleep. Across the room, an older woman was slumped over in a chair.

Bryce didn't have a weapon and looked around the room helplessly. Then he spotted the gun lying on a window ledge. He had the element of surprise and burst into the room.

Hans quickly grabbed a syringe from the table and turned his cold eyes on Bryce. "If you come any closer, I will kill your wife. It will only take one plunge into her neck." His voice was loud and ominous.

Bryce stopped immediately, his mind reeling from Hans's declaration. He wasn't wrong. Somehow, the woman lying in the bed was Doc. His beautiful, brave Doc. The woman who had coldcocked a stalker was now in the hands of a crazed madman.

Bryce put up his hands in surrender and said, "Please don't kill her. Let her live and I'll leave. I'll get out of your lives." He was stalling for time and hoped he would hear the screams of the sirens any minute. "How did you do it? How did you make her disappear?"

Hans turned away from the bed and smiled slyly. "I'm a very rich man. I can do whatever I need to do. It was easy to pay some minimum wage worker on the ship to disable the security system for a couple of hours in the middle of the night. My man, posing as a member of the ship's crew, coaxed her out of her room on the pretext that something had happened to you. She came willingly."

"No one saw them, and we lowered her down in a life raft to a waiting dingy and then to my boat. It was, as you Americans say, a piece of cake."

Bryce inched toward the bed, but Hans halted him with

his words. "I don't think you believe me, Mr. Cameron. I've nothing to lose. Without my Juliette, nothing is left in my life."

"She's not your Juliette. She doesn't belong to you."

Bryce watched Hannah slowly open her eyes, and at the same time heard the wailing sirens approaching. Hans turned back toward Hannah, when she reached out her free arm and pushed him, causing him to stumble and giving Bryce the opportunity to plow into him.

The two men fell to the floor in a life and death struggle. Bryce was quicker and stronger, and he used his military training to force the older man to drop the needle. Bryce reached for it and forcefully plunged it into the soft tissue of Hans Dreschler's belly.

CHAPTER 45
BRYCE CAMERON

BY THE TIME **Bryce got to the hospital, Hannah was fully conscious.** He assumed the needle Hans had been holding contained the sedative the monster had planned to give her to get her back under his control. Bryce had no idea what he had planned to do next, but the man was so deranged, anything was possible.

He had called Quinn moments after the police arrived on the scene, and his brother said that he and Dixie would be there as fast as they could. It was about a three-and-a-half-hour drive from Atlanta.

The detective, who was investigating the crime scene, told Bryce that he would provide a police car to take him to the hospital, and that after Hannah was stabilized, he would need to go to the station and answer questions.

Hannah had answered as many questions as she could. Her memory was sketchy, but she told them she had seen Hans inject Mrs. Jackson with something, and she remembered kicking him and the scuffle that took place between Bryce and Hans. Although she was upset and confused, Hannah was physically sound, and after hours of watchful waiting and several tests, the doctor said it would be safe for her to leave.

Bryce asked the officer to take them to his hotel, where he found Quinn and Dixie waiting in the lobby. He had never been as happy to see his brother in his whole life. Hannah took one look at Dixie and ran into her waiting arms.

They made their way up the elevator and down the hall to the room that Bryce had occupied. He opened the door and set their bags inside. Dixie took Hannah into the bedroom to get her a terrycloth robe from the closet. Then she made Hannah some hot tea and arranged a blanket around her shoulders.

Bryce called Hannah's parents and her Uncle Bill and promised to call them again in a day or two and give them all the details. He didn't want her to be alone while he went to the police station for questioning. An officer was waiting outside with a squad car, and he would have to leave soon. He had just found her again, and he was so afraid to be separated from her even for a moment.

"It's all right, Bryce," said Dixie. "I promise we will not let her out of our sight. She will be here waiting for you whatever time you get back. Do whatever you must to end this mess, so we can all start living our lives. The ones we want to live, you know?"

———

The police questioned Bryce for hours, and when morning came, he still had not returned. Quinn left a sleeping Hannah with Dixie and drove to the police station and demanded to see his brother.

After a while, an officer took him into a room where Bryce sat slouched behind a metal table. His green eyes were like bits of stone.

"Are you in handcuffs?" Quinn said. His nostrils flared with anger.

Bryce held up his hands, both free of restraints.

"Then you're not a suspect?"

"What do you mean, a suspect? I killed that man, and they know it. I am the only one who is responsible."

"Are they going to arrest you?"

"Not so far. All they've done is ask questions, but this is a damn sight more complicated situation, you know. First there are two identical twins that Hans Dreschler said he was married to, and then, a psychologist with an excellent reputation who is a kidnapper, manipulator, and diabolical killer. There are lots of things the police must figure out."

"That's going to take a long time, Bryce. Are they going to keep you here while they investigate? Because if they are ..."

The door opened, and a detective in a business suit took the seat beside Quinn. "I don't know what the end of your sentence was going to be, but you can save it. Your brother said he has told us everything he knows. We may have questions later, but for now, he is free to go home."

"Is he free to go back to Atlanta?" Quinn said. "Because that's home."

The detective paused for a moment and then said, "I don't see why not. We have a witness who can testify to many of the crimes that Doctor Dreschler committed. Mr. Cameron will not be charged. Preliminary investigation shows that he acted in self-defense."

Bryce looked up in surprise. "A witness?"

"Yes, it looks like the chauffeur is going to recover. He has a concussion, but he will be fine in a week or so. He is eager to talk and tell us everything he knows about Hans Dreschler. Evidently, he knows quite a bit."

"What about the housekeeper?" Bryce said.

"She wasn't so lucky. Not sure of the cause of death yet, but she's deceased."

When they got back to Atlanta, Bryce took Hannah to his hotel and booked the adjoining room. He knew it was going to take time for her to adjust to the new normal in her life. The last thing he wanted to do was force her to pretend that she remembered him and make her feel trapped again.

As the days went by, they took long walks and stopped for lunch in small bistros and cafés. They talked easily, and their conversations were not awkward or strange. Bryce thought they had both made a conscious decision, without even discussing it, to get to know each other as if they had recently met. They weren't calling it dating; they were calling it *walking around together*.

As they walked, her hand easily slipped into his, and she allowed him to pull her into a gentle hug each night before he went into the adjoining room to sleep. The prolonged anticipation of their becoming intimate again was agonizing for him, but he could be patient, and he would be.

They spent some of their evenings with Dixie and Quinn, and with the four of them together, Hannah was more relaxed and freer. It was on one of those nights when they were sharing a bottle of Merlot when Hannah felt strong enough to tell them what she remembered about those last few hours with Hans. "Something that keeps coming back to me in bits and pieces is that I asked him if he killed Juliette."

"You did? How brave of you," Dixie said. "Well, goodness, girl, what did he say?"

Hannah focused on the ceiling as if the scene might play out there. "He said no. He could never kill her."

Bryce tried not to sound too excited. "So, you mean Juliette is still alive?"

"I think so," she said. "He said she was never going to come out of her coma, so he put her in a nursing home in Switzerland."

"That's good news," Bryce said. "We have to find out where she is and tell her parents. They have been grief stricken without her. I think they always suspected you were not the real Juliette, and when I told them you were Hannah, they broke down in tears. I felt terrible about having to tell them on the phone. They seem like great people."

"Yes, they are," Hannah said. "I think Juliette was the luckier of the two of us regarding her adoptive parents." She took a sip of the wine she was drinking and turned to Bryce. "Sweetheart, do you think we could find her? Bring her home together?"

Bryce's eyes shifted from one person to another. He wondered if anyone else had heard her call him sweetheart. He almost lost his train of thought, but Quinn saved him.

"I don't know how we would go about finding Juliette. Where would we begin, Bryce?" he said.

Bryce recovered his composure and said, "I'm sure that nursing home is expensive. We'll follow Dreschler's bank records and find out where he was sending the money."

"That might work," Quinn said. "Dixie and I could help you."

"Well, we need to go back to Savannah next week and meet with the attorneys who are handling Dreschler's estate. Hannah must explain that she is not his wife, and therefore will not be his beneficiary."

Quinn said. "Wouldn't it be easier to take the money and put it in a trust fund for Juliette? I don't see how you can prove who you are. You're identical twins with the same DNA. Right?"

"There is a way," Dixie said. Everyone turned to look at her. "Yes, it's true that identicals have the same DNA, but they don't have the same fingerprints. You had to be finger-printed to get your psychologist's license, Hannah."

"Okay, but what about Juliette? I don't know if she has a set on file or not," Hannah said.

"Well then, we will have to go to Switzerland and find her, so we can get her prints and prove that she was Dreschler's wife and heir," Dixie said.

Quinn cleared his throat. "Did you say we?"

"Well, sure, honey. We can't let them have all the fun," she winked at him. "We've already got our passports since we were planning to elope to Mexico."

Dixie looked at Bryce and then clamped her hand over her mouth. "I'm sorry. I'm so sorry. I let the cat out of the bag and then ripped the bag up. Quinn was going to tell you. I swear he was, and then all this crap happened and ..."

Bryce took two steps toward Dixie and pulled her up and hugged her hard. "Hush, girl. I am so happy that you are going to be my sister-in-law. My brother adores you, and I think you hung the moon."

Then Bryce shook Quinn's hand and slapped him on the back as they both grinned from ear-to-ear. His happiness was all-consuming, and before he could think about what he was doing, he lifted Hannah onto her feet and started dancing around the room with her.

She threw back her head and laughed that loud, beautiful laugh that was almost stolen from him forever, and he leaned down, pressed his lips against hers, and then gently covered her mouth. She didn't hesitate, not even for a moment and threw her arms around his neck and kissed him back.

Her nearness was overwhelming. He almost missed the words she whispered in his ear because Dixie and Quinn were loudly applauding their kiss.

"I think this time, my precious husband, our story will have a happy ending."

———

We hope you enjoyed STOLEN LAUGHTER. In Book Two, TERMINAL IDENTITY, the stories of Bryce, Hannah, Quinn, and Dixie continue as they travel to Switzerland to find Juliette. Get your copy here.

Leave a review and help other readers learn what you liked about Stolen Laughter.

Claim your copy of *The Dancer and the Cop***, a delightful love story.** Subscribe to our newsletter here.

We hope you enjoyed STOLEN LAUGHTER. In Book Two, TERMINAL IDENTITY, the stories of Bryce, Hannah, Quinn, and Dixie continue as they travel to Switzerland to find Juliette.

https://tinyurl.com/TerminalID

Charlene **Tess** and Judi **Thompson** are sisters who live over 1400 miles apart. They combined their two last names into the pen name **Tess Thompson** and write novels as a team.

Judi Thompson has been writing since her early teens. She lives with her husband, Roger, in Texas. She is a retired supervisor for special education in a local school district.

Charlene Tess is a retired writing teacher and writes educational materials and grammar workbooks. She lives with her husband, Jerry, in Colorado.

Scan the QR code below and leave a review to help others readers learn what you liked about *Stolen Laughter*.

CONNECT WITH US
Facebook: https://bit.ly/3GCGoek
Goodreads: https://bit.ly/3rpLrbD
Email: NovelsbyTessThompson@gmail.com.

Books by Charlene TESS and Judi THOMPSON

- **Second Daughter (standalone novel)**
- **Secondhand Hearts series**
- **Dixieland Danger series**
- **Chance O' Brien series**
- **Angel Falls series**
- **Texas Plains romantic comedy series**

The authors also write under their own names. Visit our individual Amazon Pages to see our titles.

www.amazon.com/author/charlenetess
www.amazon.com/author/judithompson

Scan the QR code below to claim your copy of *The Dancer and the Cop*, a delightful love story, which is a prequel to our Chance O'Brien Series.

https://BookHip.com/SCFWCPV

Made in United States
Troutdale, OR
07/21/2024

21386150R00224